MACFARLANE'S LEGACY

LEGACY

BOOK ONE

(In Dreams of Caledonia)

by

J. A. Milne

Published by New Generation Publishing in 2014

First Edition

Text Copyright © J. A. Milne 2014

Cover design by J. A. Milne and James Fitt ©
Cover image taken from a painting by Barry G. Price
and reproduced by kind permission of The Newcomers' Gallery Ltd

The song words were taken from the internet.
Every conceivable effort has been made to discover the
owners of the copyright – to no avail.

ISBN 978-1-78507-178-2

www.newgeneration-publishing.com

New Generation Publishing

Contents

MACFARLANE'S LEGACY

(In Dreams of Caledonia)

Oh lips, so innocently sweet, should a man be as fortunate to be invited, to taste the honey from the bee, as nectar sweeter than the wine, so shall the mead hallow those united loins, and bring forth the sown fruits of yesteryear, vested yet again in the right that they should be.

I cannot shun, this patience 'O' rapture sublime, the maiden treads with caution until her seed combines with mine, my need is must, the time is dusk, I cannot lose a chime, or the bee will sting, the bell will ring, and the child will not be mine.

Should this yearning last a lifetime, aft the maiden flees the nest, my sorrow will not be undone, and I will hive until I rest. — I love this mortal maiden and so have made a quest that the bee should harvest honey to lie upon her breast.

And this wine which is yet sweeter, and suckled from the breast, the hallowed mead shall follow, and my son has been my quest.

PROLOGUE

"Rory, take care of Helen," Mairie smiled as she waved them away, and then turning, she returned to the cottage, gently shaking her grey head, thinking, what it was to have the joy of a sixteen year old granddaughter, not long since a baby dangling on her knee.

Each year, David had brought her to stay while he and Glynis went off touring to some exotic, far away land; — the child hadn't wanted to accompany them. She felt that Helen had sometimes felt despotic, but never in her company, and here, she were able to be a free spirit, able to roam, run and play with young companions such as Rory Cameron who was her own age.

Rory had always roamed free, his spirit was carefree, — sometimes wild, and he paid no heed to caution. He always longed for Helen to arrive, and took his bike to the station to meet the train, hours before it was due. Helen always arrived in style, — sitting sideways on his crossbar. This year, David surprisingly, had brought his daughter on his own; — he had appeared somewhat tired, staying only three days while Glynis was otherwise occupied; — Helen, she knew, would journey home alone, — she somehow felt that it would be the last she saw of her son. — She also knew that the children had taken their swimming costumes; — the loch could be quite a danger, especially the Auld Water Mill ruin where generations of children had expended their energies.

Chapter 1

Altercation

It had been a cold June day when they had buried Mairie Campbell in Arrochar's ancient churchyard, the turn out had been spectacular, the church had been full to capacity with people from the farms and the neighbouring villages, many had travelled long distances and the service had been elongated by the many eulogies which had been read.

After the service, Duncan had stood staring into the pit containing the dark oak coffin, adorned with brass handles and an inscription plaque. — For a very long time his grieving was heavy; — in his hand he held a posy of freesia's and heather, with a single red rose which he raised to his lips to kiss before reluctantly, throwing his token onto the coffin, it seemed so final; — his mother came to join him. "There will be a void in your life now, Duncan," she said, enquiring, — "There's been no word from London?"

"None," he replied. "I kept hoping that her granddaughter would break Mairies' golden rules, but not even a flower or a card, have I received, she could be feeling quite bitter."

Eleanor fondly smiled. "Helen, she was such an adorable little urchin, I rarely saw her with a clean face."

"I wouldn't know; — we never chanced to meet." Duncan sighed, he removed his jacket which he handed to his mother, undid his black onyx cuff-links and rolled up his shirt sleeves; — he signalled to Rory who joined him, he did likewise, — they each took a shovel from where they were protruding from the mounds of earth alongside, while Hannah uncontrollably sobbed, as she looked on.

To say that Helen Campbell was a recalcitrant but engaging child at the prime age of sixteen would have been testing the crowning testament of youth. She was frequently seen tossing her tangled main of auburn hair, while her Celtic green eyes turned to flashing jade lights, — and go, she would. — With her full pliant lips pouting with petulance, she would argue that black was white and that white was black, even if the colour in question was grey, but with such a positive attitude, at the later age of twenty-two, there were no grey areas in Helen's life, until the day that her solicitor stepfather, Charles Petrie, summoned her to his offices in London's Liverpool Street, which was only a stones throw away from her employment, 'The London Daily News' offices in Fleet Street, where she was a reporter in training.

The frustration sounded in her voice, "Can't you tell me over the phone?"

Charles answered, sharply ordering, "I need you here, and don't dilly-dally."

Helen sighed, as she replaced the receiver. — It had been two weeks since the devastating news that Mairie Campbell had died, — she had been Helen's last true-blue Scot's relative since the death of her father six years previously. This latter sudden tragic event had catapulted Helen's transition from childhood into womanhood overnight; — her feudal temperament was thought, by some, to be simmered. At the prime age of eighteen, she had been transported to France to finalise her piano studies, but her concentration had waned, and Monsieur Muchet had despaired of her, - and it was, - with much regret, — that he had failed her in her finals, this, in itself, was quite a blow to her confidence.

These days, the artistic temperament had become subtly hidden, especially while playing the piano or listening to other musical arrangements, — her creamy countenance would break out into a softening, mysterious smile, displaying a row of neat pearl teeth, which heightened the onlooker's fascination, — they warmed towards her, and the male of the species, found themselves fighting down an irresistible desire to protect her, and to smooth away any worries which might create any turbulence in her life. She outrageously flirted with, and then fought down those advances, and used them to her best advantage, for she was the master of all her virtues.

Charles was restless as he waited for Helen's pending arrival; — his usually steady hand was trembling, as he needlessly shuffled through the piles of paperwork, which littered his desk, — he then moved to the window to peer out onto the street far below him; — his whole demeanour shouting that he was dreading the interview which was to follow. — He sighed heavily; — the tension had been building since he had first opened his mail that morning. Parenting a teenager hadn't been his best virtue, not something that he'd slipped into easily, but, David Campbell had been his business partner, and for many years, Charles had silently loved Helen's mother, Glynis. The birth of David's child had been difficult, and so there had been none to follow.

It had also been his devastating duty to inform Helen of the death of her grandmother, but she had surprised him with her 'matter-of-fact' attitude towards this event.

"She was very old, Helen."

She had shrugged and sighed; her reply was flippant, "Well, it just means that I won't have to write any more letters, and it was her choice to sever the relationship after daddy had died. Perhaps she had begun to be ill, even then. She made some very strange remarks whenever she bothered to answer my letters; — she was always warning me, — to be wary of men."

"Senile dementia," they had surmised.

He turned from the window when hearing a soft tap on his door and the subject of his thoughts appeared before him. She was tall and slender, willowy, her wild volumed hair she had loosely restrained in a scrunchy, creating a dubious curly pony-tail which bounced as she crossed the room to greet him with a soft kiss on his cheek, — the scrunchy regularly slid down the silky texture, and he knew that she had to constantly re-apply it. She smelt fresh, despite the hot July weather, was cleanly and simply dressed, as always, in a figure hugging, short white tee-shirt and jeans which moulded her slim hips. She stood away from him to study his expression, taking in his rather morose, concerned mood as he indicated for her to be seated. — Her smooth brow furrowed into a puzzled frown. "Charles?" she questioned, with some concern, and studied him while waiting for his reply.

He nervously cleared his throat before speaking with caution. "Helen, it is my *very* difficult duty to inform you of the contents of your grandmother's *will,*" he replied, while handing her some papers, but the lawful jargon blurred, she asked for a clearer explanation while handing back the document.

Her expression was perplexed. "I wasn't aware that she had anything of value, except for the cottage, which will have to be sold."

He confirmed. "She *has* left you the cottage, but there are certain strings."

"Strings?" she echoed, warily.

"Ye...s, strings," he tentatively underlined, again clearing his throat in preparation. — She listened more attentively as he read the missive lying on the desk before him, but taking in the contents, would have been an impossible task for any lesser mortal. — Something suddenly plummeted inside Helen, — her jaw dropped, — she gasped with incredulous disbelief as the message slowly unfolded, and had sunk in. — "Mairie Campbell has left strict instructions that you are to spend six months in the Highlands, and that the cottage is to be at your disposal for that entire period."

She stared at him, wide eyed, open mouthed, momentarily speechless, and then halfway through the reading, the expected tirade burst forth, — she stood, "Wait a minute! *Six months in the Highlands*?" She loudly questioned, while pressing her balled fist into her chest, — "At the drop of a hat, — *I* ... am to live in the Highlands for six months ... why ... it ... it's ludicrous!" she exclaimed.

"Ludicrous or *not*, that seems to be the idea," he firmly replied, watching her sterling spirit swiftly rise.

"Why, the whole idea is preposterous, I ... it's futile, — I refuse to go," she stubbornly retorted, "Charles, it can't be true — read it again," she demanded, her jade eyes flashing, while stabbing with long pointing index finger at the offending document. "It can't possibly be true; it's a mistake — *read* it again."

Agitatedly, Charles snatched his horn-rimmed spectacles from his now puce coloured face, which was threateningly close to hers, as she leant over his desk, "Helen ...whichever way I read it, the *will* reads the same," he emphatically underlined. "Your gran has requested that you live in Bracken Cottage for a period of *six months*, or the property will return to the MacFarlane estates, to become as it once was, — **a-** *tie cottage*. — There it is, — clearly stated," he firmly said, indicating the now tiresome document with the stem of his specs.

She dropped back down in the chair, huffing and groaning with frustration in her dilemma. For a long moment she seemed lost for words, — she sighed and dispelled a further harrowing groan as the unbelievable message, sank in.

During this brief respite, Charles relaxed into his chair with clasped hands in front of him, and proceeded to nervously rotate his thumbs around each other, his grey/blue eyes watched warily as she rose again, her slim form straightened and turned towards the centre of his office, while thrusting her hands deeply into the pockets of her blue-denim jeans, — her whole demeanour displayed her agitation. She began to pace the plush expanse of beige carpet, while letting out yet another exasperating groan of frustrating disbelief, at the wrangle and the impracticable position, in which she now found herself; — she was muttering something inaudible. Charles held his position, anticipating further argument; — she didn't leave him a disappointed man for very long.

"It's *impossible*!" she suddenly exclaimed, stubbornly grumbling, while swinging round on her heel to face him again, her slim hands now free of her pockets were expressive.

"I simply **don't** understand ... perhaps you would *kindly* explain, just *why*...that for the last *six years* gran *emphatically* refused to allow me to visit her, giving no real reason, — and *now*, — after she's dead, — out of the blue, — she has the *audacity* to leave a *will* requesting that I *suddenly*, entirely, alter my life?" she raged, as she re-approached the desk.

He sat forward again, firmly speaking, "I can't explain, and I've never heard such a load of old piffle! Why impossible, Helen?" he reasoned. "You're exaggerating beyond belief, the request is for only six months, not for the rest of your life," he then suggested an alternative. — "Take some holiday; — they do, — still, — take holidays in the newspaper profession, — I trust."

"But Charles, even if I agree to this preposterous idea, what would I do with the cottage afterwards?"

"A problem to be met when the time comes," he replied, stiffly.

Bending to lean with hands resting on the desk, she made a soft groaning plea, "Charles, can't you get me *out* of this?"

He was emphatic with his reply, he shook his head, refusing, — "No ... I do not carry that clout, Helen, and it's hardly the verge of the earth."

Her voice still soft, still pleading for understanding, "Don't you see, Charles, I can't go *now*, — later, next year perhaps. I simply *must* convince Ryder, that I have enough experience to write his gossip column without his *constant*, irritating interference."

Charles shook his head again in rueful disagreement, remaining stern and refusing to be shifted; — he had only related one small part of the all-damning information, before she had interrupted him at the onset. He was now dreading the moment of revelation, and had to steel himself to say, — "No, I *don't* see, and what is more, next year will be far too late," the further distressing announcement came. "It has to be within the year of her death, she has stressed, emphatically."

Helen suffered another, all-telling plummet, she groaned, exasperated, at this further audacity, — her roused spirit renewed itself; her green eyes became as tempestuous as a storm tossed sea, her voice rose, "Next year ... too late?" she echoed, and resumed the tirade. She adamantly slapped the desk, arguing. — "I *can't* go; I'm *not* going to go, I *refuse* to go, I *must* stay in London; — Ryder expects a constant flow of articles; he insists upon it, to boost the circulation, and besides, the public couldn't survive without its daily dose of breakfast cynicism."

"Ryder … damned, Ryder," he muttered agitatedly "… that's all I hear from you; morning, noon and night … that man controls your life."

"That's not quite true, Charles," she pointedly replied. "I haven't seen you for over a week, and then you summon me, like … like a lamb being led to slaughter. I simply *refuse* to be brow-beaten into submission," she dropped down into the chair and tightly crossed her arms beneath her heaving chest, her pouting expression was determinedly militant.

He sighed, and once more ruefully shook his head in despair; although his voice remained resolute in his ordeal, for he knew that he had to combat this problematical situation, — he could not and would not succumb to the benediction of her employment. His gaze swept the young girl's Gaelic beauty as a concerned frown creased his noble brow, — he resorted to reasoning, "When I first suggested this Gossip Column idea, I had no intention of it taking you over, body and soul. — Why not *speak* to Ryder, Helen; I'm sure that you can come to some arrangement with him. Work on a retainer for a few months," he suggested.

She briefly glanced up at him from beneath long lashes, sulkily renewing her determination, and knowing full-well that she would raise his wrath again, she asked, — "And just tell me — what could I find to write about in a sleepy Highland village, like Arrochar?"

Her words lit the fuel to a cannon blast, she jumped, startled as he rose to the bait; — Charles exploded, postulating, red in the face again, and with a shift of his heavy shoulders, he battled on, pointing his index finger in her direction, "Saints preserve us!" he roared, exclaiming, — "Excuses! Excuses! Nothing but Excuses! — Young woman … for years, I have been subjected to a constant stream of assurances, that there's news everywhere you go, so now, — prove it," he challenged, and then again began shuffling with irritably trembling hands at the papers littering his desk, continuing, — "I am no longer, prepared to accept any further excuses, that Arrochar is any different from the rest of this miserable, motley world — and, may I add, — that for someone who insists she relishes a challenge, you are very definitely displaying all the signs of a defeatists attitude, — now!" he finished breathlessly, while slamming closed some large, leather bound ledger and banging with the flat of his hand on its cover in finality.

She jumped, startled at the impact before shouting back, — "It isn't fair to ask."

"*Fair*…what is *fair*, Helen?" he replied. "Where's your *spirit* girl, y… your sense of adventure?"

"*Adventure!*" she shrieked and chortled. "Adventure ... in Arrochar, you're surely being facetious."

The man grunted and scoffed, "I am not being facetious, not even remotely facetious, — but quite frankly, my dear, I fail to understand, — I seem to remember that not so many years ago, you unmercifully plagued your parents, every school holiday or any other available occasion that you could imagine, to visit Arrochar. And not only that, you persistently argued, and I quote, 'Please, please, pretty please'," he mimicked, "'I simply have to, I've left something vital behind' — deny it if you dare!" he threatened, and watching her expression soften into a smile, with the addition of a mischievous sparkle in the depths of her emerald green eyes, he began to hope for a breakthrough. "You may find, your vital missing link," he tempted.

Helen suddenly grinned, knowing that Charles understood her only too well. "Really, Charles, I was just a teenager; — I'd wheedle anything that I could, there is no vital missing link, and well you know it. The only vital links to life are to eat, drink and be merry, for tomorrow you may die."

"You do very little of that my girl, — you're a workaholic," he scoffed.

"It's one of life's little insidious problems, I like to work, I enjoy my job, I meet people and socialise in a different way, that's all. It isn't my style to be...," she shrugged as she struggled for the word, "cooped up in a village full of strangers. Gran's ideal, maybe, but she was a country girl; I'm town bred, and I don't want to be tied down to domesticity; Arrochar shrieks of it; — it's too placid."

"Helen, be reasonable," he pleaded.

Her voice was softly passionate, complaining; — "Reasonable ... the world is my oyster, and you're asking *me* to be reasonable. I've already been to the States and now Australia is set to be on the horizon, and Ryder mentioned an opening on a TV news channel. — Should I give all that up, just because some selfish old lady has made some ridiculous, outlandish demands?"

He studied her speculatively for a moment, her argument was sound, and he had to agree that any disruption to her career could be destructive, but this was not answering the immediate concern, — he drew breath to speak, just as there came about a strange turn of events, — she became distant, silently thoughtful, she appeared to be mulling over the situation, — he sensed an unexpected mellowing, of which he took advantage. — She suddenly flicked back an escaped lock of dark hair, asking, — "Have I got time to think about it, before I give you my answer? I would like to mull this one over with Rita for a while."

"You're expected to go in September, before the closure of the tourist season; covering the Christmas period," he replied with difficulty, chivvying, "Come on, Helen, it could be fun."

"*Two months!*" she thoughtfully, softly exclaimed.

He hastily replied, "I need to let Crawford know ASAP, he's handling all of Mairie Campbells' affairs," he informed her, referring to the Edinburgh based Solicitors. Again, he chivvied her, "Come on, Helen."

She appeared thoughtful and speculating, "I must admit I don't relish the idea of Bracken Cottage being taken over by strangers, — who's caring for it now?"

"The executor, Duncan MacFarlane, — he's the local Laird, who apparently owns most the land in the area."

She chuckled at her visions while half-rotating in her chair, "Another fusty old Laird; I don't remember him; — I wonder what's happened to old Angus, I'm sure that gran was sweet on him."

"Why not go and find out, I haven't met him, but I understand that Duncan is his grandson, and you won't be completely among strangers; — have you forgotten your gran's old friend, Hannah McPhee and her nephew, your old playmate, Rory Cameron? Hannah will love making a fuss of you. Since you've lost touch, why not write to her and tell her that you're coming?"

Her expression lapsed into a soft, mischievous smile as she remembered the fun she had had with Rory. When they had last met, he had been eighteen and a towering six-foot-three-inches high, with a head of the most unruly mop of golden curls. He loved to play tag and kiss chase and usually won; he could also play a mean duet on the piano, they even had the older generation jitter-bugging when playing the Boogie-Woogie at the dances held in the local village hall, even her old gran swayed and tapped her foot, — there was a lot of fun and laughter when she and Rory got together.

She let out a very heavy sigh, concluding, — "Well, it seems that I'm left with no alternative, okay," she finally agreed. "I'll sort something out with Ryder."

"Good girl!" Charles exclaimed, in no mean terms, while he swiftly snatched up the telephone and began dialling before she could change her mind. "I'll contact Crawford and Jackson immediately, and arrange for your pending arrival," he then grimaced, continuing, — "And in the meantime, cosset me, try a new image, ditch the jeans and go shopping with your mother for some new clothes, something feminine for a change."

"Charles … you're going too far," she warned.

"Helen, go!" he bellowed, exasperated, just wanting to end the interview.

"Okay, okay, I'll go," she chanted as she backed towards the door with a restraining hand extended, "Just one more thing … how *old* is this … Duncan MacFarlane?"

For a moment, he faltered, before bellowing, "How the *damned* hell should I know, I've never met the man, — Uh, Oh! Sorry Crawford."

Helen tweaked her fingers in farewell, "See you later."

And a few minutes later, with the prospect of Arrochar seeming a little less daunting, she began warming to the idea, as walking briskly along Fleet Street in the bright mid-July sunshine, she became overwhelmed and strongly determined to convince Ryder that she were able to achieve miracles, — but Ryder was going to be no mean feat.

Drawing level with a huge block of modern offices, she cast a glance skywards, reading the words, 'London Daily News' emblazoned across its high grey façade. Sighing softly, she entered the building through swinging plate glass doors, immediately proceeding to elbow her way through the eternal throng of people crowded in the foyer, all making steady progress to the lifts. She was now in full throttle with the idea, thinking that it would be good to get away from all of this, although her stomach felt querulous as she joined the pressing cram.

Seconds later, she stepped out of her lift onto the eighth floor. The cool open confines of the stone flagged landing were a blessed relief, before entering through another plate glass door into a vast open office, to be met by the acrid smell of stale cigarette smoke, the sound of constantly ringing telephones, the babble of high-pitched voices and incessantly tapping typewriters. — Raising a hand, she acknowledged several of her colleagues, as she threaded her way through the jumble of desks, piled high with paperwork.

Above the din, she picked out the dulcet tones of Rita White, her friend and flatmate, as she greeted her, "Hi Helen; what kept you; — good news from Charles, I hope?" she called breezily, while pouring two glasses of iced water from a jug.

Feeling hot and sticky after her midday walk, she dropped down onto a nearby chair, a trifle breathless. "Phew! It's hot," she needlessly remarked, while using a sheet of paper from Rita's desk to fan her glowing face, and smoothing back fine tendrils of hair which clung damply to her temple, before making any reply. — Although she felt concerned about her pressing interview with Ryder, she was in a strangely, joyous, tormenting mood. "Well, you'll never guess, Rita," she said, teasingly, deliberately withholding information.

Rita cast her a perceptive glance while idly biting into the green apple, which she had extracted from her lunchbox; "I won't waste your time, — I readily give in," she replied, grimacing, having swallowed the obviously sour looking fruit, and followed it with a sip of water. "Never was any good at guessing," said the bubbly redhead, who hailed from Brooklyn. "Anyway, I know you're bursting to tell me something."

Savouring the moment, rather than the apple, Helen grinned, "I'm … an … heiress," she slowly, coolly, tantalisingly informed, finding no disappointment in the reaction her words had evoked, for Rita was suddenly alert, she dropped her apple into her lap to gape at her friend with doe-like brown eyes, widened in surprise, she gasped,

"Y…You mean a fortune, we've made it at last," she asked, excitedly.

Helen softly laughed, enjoying her friend's expressive countenance, "Well, not exactly a fortune" she amended. "It goes like this …

"Oh," Rita said, sounding deflated five minutes later, but agreeing, "It does sound a bit unfair – but …," she shrugged. "So, now you have to broach Ryder with your proposition, well, I wish you luck. When do you expect to leave?"

"About September," she laconically replied.

"For the winter," Rita shuddered despite the heat. "Rather you than me — the weather in the Highlands is so unpredictable; — you'll *freeze*, — you'll be snowbound," she threatened. Then her eyes opened wide again with a new sudden realisation, — "Oh Helen!" she wailed, "I'll have to find a new flatmate, and I'll miss your company …," her voice trailed off, as Helen chuckled at friend's now woebegone countenance.

"Hold on, there's no panic," she said, raising a hand while rising in preparation to leave, "September is a long way away."

"What date in September? I'll need plenty of time to advertise."

"The ninth, — to be exact."

"That's the anniversary of the 'Battle of Flodden'," she immediately announced. "I wonder if it has any significance."

Helen raised her eyebrows in surprise, feeling impressed at Rita's lateral thinking, "The Battle of Flodden?" she echoed.

"Yes, you know … the 'Battle of Flodden', it was Scotland's bloodiest battle, — even the King died," and then grinning, she enlightened, "A High School project; I promised myself a trip, one day."

Helen grinned also, with surprise, "Well, what'll yer know? We'll have

16

to discuss this later, and do a little more research on the MacFarlanes," she said, while tucking her chair tidily into the desk, before embarking on her formidable mission to see Ryder. "It seems that we have a little mystery to solve," she said in passing finality.

Chapter 2

Alta Ego

The following evening, Helen hummed cheerfully to herself while under the jetting shower, — the pelting sensation on her weary limbs, somehow revived some of the drained energy resources, and after a day spent in the divorce courts watching a real life drama unfold, — this was sheer luxury. She stretched, savouring every droplet, while lathering her silky skin with more creamy liquid soap on a sponge.

While in her unwinding state, her thoughts drifted back to the previous day's interview with Ryder.

He hadn't been very co-operative at first. — She was letting him down at the worst possible time, he had told her, but under what seemed extenuating circumstances, had reluctantly agreed to a retainer to be reviewed within three months of her leaving for the north. — Believing that her new environment wouldn't provide many newsworthy events, she had negotiated a suitable contract which would cover general articles as well as her usual gossip, thus enabling her more scope. — Grudgingly, he had agreed to her terms, but on shaking her hand had remarked ...

"Don't leave us forever, will you, Helen? Your readers are among the most reactionary that I know."

"There's nothing like the 'power of suggestion' for creating a riot," she had said.

"I like it," Harry had replied. "And I must admit that I didn't think you had it in you. — A little soft centred, I had thought in the past, and so I'm surprised to hear myself say, — you're proving me wrong. Keep it up; — there could be a bonus in it for you when you return. You've always wanted your photograph at the top of the column."

Rousing herself from her reverie, she wrapped a large fluffy white towel around her slim form with another encasing her hair which resembled a turban, before proceeding from the bathroom, through into the bedroom to join Rita. Her companion, she found sitting at the dressing-table, concentrating on the meticulous task of painting her nails a bright tangerine. She glanced up as Helen entered the room.

"It's getting late, if you don't hurry, you'll miss your dinner," she warned.

Helen made no comment, engrossed as she now was, sorting through her meagre wardrobe for a suitable dress to wear for the concert. Sighing dejectedly, she tossed up between the only three that she owned.

"It's hopeless," she groaned. "I must agree with Charles, I've be so wrapped up with work, that I hadn't noticed that my clothes were in such a pitiful state."

While blowing on her wet lacquer, Rita glanced across the room to where Helen stood surveying the depleted, formidable heap of clothes. She rose to join her beside the cheval mirror while exclaiming in no uncertain terms, — "You daren't wear any of these! Charles will throw a- blue-fit, you've tried it before, remember, — and while we're at it, have you ever considered that Ryder doesn't think you're presentable enough to promote? There are times when you have to bend to your peers, — you don't have to be a fashion freak, just smarten up a little, and it's not so difficult to do. — I'd come shopping with you, but your mother will interfere; we don't exactly see eye to eye when it comes to clothes, — she dresses classic."

"I know, she dresses boring, — she never loosens up." She groaned, resignedly, sinking down on the dressing-stool beside her, while pulling off her head towel and combing her damp hair with her fingers. "She comes from an age where girls were cut down versions of their mothers. I never seem to have time to shop, and Ryder should understand, he gets the goods."

"How did it go today?"

"There was this interesting case in the Divorce Courts; — Charles is their solicitor; — it went on for simply hours and hours. — Do you remember the Madison couple? — They were married about two years ago. — He must be all of twenty years her senior," she estimated. "I originally wrote in the column that it was a doomed marriage, and now it seems, — I was right." She revealed, "He simply couldn't match the pace of her old flame, a much younger chap, who returned to the scene when she became a rich, bored socialite. They both attempted to well line their pockets with old Madison's money. — I couldn't believe my luck a few months ago, when I came across the devious pair, booking into Claridges for a clandestine weekend."

"Ah! Yes, — I remember your report," Rita replied, thoughtfully. "The headlines were vicious." she used her hands expressively, as if reading imaginary print, — 'Clarissa Entertains Old Beau – Madison Style' — I bet it was a real eye popper for her husband." She frowned, — "They weren't very subtle in using Claridges, were they — they were bound to be seen."

"He was out of the country much of the time, and much too trusting. He hadn't an inkling his wife had strayed from the fold," Helen explained, standing to stretch her body and yawning. "The report didn't make me feel proud of myself, but — I simply couldn't stand aside, and let the poor rich fool be swindled out of his hard-earned fortune, by his supposedly adoring wife."

Rita suddenly glanced at her wristwatch, and once again, commented on the passage of time. She would be late for her date, if she didn't hurry, — but Helen's garb for the evening had become a pressing problem. For a further moment the good-natured girl thought, — suddenly snapping her fingers and spurring into action as the answer came into her head. "I have just the thing," she announced, turning on her heel. "Wait here," she demanded, while disappearing into the adjacent room.

Helen shed the towel enveloping her and slipped into a pair of scanty, minuscule briefs, and then began the onerous task of drying her lustrous hair, while wondering what Rita would produce from her liberal wardrobe.

A few moments later, she returned bearing a dress container labelled 'Macy's of America'. "You can borrow my latest purchase, it's more your style than mine. — I don't know why I bought it, I guess I had you in mind," she said, sighing, while glancing enviously at Helen's tall, trim figure. "On second thoughts, I'll make you a present of it, — keep it as a going away present."

Helen enthusiastically gasped, "Thanks...a million," she gratefully, excitedly breathed, smiling broadly, knowing what the box contained.

"Think nothing of it," Rita answered, theatrically flicking her hand. "Anything to get that beautiful mug of yours on that page, so don't complain that I haven't sided with you. — Now, I must go; Vincent is the impatient kind, he won't wait around too long."

"You should give him the boot," she called after Rita's departing back. "Thanks again for the dress."

Half-turning, Rita called back before closing the door, "See you, Kidda! Enjoy the Puccini, and give Charles my love," she winked, followed by the after-thought, "Oh, and if Giles is around this evening, give him a big kiss from me, — you've got a lot of explaining to do."

"Giles will understand," she replied. — Helen grinned to herself, thoughtfully sighing. — She knew that leaving Rita would leave a void in both of their lives. They had shared their flat for a very interesting two years, — a span of time in which she had watched and consoled her friend through numerous, disastrous, romantic interludes, — amazingly enough, she managed to fall in and out of love with every change of weather. — She had lost count long ago of the continual stream of young men, who called to date her friend, but Rita wasn't easy virtue, — she wouldn't readily put up with the latest, expected free love, just because women were now sexually liberated, anymore than she would herself. — It was a hard task holding onto the morals of life in the modern world. — She became pensive, as she stared into the dressing table mirror and studied her reflection, naked of makeup — her thoughts took her back four years. ...

"With very little effort, Helen could look quite beautiful, if only she would take the time, and try more often," she had overheard her mother saying down in the hallway. *"Helen!"* Glynis called up the stairs, *"Helen, there's a parcel for you; — it's from your gran."*

"She's sent them!" she exclaimed, excitedly breathless, after running down the stairs.

"For heavens sake, — sent what?" Glynis also exclaimed.

"Why, the hair combs, — of course."

Glynis appeared amazed, *"You're actually doing something different with your hair?"*

"Well, I can't arrive at the school party looking like a gypsy; — all the girls will have made a special effort, and they've asked me to play."

"What are you playing?"

"A Prelude," she replied laconically, whilst in the process of un-wrapping the parcel.

"A Prelude...a prelude to what?" Glynis asked impatiently.

Helen shrugged; — her reply was evasive, *"Whatever they ask for, mother."*

"Well...well, can't we come and hear?"

"You would be a distraction, and no-one else's parents will be there; — I'll get them to record it and gran can have a copy as well."

"Has she something to play it on? I've only noticed some old gramophone."

"Rory will help her with that, his equipment is up-to-date. "She suddenly gasped, excitedly crying ... "Just look at this — isn't this just so beautiful?"

"Why, it's a Victorian aigrette and there's a corsage, —" and taking

them to admire, Glynis inhaled the intoxicating perfume. "Mmm, my, red
roses and white heather, tied with a tartan ribbon; — have you got a secret
admirer?"

"Gran admires me, and it was probably Rory's idea to send the flowers;
— they'll be from her garden, and it's not a corsage, it's a hair ornament,
— part of the aigrette, look, — there's a picture of a grand Victorian lady
wearing these very pieces of jewellery, as an example."

Glynis studied the likeness, remarking, "I don't recognise her, she must
be a relative of your grandfathers."

She chuckled softly, shaking herself away from her reverie and then suddenly spurred into action, as the clock again, caught her eye, — she sighed with the awareness that she was finally yielding to her peers.

She pulled a face at herself in the mirror, screwing up her neat straight nose, — first applying mascara to a long fringe of dark curling lashes, beneath an arc of neatly trimmed eyebrows, — she then lightly brushed her smooth rounded cheeks with blusher, and after applying a glossy soft orange lipstick, nipped her mouth into a prunes and prisms effect, and then, — a final spray of favourite perfume for good measure. — She removed the box lid, unfolded the tissue wrapping and extracted the dress, made in shimmering shades of peacock-blue. She then hastily dressed before the cheval mirror, being totally aware that the silky soft lines of the light summer gown, draped, moulded and emphasised the feminine contours of her trim form, — the dress wasn't restricting, and felt very comfortable to wear; — the silk lightly brushed her skin, making her feel expensively dressed and confident. The bodice was sleeveless, a raglan, cutting up to a tight polo neck, leading down to a front split, provocatively revealing the surface of lightly tanned breasts, — she finally brushed her luxurious cascade of chestnut hair into a shining, wavy profusion, and then shrugged at the final effect. "I'll do," she softly murmured.

After casting a last glance around the room, she snatched-up her car keys from the dressing table and hurried from the flat, lightly running down the stairs, with low-heeled silver sandals clattering on stone steps. Within minutes, once on the street, she gained entry to her red mini, and set off to drive through the bustling city centre, towards a well sought after area in Hampstead. Fortunately, the rush hour traffic had eased and only half-an-hour later, she drew up outside the Petrie residence. — The black wrought iron gates were laid open, awaiting her arrival.

Tall Chimneys' was a large, smart looking white painted corner house built around the 1920s. It was an unusual design, with irregular, — many turreted red tiled roofs, inset with garret windows, beneath which, were cornered latticed casement windows projecting from the upper walls. — Just as Helen drew to a halt, the front door opened, both Charles and her mother came down the path smiling a greeting, and stepping out of her car, she received her mother's welcoming embrace. "Darling!" she profusely greeted, while placing a kiss on the proffered cheek. "So good to see you again; — it's been so long." She continued complaining, "I do *wish* you would honour us with your presence a little more often." — Helen opened her mouth to reply, only to shut it again as her mother still continued, "I *know*, — its pressure of work," she acknowledged, taking the words from Helen's mouth, while the subject of the appraisal was trying to appear patiently understanding. — Glynis continued to continue speaking while sweeping her daughter with an affectionate, scrutinising look of surprise. "Why, you *do* look nice, dear, — very elegant," she commented favourably, turning to her husband for his supporting opinion, — "Charles, you must agree."

Helen impatiently raised her eyes at the fuss, feeling her cheeks tinge to a delicate rose-colour, as she self-consciously met Charles's gaze. He grunted and winked his silent approval.

They entered the house and passed down the hallway, leading through to the living room, a room which was partially book-lined and tastefully decorated and furnished with large cream leather sofas, sitting on a woodblock floor, which was scattered with red Turkish rugs; — the ladies seated themselves. Helen's piano stood near a wall of sliding glass doors, although now closed, they opened onto a large airy verandah which stepped down into the tree and heavily bushed garden. Charles enquired while he poured the drinks …

"How did you get on with Ryder?"

"Only fair, he drives a hard bargain," she replied, sipping at her white wine while carefully detailing her agreement with Ryder. Charles listened attentively, and, was, as she knew he would be, — dissatisfied with the flimsiness of the contract.

"Only three months …?" he looked thoughtfully disgruntled, but then shrugged. "Well, I suppose it's a start, though we must keep this to ourselves," he said, glancing across at her, his voice lacking enthusiasm. "To anyone else, — you understand, — you are on an extended holiday, and I only hope for your sake that a story of some consequence occurs, which will whet your gluttonous readers' appetites and seek to satisfy,

Ryders inability to find total confidence in your work, — can't understand the *makings* of the man," he muttered. "You need this break; it will do you good."

"Yes, I agree," her mother chipped in. "I feel quite excited on your behalf, inheriting your gran's cottage. — Of course, I'm not *really* surprised, your gran always did adore you," for a moment, she appeared thoughtful, "… although, I could never understand her not wanting you to visit Arrochar, after your father had died. — Your letters must have seemed small compensation, in return for the loss of her son."

"Gran was happy with the situation as it was, I suppose," Helen replied, her voice, lack-lustre. "I know her request for solitude seemed strange, almost as strange as her demand for me to spend six months in Arrochar, now she's dead. But I can honestly say, that I believe she had a reason," she concluded, thoughtfully, silently questioning, — 'but what was that reason' she wondered, not for the first time, — and what is all the secrecy about?

"Yes, of course she had, dear," her mother agreed, and then continued with another line of topic, craftily suggesting. — "Before you go north, we must go on a shopping spree; you'll need a lot of beautiful clothes to wear."

Helen raised intolerant eyes, while she groaned and tutted with impatience. The issue of clothes was fast becoming a pressing fact, but it wasn't a fact that she was prepared to admit to Glynis; — she answered mutinously, "Mother! I can't imagine that a village tucked away in the heart of the Highlands, would require a West End type wardrobe."

"Nonsense, stop avoiding the issue dear, we need clothes to boost the feminine moral, and Arrochar is a tourist village; — the locals aren't exactly adverse to a little sophistication."

She firmly argued, "In Scotland, tourists wear casual, comfortable clothing, some wear wet gear and walking boots, — I don't see myself in tweeds."

"I never mentioned tweeds, and I simply abhor those unfeminine walking boots."

Helen sighed in resignation; — she surreptitiously studied her parent. — Her mother always managed to be well turned out in smart suits bearing quality labels, and her short pretty fair hair beautifully styled. — It had just a hint of grey in it these days, she observed, knowing that she would 'wax-lyrical' on her various trips to the U.S. and had succumb to the odd chin tuck and the latest hair dying techniques, none of which she felt would enhance her own virtues.

Glynis's cook then blessedly made an appearance, to announce that their meal was ready. — They removed to the dining room, where Glynis suddenly smiled at her, waiting for her decision, "Well, Helen?" she prompted. "It's a good opportunity; — it's about time you took yourself in hand and spoilt yourself; — spend some of your mounting hoards."

Sighing again, while feeling that there seemed to be no escape; — she grudgingly replied while counting on her fingers. "Alright, you win, but it's going to be difficult, I still have to complete another two months with the paper; — I'll just have to steal the time for shopping."

Glynis looked at her daughter with positive jubilance, "Excellent!" she exclaimed. "I shall look forward to it," and then fell silent, a happy sparkle lighting her eyes, while she tucked into her crab and avocado salad and in between mouthfuls, chatted to Charles.

Glancing thoughtfully from one to the other of her parents, both now engrossed in their meal, a shrewd smile played about her pretty mouth. — Her inheritance was going to make radical changes to her life, which obviously pleased them. — They had never, exactly, one hundred per cent, approved of her choice of career, and had shown disappointment when she had given up her piano studies to pursue journalism. "There's no future in music," she had argued, knowing that her father had held very different views. He had always taught her that, — music was the melting pot of life.

"But a journalist, Helen, all those terrible murders and dull politics to report on, — so depressing," Glynis had remarked at the time, giving a convincing shudder at the abhorrent thought.

Charles had been a little more encouraging; —*"It wouldn't be so bad if you could work on the Gossip Columns. — If you really insist on this idea of yours, why not call on Harry Ryder. — He's the Editor of the 'Daily News'. — I'll speak to him on your behalf, — if you so wish,"* he had suggested.

She had replied; feeling startled at the suggestion, and had raised an adamantly protesting hand, *"No, no thank you, Charles, — this is something I would like to do for myself."*

It was very difficult not to hurt them on occasions. The Gaelic side of Helen sometimes rebelled at their solicitude for her welfare. Understandably, — she supposed, — as after the shock of her adored father dying so suddenly, she had fretted deeply had been unable to eat or sleep, until eventually she had contracted pneumonia. — Her mother had immediately, whisked her away to Switzerland to convalesce for three months, thus taking the opportunity to rest herself and review her changed circumstances, after which, they had returned to England. — A further six months had elapsed before Glynis had married Charles, a natural turn of events which had privately pleased Helen, as Charles had always been in her life. — She had often felt that she had two fathers, although a polygamous relationship would have been far from her mother's mind. The things that weren't far from the mind of Glynis, however, were matters that she couldn't fathom, and Helen toyed and teased with this aspect of her mother's nature, she avoided her probing tactics with great skill.

"We don't want a repeat of all those terrible dreams that you suffered," Glynis remarked.

"What dreams?" Helen enquired evasively, her voice indignantly rising.

"Well, you had such a high temperature, your mind was wandering and you kept calling out someone's name, no-one that I recognised, of course."

"Dreams are private affairs, mostly woven around the imagination," she replied, *"A teenager's lively mind. I had a crush on a boy down the street; and I don't think they were so very terrible."*

Glynis immediately latched on, "What boy down the street? You never said anything about a boy down the street."

"That's because, you would never have approved."

Her gran had refused all offers to live with them in London, preferring instead her beloved Highlands, and Helen concluded, that whatever had been her reasons for remaining a semi-recluse, had gone with her to the grave.

Giles Erskine, at twenty six, was a reporter and commentator on musical events, such as the Promenade Concerts. He was an avid follower of the Scottish National Orchestra and, on hearing Helen's news, keenly insisted on accompanying her to Edinburgh, where they could spend an evening wallowing in Mozart's piano concertos. Giles was studiously handsome, his ash blond head stood a few inches above Helen's and he had the most mesmerising blue eyes which drew the girls, but he currently only had eyes for Helen. — He made a wonderful escort, was lively, sociable and entertaining in mixed company, but on a one-to-one basis, he wasn't a conversationalist; they had met during an interval at one of the Proms. Helen soon realized that he was becoming a habit that Glynis was keen to promote.

The following six weeks passed in what Helen considered — sometime later, — to be a chaotic flurry of excitement. — Under her mother's strict supervision, — after she had come through the gruelling experience of being re-processed, — suffering the treatment of numerous beauticians, throwing on this face-pack and that cream. "Good protection against the Highland weather, dear," she was forced to accept. Her nails manicured, "Hands and feet," her mother insisted. It seemed the bitter end after several sauna treatments to be pushed and pummelled into orderly shape by a matronly masseuse.

"Mother ... I swear to impunity that you're enjoying all of this," she mutinously accused, while laying face down on the beauty parlour couch, with only a large fluffy towel to cover her modesty.

Her mother gave a tinkling laugh, admitting, "Of course I am, my darling, — now, *just* relax, and enjoy yourself. It's high time you were taken in hand, — is it *really* so very terrible?" She asked.

Helen merely grunted in reply.

Her mother's inexhaustible enthusiasm, led them to a further week of invading countless boutiques and department stores, until she became giddy from trying on clothes, twisting and twirling for the older woman's approval, until the inside of her head whirled, and drummed out the rhythm of a train, hammering down the tracks — dresses for day wear, dresses for evening wear, suits, blouses, jumpers, skirts, undies and shoes for every conceivable occasion, but not one pair of trousers in sight; — a small fact which she intended to remedy at a later date. — "You simply must have that long white one, Helen," she said, giving a secret smile. "You look so charming in white; it's all I ever dressed you in when you were a little girl."

Helen raised her eyes, "But mother ... I'm *not* a little girl now, and I don't want to resemble a milk bottle." was her disgruntled reply. "I would rather have gone shopping with, Rita."

"Rita has such an appalling taste in clothes," Glynis retorted, shuddering. "Everything she wears is so loud, acid lime greens and orange; you can see her coming from a mile away."

"She's colourful!" Helen indignantly exclaimed. "And they **are** the fashion colours this season, it's all in Vogue, — why do I have to look so boring?"

"I'll buy the dress for you," Glynis decided.

At the end of the tortuous week, Charles met them for lunch in the Café Royale, "Oxford Street and Kensington High Street, can't have a single thing left!" he laughingly declared, seeing their heap of parcels.

Glynis gave him a satisfied grin in welcome, while Helen just grunted, knowing that her Mini would be groaning under the weight of numerous suitcases, — however, her knowledge was to be short lived …

"Well, Helen," he continued, after seating himself to begin the familiar ritual of consulting his diary to reveal the next stage of Mairie's instructions, "The arrangements are — that you travel to Edinburgh by train in ten days time, where I've booked you into a hotel for one night. Crawford is expecting you to call on him to sign some papers. — Your car, I have arranged to arrive by motor rail, two days after you yourself arrive in Arrochar. — Now, is there anything else further, that you wish me to do, or is there anything that you don't understand?"

Helen's usually smooth brow creased, she became further perplexed, sitting up pert, she warily echoed, questioning, as the information on the car sank in, "Train … did I hear you say… train?"

Charles nodded, "That is what I said, Helen … train."

Helen puffed out her cheeks, followed by blowing the air through pursed lips; showing her intolerant, impatient disbelief, — her indignation was obvious, "I'd rather drive myself," came the complaining reply.

Charles was immediately on his metal, "May I remind you, that it was your usual mode of transport, and in your own *eager* words, spoken on the station platform, 'It simply fly's me up to Scotland'. We will carry out the instructions in the *will* … to the letter … its imperative!" he informed her gruffly. "And, no buts," he warned, observing her next intake of breath. "*That's,* the way it is … and *that's* the way … it's going to stay," he ended firmly, giving her a challenging glare.

Helen pouted again, appearing annoyingly thoughtful for a moment. The mystery deepens, everything seemed to be out of her hands, out of her control, and she suddenly had a suspicion that Charles may know more than he was prepared to let on. — His next remark revealed that he must have read her mind, "I don't know anymore than you do," he hastily confirmed, displaying his knowledge of her by pre-empting another outburst.

"Are there anymore surprises, Charles?"

Charles grunted, clearing his throat, before he swiftly answered, "Not this end."

Helen succinctly echoed, "Not … this end?"

"Champagne everyone?" he asked, breathing a sigh of relief when the waiter called for their order, "We must make a toast."

"A good idea, Charles," Glynis agreed.

And, lightened by the moment, "I'll get giddy," Helen remarked, forced into relaxing while giving a chuckle.

"I'm already giddy," Charles reciprocated. "I must have the giddiest, most effusive step-daughter that any man has ever been blessed with."

Suddenly, a warm welter of affection flowed through her, a hint of merriment lit her sparkling eyes as she leaned towards Charles, in a mood to tease, "You're an absolute *darling,* Charles," she said, with alacrity and deliberate emphasis on the affectionate word, knowing it would have the desired effect.

Looking abashed, Charles sat back in his seat to bluster his confused way out of her remark, but suddenly, his face relaxed into a slow beam and he joined in the gales of laughter now surrounding him, "I shall miss you, Helen, I shall miss you. It's going to be *far* too peaceful, no-one to argue with."

"You can argue with mother," she grinned.

"It's not *quite* the same thing," he pointedly remarked.

Chapter 3

Edinburgh in the Autumn

Helen awoke early in her hotel room and leaping from her bed, crossed the floor to gaze from the window. The early city bustle had already started, working to meet another day.

Edinburgh Castle was in full view, reminding her that she had missed the hectic three weeks of the traditional, Edinburgh Festival and the Military Tattoo, to which her father had brought her, many years ago. They had fitted in as many concerts and musical events as they could, thus wetting her appetite for the classical music and the jazz that she'd played so studiously. — She looked down at her slender fingers, knuckling and flexing them, using the window ledge as an imaginary piano. — The previous evening, she had spent with Giles listening to Mozart's piano concerto's No 23 and No 25. — Afterwards, he had argued that he wanted to accompany her on the rest of her journey, but she had adamantly told him, — that in no uncertain terms, — could she allow his intrusion into the terms of the *will,* — this was something between herself and her grandmother. Giles had reluctantly conceded, and had departed for Glasgow on the early morning train. — At her bedroom door he had kissed her goodnight, and tried to make her promise to keep in touch, "Journey's end," she had murmured, apologetically.

Chuckling to herself, she turned from the window and sighed, turning her thoughts towards her morning arrangements. — She had a lunchtime appointment with Crawford, and so there was more than enough time to prepare.

She showered, and dressed casually in newly purchased golden beige linen slacks, teamed with a sleeveless white clingy tee-shirt with a polo neck, while making the decision to use the hotel's hairdressing salon, after her usual breakfast of coffee and croissants. — The skilful stylist worked patiently with the lustrous strands, winding, binding and pinning her hair into a sophisticated, swirling upswept style, creating a coronet of large curls to the crown of her head, and to finally, thread through a band of cream coloured velvet ribbon.

Almost two hours later, Helen was passing through the reception foyer, which was milling with people and was littered with newly arrived Louis Vuitton matching luggage; there was a commotion at the desk, caused by a group of demanding VIPs who didn't seem to have booked rooms. The lady had an embarrassingly lashing tongue, — it turned curious heads, and soon had the porters' scurrying to collect the luggage and transport it to the allotted rooms. The kilted commissionaires' turned heads with faces full of disdain, it was a mean scene to a reporter; — she was burning with curiosity.

"Who's the lady?" Helen asked one of the porters.

"I don't know Miss, but she's no lady."

"What's on the luggage label?" she eagerly whispered.

"It just says, 'APC' Edinburgh. — I must move it, Miss," he said, apologetically concerned, "I don't want to lose my tip."

Moments later, the aloof lady and her entourage joined Helen in the lift, it was a little crammed with an overbearing, stony silent, tense atmosphere. The party departed from the lift on the floor below hers, which was damning.

Back in her room, she turned her attention to personal matters in hand. Accompanied by Rita, the sombre black Chanel suit which Glynis had selected, had been duly returned to the store and exchanged for a refreshing Cornish cream, teamed with a navy-blue blouse, littered with cream poker dots; this she meticulously donned. She slid on silk stockings, high heeled, navy patent leather court shoes, and from the bed, lifted a matching clutch bag, finishing the touch, by draping a navy cashmere swagger coat about her shoulders. Viewing her now elegant reflection in the mirror, she wondered whereto, had her hippie image disappeared, there wasn't even a mere trace, it was new guise. — Could this really be, — Helen Campbell, she thought, determined to display the differences between town and country living?

An hour later, she passed back through the reception and, while handing in her room key, she furtively craned her neck to read the guest book which said, 'Runcorn Productions – Hollywood - USA', of which she made a mental note, some research wouldn't go amiss.

Moments later, she mingled with the cosmopolitan tourists strolling along Prince's Street, until she wandered into the Georgian New Town where her footsteps led her towards the citys' offices, amid the fashionable addresses of Moray Place, and seeking until she found herself outside her destination.

She gazed about her, admiring the elegant tree-lined square, surrounded by a crescent of grey-stone eighteenth century Georgian houses. Lifting her eyes, she surveyed with interest, the handsome neo-classical façade of the building in front of her. The scrubbed steps, the shiny black railings displaying the smart gold insignia plate of: - 'Crawford and Jackson - Solicitors and Commissioners' of Oaths' — it informed its readers.

So this was where her father had begun his career, she reacquainted, as she moved towards the matching, shiny black door, adorned with brass door furniture. It was ajar in readiness to admit potential clients.

Entering the green carpeted hallway, she then entered the welcoming open doorway of the Reception Office, where a rather stern looking secretary greeted her. — The matronly lady appeared puzzled while making a study of her fob watch, which was pinned to the lapel of her sombre black suit, relieved by the hand crocheted white lace collar of her blouse; — she then levelled her eyes at her visitor, above half-lens specs, saying …

"Yeel be Miss Campbell," she surmised. "Sit you down; I'll just away to find Mr. Crawford. Though you're a trifle early for your appointment, — 1pm, on the cannon blast, — 'twas arranged and it's only 12.00 midday, — mind, he may not see you … lunch … you understand," she said protectively.

"Thank you," said Helen, feeling slightly amused while deciding that Miss MacNab, — as her desk label informed her, — must be a solid part of the office furniture. "I can wait," she laconically informed.

Alone for a moment, she wandered over to the window to peer out onto the square. — Her eyes became misty, thinking again of her father enjoying the same view, not so many years ago. — Deep in thought, she failed to hear the opening door, — startled for a moment at the loud robust greeting; — she jumped at its alacrity and whirled round on her heel to face an equally robust figure.

"Ah! Miss Campbell, delighted, delighted to meet you at last," said Mr. Crawford, keenly, effusively, approaching her with his arm outstretched, ready to grasp her hand in a firm, vigorous handshake. — He cast scrutinising eyes over her, saying, "And unmistakably, you *are* a Campbell, — there can be no doubt of that. — I remember your father well, one of our more successful protégés. — We share you losses, my dear," he said. — Then not wishing to dwell too long on past grief, his ruddy complexioned face broke into a kindly smile.

Returning his smile, she thanked him for his felicitations as he ushered her past him through a door at the opposite end of the office. — Miss MacNab had obviously, got it wrong, she thought, as he led the way across a further narrow passageway and through another door, which led into an enormously high-ceilinged, book-lined office. — It was sparsely furnished, with a very large, littered oak partner's desk backing onto the window bay and dominating the room. Either side of the desk were the customary chairs, with two conveniently placed filing cabinets standing abreast of the window. — Unlike Charles city office, all appeared very Dickensian, worn and musty.

"Sit you down, Lass," invited Mr. Crawford, indicating the chair on the near side of his desk, while dropping his ample frame into the other. — The chair creaked under his weight, and Helen idly wondered if it would support him, — "Now, let me see," he thoughtfully remarked as he rummaged amongst his paperwork. "Ah! Here it is," he suddenly, jubilantly, exclaimed, holding up a buff coloured folder, bearing the title, — 'Mairie Campbell-Deceased'. — "I have quite a few documents for you to sign, Miss Campbell."

"You'll need these," she said, while opening her bag and withdrawing a wad of papers to hand them over the desk, "My birth certificate and father's death certificate."

"Excellent! Excellent! A mere formality, — you understand," he explained, scanning the documents and writing copious notes with a fountain pen, on papers taken from Mairie's folder … he continued, "She was a grand lady, your grandmother, I was proud to know her." He briefly appeared thoughtful, he murmured aside, "such a pretty lady," while a watered crimson hue, rose from beneath his stiffened shirt collar, to rise again and pallet itself on his mottled cheek; he then gruffly, cleared his throat before continuing. "You didn't see her for sometime, did you lass? — strange, strange, such a peculiar kettle of fish," he again remarked, frowning and shaking his head as he placed some papers in front of her. "Please read these, make sure that you digest them, then sign at the bottom," he indicated.

Sighing, she complied with his instructions, feeling as though she was signing her life away, but there was no turning back. Thoughts of loyalty and dedication to duty held her silent.

With the formalities completed, he passed over some parchment papers; "You are now the proud owner of Bracken Cottage," he said. "These are the title deeds and I want you to understand, that you are committed for the entire term assigned. — I'm sure that you will enjoy yourself." Continuing,

"I now have to hand you these letters."

Enjoy myself under these circumstances; she wretchedly thought as she took the proffered envelopes, but I must have confidence in myself and in my beliefs, so that I can fulfil my own ambitions, — there's no other way, she self-instilled.

And scanning the familiar writing on the first envelope recognised her gran's handwriting. — Will all be revealed, she silently wondered? "I'll ... read it, later," she stiltedly announced, aloud.

"I have no idea what it says," he conveyed. "It was handed to me after the burial."

The second envelope was typewritten and bore the address: - Mr. D. MacFarlane - The Loch House - Arrochar. "What's this?" She quizzed.

"That's your introduction to the Laird, but judging by your family resemblance, I feel you won't be in need of it, — just another formality," he repeated, smiling. "Now, is there anything else that I can help you with?"

She shrugged, "Possibly, I don't remember a- Mister Duncan MacFarlane, gran didn't ever mention him in her letters, I vaguely remember a- Robert; and what has become of the old Laird, Angus, I believe was his name?"

"He died some years ago, Robert was his son, but the hand of fate stepped in and shuffled a few things around, but again ... I can confidently assure you that you will find Duncan an admirable executor to the *will*," he confirmed. — "He has such tremendous business acumen. I'm sure, if you have any problems at all, he will be only too pleased to help."

Helen became anxious to assure the solicitor of her independence, "I ... err ... don't think that I will be asking any favours, especially of the Laird. We've been enough trouble to him already, and I'm sure that his impressions of Mairie Campbells' relations must find us very wanting, lacking in any human compassion for our elderly relative, and it just wasn't the case," she blurted.

Crawford was taken aback by her sudden outburst, which he detected as some irony of guilt; — his brow furrowed in concern and he hastened to reassure, "MacFarlane is fully acquainted with the situation, so you may have no fear of finding yourself ill-judged. Mairie Campbell was clear in mind and emphatic to the bitter end about her wishes, both during her life, and with her requests after it. You were far too young to do anything in the way of caring for her, and at a guess and mind, it is only a guess; — she didn't want you missing any of the opportunities of youth, for her benefit."

Helen warmly smiled with grateful affection. "Like father, she would never ask for help. Campbell pride, I think they call it."

Crawford smiled again, cocking a bushy eyebrow, "May I say, Miss Campbell, that upon our very short acquaintance, I don't think that they were the only ones to suffer from pride, — don't let it blind you too much, — will you?" He opened the folder again to withdraw a key, which he ceremoniously handed over to her. "This is one of the cottage keys and MacFarlane has the other one. The arrangements, according to the *will,* are … that he is to meet you at Talbert station, so if you would kindly give me your estimated time of arrival, I will contact him, immediately.

Ten minutes later with their business completed, and her letters safely tucked with the precious key in her bag, she made her departure back though the corridors to the reception where the maidenly secretary sat typing. Miss MacNab arrested Helen's attention as she was passing through,

"I beg your pardon, Miss Campbell, I hardly recognise you; — you look so very different. — It was many years ago, I only glimpsed you through the window, you were just a young lassie, you were here with your father; — he'd made a nostalgic detour when you were en-route to Arrochar. I fear that he must have felt that he had little time left to him."

Helen smiled, "He made a last flying visit to see his mother."

Suddenly, they were both distracted when Mr. Crawford reappeared, "Your gloves, Miss Campbell."

Thanks," she said.

He inclined his head and then turned his attention towards Miss MacNab, issued some brief instruction and, with a final farewell, he disappeared.

Miss MacNab glanced up briefly from her task on the telephone and nodded as Helen called out a cheerful farewell, wondering yet again, if the lady were the nuts and bolts of Messrs Crawford and Jackson, Solicitors.

Once outside the solicitor's office, the wind struck cold after the confines of the building; she involuntarily shivered and pulled her coat more closely around her. — Feeling anxious to read her letter, she made a quick assessment of her bearings. — It was only a short walk to a small coffee shop which she had noticed upon her arrival.

Moments later, comfortably settled in a secluded alcove, while waiting to be served with a welcoming cup of coffee and girdle scones, she plucked the letter from the depths of her bag to neatly rip open the envelope with her nail file; — it was dated a few days before Mairie's demise, — the writing was shaky, — the brief words on the page were very nostalgic, full of expectancy, but they neither revealed nor conveyed anything, except a protracted, confident knowledge that she had tightly sewn up her granddaughter's near future.

My Dear, Helen,

As you read this letter, I know that you will be over the Borders, possibly in Arrochar, itself.

As my last surviving relative, I'm pleased to leave you Bracken Cottage.

Live there, my deere, allow it to embrace you as I did, and when you require them, you'll find peace and contentment within its walls.

I have read all of your letters so many times, and feel that you have shared your life with me, they come so full of vitality and youthfulness.

I am content in the knowledge that you'll now breathe the air of the

Highlands. Look into your heart, Helen, for I am certain, that you'll be welcomed into the heart of Arrochar. God bless you my deere – Mairie Campbell.

Helens' thoughts on this matter were that her grandmother could not have written the letter without assistance, enquiries would be in order. — She then turned her thoughts to Mr. Crawford; he had obviously drawn up the *will*, but the contents weren't his to question, he also had a soft spot for Mairie, who had remained a widow for several decades, despite the attentions of more than one admirer. She had also observed that Crawford and Miss MacNab had conflicting views as to her appearance.

Sighing, she read the letter once again; it still explained nothing more than the words on the page. — She slowly refolded the missive and then replaced it back into the envelope, first gazing at it thoughtfully before returning it to the safe confines of her bag. — What does it all mean, she silently questioned, — why has she done this? "Oh, Mairie Campbell, Mairie Campbell," she murmured, and suddenly startled along with the whole clientele in the restaurant, when a loud explosion smote her ears, "what was that?" she sharply asked the waitress who had brought her order.

The waitress smiled brightly, it was a customary question. "It's the one o'clock cannon, firing from the Castle Rock," she informed her. "It fires everyday except for Sunday."

"Oh, a tourist attraction."

"No miss; it's an ancient piece of history, the sailors of Leith set their chronometers by it."

"Oh, thanks!" she smiled.

The journey from Edinburgh, via Glasgow to Arrochar seemed endless on the branch line train. As a diversion, she listened to the conversations of her companions, obviously rambling tourists, who were excited by their forthcoming exhortations, before also turning her attention to the passing raggedness of the landscape. And, in a vain effort to join them, from her small case, she withdrew a survey map she had chanced to purchase in Edinburgh, trying to identify the high peaks of the Ben Mountains, and various famous lochs as the train slowly wended its way around them.

Disheartened, she realised that her geography was sadly lacking, and made a promise to herself to take a guided tour of the area before winter set in. — For a few more minutes, she idly flicked through the pages of a glossy magazine called, 'Highland Life' it was full of profiles, stories of country people, which she read with interest.

Romantic Scotland, she had the passing, fleeting thought, and lulled by the rhythm of the train, drifted into a light sleep, filled with the shadowy images which had long ago been created by Rory's colourful imagination. He had leapt out of so many doorways, simply to scare her, only to kiss her better. — Despite herself, she was longing to see him again, and wondered if he had married. Hannah's reply to her letter had been brief; she conveyed that all news would be revealed in person, — her memories assailed her…

Helen passed through the castle gates and then hurried between the open portals of the oak doors. Inside, she took the stone steps that led down to the dungeons, and with trepidation, passed through the caverns of stone archways with partially lit sections, displaying wax tableauxs' of prisoners in wall-iron restraints, sitting or laying on straw, with a suitable amount of blood curdling from their tortured bodies. — She cringed as she passed through the torture chambers, depicting victims in various stages of agony until she had reached the bottom most cell, with a door of oak set with a window of latticed iron bars.

She could see the nameless lady dressed in her medieval cloak, embroidered with elaborate Celtic designs, the hood hung long and heavily down her back. Her auburn hair, which hung in thick plaits, fell forward over her shoulders. She was leaning towards the grilled door; her lips were pursed in a receptive kiss. The man on the other side, within the cell, who was leaning his face through the grill to receive the kiss, was Viking; he had a blond moustache and long straggly matted hair…

The prison warder who had obviously allowed the clandestine meeting of the lovers, stood at a discrete distance, — was he in on the plot? She wondered…

The explanation of the tableaux was posted on the outer wall of the dungeon; Rory had read it out to her …

In 1263 there was a Viking invasion in this area under the command of King Hakon of the Orkney and Shetland Islands. — he is said to have sent 60 ships up Loch Long, — they are thereafter, said to have dragged their boats over the two miles between Loch Long and Loch Lomond using wooden rollers, then re-launching their boats in Loch Lomond, his men landing at Arrochar, where they proceeded to launch an assault on the local inhabitants. It is suspected that a battle took place between the Vikings and the early MacFarlanes. In evidence, there is a burial ground midway between Arrochar and Talbert which has all the appearances of being the grave of a Viking leader.

Chapter 4

New Horizons

"Talbert ... Talbert Station, this train terminates here, — all passengers returning to Edinburgh, — please board now,"

Alerted, Helen woke from her doze with a start, hearing the familiar nasally public address system announcement. — Now fully awake, she hastily collected her hand luggage, leaving the hastily vacated carriage behind her to step onto the bustling platform; — her glance witnessed the porter unloading her smart, matching suitcases from the luggage van. "Seven pieces, lass," he reported as she approached.

"How did you know these were mine?" she enquired.

The porter removed his cap and scratched his head, saying, "It stands to reason, most travel light in these here parts, but you seem to have come to stay. Everyone else has rucksacks and is dressed casual like, you're dressed as a city dweller, — those heels are no good for climbing mountains, they'd snap in no time, if you'd take my advice, Miss Campbell ...." The porter waned when Helen silently, with enforced patience, raised her eyes at his revelation, "News travels fast in these here parts," he hastily remarked. "I was instructed to keep an eye open for you."

She nodded her thanks and handed him some coins, after which, she gazed about her, wondering where this illustrious stranger was, as the platform was now empty. — She was just considering a taxi, when suddenly her attention became alerted towards the station's brilliantly white painted picket fence and then over to the road beyond, by a shattering squeal of brakes renting the air, disturbing the peace. — The noise belonged to the battered blue estate car, now screeching to an unceremonious halt alongside the little picket gate.

Helen watched with mounting trepidation as a small, plump, middle aged lady with greying hair, and a tall young man of her own age, clad in fashionable blue-denims and a blue check shirt with sleeves rolled up, displaying rippling tanned muscles, stepped out. — As the pair walked through the gateway smiling in her direction, she hurried towards them with arms outstretched.

"Hannah! Hannah McPhee!" she exclaimed in delight.

"Helen … cried the lady excitedly, engulfing her in her plump arms and then planting a kiss on her proffered cheek. "Oh my, lass, it's so grand to see you again, it's been so long," she said excitedly, her eyes filling with tears. "Here, let me look at you," she requested, holding her at arm's length, while chatting on. "My, you are bonnie, just like your grandmother in her young days, or *maybe* a tad more sophisticated, I think. I wouldn't have recognised you from the last time that I saw you, — such an engaging child," she prattled on, while fumbling for a handkerchief to wipe away a stray tear from her homely cheek.

Rory had politely stood on ceremony with hands on hips, and although he was longing to draw Helen into his arms, he was suffering from an unusual bout of shyness; — his deep grey eyes were sweeping her appearance in awed wonderment, she didn't appear as approachable, until the long awaited moment came …

"Am I going to wait forever?" she said, invitingly stretching out her arms for the expected welcome.

He didn't need asking twice, he shook his head while grinning, his large hands lifting her from the waist with ease; — he tightly embraced her and swung her laughing form around, and as he rested her back onto her feet, he bent his tousled head to plant a swift kiss on her cheek, and despite his outward bravado, she felt him trembling, "Wow," he exclaimed flirtatiously, "I knew that Arrochar was missing a Princess, but I didn't expect her to turn up in the shape of Helen Campbell, — and *what* a shape."

Feeling the hot colour suffuse her face, Helen also flirted, "You look a might improved yourself, Rory Cameron, — if I may say so," she said, catching his wink while giving him a saucy curtsey, her pointing finger under her chin.

"You may," he replied, giving a slight mocking bow in return.

"Rory Cameron … behave yourself," Hannah chastised. "Away with you and pack Helen's suitcases in the car." And turning to Helen, "And you'd do as well, lass, to save your curtsies for the Laird."

She frowned, puzzled, "Oh, I don't think I'll be curtseying to the Laird."

"He commands plenty of etiquette." Hannah sternly informed.

Giving a wicked chuckle, Rory draped Hannahs' shoulders with his arm, squeezing her affectionately before picking up some of the baggage, commenting, "It's just as well I didn't bring my bike," and within minutes, everything was stowed neatly into the well-used Ford. Helen sat beside Rory in the front seat, while Hannah settled herself with some of the luggage in the rear.

Hannah reminded her as they set off, "The distance to the village, is just over a mile, but it makes a pleasant drive. — The Laird sends his apologies for not meeting you himself; he left last evening on some sudden, urgent business. He's been detained, and so arranged for us to meet you, instead."

Helen turned to smile at her, "It's good to be here, and to renew old acquaintances," she admitted, and sighing, she happily relaxed, "there's plenty of time to make new ones."

The conversation during the drive briefly covered the missing years since Helen's last visit. — She learned that Hannah was the Laird's housekeeper, a piece of news, which wasn't altogether surprising, as she had previously worked for the old Laird, at the Castle Drumbrae.

"Oh, Aye," she informed. "Since old Angus MacFarlane died, the castle has become a historical monument, you know, a tourist attraction; — during the summer months, Rory and his father work as the gardeners and caretakers; they still live in 'Mohr Cottage' attached to the castle walls, — my brother is a rose specialist."

"We are called 'Gillies'," Rory informed her, "... commonly known as the Laird's attendants."

"And what do you do in the winter?" She enquired.

He laughed humorously, "In time, yeel find out."

During a short lull in the conversation, they rounded a bend in the road where Helen let out a soft, pleasurable gasp at the sudden view; — her raking eyes scanned greedily, absorbing the entrancing scene, thus renewing her acquaintance with a familiar landmark, that of a sleepy looking loch. "Oh, it's still *so* beautiful!" she softly exclaimed, while peering through the windscreen, admiring the tranquil, breathtaking scene. "It's just like a painting!"

"It's been done a few times," Hannah remarked.

"Rory, *Stop! Stop!"* she urgently cried, eagerly wanting to absorb more of the view.

At her command, he swiftly skidded to a startling halt, — she immediately opened the door and swiftly stepped out of the car, Rory came to stand alongside her, "Oh, how wonderful!" she breathed, exclaiming softly. "Could anything be more perfect?" she exclaimed again, her heart racing

41

as she keenly stared from the roadside at the scene spreading before her.

There were rush grasses along the near shoreline, leading to a reflected, mirror image in the crystal water, of blue sky and white fluffy wool cloud; the drifting reflections seemed to breathe like a silent, sweeping, velvety sigh, darkening into shadows over the purple clad peeks. A tiny castle ruin stood to the left, with grass covering a rock mound; a line of trees ran from the castle to the right.

Rory was leaning against the low rugged wall, his eyes warmly caressed her face, and taking in her sparking jade eyes, her rapt expression and her heightened colour, evidencing her excitement, his young heart quickened, as she raised her hand to shade her eyes to see several yachts gliding in full colourful sail. "And the diving rock is still there."

"We could hardly move the rock, Princess," he chuckled. "The waterfowl would complain."

She pointed, "*Surely* that was the Auld Water Mill; it was a crumbling ruin six years ago."

"Aye, lass," Hannah confirmed, smiling her mutual pleasure. "That's right, it was, but Mr. Duncan had it rebuilt and he now lives in it. He's renamed it, —The Loch House."

"I don't think I want to leave," she reluctantly complained, when Rory suggested that they move on; he had other duties to perform and he had received instructions from his employer that he wasn't to dally.

"You've plenty of time to come again," he replied. "We can go sailing, I have my own boat."

As they drove on, she impulsively, peered back over her shoulder at the rambling white buildings by the water's edge, idly wondering when she would meet its mysterious owner, and as if in answer to her thoughts, Hannah spoke,

"I daresay, he will come and visit you as soon as he returns."

"Oh yes, of course," she replied in passing.

They drove on over the brow of a hill, Helen sat foreword eagerly when Arrochar came into view, its white painted buildings nestling comfortably in a small vale. — Slightly to the left, Rory pointed out the 15th century castle, set high on a brae. She followed the direction of his pointing finger, while dreamily speaking her thoughts, "Nothing's changed, it still looks just as enchanting," she sighed, "Proud, magnificent and secretly protective, too, — don't you think so, Hannah?" she enquired, at the end of her romanticising.

"I don't know about all of that," came Hannah's, dour reply. "But it's the best money spinner that anyone ever invented."

Rory replied, "You can say that again, Hannah. — Now that the Laird has leased it to the film company, it will make even more of a mint. The tourists are bound to flock to Arrochar just to see the location used in the film."

"Who's starring?" Helen eagerly asked, pricking up her ears for items of news.

"A onetime local lass," Rory replied. "Alex Craig; she's a stunner!"

"Alex Craig," Helen murmured, echoing the name with quizzical interest. "I know of her, I've read about her in some American press reports. I've never chanced to meet her, but for some reason, I seem to vaguely remember her father, James," she said, thoughtfully.

"Aye, lass, you would. He was a frequent visitor to Bracken Cottage in your gran's day. — You would remember him," Hannah confirmed. "At onetime, father and daughter were very close, he doted on her, spoilt her, she had everything her own way. — But it was easy enough to understand, as Mr. Craig reared her single handed, his wife dying as she did, when Miss Alex was born. — He never did remarry."

"How very sad," Helen laconically remarked, turning her attention back to the scenery.

To reach the cottage they had to drive through the village, past the Farriers courtyard with his anvil signage, and the grain merchants, displaying a yellow and brown sign, announcing, 'Spillers' Balanced Rations for Cattle, Sheep, Pigs and Poultry. — In the High Street, there were still a good few late holiday makers, milling about the tiny gift shops, browsing leisurely at the enticing goods colourfully displayed in their windows: — Tartans and Shetland wool jumpers, made in Arrochar's own mill, — the old Woollen Mill being the only industry that the village boasted. — Large displays of Celtic jewellery also caught the eye, plus many interesting items fashioned from dykes-head horn, kindly supplied by the Highland cattle, and plenty of postcards bearing local views of interest.

Rory turned the car down a lane, just off the main road. It was sign-posted, 'Bracken Lane – To the Kirk and the Castle'. A few yards along the lane, standing in its own grounds; he came to a halt alongside the most charming rose covered cottage.

The small front gardens surrounded by a waist high white picket fence, were still a riot of glorious colour with rose bushes of every hue. — Their perfume intoxicating as Helen stepped from the car to admire, what was now unbelievably her home.

She smiled softly, commenting, "It's very well cared for," showing mild surprise as Hannah came to stand beside her. "I seem to remember that it was a little run down."

"Aye, lass, your grandmother made sure that all would be restored to order; — she loved her home and Arrochar," she replied. "I think that she desperately wanted you to be happy here, — come now," she alerted, gently patting her companion's arm, "I'm sure you must need a cup of tea after your long journey."

Helen followed her the few yards along the crazy-paving footpath, admiring as she approached, the glossy red front door, a stark contrast to the grey flintstone walls, — she raised her eyes to read the date carved into the stonework '1735'.

A few moments later, Hannah bustled about making tea in the kitchen while Rory brought in the luggage, disappearing through a small doorway which led to the upstairs, while Helen explored the lower quarters of her new abode.

She waited for Rory to come down, before wandering up the small steep staircase, touching the warm low oak beams as she went. — The first and largest bedroom had been her gran's room, with its comfortable looking Victorian brass-framed bed, the second, she stood in the centre of — gazing about, enchanted. — Time has stood still in the little room decorated in lemon and white, with matching sprig muslin curtains and bedcover, the pattern, repeated in the valance around the kidney shaped dressing table, upon which her eye rested in curious surprise.

She moved towards the table, reaching out to pick up the familiar silver backed hairbrush which belonged to the dressing set. — Studying its back, she looked more closely at the monogram engraved on its shiny surface, reading 'HC' in scroll lettering. — She knew that the brushes had been her grans', but the lettering had been expertly changed, and so made a mental note to enquire of Hannah.

In the third bedroom, she had another surprise, for it had been tastefully converted into a slate and pine bathroom with all mod cons, including that of a shower, the smell was of new tile cement and paint. — Someone had been very diligent, she thought.

Continuing her exploration, she returned downstairs and peeked into the newly refurbished kitchen, where at onetime, a smell of warm baked bread and griddle scones had permeated the atmosphere, emitting from the wood burning stove, which had been replaced with a more modern powered version. — It seemed that no-one was about and, seeing the outer door open, she sidled across to peer out across sprawling green lawns, past the overhanging willow trees and towards the trout stream, which bubbled its way past the bottom of the garden, and noted the horse tethering post set alongside, — she warmly stroked the ancient wood, while peering around, Hannah was nowhere to be seen.

Re-entering through the kitchen, she strolled through into the dining room with its highly polished refectory furniture, and collection of horse-brasses. The dining room led directly into the front garden. — In the adjacent sitting room, Helen could only stand in renewed pleasurable awe at the inglenook fireplace, the sides of which, were large enough to comfortably seat two people, and with a large, generously filled log basket set to one side, she could toast her toes in defiance of Rita's dark threat echoing, *"you'll be snowbound in the winter."* Hugging this thought close to her, Helen smiled, as removing one of the bright cushions; she sat down on the Harris Tweed covered settee, imagining the cosy room in the depths of winter.

Suddenly, she was drawn from her thoughts by voices drifting through from the kitchen. — Thinking it was Hannah and Rory, she rose to join them, pausing briefly at the door, taking in the small group. Hannah glimpsed her; enter the room. "Ah! There you are!" She enthusiastically exclaimed, anxious to introduce the newcomers.

"This is our very distinguished doctor … Iain Roach and his wife, Jean," she keenly announced, as Helen extended her hand to each in turn. — Courtesies completed, Rory called the doctor into the garden, leaving the women to their chatter.

"We were so looking forward to meeting you, that we considered you wouldn't mind us calling so soon," Jean said, pleasantly smiling.

"No, of course not," Helen assured, displaying genuine pleasure. "I'm delighted."

"It was a mite unfortunate that Duncan was called away so unexpectedly, he was so anxious to meet you himself. It's a tradition that the Laird personally welcomes all newcomers to his village, and he is a stickler for upholding traditions," she chuckled, shaking her head, while murmuring, "So quaint and old fashioned."

"I was quite happy with Hannah and Rory," she again assured. "Have you time for tea?"

Making a hasty inspection of her watch, Jean apologetically replied, "I'm afraid not, surgery is due to start, — but we're holding a dinner party this weekend and we would like you to come. It will be an ideal opportunity for you to meet a few of the locals. If it's all right with you, I'll call again tomorrow morning with an invitation. We can have a long gossip then, and don't forget; — I want to know *all* about you."

"Thanks, I'd be delighted." Helen replied eagerly, on all counts. "I'm already looking forward to it, — but there really isn't very much to know."

"Town life is very different to country life," Jean sceptically remarked, "We're very laid back; — you could find it a little frustrating."

Helen brushed this remark aside, "Oh, I'm very adaptable, London is much closer to the countryside than people realise; — I have friends in Hertfordshire."

Jean nodded, "Then, you'll be quite at home," she replied, and called out to her husband, alerting him as to the time. — Moments later, Helen accompanied them to the gate. — She waited while they settled themselves into their old Shooting Brake, to stand waving until they had driven out of sight.

Jean called the following day, duly delivering the promised invitation, and as they chatted and drank numerous cups of steaming coffee, Helen briefly studied her new friend, a slim, attractive, smartly dressed woman with short fair hair and softly accented voice; — she guessed her age to be around thirty-five. Iain was six years her senior; they had only been married for a few years, and, as yet, had no family. "But, there is still time," she confided, followed by the revelation that she filled in her time between the surgery, and being involved with the village social life. "We could do with some help," she said, sighing, "If you can spare the time, why not give me a hand with the children's Christmas party, and I know you're musically talented, the choral group could do with some professional guidance, — work with young Rory, he does a grand job doubling as Choirmaster and Youth Club Leader," she surprisingly revealed, and mused as she chatted on, "I sometimes feel he's missed his vocation, but he's bent on farming eventually, which is just a well, so many of the young folk leave the village and head for the racy city life, where there's more scope."

And Helen silently, couldn't agree more to the latter. "I would like to help," she replied, wavering, with a note of sadness in her voice, "but I don't know whether I would be ... good enough," she hedged a reply. "I failed my exams; something was missing," she shrugged, "I just lost heart."

"Then, perhaps you'll find your heart again in Arrochar," Jean coaxed, smiling at her.

"Well, I suppose I do need something to do," she said, sighing thoughtfully while frowning, feeling so afraid of failure, — she had refrained from giving a positive answer.

"No-one expects perfection," Jean remarked, encouragingly, she also sighed, "I sometimes wish that Duncan would get married, — usually the Laird's wife is responsible for organising these affairs," she revealed.

"He isn't married?" Helen gawked, sounding amazed, never having considered that a man with such vast estates could be single, usually, they felt duty bound to produce heirs as soon as the opportunity presented itself, — but that thought was immediately replaced by, — perhaps the opportunity hadn't presented itself. With the village youngsters leaving in such droves, the population would be seriously depleted, both in the past, present, and in the future.

"No, not Duncan, he heavily relied on his mother, the Lady Eleanor MacFarlane," Jean replied. "She was a widow until recently, but having remarried, she left Arrochar to live in Edinburgh, nearer to her husband's job. Leaving the village was the one thing, which greatly concerned her, as it so removed her moral support from Duncan, but he insisted that she took what happiness came her way, and wasn't to consider the estates at all."

"I *can* understand," Helen replied, feeling a curious empathy for a woman that she had only seen from a distance. "She must have suffered from divided loyalties."

Jean nodded, "It eased her mind, knowing that Hannah and I would be on hand to support Duncan, whenever the need arose."

"Then, I think he's very fortunate to have such reliable friends," Helen replied. "Has he never considered getting married?" she curiously enquired.

"I'm not at all sure," Jean said, in a vague sort of way, "I think he's had a few lady friends passing through over the years, but nothing of a permanent nature, you would need a special kind of stamina to remain here, or perhaps, he's just determined to become a staid old bachelor, but on the other hand, it isn't any secret that he's leased the castle to a film company, and that his old flame, Alex Craig, has the starring role, no doubt, they'll be picking up from where they left off, - some five years ago."

Helen was now becoming really, curiously interested, she pricked her up ears, — could there be a story, she silently wondered, — and enquired further, "Were they engaged?" she eagerly asked, sipping her coffee, while listening intently to the reply.

Jean's smooth brow slightly furrowed, showing her uncertainty, "I'm not at all sure … they may have been. — I was new to the village, still a dreamy bride, I didn't pay particular attention to the affairs of others, — but it *was* rumoured that they were going to marry, until one day, Alex met her American director." She appeared thoughtful, "I believe his name was

Arnie Browning, and the tittle-tattle had it, that he must have enticed her away with promises that she simply couldn't resist, for in no time at all, she had upped and left Arrochar for America."

"Sounds *very* intriguing," Helen mischievously remarked.

"Oh aye, village life survives on intrigue and gossip," Jean flippantly agreed, suddenly grinning. "You have to separate the wheat from the chaff, so to speak, something of which you must be a connoisseur; — no-one ever really knows the real truth of the matter, except for the people concerned, and then you have to be very wary that no-one attempts to wheedle true matters from you, and then it's necessary to bend the truth a little, — but, as for Alex, I would never typecast her as a farmer's wife, even though, she *is* a farmer's daughter."

"Perhaps, she didn't love him enough to try, it would seem so to me," Helen replied, siding with a woman's career, "… and the temptation of a successful, glamorous career, would quite naturally surpass marriage to some 'dull, pompous, old Laird' everything that an aspiring actress would hate," she exclaimed.

Jean's eyes sparkled with merriment at the younger woman's rendition, her voice tinkled musically with amusement, as she replied: - "Well, everyone has their good side, Helen, — even a- 'dull, pompous, old Laird'."

A while later, after she had left, Helen's mind dwelt heavily upon her conversation with Jean; — In the past, Alex Craig had never stirred up very much interest with the British press, never having aired her talents in the country. — But now it seemed that everything was going to change, and Helen was beginning to smell the opportunity of an inside scoop, especially if the actress were to be romantically involved with the Laird. — With this in mind, she decided that she wouldn't be at a disadvantage, if she were to give Ryder the 'tip-off' on Alex Craig's pending arrival. He would use his own methods of discovering exactly when it was to be, and advise her accordingly.

Satisfied with her decision to phone Ryder, she suddenly let out a mild expletive, realising that the cottage didn't boast a phone. — A trip into the village was now necessary, she had noticed a phone box by the Farriers, — and then momentarily transferred her concentration to the dinner invitation, which, once removed from its envelope, proved to be a smart white card, edged with a decaled gilt border, the gilding was echoed in the coats-of-arms regalia. The embossed words, *'formal attire'* stared up at her. — She felt a sudden rush of gratitude for her mother's insistence on shopping for clothes. But now, with so much to choose from, and so much newly on her mind, she decided to postpone any thoughts of dress for the following evening. She would consult Hannah later, as to what's best to wear for her first social occasion in Arrochar, for now, a more important issue was pending.

Chapter 5

Tempest

Saturday morning soon arrived, — the day of the party; Helen slept later than usual, only waking when a soft tap came on her bedroom door. — Sleepily, she called out, "Come in Hannah!" she yawned and stretched luxuriously, as the door opened a crack, and then wider to admit Hannah's ample figure, plus tea tray, through the opening.

"It's a raw morning, lass," she announced in her dour Scot's tone. "The mist has settled low over the mountains, and the fallen leaves are wet and slippery underfoot, so if you still have your mind set on that walk to the Kirk, then I advise you not to leave it very much longer, as the mist could increase."

"Thanks Hannah," she enthusiastically replied, feeling a return of the gratitude she had previously felt, at Hannah's insistence on popping in to help her start the day.

She drank her morning tea in between nibbling hot buttered toast, while reading her air-mail letter from Ryder, he had moved rapidly, — excitedly, she read with mounting interest: -

Helen

Your timing was spot on. I followed up your information regarding the Craig/Browning film, and immediately set Rita the task of researching the company, and, they are indeed 'Runcorn Productions'. Chester Maxwell interviewed Alex Craig in Edinburgh.

Miss Craig, surprisingly, lacked her usual blasé attitude adopted by her kind, meeting the tirade of questions on any future plans of matrimony with a cool, 'no comment' but she did indicate plans for a Press Conference in the near future to launch the commencement of filming – to be advised. I will secure you an invitation, in the meantime, I suggest you keep a low profile on the subject. Collect all the information you can, if there's a story to crack, then crack it at the conference, and you can be certain, I'll review your contract for a further three months, at the end which, the column is yours. Harry R.

She read the contents once more, before dropping the missive thoughtfully onto the bedcover. — The Laird's absence coincided with Alex Craig's arrival, which pointed to one obvious conclusion; — he must have been keen to resume relations with the actress, hence, his inability to follow the old traditions of welcoming newcomers to Arrochar. — But, although left with a slight feeling of neglect, she supposed that he couldn't be in two places at onetime, and so he attended to the first and most important issue, — his bride to be. However, she decided, it wasn't going to let the situation peeve her, as the contents of Ryder's letter were sufficiently overriding in consolation.

Stirred by a surge of joy, she leapt out of bed to peer through the window, agreeing with Hannah's weather report. — It *was* bleak and misty; however, feeling undaunted, she remained resolute on her decision to walk to the Kirk, with the intention of visiting her gran's grave.

After a quick shower, she donned a pair of her old jeans, smiling at the furtive way in which she had slipped them into one of her suitcases, after her mother had checked the contents. She topped them with a thick Arran sweater — newly purchased in the village. — While humming tunefully to herself, she wound up the thick length of her silky hair, securing it with a doubtful single pin onto the crown of her head, over-which, she pulled a woollen bobble hat, well down over her ears. A similar matching scarf, she wound around her neck, finally pushing her feet into stylish high heeled, knee-high boots. — Thus attired, she was certain to be well muffled against all impeding elements.

Hannah was in the kitchen, tidying the last of the breakfast washing up, and so engrossed, that she didn't look up immediately. — She was staying for just a few more minutes; — Helen was duly informed, before leaving for The Loch House. — Hannah turned from her task and laughed merrily upon seeing her, exclaiming! "Oh, lass, you look all-of sixteen again; — clothes make such a difference," she finished, staring dubiously at the boots.

The housekeeper was unaware of her recently enforced new image, "I feel much more comfortable," she replied, while giving her a spontaneous, affectionate hug before strolling together to the gate. "… and perhaps, Rory won't look at me as if I were some alien from outer space."

Hannah laughed, "He'll soon get used to you again, you mark my words, and he won't stand on ceremony for long, — waiting to be asked."

And with Hannah's warning to take care, ringing in her ears, she set off up the lane, turning occasionally to wave back to the housekeeper, until she had walked out of sight, over the small bridge which spanned the stream.

The Kirk was half-a-mile away from the cottage, and she estimated that it would take approximately fifteen minutes to cover the distance, if she strode it out.

Suddenly, she shivered, feeling the chilly dampness penetrating the thickness of her jumper, causing her to speed up her step as she rounded a bend in the road. — Panting slightly from the exhorting exercise, her breath came in short puffs of white billowy steam hanging on the atmosphere, only to disappear again as it mingled with the light descending mist. — Feeling the minute moist droplets collecting on the tips of her lashes, she blinked to clear the silvery blur impeding her vision, and was so intent upon her mission, that she didn't hear the soft drone of a car's engine behind her until it was — too late …

A shrill scream rent itself from her throat as she flung herself aside, only to pitch headlong into the wet, muddy ditch, while the vehicle swerved past, skidding and screeching to an ear-splitting halt, a few yards further up the lane, — the spray from the road showered over her.

For a moment, she lay stunned with heart thudding shock, then recovering sufficiently, managed an undignified, slippery scramble back onto her feet and solid ground. — Only reasonably stable again, she stood, her heart still thumping wildly against her ribs, her legs uncontrollably trembling with a mixture of fright and rage, as she looked helplessly down, at the now indiscernible colours of her muddy soaked clothes, — "Oh, no!" she loudly groaned, as with shaking hands, she began brushing vainly at her front, but it became painfully obvious that nothing would re-enhance their freshly laundered appearance, immediately.

Her chest heaved with anger; — she turned her head and glared in the direction of the car, a white mud splattered Rover, whose sole occupant had just leapt out, and after slamming the car door shut behind him, strode his way back towards her, — his face dark with fury. Momentarily swayed by his unjust attitude, Helen cowered back a little as he approached.

"You little fool!" he raged at her, "Don't you know any better than to walk on the *wrong* side of the lane? You should *face* oncoming traffic; it's a code of the countryside."

She stood, staring dumbstruck for a moment, and then suddenly, something snapped inside, incensed now with rage and indignation, her hands balled into small fists at her side, as she fought down the desire to strike the arrogant face above her, "H ... how *dare* you speak to me like that? Look what you've done," she rasped, peering down at herself. "Y ... you nearly ran me down; in fact you *did* run me down."

Standing, hands on hips, the stranger glowered down at her, "I might have known," he scoffed. "You tourists just wander around regardless of anyone, and look at those non-sensible boots."

Wide eyed, she struggled for a retort, "And you shouldn't speed around lanes, like ... like some *mad* thing, this isn't ... Brands Hatch," she retorted, while drawing herself up, desperately trying to recover some of her miserably lost dignity, — and as if to prove a point, dragged her hat from her head, tossing her cascade of hair free as she replied. "And I'll have you know, I'm not a ...," but she didn't complete her sentence, as the man turned on his heel while shouting back.

"Have more care!" He warned. "Next time, you may not be so lucky."

"Next ...," But before she could finish her indignant reply, he'd climbed back into his car and had driven off, his engine's roar fading with the lengthening gap between them.

For a moment, she just stared into space, her mouth gawped open, disbelief written on her every muddy feature. — Then, as if suddenly spurred into life by her insatiate fury, she kicked the ground, fuming to herself, while turning to walk home again, outraged and chuntering, "How dare he speak to me like that; the ill-mannered oaf, just leaving me, without even a *shred* of 'common decency' to ask if I'd been hurt. — Why, if I meet him again, I ... I'll ...," she said, addressing the trees. "Drat the man! drat! drat! drat!" she let out the expletive, when suddenly her ankle turned and she heard and felt the squelch of the soaking moisture in which her feet were contained, she groaned again in despair, feeling choked with angry tears.

By the time she had reached the cottage, her temper had cooled, just a little, sense having decided that she'd had a lucky escape after all, although, she still felt resentful towards the arrogant stranger. — It was at the door when the heel of her boot snapped, sending her deeper into despair.

On entering the kitchen, she found a note from Hannah propped against the teapot, informing her that she would call again later that evening, and that Rory had returned from Edinburgh with her car, which he would deliver to her door that very afternoon. This information led to the anxious thought of: — in what condition would her car be when it arrived?

She struggled out of her squelching boots, made a brief study of the snapped heel, and then sighing, when realising they were rendered useless, — she slung them across the floor in distaste; — whipping her jumper quickly over her head, she peeled off her slim fitting jeans, and then ran upstairs to quickly shower and change into a fresh blouse and slacks. Returning downstairs, she whipped up the discarded clothing, to unceremoniously bundle them into a sink of hot soapy suds, "Ugh, tourists, indeed!" she grimaced, while thoroughly pummelling at the wet muddy mass, after which, frustrations satisfied, she filed the disastrous incident to the rear of her mind.

Sometime later, Rory duly arrived as expected, and stayed just long enough to hand over her car keys and a cellophane box, which contained a spray of freesias and heather. "You can wear them this evening," he said, and bending his large frame, she gripped his shoulders and while lightly holding her chin, he dropped a gentle kiss on her lips, — and the warmth of his expression was obvious.

She also warmly smiled, saying softly, "I'll see you later."

He nodded in agreement, to silently pause by the door as if reluctant to leave, before he finally left.

Hours later, she had just stepped out from the refreshing depths of a perfumed bath, which relieved her bruised and stiffened limbs, when she heard Hannah calling up the stairs, thus announcing her arrival. — Hastily, she wrapped a towel about her freshly washed hair and slipped into a towelling bathrobe, tying it snugly about herself before padding barefoot downstairs, to enjoy one of Hannah's numerous cups of tea, and as she guessed, nibbles of home-made shortbread, she was busy arranging some flowers in the kitchen, and half-turned on hearing the soft footfall.

She spoke with exuberance, "Oh Lass, I was fair dying to tell you …,"

"What beautiful roses!" Helen exclaimed, diverting Hannah's conversation on further entering the room, to be greeted by an intoxicating perfume.

"They're from Mr. Duncan," the housekeeper informed.

"Oh, he's back, is he?" Helen laconically acknowledged, displaying a daunting lack of interest.

Hannah nodded. "I see you're spoilt for choice," she said, having seen Rory's corsage.

"I like the modesty," she loosely remarked.

Hannah romantically, warmly smiled, "A corsage is meant to be worn over the heart." — Once finished with the flowers; she began preparing the tea tray, her voice faded into the background while Helen became absorbed with her gift; — she inhaled the exotic aroma of the blooms and extracted the accompanying envelope from the bouquet.

First scanning the pale grey envelope, and admiring the neat scroll handwriting, *'To Miss Helen Campbell'*, she read, after slitting the seal and removing the matching sheet of paper. — Impressed, she noted the address embossed in black lettering on the left-hand corner. The message, written in the same neat hand as the envelope, was brief but formal: -

Dear Miss Campbell,
I write my apologies for not having been able to meet you as arranged.
Unfortunately, I was unavoidably detained by business, but I have learned from Hannah, that you will be attending the Roaches party this evening, where I shall look forward to making your acquaintance.
Until this evening — Duncan R. MacFarlane

'How quaint' she thought, while replacing the missive into its envelope, and then carried the flowers into the dining room, where she placed the vase in the centre of the table, and then seated herself, her mind lingering with thoughts that she was finally, to meet the Laird that evening. — Her notebook was on the table in front of her, it was covered in copious notes from her afternoon's musings. — Hannah bustled in after her. "You were saying, Hannah?"

Hannah tutted, but she was still itching to spill the gossip, she was all agog that … "Alex Craig has arrived back in Arrochar, and Jean has invited her to the party this evening, and of all things," her voice rose ecstatically, "Mr. Duncan is to escort her."

This information spurred a second thought that not only was she to meet the Laird this evening, but as a bonus, Alex Craig also. — Things were becoming a broiling hotbed as it seemed, and they weren't wasting anytime in resuming their relationship, — and publicly too, so there must be something in the rumours of bygone years, — interesting, she thought, keenly prompting while helping herself to one of the shortbread melting moments. "I suppose she's staying at the hotel," she casually suggested.

Hannah's voice rose in incredulous astonishment at a question with such obvious answers, - she cried … "Why should she do that, when she can stay with her father at Craigiemhor Farm?"

Helen appeared flippant, "Oh, it was just something that Jean said."

Hannah shook her wise head at this announcement, "And just *what* has

Jean been filling your head with?" she asked suspiciously.

She shrugged, cautiously replying, "Very little, really; she still had her head in the clouds when it was all happening. — She seemed to think that the Laird and Alex Craig had a romantic interest in each other a few years ago, — and well, she may have stayed with the Laird."

Hannah raised her eyes aloft, "You young people of today," she chastised, "Have you no sense of propriety? — This is Arrochar lassie, and I'm sure that the Laird will steer clear from rekindling empty gossip, and making displays of public affection."

"But Hannah," Helen arguably reasoned, "... he's already done that by leasing the castle to Miss Craig and her film company."

"That's as maybe," the housekeeper replied bluntly, showing her obvious distaste. "The Laird is a very private person."

Helen displayed incredulous disbelief, "Why, the man sounds positively fusty, narrow minded, and slow on the uptake. — Here we are in the middle of the 20th Century, not the Middle Ages when women were forced into wearing chastity belts. — I really can't believe that Arrochar hasn't progressed a little as well," she said, while pulling the restraining towel from her head, to begin combing through her damp hair with her fingers. — After all, she didn't know the Laird, but she was learning about him, "There's no smoke without fire," she coaxed, "... and a little rekindling doesn't hurt? — And if you don't tell me, Hannah, I'll find out anyway. I guarantee that the whole village chewed the bones bare on this one, and will do so again."

The housekeeper felt concerned at this new turn of events, "I don't know about that," she warily replied, sighing, while silently thinking that Helen was right, — the gossip was rife in the village; she had met Mrs Duniclieff in the butcher's shop only that morning, she was wide eyed with enthusiasm, there were rumours of a secret engagement, and before long, she had been surrounded by quite a gathering in the tiny shop, all wanting to know. — It was a rare sight to see a silver Cadillac purring down the High Street; it was so out of place in such a rural setting. — She considered … "Best it comes from me," She said aloud, and proceeded …

"Well … folklore had it, that they were supposed to marry, and then Miss Alex broke off their relationship to follow up her screen career. It appeared that she'd left him high and dry."

"And, I suppose she broke his heart," Helen commented. "And, I suppose again, that he still cares."

Hannah raised her eyebrows, "Goodness lass, who can tell about these things? He isn't one to show his feelings, either way," she confirmed. "All

I know *is* he's better off without her, but that's only *my* opinion, — their respective fathers had other ideas, — it was widely rumoured that they were desperate for the match. — A right conniving pair they were, until they had something of a row, and the Lord only knows what that could have been about. But their speculating does make a fair amount of sense, you see," she informed, "… Craigiemhor Farm lays 'smack-bang' in the middle of MacFarlane land, and if Miss Alex and the Laird were to marry, then it would eventually unite the lands, and so complete the estates. — It's a perfect match, you know, a business match," she finished.

Helen smiled, while shaking her head in disbelief, "You mean a marriage of convenience."

"Is that what it's called?"

Helen nodded, she was indignant, "It's so antiquated, — I couldn't imagine anyone agreeing to such a cold-hearted arrangement, all for the sake of land gain, and I certainly wouldn't consider it to be a perfect match. — Prince or pauper, if ever I marry, it would have to be … for love."

"Land is power, Lass, whichever way you look at it, and there's no room for sentiment when it comes to gleaning more, but then..." she added, shrugging, "people do become fond of each other in the strangest of circumstances."

Helen appeared thoughtful, she murmured softly, "And money is the root-of-all evil," concluding, — "The man's a mercenary."

Hannah frowned, she echoed, querying, "A mercenary?"

"Someone who fights for only money and possessions," she explained. Her curiosity furthered, she enquired, "How did his father die?"

"Och, such a terrible tragedy it was, he slipped one day while trying to rescue a sheep. The animal had fallen over a crag, in a mist, on a day such as today. '*Rab's Crag,*' they now call it, being as the Laird's father was named '*Robert*'," — and Helen recalled the signature on her letter - 'Duncan R. MacFarlane' - 'R' for Robert, she correctly surmised as Hannah continued with her tale, — "His wife, the Lady MacFarlane, Mrs Graham, as she now is, was deeply grieved at her loss, but as time passed by, she came to terms with it. — Immediately after Robbie MacFarlane's accident, they had to bring Mr. Duncan back from his studies in Aberdeen University to run the estates, especially as Angus, the old Laird, was ailing fast. — The shock of his son dying so suddenly, hastened his own end less than a year later. — Mr. Duncan shouldered his responsibilities with a true Chieftains strength and courage," she said, sighing, — "But … all that was six years ago, just after your last visit, and around about the time of your own poor father's untimely death."

Helen's eyes momentarily clouded, and seeing this, a slight concerned frown creased Hannah's brow as she realised, that she had reawakened the girl's own grief, — she admonished herself, "Forgive an old woman for aimless prattle," she said in apology.

Brightening again, Helen smiled her forgiveness, she sighed, "It was a long time ago, and life must go on. — I'm quite sure that the Laird has got on with his," she practically replied, and as a diversion, continued her questioning, she enquired, "What was the Laird studying in Aberdeen?"

"Farm management, by all accounts, not that he needed, he'd had plenty of hands-on experience; — he never completed the course, but the estates haven't suffered from the loss of his scholarships."

"I'm quite sure they haven't," she murmured, with a slight sounding scoff, "He sounds so boringly perfect, just a little lacking as a host ... I think."

Hannah grinned at this rendition of her employer, she thought that Helen was embroidering romanticism, — she was a past master at it, a fine trait for a news reporter and felt obliged to put her right, "Och, he's really quite human, Helen, and far from perfect, he gets into a temper when things don't go smoothly, and then everyone has to watch-out," she finally remarked, while glancing at the mantle clock, and with a sudden sharp intake of breath, she diverted the conversation, "That's enough gossip for one day. — Away with you now, we have to get you into your dress, or you will be late for the party, unless it's your prime intention of attending this function in the raw, that should turn a few heads," she grinned.

Helen chuckled again, and feeling a welter of affection, immediately sprang up from her seat to plant a warm kiss on the embarrassed, housekeeper's cheek, "you're so wonderful, Hannah," she said, to which the housekeeper replied ...

"Och, dinnae be so *daft,* away with you now. I'll clear these cups while you're gone, and on the way to Jean's, you can give me a lift home, now you have your car with you. I would guess that you're a far more reliable driver than young Rory," she said, grinning. "He terrifies me."

As she potted about, Hannah reminisced about her nephew, — she remembered that poor young Rory's heart had suffered when Mairie had told him that Helen would visit no more, — he'd moped around for a wee while and took himself away hiking as much as his duties would allow, he seemed to find solace in solitude, but Mairie sharpened his wits, she bade Angus to take the boy under his wing. — When the castle became vacant of its tenants, Rory became its caretaker, — the repair work was a massive undertaking, this also repaired his heart and his spirit, — it would seem kinder if Helen had grown in distance from him; — she was worldly, whereas he was not.

Alone in her bedroom, Helen pondered briefly on Hannah's tale, — she had, she was aware, — reached the same conclusions apparent to the whole populations of Arrochar. — The ambitious Laird would be anxious to secure Alex Craig for his wife, — and by Alex's 'no comment' to Maxwells' marital questions, she sounded as though she were very likely in agreement with the proposal now, — if she hadn't been a few years ago. Her evening at the surgery was not only going to be sociably interesting, she thought, but invaluable to the career stakes also. — And, with a self-satisfied, determined air, Helen transferred her concentration from future article pursuits, to the more immediate concerns of dressing.

The French silk undies, had at the time, seemed a wanton waste, but now another feeling of gratitude welled at her mother's insistence, — unlike the boots, — that they were necessary to feel completely feminine.

Thus scantily attired, she sat at her dressing table brushing out and rewinding her hair into several different, unsuitable styles. Suddenly groaning with frustration, a wish for the Edinburgh hairdresser surged through her until, vainly trying again, this time, using its generous length and finding her attempt at a Victorian roll was more successful, held into place by the ornate combs, she had found in the dressing table drawer.

The swept style highlighted, smooth, finely shaped cheekbones. She teased with her fingers at her hairline, releasing tiny softening tendrils, which framed a face of gentle, innocent beauty, and in completion, clipped an aigrette filled with Rory's freesias and white heather to her side hairline. After applying a light touch of make-up, she zipped herself into her dress, slipped bare feet into golden sandals, and then added the final touch, just a few subtle dabs of Chanel No 5.

First tapping softly on the door, Hannah entered the room to survey the final results, she sighed, admiring, "Ah … you do look bonnie, lass, indeed you do. Your old gran would feel prideful to see you tonight. — I think we've made the right choice of dress," she remarked, "I hung it outside of the wardrobe in the hopes. …"

Helen self-consciously blushed, and turned in skirts of swirling soft folds of white crepe that lay against her sulphide curves. The high front neckline of the bodice, gently sweeping across the column of her throat, down to a low 'V' at the back, reaching almost to her waist and revealing her soft creamy skin, lightly tanned to perfection. — The gown was sleeveless, giving show to a wide gold bracelet, she had clasped to her forearm.

"I have a wee gift for you, lass," Hannah said, producing a box from her apron pocket and handing it to her companion, "This is rightfully yours. It belonged to your gran. She left it to me, but I will find no use for it, and so I'm returning it to you."

Charmed, but curious, Helen removed the box lid, gasping with pleasure when revealing a large white-gold fly plaid brooch, "I ... can't take this," she said, hesitantly.

"You *can* and you must," Hannah commanded. "The stone is a Cairngorm. This is your clan stone. Now, wear it with pride," she said, taking the brooch from the box herself to pin to Helen's left shoulder.

She raised a hand to lovingly caress the jewel, when Hannah suddenly cried out, concerned," Why lass, how did you graze your hand? It looks sore, here let me see."

"Oh that," she replied, peering down jointly at the wound. "I had a bit of an accident this morning, on the way to the Kirk, I ... never quite got there," she said, evasively.

Hannah grunted, "Judging by the state of your clothes in the sink, I think it was a mite more of an accident than you're telling; I'll take them home with me to dry. — But, so long as you're alright, I'll say no more," She smiled wisely; *boots* were on the communal minds. — Hannah had seen the devastation in the kitchen, where Helen had randomly left the scattered, offending articles on the floor.

Helen nodded while waiting for Hannah to assist her with the enveloping folds of her green velvet evening cloak, lined with green Campbell plaid, "I'm glad your gran left this cloak," she said soberly. "You would fair catch your death of cold without it."

Helen sighed with happiness as she appreciatively turned, to drop a kiss on Hannah's cheek, her eyes sparkled, reflecting to jade, she suddenly felt a burst of overwhelming excitement, "I'm *so* happy, Hannah," she exclaimed, unnecessarily, "Everyone has been so very kind and helpful."

"Aye, well, that's as maybe, we don't want you homesick," Hannah replied. "Come on now, we must away before you become daft with sentiment," she bustled.

Chapter 6

Symbolism

Half an hour later, Helen turned her car into the driveway of Talbert House, fondly referred to by the locals as the Old Surgery. Although not quite dark, approaching the sprawling pastoral Georgian House, she felt appreciative of the welcoming lights shining from the many square latticed windows. The lights cast bright beams across open lawns, strewn with glistening wet leaves which had fallen from the branches of an avenue of Pendunculate Oak trees, standing like regal sentries on either side of the drive.

She drew to a halt directly in front of the house, stationing the car alongside several others parked on the forecourt. On leaving the confines of car, she realised that the mizzerling afternoon rain had ceased, and drew in a breath to inhale the good, fresh dampness of the earth all about her. — Hoisting her long skirts to her ankles, she stepped towards the house, only taking mild interest in the car now progressing along the drive towards her, its headlights changed to a dipped beam, making its identity in the shadows, impossible to determine.

Tugging at the brass bell-rope to announce her arrival, the freshly painted white front door was immediately opened to reveal Jean, smiling a friendly welcome. She was dressed very becomingly in an expensive designer dress of primrose yellow chiffon, "Welcome, Helen, — Welcome to our home," she brightly said, while glancing beyond her shoulder, and warmly dropping a kiss on Helen's cheek, as the latter stepped over the threshold of Talbert House for the first time.

"Thanks, Jean." she replied, responding with a soft smile as her hostess stood aside, allowing her to pass further into the wide, well lit hall, the door, she left ajar. — Helen appreciatively glanced around her, taking in the hall's expanse of cool mint green carpet now beneath her feet, and acknowledged Iain standing a few feet away; — he was in conversation with a gentleman, whom judging by his attire, was very obviously the local Vicar.

She paused, while waiting for Jean to finish speaking a few soft words to her husband. In the background, a hubbub of cheery high-spirited voices and soft music floated to her ears, as her hostess led the way across the hall, up a winding staircase, and finally into one of the many bedrooms which had been set aside for the use of female guests, and there were quite a few, as Helen soon discovered, by the amount of coats hanging in the wardrobe.

"You have a beautiful house," Helen remarked.

"It was the Factor's house," Jean informed. "Sir Robert MacFarlane and The Lady Eleanor lived here, until she re-married.

"The Factors?" she questioned.

"The Factors are the Scottish landlords, — they collect the rents and look after their tenants' homes, but in times past, if the tenant failed to pay his rent, then unfair justice was done. — Thankfully, we do not wallow in such practices today. — The Surgery area is in the allotted fours rooms sectioned off from the main house, the latter is open to tourists, — some of the village people are enthusiastic tour guides and a treasure to the estates." Jean waited while her companion tidied her hair, "The new style suits you, it's softer around your face," she remarked, while feeling a rising fascination at the younger woman's likeness to her grandmother. — She felt like staring at her, — studying her in depth, to catch the refined, gentle mannerisms that had so set apart Mairie Campbell from other women, — hers had been an undiminishing beauty that even old age had failed to fade, and here it was again, — in Helen.

"Thanks." Helen simply replied, while giving her hair a final pat for good measure. "It's just for this evening, very reminiscent of prom balls and grand concerts. — I think the style rather old fashioned, but its back in vogue."

Jean suddenly expelled a concerned gasp, "Helen, you've injured your hand; — here, let me put some cream on it for you," she fussed in a nurses way.

"It really isn't serious, just a small scratch and I did treat it myself; — I wouldn't want to smell of disinfectant all evening."

"How did you do it?"

"I … it really was my fault," she related the incident, ending, "… and my mother abhors walking boots and anything that isn't remotely feminine, I try not to listen to her." She suddenly grinned. "He really was quite fearsome."

Jean appeared thoughtfully amused, it shone in her eyes, "A white Rover, you say?" she underlined. "Well, so long as you're otherwise unscathed. …"

Helen nodded, "He wasn't really speeding; — I just wasn't paying attention, — I possibly frightened him; — but I didn't expect him to just *run-off* like that."

"You're very understanding, Bracken Lane is narrow and winding, the locals should know better. — I'll have a word with Duncan, — perhaps we need more road signs, just to make the rules more clear for everyone."

"Has the Laird arrived, yet?" she enquired, curiously. "I'm anxious to thank him for the restoration work that's been done on Bracken Cottage."

"Not yet," Jean sighed. "There was a problem at the airport, it seems that Alex's plane couldn't land on time, and I also suspect that she's kept Duncan waiting long enough to make an entrance worthwhile. — It must be said, as he's duty bound to arrive early at social functions. — You can usually set your clock by him," — Yet more evidence, Helen thought, with a furthering of interest at the now unfolding contents of her article, and then drew her attention back to Jean's conversation, — "Duncan won't want any thanks, he likes doing nice things."

"There are … other reasons, Jean."

"*Other,* reasons?" Jean questioned, with a slight concerned frown, while wondering what the other reasons could be.

"Well, I don't wish to be obliged to anybody," she explained, "My family feels quite concerned that the work may have been under-funded; — it's very likely that Mairie may not have foreseen a rise in current day prices when she made her *will*; — I would feel very uncomfortable were I to find that I owed him money."

"Then, you're under a misapprehension, Helen, there was never a shrewder woman born than Mairie Campbell, — and we really can't allow *you* and Duncan, to spend *your* welcoming party, discussing matters of business."

Helen was suddenly aghast, at this all-revealing announcement, — a certain amount of intrepid fear swept through her, — she turned large, surprised, questioning eyes on Jean, as she smiled broadly in admittance of her, — up until now, — well kept secret. "I … don't understand; I'm not famous, or anything like that." she stiltedly replied, stepping forward to give her companion a kiss on the cheek.

"Well, you're famous now; — it was the only way," she announced. "So many people expressed a wish to meet you, that Duncan suggested a party, and I insisted on keeping it a secret," her hand swept towards the door, —

"So … come and meet your public, — Mairie Campbell's granddaughter," she finished, with a soft laugh.

Apprehensively, Helen followed Jean from the room, her companion's cool calm exterior provided the much-needed moral support, and within a few more seconds, she had cast aside her trepidation, laughing and chatting happily and confidently together, as they strolled along the landing towards the top of the stairs, and upon their descent, their flowing skirts were trailing the steps behind them, it was a regal entrance.

Reaching almost to the foot of the stairs, they paused, Helen glanced around, in the hopes of seeing Rory, but his presence was nowhere to be seen. "Ah, there's Duncan," Jean murmured, "… and not before time."

Helen's gaze followed the same direction as Jean's.

Iain, who had remained in the hallway being a dutiful host, was speaking at great length to a newly arrived couple whose faces, Helen was unable to see, as they partly had their backs turned towards her, but there could be no doubt; — they were a striking pair.

The tall, slender woman had dark red hair, caught back in a severe chignon at the nape of her neck; she was very sensuously dressed, entirely in a gown of midnight blue satin, a perfect foil for her diamond drop earrings, shimmering as she moved her elegant head. — The shimmering diamonds were repeated again in the broad matching band of bracelet, clasped onto her left wrist, with long tapering fingers holding the edge of an expensive cream mink stole, draped casually across her slim shoulders; — she was displaying a sapphire and diamond engagement ring; — the scene was very emblematic of the red carpet at the Oscars. Her presence in the hall commanded the attention of other milling guests, heightened by her male companion to whose arm, she possessively clung; — she was very definitely, — the formidable woman in the lift, — without a doubt, this *was* … Alex Craig.

Her companion was taller still, raven-haired and, as the other men, suavely dressed in a well-cut evening suit. There was something vaguely familiar about him, Helen studiously thought, and as he turned, looked down and then sharply looked up again, he inclined his head to acknowledge them, immediately catching her unwavering gaze; — blue eyes met green and fused across the distance. — As he began moving towards her, — horror swept through her, her hand flew tremulously to her mouth; she caught her breath at the sight of the arrogant stranger, — her eyes narrowed; her fuming temper returned; any thoughts of forgiveness were forgotten. The fact that she would meet him again hadn't even remotely entered her head,

— although, on second thoughts, — in a village as small as Arrochar, it had to be as inevitable, and as obvious, as the uncomfortable warm flush of colour, that had maddeningly suffused her face. — She hesitated, it was only a moment, but it seemed an hour, so transfixed was she across the short distance.

In self-defence, Helen haughtily drew herself up to her full height, — doggedly determined that she would remain aloof and impervious of him; — she remained standing on the bottom stair, her right hand on the banister — Jean had left her side; she had joined the small group and was warmly, enthusiastically, welcoming her guests, leaving Helen in no doubt as to whom they were, — she was expected to follow, but an element of panic set in, her treacherous heart began racing when she became aware of him, politely leaving the group and moving towards her, — her eyes frantically searched for an escape route, but she was an animal trapped by her prey. — She turned to hastily retrace her steps, but suddenly, a soft, anxious, male voice alerted her, — he spoke her name, "Helen." She further, haughtily pulled herself up, her nose pinched, her lips petulant, as he came to stand in front of her. "Helen, I've so been looking forward to meeting you. — I can't tell you how very sorry I am, that I couldn't meet you at the station."

It was an awkward situation for all concerned, she wanted desperately to move away from his domineering presence, which was rendering her breathless, forcing her in vain to regain some of her lost composure, to steady the conflicting, raging, passionate emotions, which chased through her one by one, — but which one, would win?. — She became stiffly polite, "I … seem to be at a disadvantage," she tersely answered.

Jean, who had accompanied him, was beaming with exuberant pleasure, "Oh, let me do the honours," she said, affectionately holding onto his arm in a familiar way as she spoke. "Helen … I would like to introduce you to your host, our noble Laird, Duncan MacFarlane, also known as Lord Lennox."

She inclined her head, "Good evening," she said, a trifle curtly, hesitantly holding out her hand, while trying to keep her voice level and her hammering heart still, as he now gazed down at her from what seemed at such close quarters, to be a great height, — and, becoming engrossed in conversation — his blue velvet gaze was embarrassingly penetrating, raking, *kissing*. — She managed to speak with controlled tones of derision, and with some uncertainty, "I'm … very pleased to meet you, at long last."
— His sudden smile caused his eyes to pleasingly crease at the corners, — surprisingly, there was no hint of mockery, only apologetic, kindly

65

concern, she observed while trying to hold his gaze, and continuing in engrossed conversation, became conscious that he still held her hand and was rhythmically, disturbingly, caressing the porcelain skin with his thumb.

"I hope that your journey was a pleasant one," he politely enquired.

"Well … most of it," she replied, sighing, while struggling with her inner-most turmoil. "There …was a slight mishap at journey's end, — but thank you for the roses," and smiling stiffly, retrieved her hand. "It was very thoughtful of you to send Rory and Hannah to meet me."

His brow slightly furrowed; his eyes became a misty purple in his showing of concern. "A peace offering; it was the least I could do under the circumstances," he said in a regretful way. "I was reluctant to leave you to Rory Camerons' tender mercies. He isn't the best of timekeepers. — I … hope … he wasn't late."

She deliberately smiled in an affectionate, knowing way, replying, "He was already at the station, and, I've never known him to be late, he is very keen; —you probably did him a favour."

Duncan gave a small shake of his head; he appeared mildly abashed and sceptical. "Are we … talking about the same person?"

Helen nodded. "Rory is Rory; — we … go back a long way," she sighed on the sentence in defence. "He's got me into some terrible scrapes. I don't think that he's going to change now."

"I hope that he doesn't get you into any more," he pleasantly chuckled, covering an unfamiliar painful surge at her words.

"Oh, I have this distinct feeling that he will."

She wanly returned his smile, despite herself, enjoying his pleasantly deep Scot's burr, — and deny it though she tried, it spread trails of glowing warmth coursing through her veins, thus melting some of the ice which had formed around the region of her heart.

Jean's jubilance was to be short lived when Alex Craig joined them, — the atmosphere was immediately charged with tension, — intensifying, when the actress possessively twined her arms through one of the Laird's and seemed to tightly hug it with both arms, — he briefly raised one eyebrow, while his closed lips stretched around his teeth, and with slight showing of impatience, immediately, politely, disengaged himself away from her grip, — it seemed like a silent warning. — Her grin was sardonic, intending to leave the recipient bereft of confidence.

For a moment, Helen felt puzzled, but she then remembered Hannah's descriptive words, — that he disliked public displays of affection.

Alex then turned her smirking attention towards Helen; she was staring

66

at her with a rude curiousness.

But, Helen drew herself up to her full height; — she had swiftly got the actresses measure; — she was determined that she wasn't going to be swayed.

Jean hadn't moved throughout the unfolding scene, — she was cautiously buttering the situation. "Helen Campbell, I would like to introduce you to the very famous, Miss Alex Craig. - Helen's a journalist, Alex."

Helen assertively stretched out her hand. "I'm very pleased to meet you, Miss Craig."

Alex moved the fingers still holding the edge of the stole, the rings' stones brilliantly twinkled, and with obvious reluctance, she reached out her right hand and condescendingly reciprocated with the briefest and lightest of touch. — Her haughty manner was apparent; — her tawny eyes were sweeping and wide with disbelief, her expression continued to be sardonic, "Ye … s, of course, you would be," she trailed the word slowly and thoughtfully. "I wouldn't have expected anything *else* from a journalist, always on the look-out for a new angle."

Helens' eyes narrowed warily; she hastily, flippantly replied, "Oh, there's no angle here, Miss Craig; — I can assure you."

Alex stiffly nodded her head towards her, continuing to be sceptically, quizzically thoughtful, — she spoke again, "I feel that we've met somewhere before, unless my eyes are deceiving me."

Helen shook her head. "That isn't possible," she laconically assured.

Alex never missed an opportunity, — she still continued to be amused. "Then, I must be mistaken," she conceded.

"*Very,* mistaken," Duncan murmured.

"Darling, you could have warned me."

He seemed surprised, responding — "Warned you …warned you of what?"

"Well, I didn't expect to face a resurgence of Campbells when I came home. I was given to understand that Mairie Campbell had died, or had passed on, — as they say." She then redirected her complaint to Helen, "You could only be her apparition, some-kind of a- reincarnation," she said maliciously, her curling her lip in distaste. Her final remark was cruelly spiteful — "The Campbells always seem to *manifest* themselves, — in some way?"

Helen immediately felt a searing stab; she rose in defence of herself, she appeared perplexed as she absorbed the actresses maligning, insulting remarks, feeling at a further disadvantage, she answered cautiously,

— "Have you ever had a dirty face, Miss Craig? They really **are** *quite* fashionable. My grandmother's views on this situation would be; — don't say anything, unless it is worth saying."

Alex's amused eyes swiftly flicked around, she remarked, — "Everything is worth saying."

Duncan anxiously interjected; — he was desperate to say something of a- mitigating nature to the formers remark, — "Helen, I must declare that I totally disagree and wish to assure you, that all in the space of a single moment, your gracious presence has swept back nearly a century in time."

Helen replied, "Thank you, but *my* presence seems to have caused *quite* a stir."

Alex swayed towards the Laird, still smirking, — "How very gallant of you, Duncan."

Jean mercifully chipped in, coming to the rescue by brightly saying, — "I wish to assure you Alex that your vision is quite perfect, but if you have any doubts, — no matter how small — I'm quite sure that Iain will be very pleased to advise you. — Helen has her family resemblances, like anyone of us; it's … just that *some* have a more pronounced likeness than others … and that is all … shall we … proceed?" — Jean brilliantly smiled, and turned to address the Laird. "Duncan, so as to avoid any further calamities, would you be a- deere and get yourself and Helen a drink. I'm sure that our guest of honour must be dying of thirst by now, and we don't want her fainting from dehydration, — now do we? And I have no doubt that you can do with a *stiff* brandy yourself, — a *nice* relaxing drink," and smiling from one to the other, she then led Alex away.

Both Helen and the Laird watched their departing backs, until they'd reached the bend in the stairs, where Alex briefly turned to glance back at them, and if there was malevolence in her glance, then Helen wondered why, for it left her with a distinct feeling of unease. Could it be, — that as a reporter, — Alex Craig felt her to be a threat to her privacy, — but then of course, — she was, — she privately conceded,

"Shall we go?" he suggested, feeling an immediate flood of release, from the heinous situation and his divided attentions.

She was trembling slightly when the Laird proffered his arm, and nervously returned his reassuring smile as she lightly held his elbow, feeling as though she had entered a ridiculous game of charades, as he *still* hadn't given any real indication that he recognised her from their morning encounter, but splattered with mud as she had been, she had been virtually beyond recognition.

Chapter 7

Lord Lennox

He led her through into the milling party's throng in the lounge, which upon entrance, proved to have a vastly high white ceiling with pastel green walls. A room which during the day, was divided by white louvered doors stretching across its width, — they were now folded back, allowing the room's fullest possible use. Iain was opening the French windows which led into a large glazed Victorian summerhouse; — the damp grounds beyond were floodlit and beyond them, were darkening views of rolling green slopes.

A few couples were dancing in the far area cleared of its furniture for the evening, and were at first oblivious of any newcomers to the gathering, but not so the people in the immediate vicinity, for Helen began to feel herself, self-consciously blushing again under their curious stares and glances. — The Laird of course, knew everyone, and stopped several times to introduce her to a large number of guests, — once introduced, they ceased to stare as if assuaged, Rita would have concluded, 'It's the new girl on the block'.

"I'm finding this very difficult," she complained, during a brief interlude of what had now become a reception, as they were invited by a very smartly dressed, uniformed waiter wearing white gloves, to select a welcoming drink from his silver salver, bearing a choice of Martinis, Sherries and Champagne. Helen took a cool looking Martini; Duncan favoured the Champagne. "A toast to your arrival," he acknowledged, raising his glass, while inclining his head in a polite bow.

Helen was obviously still feeling disgruntled. "A few hours ago, I was a hippie," she exaggerated, a trifle caustically. "Would you have given this much time and attention to such a class difference, for which I suspect, you have little or no regard?"

"I have a high regard for all women, I just wish they would make up their minds what they want in life; I was told that you didn't want to come."

"Arrochar was just a playground, a summer retreat, and *snap* decisions are a male trait; — very often they live to regret it," she replied, led by the obvious reference to Alex.

"I hope that I don't regret becoming the executor of Mairie Campbell's *will*," he replied, acknowledging her haughty indifference.

She momentarily mellowed enough to reply, "Charles was very persuasive."

"Oh and how did Charles persuade you?"

She answered with care, "He convinced me that it was a matter of duty." She then became acutely conscious of him studying her again, until he suddenly startled her by leaning forward and speaking quietly, so that only she would hear, concluding …

"Are you nervous?" He enquired.

"I feel very much on display," she tersely replied.

"You should be used to such situations, playing in concerts," he pointed out.

"Being viewed in a goldfish bowl isn't to my liking, and that's a very painful subject and it's not quite the same thing," she brushed a trifle stiffly. "You also seem to know an awful lot about me."

"Mairie Campbell was a friend, and you lassies love a good gossip. She was proud of your achievements."

"I see my fame has come before me," she replied, smiling and inclining her head at *yet* another passing guest. "I'm at a disadvantage and you forget, — *gossip* dominates my life."

He shook his head; "Newspapers are hardly private issues; — your column is very well read."

"You mean, you've read that also," she said, astonished. "I would have thought that gossip was beneath you."

"So long as the gossip isn't about me — I've read every line, your column is very controversial," he chuckled. "Now, are you going to *admit* that you're feeling nervous?"

Helen gave a soft facetious laugh, replying, "I'm not sure just *how* I feel at this very moment, a little bristled perhaps; — is Miss Craig usually so 'bruyant' towards virtual strangers?"

"Miss Craig is responsible for herself," he hastily replied. "One learns how to handle her."

"What did she mean?"

"Mean?" he echoed warily.

"Yes … mean … about the reincarnation."

Duncan uncomfortably swallowed, as he fiddled with the restrictions of his bow tie, it was the moment that he'd been dreading, — his reply was cagy, he managed to sound surprised, "I … it was a terrible choice of words; — I thought that Jean had corrected that."

Helen then caught sight of Alex as she entered the room holding onto a man's arm, — she poised in the doorway, glanced around her and when catching sight of Duncan, she began to move in their direction, but she was waylaid by an autograph hunter. — Helen thought that she'd heard a small sigh expire from him; — she immediately felt as though she were detaining him.

"She's very beautiful; — please don't neglect her on my behalf," she suggested.

His reply was flirtatious. "She isn't the most beautiful woman in the room," he swiftly said, his eyes were warmly caressing while casting her more than just a passing glance.

"If I didn't know any better, I would have a sneaking suspicion that you were trying to wheedle your way into my affections."

"And … are you saying that I'm wasting my time? You can't blame a man for trying; — you could turn any man's head, — and you're blushing again," he observed, noting her heightened colour.

"*No,* I am not," she denied indignantly, haughtily, flicking away a tickling tendril of hair from her neck, "I *never* blush."

"You could have fooled me," he chuckled. "I've never seen a face look so rosy."

"You're quite mistaken; I'm warm from the wine," she replied hastily, evasively, knowing that it was her restrained anger, causing her to flush, "Piano's … are my instrument, my Lord, not second fiddles; — you seem to be suffering from a bout of divided loyalties."

"I would be disloyal to myself, were I to shift my preferences," he replied.

"Then, I … think that we need to change the subject, Mr. MacFarlane," she suggested, evasively. "Perhaps I should thank you for the party instead, as I understand that you were responsible for the idea."

He maddeningly chuckled again, sweeping a hand, referring to the guests, "They were all curious to meet Mairie Campbell's granddaughter, and *please,* do we have to be so formal, my name is *Duncan,* and I refuse to answer to anything else."

Rita would have cold-bloodedly called him 'Mac' upon introduction, came the spurious thought, while chastising herself; — he had taken control of the situation by stunning her with courteous romanticism, which was unequal to any modern day, 'leading-to-the-lair' banter. — He was baiting her, and she was consciously falling for it, and considered that it was his way of calming the tempest.

She thoughtfully sipped at her Martini and despite her inner turmoil, wished to savour his name on her lips, along with the Martini, but instead queried its meaning, "It sounds regal. What does it mean?"

He replied, "It means 'Brown Warrior' and you could be right about it sounding regal, as *I* and many counterparts share it with two Kings of Scotland."

It was an apt name for a swarthy Scot, she thought, as he continued, knowing that he possessed the arrogance of Kings. "You should brush up on your Shakespeare, and I suggest that you begin with Macbeth, as it was he who murdered Duncan 1st, thus enabling him to succeed to the throne. My forbears, the 'Earls of Lennox' largely feature in the story."

And she could have murdered *him* this morning, came a further spurious thought, although safely replying. "I must admit that Shakespeare was never my strong subject; I was one of the witches during an all girl performance at school." She spontaneously, mischievously, smiled, revealing, "It was an absolute disaster; — I forgot my lines and ended up thanking the prompt for her assistance. — I'm no actress."

"Your name, 'Helen' means the *bright* one," she caught his smile, as she glanced up, thinking, here it comes again — she hadn't been very *bright* that morning.

"Oh, I only have one name;" she brushed. "I was christened after my paternal great grandmother. — It becomes very confusing sometimes, trying to sort out ones' relations," she admitted, giving another soft amused laugh. "Our branch of the Campbell's has always been a piece of enigma to me, and Mairie Campbell has been no different. — Her strange behaviour over the last few years, I had put down to some-kind of senile decay, brought on by my father's death, but Crawford assured me that it wasn't so."

"He was so right," he confirmed. "I was with her to the very last; she just faded peacefully away, and for the years that I knew her, I found her like most of ye lassies, an enigma only when she chose to be."

"A woman's prerogative," Helen chuckled, despite her inner-self, — she was beginning to relax, mellowed by the alcohol. "Good for gran."

He shared her amusement, after which, the Reverend and his wife who approached to be introduced, briefly interrupted their conversation.

Formalities completed, they moved away again.

"Is it *always* like this?" she complained.

He spontaneously, broadly grinned. "I'm expected to stand on ceremony, the older generation expect the protocol, yeel have to get used to it, — it's happening all the time."

"It's so bourgeoisie, they could do with a little loosening up," she commented, while sipping her drink and savouring the refreshing cool liquid, which moistened her dry throat, and then stared down at the fine crystal glass as if fascinated by its thistle shape. — As she studied its prismatic colours, she felt oddly conscious of the man standing so attentively at her side, momentarily lost for words, she suddenly said, "Oh, I've just remembered, I have a letter of introduction from Mr. Crawford."

"I hardly think, that there's any need for such a formality, do you?" He asked, confirming, while raising a dark eyebrow in surprise, "Very clearly, you *are* Helen Campbell and not an impostor."

Helen gave another soft laugh, "Yes, I suppose I am," she replied, answering as if not quite convinced herself, while all the time hating him for being so irritatingly confident, whereas she was not. — He was just doing his job, she conceded.

"My mother sends her apologies for her absence, she's in the throws of a cold, and didn't feel well enough to travel from Edinburgh."

The music suddenly changed to a romantic song, — a crooner singing an old popular theme song which had the name Jean in the title, it must have spurred a thought. Helen swayed invitingly to the lilt.

"Jean," he explained needlessly, "Its Iain's favourite, 'Come into my arms bonnie Jean' and she certainly did that, — without a moment's hesitation, she just walked right up to him and kissed him, deed done."

"Really, it all sounds quite boring and very forward, and it would risk a rejection, and the name, 'Helen', doesn't exactly lend itself to musical attributes," she sighed.

"Oh, it isn't boring," he replied, in reference to the former. "It's just getting your life in order, and then moving onto the next thing."

"Life isn't exactly in a rush here," she observed, beginning to feel amused with the situation.

Duncan quietly studied the glowing creaminess of her skin, he could not get enough of her, he was mesmerised, and despite his outward demeanour, he was feeling awkward in her presence, mostly caused by thoughts of the afternoon's accident, which she surprisingly hadn't mentioned, but how to put matters right was beyond him, especially as Alex had deliberately perpetrated a situation which had furthered his discomfort. — His male senses were being tantalised by her close proximity, he desperately wanted to inhale more of his companion's freshness, he wanted her in his arms — most of the dances were of the more 'pop' variety where couples moved and gyrated separately, but this was an ideal tune to smooch to — bravado and assertiveness then overcame him; — there was only one thing to do — he removed her glass from her nervously toying fingers, and placed it with his own on a conveniently passing waitress's tray — and without, so much as a- 'by-your-leave' he slid his arms about her and glided a very surprised young woman into a waltz.

It was just as well she could dance, she thought, as she managed without very much effort, to match his skilful, fluid and rhythmic steps with those of her own.

They continued the dance in communal silence, while Helen's eyes strayed irresistibly upwards, — shielded by her lashes, she was able to surreptitiously study her partner, deciding that he wasn't really a handsome man, more rugged would be a fairer description of the Laird, — his complexion, swarthy, she supposed from working in the open air, — his closely cut dark hair had a tendency to wave and was fashionably longer, curling at the nape; his rather generous, sensuous mouth seemed ready to smile when he wasn't yelling at her, and those magnetic blue eyes, fringed with dark lashes. — She surmised him to be aged a little above thirty, as her own eyes came to rest on the strong, clean lines of his jaw.

She lowered her eyes as the music melted into a soft stirring end, where he twirled her, and still holding her fingers, she sank into a deep, slow curtsey. He grinned as she softly laughed, and then bobbed up again to be encircled within his arms.

. They stood, as it seemed, locked together, suspended in time, alone in the middle of the dancing area, all sound faded away, their lips so temptingly close as his velvety blue eyes greedily absorbed beguiling eyes that were alight, sparkling with vivacity and merriment, above a nose which could only be described as pert, and below the pert nose were glossy, tempting, suppliant lips just waiting to be kissed, the urge to kiss her was overwhelming; — he sighed heavily, the open verandah was only a few steps away, but so was Alex, and her intentions were all prevailing.

"Helen …," he began. — She smiled up at him, expectantly waiting, but whatever the Laird had been about to say, she wasn't to find out, as Alex approached them holding the arm of a man who was very definitely, of Transatlantic stock.

"Damn!" Duncan let out the soft expletive, appearing annoyed, as the spell was broken. — He reluctantly released her, while Helen forced her attentions away, to concentrate on their unwelcome intrusion.

"Helen Campbell, may I introduce you to Arnie Browning, my director."

Helen nodded to Arnie and shook his hand. — He wasn't as she would have expected directors to be; — the ones she had encountered in the past had mostly suffered acutely from over indulgence, something that she felt that Arnie Browning would never do, for he was tall and thin, reminding her of a greyhound, and dressed smartly in a green plaid evening jacket matched with plain black trousers; — he was typical of many Americans who flocked to Scotland.

He was fair-haired, in stark contrast to the Laird, and his eyes seemed to be a hazel brown as he peered through rimless specs, perched on his too bony nose. A plain man in fact, but although he was pleasant, it certainly hadn't been Arnies' good looks that had captivated and lured Alex away all those years ago.

The music started up again. Alex took the Laird's arm, eagerly pulling him away; obviously, she wanted to dance, thus leaving Helen and Arnie watching them for a moment.

As they drifted away out of earshot, Alex provocatively bent her head upward in conversation with the Laird; — a sultry expression on her face told everything. — It was apparent she wasn't wasting anytime in rekindling their relationship, — and first laughing at her words, he then lowered his dark head nearer to hers, as he replied.

"She's complaining about his lack of attention," a voice beside her said.

Helen stood talking to Arnie for sometime about his film, and despite her rather closeted former opinion, she found that she liked the director, he was amusing and witty in the American sense; — his accent wasn't as corn-brash as some Americans whom she had interviewed.

During the course of their conversation, Arnie told her how pleased he was that the Laird had allowed the castle to be used for the film. "We wanted to use it several years ago," he explained, "… but the old Laird, Angus MacFarlane, refused to allow it. There was some kind of a feud going on at the time, between James Craig, Alex's father and the older MacFarlanes, and so we shelved the idea for a time, until Alex decided she felt homesick enough, and the present Laird seemed pleased to welcome her back into this '*dumb*, one-horse-town' of his." — And Helen, following the direction of Arnie's glance, saw that Alex was still dancing with the Laird, her arms now entwined loosely about his neck. — She had obviously found the cure for her homesickness, and the Laird, very definitely, wasn't raising any objections. — Obviously again, she further thought, — whatever the feud had been over, must be settled now.

Happily relaxed, she continued chatting to Arnie for a while until the Reverend and his good lady approached them, with the obvious intention of speaking to Helen, — when at the same time, a mountainous looking, over-bejewelled woman, who declared that she *simply* adored Americans, then side-tracked, Arnie; — he obviously had little or no hope of escaping her captive charms again that evening. — Helen stifled her amusement, seeing the odd looking pair, — the widow whisked him away.

The Reverend Adams and his good wife made a great fuss of her, and hoped she would take up her grandmother's pew in the Kirk, and they couldn't have been more delighted when she told them, that she intended assisting Jean with the Christmas entertainment.

"Did I hear my name mentioned?" laughed Jean, as she good-humouredly came to join them.

"Why *yes,* you did," Helen cheerfully admitted, while explaining.

"Wonderful, news!," Jean exclaimed, showing her joy at Helen's final decision, and spent a further few minutes discussing the latest features planned for the Harvest Festival, until the Reverend had his attentions drawn elsewhere.

"Let's find some peace and quiet," Jean said, gesticulating, while hastily leading the way to the stairway and some seclusion, — something they found in the Wedgwood room.

When alone, she turned to Helen, all eagerly agog, "Well?" she enquired, chuckling mischievously. "What do you think of our, 'dull, pompous, old Laird' now?"

They seated themselves before the dressing mirrors, Helen realising that her new friend had obviously been teasing her, — cagily, she replied, feeling the colour heighten in her face, "You might have warned me, letting me go on like that," she chastised. "I hope that you haven't told him."

Jean shook her head, "It was just girl talk, and you were so adamant that Alex has such a poor bargain, I just hadn't the heart to shatter your illusions, they were rather amusing, — but … now that you've met him," she shrugged, "well, you can find out for yourself."

"I feel uncomfortable with him," she honestly announced.

Jean seemed surprised, "Uncomfortable … with Duncan? He's probably just as nervous as you are; he's really quite a lamb, just ignore his title. — Alex puts her feet into everything and always leaves someone else to sort out the mess; — she's publicly put him on the spot and he's probably trying to worm his way out of it."

"Why should he be nervous of me?"

"Take a look at yourself in the mirror."

"He's a stick-in-the-mud; an older wife would suit him better."

Jean smiled, "Should we hamper him with such things?"

As she renewed her lipstick, and while glancing at her companion through the mirror, she asked the question which was foremost on her mind, "I didn't know whether to congratulate them or not. — Will they be making an announcement this evening?"

"All-in-good-time, I would suspect. — James isn't here, nor the Lady Eleanor, — both, would wish to be in attendance at such an important occasion."

"Alex would have to give up a very successful career when she marries the Laird," Helen observantly remarked.

"It's fundamental, there is simply no choice in the matter, she will have to comply," Jean replied. "There comes a time in every woman's life when she hankers after a husband, home and family and Alex is no different than the rest of us, — besides, she's approaching thirty, if she leaves it very much longer; she'll find childbearing all the more difficult. — Its something that I know about," she finished, sadly.

"And the Laird must have heirs," Helen concluded.

"Yes," Jean replied. "He's acutely conscious of his need to be married. If he doesn't have children, then his lands will automatically be referred to the state when he dies, and that would be ironical, as the MacFarlanes' have been fighting for centuries to retain their lands."

Helen mindfully conceded, — it was small wonder, that the couples respective parents were so desperate for the match, and the Laird would quite naturally be of the same frame of mind, and in conclusion, decided that Alex did him some injustice by leaving, in more ways than one, — but come what may, she could not imagine Alex Craig changing nappies.

She changed the subject, sounding disappointed, "Jean, why isn't Rory here, I fully expected to see him, even if he was on duty?"

"I can't really explain," she replied, shaking her head. "Duncan makes those kinds of decisions, no-one questions him."

"It must have been very last minute," she observed. "I saw Rory this afternoon, and to all pretence and purpose, he was coming; there was no mention of him, not."

Suddenly, a dinner gong smote their ears, interrupting their conversation, and Jean immediately displayed urgency, "We must go," she hastily said, "... dinner is about to be served; we follow protocol."

They made their way downstairs, where Jean ushered her through to the door ahead of the gathering crowd. Iain and the Laird with Alex and Arnie were waiting for them.

Helen, felt hesitant, she seemed to be the only one unsure of what to do, and she must have appeared a little lost, for as if aware of her dilemma, the Laird smiled indulgently down at her, and taking possession of her hand, tucked it through his crooked arm. His warm hand covered hers, thus renewing the confusions.

Feeling at first surprised by his unexpected action, she then considered he was merely being courteous, but it didn't stave off the acutely conscious feeling of Alex Craig's presence nearby. — Helen stiffened when the actress momentarily glanced her way, as she attached herself to Arnie's arm, and then Helen's attention was drawn elsewhere, as the party led by Jean and Iain, moved steadily into the softly lit dining room.

Once having seated her beside Arnie, — to her left, the Laird moved directly to the opposite side of the table to seat himself, with Alex to his right.

Content to observe, Helen allowed her eyes to roam about the room. — The Roaches obviously favoured pastel shades. — This room being a shade of pale buttermilk and furnished with French gilt furnishings. — The ceiling was high and painted white, and from its centre, hanging from elaborately carved stucco rose, was a dimly lit crystal chandelier, shedding a million sparkling prisms above her head.

Lowering her eyes again, she met those of the Laird's blue penetrating gaze, for what seemed an eternity, until managing to avert her head by casting a glance along the glittering, snow-white clad table, in an attempt to settle her concentration on Alex's cool-aired confidence. – It was obvious that she loved being the centre of attention.

She was quite beautiful in a sophisticated Hollywood style, but her clean-cut features were clearly displayed by her severely drawn back hair, which highlighted her high, sharp cheek bones, — her thin lips were skilfully outlined in an attempt to suggest fullness, — her voice, as she addressed the company, held no trace of her original northern accent, and her Americanisms seemed just a trifle theatrical, as she monopolised the conversation, answering questions at great length about her film, until Jean from the top end of the table, pressed her for more general information.

"When does the film unit muster, Alex?"

Alex sweetly smiled; her diamond drop earrings swung crazily when she sharply turned her head towards the Laird, her doe-like eyes caressed his features before replying, — she again, possessively slotted her arm through his, but this time, he didn't remove it. "Duncan has agreed to a date in late November, — haven't you darling? — It has to be then, we need the winter climate to set the first scenes, and we'll make the party, a- Ceilidh, plenty of Highland music, piano accordions playing reels and the wig … waggling of kilts, which I fully expected Jean to have organised for my homecoming," she admonished. "Until then, I shall enjoy a short vacation."

And try as she might, Helen could not imagine the actress letting her hair down, — her eyes held amused sparkles, as bright as the diamonds in Alex's engagement ring and the prisms above her head.

"We're sorry to disappoint you," their hostess softly replied. "We decided that Helen might feel more at home in a more traditional English setting, although the cuisine is Scottish."

"Home is where the heart is," Helen laconically replied. "I am well travelled."

Alex's reply to this was: - "I left my heart in Arrochar, and now I'm here to stake my claim."

"And, where is your lost heart, Helen?" Jean asked this very leading question. "London, France, Switzerland, America or perhaps, also in the Highlands," she suggested.

Helen mysteriously smiled, as she briefly flashed a glance in Duncan's direction; — he seemed to be waiting anxiously, pensively, for her reply, he sighed when she cagily replied. "My heart is still in my own keeping; it isn't time to leave it anywhere, just yet."

"A cagy reply," Jean acknowledged.

Alex interrupted, she had had her say on the tiring subject, and that was enough, she was impatient to return to her own plans, alerting, "Helen, a date for your diary. — We plan to hold the Press Conference, — the evening before the party. I shall see to it that you receive the very first invitation."

Ryder had been very busy; she realised. — Very much back on the alert, she opened her mouth to speak, and then the unexpected happened …

Duncan chipped in, sounding anxious, "I'm sure that Helen is mightily grateful, Alex, but she's on holiday, and I'm not going to allow her to fill up her diary with anything other, than sociable pursuits."

Alex swiftly replied, gloating, damning, revealing, "I think that Helen's Editor may have a very different opinion. — I had the opportunity of speaking to a Daily News representative in London," — she then addressed

Helen, who was aghast at the interference. "Your Editor is expecting great things of you, — isn't he?"

Helen was immediately on her guard against Alexs' probing tactics, she was in a corner and confused as why Ryder should have discussed the personal affairs of an employee with a colleague, — and seeing her dilemma, it was obvious that Alex's face bore another sneer of triumph, which was immediately, wiped off, when Helen just as swiftly answered: - "But … why wait three months for your conference? I would have thought you'd be *eager* to set the publicity wheels in motion, — just say the word, and I'll have the *whole* of Fleet Street listening to you."

Alexs' eyes, viciously narrowed, "I've taken the trouble of reading some of your back issues, — you're quite the little '*hot-shot*' aren't you, Helen? Roland Barrett happens to be a friend of mine," she revealed, mounting the tension.

"Then, you know some very shady people, Miss Craig."

"Newspapers can be such a *sluice,*" Alex retorted, while her sharp features screwed up in distaste.

Helen coolly replied. "Then, I am surprised that you're prepared to risk your reputation, but of course, your vanity will far outweigh your fear of the press."

Alexs' eyes wildly flicked as she replied. "You like challenges — I trust you to make it good."

Duncan turned to her, sharply saying, "This isn't going to happen, Alex."

Helen put up an arresting hand, she murmured, "I can manage."

"Are we going to be allowed to know the plot of the film, Alex?" Iain enquired, in a vain effort to mercifully change the direction of the conversation.

"It's non-other than — Medieval," she replied laconically, before continuing, "What else could you be doing in a castle setting, but damsels in distress … bold knights in shining armour; — of course, chivalry is long since dead."

"Really, Alex, on behalf of the gentlemen here present, I *must* protest," Jean retorted. "Perhaps, something in your manner has prevented it from coming your way."

"You sound like the last of the romantics, Miss Craig," Helen interjected, along with a sudden mischievous smile, enjoying the lively vision of Alex wearing blonde plaits, *kissing* her lover through iron bars. "Are you sure that you aren't miscast? — I'm just longing to see the scene in the dungeons. — Rory and I spent a *whole* summer, just painting poor blood soaked souls, — of course, all enemies of the MacFarlanes', there were a few who underestimated them, especially… disloyal women."

"I'd be on your guard, Helen Campbell, if I were you, there is such a thing as slander, and you have a reputation for casting aspersions, but that's the journalistic psyche for you, always getting down to brass tacks."

"Then … let him beware, — he who casts the first stone," she replied, aware of the remounting tension.

"Oh, Alex where's your sense of humour?" Jean interjected.

Arnie coughed, he raised his hand to insert a finger in his uncomfortably tightening collar while saying; "Alex left her sense of humour back home in the States, where humour is far more diverse."

"The British use double entendres, it's more subtle," Helen offered.

"You tell us, Arnie," Jean suggested.

"A synopsis would give too much away, but just briefly, it's based on the history of the early MacFarlanes and the Viking invasion; we still haven't found a leading man and we still haven't decided on a name for the heroine."

"Then, Duncan would be ideal," Jean suggested, referring to the former, while thinking of his historical namesakes.

"Saints preserve us," Duncan was heard to murmur, "I think I share Helens' sentiments on acting, — even if I could act, I couldn't face the critics, I'd rather not have my name in the headlines, — thank you kindly, but I must decline the offer."

Helen probed Arnie, "And the title of the film, is …?"

"Nothing is settled," Alex swiftly, sharply, interjected.

Helen was unperturbed; she gave a sly smile of triumph. "I think it should be called, 'The Lennox Line' just in case it all stops here."

"What a wonderful idea," Jean remarked, "… but I don't think that the line will be stopping."

Duncan grinned broadly, his eyes met, yet again, with Helen's, his next remark, spontaneous, "Oh, I categorically underline that," which met with gales of laughter.

"I'll add the title to the list," Arnie announced.

As a diversion, Alex returned to her gushing self. "I would like to take this opportunity, of inviting simply everyone to our muster party," she said, in low velvety tones, again turning wide-fawning, adoring eyes on the Laird. "That is, that you my darling, agree to us using the Great Feasting Hall, as the castle is the only place in Arrochar large enough to cater for parties of any such consequence."

Helen felt a stab of indignation on Jeans behalf, at Alex's tactless remark, but she appeared to be the only one who had noticed. The Laird was now smiling indulgently at the actress, although *his* voice, as he replied, held an undertone of concern, his accent thickened, "I cannae see any reason to refuse your request, but I trust the Film Unit will start as they mean to carry on, by showing respect for a historical monument, such as the Castle Drumbrae."

"But, of course they will, darling," she said a trifle indignantly. "And you will be there to protect your fortress, personally."

Still listening quietly, Helen could sympathise with the Laird's concern on the matter of muster parties. — She had attended a few in her time, and some of them had turned out to be wild, boisterous affairs, creating a disturbance in neighbourhoods near and far, and now, Alex's subtle invitation to the dignified company here present, she knew would alter the party's tone considerably.

"Thank you for your invitation, Alex," Jean replied. "I think I can safely answer for all and sundry, and say that we're *already* looking forward to the party that will end all parties — it will make a *grand* beginning to the Christmas festivities."

"There … it's all settled," Alex confirmed, with absolute satisfaction.

Chapter 8

Confusing Conspiracies

Mercifully, the waitresses and waiters then appeared to serve the meal, thus breaking the tension, and made a welcome distraction, — the conversation turned into appreciative exclamations and praise on the cuisine. — Helen's appetite rose at the sight of the delicious local caught salmon cooked in wine and topped with creamy cucumber sauce. — The main course was pheasant and fresh vegetables, followed by a choice of desserts, the favourite being a pear and ginger wine dish, served with fresh double cream. — But feeling well fed, Helen declined the sweet and plumped for cheese and biscuits, grateful at the end, to wash it all down with a- creamy coffee, served in delicate bone china cups, bearing the MacFarlane's gold crest.

She then entered into conversation with her companion sitting to her right. — Peter Dundas was a young man in his mid twenties, and she soon discovered that he was an enthusiastic Jazz musician, "Are you from this village?" Helen keenly enquired.

He indicated the couple sitting adjacent to him. "My parents live in Carrick; — it's the next village. I live in Aberdeen when I'm in town, but I'm on tour most of the time, and just to remind you, I ran into you a few years ago, you certainly made that old village hall piano swing, I played the horn; — it certainly livened up a few things."

Helen brightly snapped her fingers, "I remember, Rory Cameron's friend."

Peter suddenly, pleasantly, chuckled, "We didn't see much of Rory when you were around; — he kept you to himself, especially when I asked him to put in a good word, — if you fancy a session anytime, I always carry my horn."

"Then, tomorrow evening," she excitedly suggested. "There's a piano in the hotel."

In conclusion to the meal, there were liquors to be served in the lounge for those requiring them, and as Helen stood to leave, — still in sparkling conversation with Peter, — she noticed that a few of the gentlemen were remaining in the dining room to enjoy a smoke, and among them, the Laird. She hesitated for a moment, surprised and fascinated when he withdrew a pipe from his breast pocket, and proceeded to slowly, methodically, fill it with tobacco from a pouch, which appeared from somewhere inside his jacket.

A fleeting soft smile crossed Helens' lovely features, as it brought back happy memories. — Her father had smoked a pipe; it was so … quintessentially a male's prerogative, she thought, and with it, there came a certain, self-satisfied air of contentment, — and she noticed that the Laird, were as all men.

He glanced up as if suddenly aware of her watching him, — the hot colour suffused her face again, as he quietly, unwaveringly, studied her through a thin veil of smoke, and feeling the return of her confusion, she turned a haughty head, making a swift, but not ungracious, beeline for the door, seeking refuge among the other lady guests now in the lounge, where Alex sought her out, — the conversation was cutting …

"I'd like to have a little private *chat* with you," she said caustically.

"Well, here I am, so *chat* away," She invited, sighing, while observing the gathering from a distance, "but I don't think that we have anything remotely in common."

"Then, let us find something, and I warn you, I'm not going to *mince* my words.

Helens' eyes narrowed. "I'm quite certain that you're a very stirring, unsavoury *cook*, Miss Craig, I also think that you're chancing your luck, — may I remind you, that I have the power of the press behind me, I could make or break you."

"Then, let us see who will break first, and I shall begin by saying that you're a soft, emotional, romantic little fool," Alex scoffed. "That was a wonderful entrance you made, — swanning down those stairs, Helen Campbell; — a Busby Berkley film set couldn't have presented a more picturesque setting, — and *all* for Duncan's benefit."

Helen frowned and screwed up her nose, her expression perplexed. "Thank-you for the compliment, but Busby Berkley was a little before my time — more my grandmother's, and you really shouldn't let your imagination run away with you, Miss Craig: — until that very moment, I hadn't *met* the Laird, and may I remind you, that you were both engrossed in a conversation with Iain, when Jean and I — came down — those stairs.

"A little tactful distraction; — I'm quite sure that Jean Roach pre-arranged it. Iain Roach kept us chatting for an unseemly length of time," she bitterly accused. "We saw you go upstairs, you took more than five minutes."

Helens' scrutinising eyes scrolled up and down Alex's form, while saying, "You're feeling just a tad annoyed that you've been upstaged. — I haven't the faintest doubt, that you managed a very stunning entrance *all* of your very own, benefiting your status, before you reached Talbert."

"It's just a friendly warning, don't get your hopes up, Duncan gets a little bored and lonely sometimes, — he's accustomed to diverting his attentions towards other women, but all that will change, now that I'm back home."

Helen gasped at her companion's audacity; she was shaking with inner rage, but her exterior was calm, her words, positive, "Then, let me enlighten you — In the first instance, it wasn't my idea to come here, the situation was foisted on me, and, unlike you, I have no current plans to get married, — I'm too young to make such a leap, I have a lot of things to achieve, — perhaps when I've reached your great age, — and again, if he only has you to rely upon as a prospective *wife,* — then he's better off, bored and lonely, and he does well to divert his attentions, — men seek warmth in relationships; — you're a cold, calculating woman, Miss Craig."

Then, let me also do some enlightening, — he had quite a fetish for Mairie Campbell, he couldn't keep away, and now *you're* here — as her replacement, — you're her very effigy," she sneered.

Helen felt that she'd heard enough. "You sound very insecure, — you cling onto his arm for support so often, that I could suggest, you have a fear of falling, use a- walking stick or perhaps even more secure, some handcuffs so that he can't get away — and if you're so afraid of him wandering my way, then your wasting your energies, you will be here, long after I have gone."

"Then, perhaps we should shorten your visit," Alex spitefully replied. "And lessen your sentence; — money always speaks."

"Oh, no, I intend doing *everyday*; I'm not turning down a challenge, and it was *you,* who made it."

"So far, stalemate." she replied.

"I think, Miss Craig," Helen coolly answered, "that we should draw an end to this rather unfortunate incident, — now, if you'll excuse me, I'm expected to circulate, and I've already spent far too much time in your company." She turned to leave, but Alex arrested her. …

"Just one more thing, Helen Campbell … could we keep this conversation — between ourselves?"

"It's already forgotten … I won't tell, if you don't."

Helen turned, relieved to be engaged by Peter Dundas asking for a dance, leaving Alex gloating alone. — Peter was a wow! at jiving, leaving her and the other on-looking guests breathless.

A short while later, Helen was dancing with Arnie Browning, the American was non-too-light on his feet, she found, and several times during their dance, her toes suffered unmercifully from their mismatched steps. "Shall we start again?" she suggested.

"Gee! I'm sorry, Helen honey," he said. "… born with two left feet, I guess. Alex rarely takes the risk of dancing with me; she reckons it's like dancing with some kind of a broom-handle. — I can't relax, unlike the Laird, over there." He appeared downcast as he nodded past her shoulder, and they turned in dancing so that the Laird and Alex came into view. — They weren't really dancing, just swaying on the spot as they spoke, but Helen sensed Arnie's envy, and a feeling of pity welled up inside of her. — He was hopelessly in love with Alex, she realised, so much so, that he would do anything to please her, even to the point of bringing her back into the arms of a rival against whom he could have no possible chance.

"Don't be so hard on yourself, Arnie," she softly sympathised; — genuinely concerned that Alex could have been so cruel, so personal, to a friend.

Arnie glanced down at her, smiling as if resigned to his fate, "Awe, chucks! You're just being kind to me, Helen. — I know that I can direct Alex through a thousand dramatic film sequences with ease, but I just can't direct her feet on the dance floor."

'Or her heart away from the Laird,' she thought.

Arnie continued, hopefully inviting, "If ever you need work, give me a call. There are plenty of roles for beautiful women," he winked, before she was whisked away and felt herself gathered into other, more restraining arms.

"Now, where were we?" Duncan asked, pressing her more closely to him than was sensibly comfortable, unnerving her and annoyingly stirring her pulse rate by having to inhale the slight, masculine aroma of his pipe tobacco, mingled with his 'Givenchy' after shave.

"I … think, you were about to ask me something," she reminded him.

"Oh, yes," he acknowledged, his cool breath fanning her cheek as he lowered his head, continuing to speak to her, his concern showing in his tone; — it became obvious that he had seen her together, with Alex.

"Helen, just ignore Alex," he said positively. "She has this unfortunate attitude that upsets everyone, — she's a past master at it."

"I don't *think* that Alex Craig is going to allow me to ignore her, — and it isn't helping that you keep giving me *all* this attention," she pointedly admonished.

He sounded mildly indignant, "You're my guest, a very special guest and so far, I don't feel that I've been the best of hosts, — I would like to make amends, which brings me to ask, — how are you getting home?"

"I … err … I have my car with me," she answered, sounding surprised, puzzled and confused that he should ask.

"Your stepfather made a wise decision by not allowing you to drive all the way from London, — it can be very tiring, if you're unaccustomed to long journeys."

"Charles is inclined to *fuss*, — and anyway, they were grans' strict instructions, — although, heaven knows why, — you surely knew that?" she asked, again sounding puzzled.

He flushed, — she had unwittingly kicked his Achilles heel, his reply was awkwardly brushing, "Aye, I did," he admitted in a culpable way, while glancing down at her. "Charles isn't alone with his concerns, — the lanes are very dangerous to manoeuvre at night, and so perhaps, I should drive you home."

Helen couldn't help her next thought, that the lanes were just as dangerous during the daytime, when the white Rover was on the road, — she was a trifle swift with her refusal, "Oh, … no, … no, no, … I assure you, … I can manage. I'm a very competent driver."

"I insist," he annoyingly replied.

And again, not wishing to be an inconvenience, she attempted a further misplaced refusal, "Thanks, but there really *is* no need, — the lanes won't be a problem," she assured. "I manage to drive through the City of London every day, without any mishaps."

Swift with an answer, he replied. "The city is brightly lit up at night, whereas Arrochar is not, and I couldn't run the risk of any dangerous encounters on your way home."

"And, I wish that everyone would *stop* taking *my* best interests to heart," she snapped irritably, at his remark, firmly underlining her previous thought, insistently, authoritively saying, "I *said,* I can manage."

"If you carry on this way, Miss Campbell, I shall think that you don't want to be alone with me."

"How did you guess?" she laughed softly, to lesson the blow of flouting his authority. "Then … allow me to suggest a compromise."

"Which is?"

"I'll drive my own car, and … you can drive ahead of me."

"Are you usually this stubborn?" He stiffly asked.

"I'm in control of my own life; why shouldn't I make my own decisions?" she haughtily replied.

To which *he* replied. "Don't argue, or shall have no alternative but to take very stringent action."

Helen's head snapped up to catch his expression and his meaning, but he was smiling down at her, and so she relaxed again. "Would I dare?" she questioned, murmured softly, feeling that she was in a production of: - 'The Taming of the Shrew'.

"Yes, you would," he said, while gently removing her hand from his shoulder, to briefly study her scathed palm, and then raising it to his lips, placed a soft, velvety, warm kiss in the region of the wound. His eyes raked her features, questioning, almost pleading, but he uttered nothing.

"You're incorrigible," she recognised.

"It has been said many times," he replied. "I'm not very good at taking *no* for an answer."

"Then, I won't argue with you, if you agree to my terms."

"You drive a hard bargain." He smiled, sighing softly, and pressing her closer as they continued dancing in communal silence.

Without thinking and regardless of Alex, she sighed also, nestling her head onto his shoulder, to briefly feel her hair stir, while gentle, erotic, sensitive fingers caressed the silky textured skin on her back. — She was beginning to feel very comfortable in his arms. — She suddenly laughed softly, listening to the music, she whispered, "did you choose, this tune?"

"I had a hand in it. Do you like it?"

"Yes, I do, it's a nice melody," she warmly replied, along with a mischievous, secret smile, while briefly glancing up at him, prompting, "And it's very apt … September in the Rain," she teased.

He chuckled as he spoke, "I think I might disagree on that matter, it isn't remotely like it."

"Oh, so you know something about music."

"I know most things about Scottish tunes, many of them have the lilt of the Viennese waltz, you may have noticed, — this one is called, 'Leaving Lismore'."

"And *where* is Lismore?"

"The island of Lismore is one of the many 'holy' islands of Argyll. — In Gaelic 'Lismore' means 'the great garden' and if you pay a visit, laying as it does, close to the coast of Lorne, you will find yourself standing on one if the most fertile islands in Scotland."

"Much like 'Kent' being the garden of England, I suppose," she lined up.

"In a round about way," he softly laughed in agreement.

"Perhaps, I should follow the singers' pursuits," she suggested.

Duncan stared down at her, amused, he felt teased, he now knew that she was totally relaxed with him, she was warm, comfortable and mellowed, — he pressed her closer and rested his cheek on the crown of her head, while inhaling the tantalising fragrance of her hair.

Just after midnight some of the guests decided to leave. It seemed to be a signal that the evening was at an end, as a steady stream of happy tired people came to bid Helen and their hosts a goodnight, among them Peter, who enthusiastically kissed her on the cheek, while reminding her about her promise the following evening, with a possible news article to follow. — Alex had also decided to retire early with Arnie. — They'd been travelling for many days, she underlined, and made a heartfelt declaration that she wanted to catch up on her beauty sleep, as she was very definitely suffering from a serious bout of jet lag. Helen thought that she looked very well, despite her complaints, and took it that it was just her excuse for leaving; — she was unaware that Duncan had manipulated this.

"I'll meet you for that game of croquet," Arnie mentioned, as he bid Helen a farewell, reminding, "You promised to teach me."

It's been a wonderful evening, Jean darling. — A wonderful party and such wonderful people," Alex gushed. "I can't thank you enough for holding a party especially for me, — such a surprise, — and I forgive you Duncan, for not seeing me home," — condescendingly murmuring, "… so duty bound." And glancing at Helen, "So acidly *sweet*," she finished.

Helen shrugged, standing in silent amusement and then was re-alerted, "Goodnight, Helen," she said again, giving an equivalent amused, sweeping glance as if not quite certain of what she saw, "We'll meet again, no doubt."

"No doubt, Miss Craig," she replied, refusing to allow Alex to further unnerve her … and undaunted, held out a hand. "Bracken Cottage will extend its hospitality now, as in the past," she courteously invited.

"Ye … s," Alex trailed, suspended in thought for one tawny moment, and condescendingly touched Helen's fingers, before returning to the Laird and laying a gloved hand gently on his shoulder, as she raised her face to receive his kiss on her cheek. "Goodnight, Duncan, I shall look forward to seeing you on the morrow lunchtime, there are matters of great importance I wish to discuss with you." And then, she suffered an after thought, "… Oh, and I don't think that I thanked you properly, for the roses, — so sweet of you."

Helen felt a searing stab in her stomach at this revelation, — it momentarily showed in her pained expression and her demeanour, Alex triumphantly noticed this.

Duncan raised his eyes at this further, heinous, gutting remark, his discomfort apparent, displayed in his flushed tell-tale colour, — positioned as he now was by Alex's all-revealing, tactless remarks.

"I wondered why Rory has been roaring about the village like a mad man," Jean swiftly remarked, once again, saving the situation. "He's now become a florist."

Helen gasped; she had recovered enough to stifle a laugh and mischievously enquired, "How many roses, Miss Craig?"

"Why *ten*, of course," she replied, sounding surprised. "Isn't this the number which is tantamount to a bouquet, these days?"

Helen gave a sly smile as she casually replied. "I received the traditional dozen."

"Perhaps, Rory can't count, or he hasn't caught up with the times," Jean hastily remarked.

"I really think that it's about time that Alex was going," Duncan injected in an attempt to avoid any further spearing issues. — Moments later, Helen and Jean watched his tall, broad shouldered figure with tapering hips, strolling easily across the hall as he steered the departing guests towards the door.

"*Well,*" Jean breathed a sigh of relief, "now that everyone has left, I think I'll go and organise a pot of coffee, or you may prefer some mulled wine. — what about you, Duncan, you could possibly do with a stiff drink?" she called, as he approached, — and suggesting, "Take Helen into the salon, there's something in there, that she may like."

He nodded in agreement, "My pleasure," and taking a hold of his companion's proffered hand, he led her into the Salon, ushering her past him through the door, to stand slightly behind her shoulder.

She let out a soft, delighted gasp at the scene before her; "This house must have everything!" She cried, taking in further tasteful cream and gold decoration. — But the centre of her attention, focussed on the ornately painted *Spinet* so charmingly standing on a dais, backed by gold brocade curtains.

Immediately drawn towards the pretty instrument, she spread her skirts to seat herself upon the stool, and flexing her fingers, tinkled at the keys. — She was aware of Duncan standing near her, she indicated for him to join her, "Begone Dull Care," he recognised, while placing a chair to sit slightly behind her, ever conscious of his studious blue velvet eyes, continuing to unnerve her.

Without thought, her occupied hands adroitly slid into a 'Gavotte'. She closed her eyes, momentarily enjoying the experience, listening to the pretty tinkling sound coming so perfectly from the instrument. — She smiled with pleasure, knowing that she was sharing her pleasure elsewhere, "Oh, Duncan," she sighed softly, not realising that she had spoken his name, "… if you close your eyes, you will see them all dancing. — The ladies in their beautiful, colourful, silken, Georgian gowns and the gentlemen, all wearing heavily embroidered suits and periwigs, — they look so graceful, nodding to each other and playing with their fans," she colourfully romanticised, referring to the Baroque period.

"Helen, if I close my eyes, I won't be able to see *you* and I quite like what I'm seeing." he said, of her entrancing form.

She gave a soft laugh, swaying from side to side with the flowing rhythm, her hands rising and falling, creating the gentle music until she came to the finale, making a run of notes along the piano to the end of the keyboard, towards him, in a flirtatious way, it was the cue for a spontaneous kiss, but she stopped short, and straightened, to busily shuffle music sheets.

"How on earth did you fail?" he exclaimed.

She slowly replaced the lid, thus covering the keys, "It must be the instrument," she answered evasively, while standing, "It has magical powers." They both realised then that Jean had quietly entered the room; they went to join her.

"That's just *how* the instrument is meant to be played," she remarked. "It sounded like Mozart."

"Yes," Helen replied.

"He certainly left us a heritage, and dying so young," Jean commented, while busily pouring the coffee."

"He was passionately in love with his wife," Helen informed. "She was the adrenaline behind all his works, it will endure forever."

"And here we are, still enjoying him today," Jean said. "It's a pity that we can't thank him."

"I think that Helen just has," Duncan chipped in. "What's happened to Iain?"

"He's been summoned to Mrs Laurie's confinement. — Twins, I think, so two more subjects for you, Duncan."

He chuckled, "You're so right, Jean," he replied, while absently twisting the heavy gold signet ring which he wore on the small finger of his right hand. —Helen followed his movement as he reached out to take his cup from the table, allowing her to see the design on the ring. — She recognised it as his coats-of-arms, realising that he must have used it that afternoon to seal her letter, while at the same time, noting his hands. — They were well cared for hands, broad and strong, but somehow, — she knew that they weren't work-shy hands.

Jean reclined into her chair to thoughtfully sip her drink, silently observing the handsome young couple.

Their drinks were forgotten, their two heads were now laid back on the settee, facing each other. — Helen was relaxed and radiant; she couldn't fail to notice; — Duncan's eyes were greedily studying his companion's lively animated features as she spoke, — both, so deeply engrossed in their own conversation, oblivious of her, — there seemed to be so much to say. — The subject was the delights of Paris and some juvenile escapades along the banks of the river Seine.

The evening had been a satisfyingly successful one, but she felt that all wasn't going to be plain sailing during Helen's visit. — Duncan was unconsciously holding Helen's relaxed hand between them, — she also felt that he must never let go of that hand, for it would tear the heart out of him, and the bleeding heart from Arrochar, he was bereft. — Had Mairie Campbell done the right thing, insisting that Helen came to the village, as she did? — She was already a woman of the world with a promising career, — so how would Duncan persuade her to stay? — It was a strange turn of events; — Duncan wasn't usually given to making rash decisions, she concluded, and with his latest pending arrangements with Alex, — and Helen gave such a sparkling performance with young Peter with more to follow, — and then there was Rory, the latter having worked like a Trojan on updating the cottage since July, it was now a rather crowded equation. But she had noted that Helen had swiftly changed her mind about melting into the village social organisations, once she had met Duncan, a livelier time seemed ahead.

Duncan rising, and pulling Helen with him stirred her from her thoughts, "We had better make a move Jean, Helen's had a long day."

Helen was about to say that she wasn't a bit tired, and that she didn't want the day to end, but she said none of that.

Within minutes, they'd gathered in the hall, Jean had already fetched Helen's cloak from above stairs. — She waited while Duncan helped her on with it, before receiving a light kiss on her cheek, and grateful thanks from them both.

She gave Jean a last breezy wave through the car window, as she followed the red tail light of the Rover down the driveway. — Once turned into the lanes, she peered through the windscreen into the darkness; her concentration on Duncan's silhouette lit up by the headlights of the Mini, and thought it a strange end to the day. — Only a few short hours ago, she had been so prepared to dislike him, but now, she shrugged to herself in the darkness, now she wasn't so sure, and sighing, dismissed the shattering effects he had had on her, as first night nerves.

Presently, they passed the Kirk on the right hand side of the lane. She slowed down to manoeuvre the bend, shuddering slightly as she passed the wretched spot. — Moments later, on their approach to the bridge, the cottage loomed eerily from the pitch-blackness, — evoking the sudden wish that she had had the forethought, to leave a friendly light on somewhere inside.

Observing the red glow from its brake lights, she steered past the Rover, turning to run up on the grass verge, alongside the garden fence. — After switching on the interior light, she rummaged in her bag for her door key, and having found it, stepped out onto the damp grass, wetting her sandaled feet. —Suddenly, a torch beam shone onto the ground, encircling her feet, allowing her to see more clearly where she was treading, while Duncan held open the gate for her to pass by him into the gardens.

Helen's heart treacherously pounded, as he took the key from her trembling fingers, to open the door. — Then reaching inside the room, found the switch, immediately, flooding the porch with a friendly yellow glow.

"Thanks," she said, as he handed back her key, — she hesitantly moved to enter the cottage, "Goodnight," she said, softly. "It was a wonderful party, Duncan."

"Helen," he spoke her name quietly, detaining her, and then pausing as if he couldn't find the words which he wanted to say, while looking down at the now unlit torch between his hands. — His face in the shadows, she couldn't determine, realising that for the second time that evening, he had something to say, and yet, there he was stumbling for words again, Alex had prevented him earlier, so what prevented him now, she wondered, while waiting for him to continue?.

He heavily sighed, — almost in resignation. "I'll see you on the morrow,

I have some things which Mairie left you," he informed. "Sleep well." And lifting her hand, raised it to his lips to kiss before hastily turning to leave.

She hesitated, sucking in her breath, wanting to call him back, the words dying on her own lips as she watched him departing, before disappearing into the darkness of the lane, there to become a mere shadow. — Moments later, she heard the car spurt into soft purring action, — whatever he had wanted to say, had once more been left unsaid, — and, pondering further, wondered what it was he found so difficult, for he wasn't at a loss for words; — these bouts of shyness seemed alien to him.

With so much on her mind, Helen spent a restless night, still puzzling at the curious stares and glances that she had received. — It wasn't so unusual to resemble ones' relations, but the people of Arrochar seemed to be more than overtly curious. — And Alexs' many cutting remarks still dwelt on her mind, as much as Duncan's mitigating statement at the time of their meeting.

Alex had known Mairie Campbell, of that fact she was well aware, and possibly had known her as well as Duncan, but neither would have known her in her former years, so any resemblance of a youthful quality would have long since faded. And it also seemed that a few years ago, any resemblance couldn't have been so acutely striking, for nobody had ever mentioned it then. — Rory, she suddenly thought, — I'll ask Rory, he must have a tangible explanation, if indeed there was a tangible explanation.

The turbulence continued throughout the night, now dwelling on the more pleasant events of the evening, with Duncan invading her every dream. — She felt strangely euphoric and admitted to herself that she was longing to see him again, a feeling that she had never felt before about any male. — She sighed and turned, lying on her back to stare at the window with its open curtains, letting in a clear full moon shining down. — She rose by the dawn's early light, to peer through the window as an owl hooted, and the twilight world, prepared to disappear.

Chapter 9

Competition

The following morning, she made an inspection of her garden, dampening some of her newly found, 'joie d' vie' while sighing at the sight of the lovely roses, some becoming very bedraggled and in an obvious need of a prune. — Also, the grass was beginning to resemble a hayfield, — but it was too wet to cut, and the heavy mower which she knew lurked in the shed, would only tear at the lawns. There was no alternative, only to content herself pruning the roses, and she was doing just that when Rory came screeching down the lane, skidding to an ear splitting halt alongside the picket fence.

She waved and called out gleefully to him as he hopped from the car, — and then her jaw dropped, she gasped, for instead of entering by the conventional method; the young man neatly leaped the gate, only to precariously wobble on one leg, before regaining his balance.

She laughed, melodiously, "Rory Cameron, after all these years of practice and you still haven't perfected that stunt."

"It must be the audience; — it goes very well when no-one is watching."

"It's just as well you weren't wearing your kilt; you'd have been hopping around a bit if you'd fallen into the rose beds."

"Ah, yes, but Helen, you would have made a wonderful nurse."

"None of your nonsense, Rory Cameron," she humorously chastised.

His dove grey eyes mischievously, endearingly, caressed her features, "you've narely changed; you look more like the old Helen that I have mirrored in my heart, wearing Hannah's apron and with mud covering yer countenance."

Chuckling, she curtsied coyly, with her pointing finger under her chin, as she looked down at herself, displaying Hannah's volumous flowered apron, wrapped around her slim shape. — It covered her virtually from head to toe. — Her hair was caught back by a small green tartan scarf, tied under the glorious cascading tangle behind her shoulders.

Rory bent his head to kiss her rosy coloured, raised face while gently tugging the scarf free, "Oh," she gasped in surprise and snatched into thin air to retrieve it.

"You fall for it every time," he teased, gripping the scarf tighter while backing away; — he then turned and started slowly running towards the stream.

Still laughing melodiously, she chased after him, coming to a panting halt before him, still tussling for the scarf, "A kiss," he bargained, "… then I'll give it to you."

Deciding on a ploy, she declared breathlessly, "You've just had a kiss … Oh, you can have it," she said, referring to the scarf, but Rory was swifter with his measure at the time old trick, he wagged his finger, — still holding onto the scarf, seeming to come to a sobering halt, he diverted from the game. "How did you find the party?" He asked.

"I expected to see you there," she replied, "in loyal attendance of the Laird."

"Oh, aye, I was invited, but the Laird had other ideas."

"Other ideas?" she echoed, her voice displaying interest.

"He's worrying about something, but not telling, — it's best to keep out of his way when he gets the bolshies, so I was grateful when he told me that there was a new batch of anglers arriving to deal with."

"You missed a good do," she said.

"Och, aye, Mrs Roach's flings are usually the height of success and the talking point of the village for weeks to come, — right from the doctor's new diamond stick tie pin to the Widow Calhouns' latest winter warmers, needed to safeguard her ample proportions against any possible attacks of lumbago," he chuckled, breathlessly, ending, — "She usually takes it all off with her coat."

Could you say all that again?" Helen grinned, this time with returning memories of the previous evening. — The Widow Calhoun was the large lady, who had declared that she 'simply adored Americans' and the idea that she possibly had been wearing red flannel underwear beneath her bejewelled exterior, was too much to be polite about.

Rory immediately took an intake of breath, with the intention of repeating his colourful description of the ample lady, when she raised an arresting hand, "I think, Rory, we should allow the Widow Calhouns' winter requisites to rest in peace," she replied, when their levity had subsided, and went on to explain how elegant Alex Craig had appeared, knowing she had a fan in Rory, but she refrained from dampening his impressions in view of her own enlightening view, as he was keenly looking forward to the commencement of filming, and would no doubt be in charge of the castles upkeep when the film unit took over, and so able to see his goddess everyday, from close quarters.

In conclusion to her resume, she mentioned how self-conscious she had felt on occasions and the odd things that were said, "Like … she's a spitting image and quite a chip of the old block. — Gran always hated to be photographed, she avoided it like the plague, — there can be nothing to compare."

"There's no mystery, Princess. — In the first place, they would stare at a gorgeous girl like you, and in the second place, your granny may not have liked her photograph to be taken, but she can't have objected to being painted at onetime. — There's a large portrait of her in the castle gallery, — painted, I should think, some sixty or possibly even seventy years ago, she looks about your age, now."

"A portrait," she echoed in puzzled surprise, "I was told nothing of a portrait. Where did it come from?"

Rory picked up some loose stones which were partly buried in the grass and began to skid them along the stream as he replied, "My father and I found it a few months ago amongst a heap of old canvases in the castle vaults. Many of them were of villagers, but your gran was a particular friend of the MacFarlane's, and the present Laird felt it fitting to hang it alongside the portraits of his own family as a memorial to her. And, I happen to know, that Miss Craig went to the castle with the Laird yesterday morning, — she no doubt saw the portrait then, and I should think that her remark was fairly well justified, for you could have …"

She interrupted, latching onto what was foremost on her mind, "That's interesting," she thoughtfully replied. "About what time did they make their visit?"

He shrugged, "Ten or thereabouts," Rory replied, "Before the castle opened to the public."

And it was just before that, Helen thought, when he had bowled her over in the lane, — so that was the reason he was in such a tearing hurry, — to keep his appointment with Alex, and he's a man who hates to be late, Jean indicated as much. "Are the MacFarlane portraits on general display to the public?" she lightly enquired, just to acknowledge his information.

"Yes," he replied. "They're in the upper gallery, on the first floor, but you won't need a ticket, Helen; I'm sure, if you ask the Laird, he will be pleased to either show you himself or to issue you with a local pass ticket to fix to your car windscreen, or you can come with me, now," he suggested.

She was dismissive, she had his answer and passed onto current issues, "Oh, there's no great hurry, I have six months in which to look at portraits," she flippantly replied, while unfolding his fingers and taking the last stone from his large hand. — And letting out a tinkling laugh, flung the stone into the stream after the others, to land with a feeble plop.

Rory shook his curly head in despair, "Oh, Princess, not like that," he said, as he bent his large frame, — but instead of picking up stones, she let out a loud shriek as unsuspectingly, he scooped her up, one arm about her waist and the other under her knees, "… like this!"

"Rory no!" she laughingly, loudly shrieked, as she clung on with arms about his neck, as he made to drop her into the water. "Rory, no … *put me down*," she demanded, — instead, he swung her around in a double circle, "No, No," she laughed and shrieked again, kicking her legs, "I'm getting giddy," she giggled.

If you do that, Princess, I'll drop you." He swung her again, only this time he came to an earth-shattering halt, staring ahead of him. — His expression, one of guilty horror as he let out a low groan, "Oh ... heck!" he softly exclaimed, "… I'm supposed to be on duty in the castle," he murmured, while setting her back onto her feet.

"It's the Laird," she said, needlessly, feeling her pulse rate soar to heights that she hadn't deemed possible for one so rational. — And heart thudding, braced herself to meet him.

They both stood, sharing their mortifying discomfort while watching his approach. — Rory anticipating the lecture which he knew he would receive, and Helen anticipating, she wasn't sure what, on Rory's behalf, as Duncan strode easily towards them across the lawns.

It struck her how very different he appeared today, his evening suit now replaced by classic casuals. — A cream checked shirt, open at the neck, revealing, a tanned column of throat; he'd teamed with close fitting brown cord slacks, a tone darker than his Bladen jacket, which he was in the process of casting over one broad shoulder — as he drew nearer, his blue eyes were hardened to shards of ice, his jaw set granite.

"I've been standing over there for at least, *five* minutes," he said, breathing heavily while using his thumb, backward pointing sharply toward the gate, while addressing his errant employee, "I'm glad you seem to have the *time* for horse-play, Mr. Cameron."

Without thought, Helen immediately, recklessly, leaped to his defence,

"Oh, *please* don't blame, Rory?" she pleaded, twisting her tremulous hands within the folds her apron, "I … I detained him," and scanning around swiftly, searching for a plausible reason, "*The grass* … it needs to be cut and Rory was just explaining that it's too wet to …," her hapless voice just trailed away as Rory just stared at her speechless, and the Laird listened with one dark eyebrow cocked, "I think it's time to disappear," she murmured, her face suffused in colour. Then turning on her heel, made a hasty retreat towards the cottage, overhearing …

"It seems that today, you're wearing Helen's favour," Duncan caustically remarked.

In the kitchen, she glanced through the window at the two men talking in the garden. Duncan was now holding her scarf and by the sheepish expression on his face, Rory was obviously in major trouble, and she was well aware that she hadn't helped his situation.

A moment later, they both began walking towards the cottage, but before they'd reached it, Rory diverted his steps to hastily walk away towards the lane. She felt a distinct upsurge of annoyance at having been denied the opportunity of bidding him a proper farewell, "I would have appreciated saying goodbye to Rory," she irritably complained, as Duncan entered the kitchen.

His misty blue eyes narrowed slightly; he was trembling with rage, he said something completely unexpected, — "You kissed him; wasn't that enough?" he accused, indignantly complaining in return.

"I couldn't stop him, I didn't want to; I enjoyed it; it was fun; is there something wrong with that?"

"It would have gone further; and he's wasted enough of my time on socialising, but it will be made up during the coming week, — **and**, I *daresay,* that he will give you plenty of other opportunities of saying, 'hello *and,* goodbye' in the future."

Her small chin and pert nose rose in defiance, and remembering Duncan's arrogant attitude in the lane the previous afternoon, she bravely made another misplaced attempt to rise to Rory's defence, "I'm in no moral danger from Rory — has he done something so dreadful in paying me a visit, before he started work?"

"He's late, and time is money … and *don't* ask questions."

"That's a mercenary, remark," she scoffed, jade eyes flashing. "And what punishment do you inflict upon your poor unsuspecting subjects, when they fail to do your bidding?"

"If you carry *on* this way, Miss Campbell, yeel soon find out. — Now don't interfere," he warned, tapping the end of her nose lightly with his index finger, "Rory has worked for me long enough to know the consequences, 'little miss fix-it' and your face is dirty."

"Oh!" She exclaimed with gusto, as again hot colour suffused her face.

Feeling agitated, her hands were trembling; she turned away and began busying herself by filling the kettle with the intention of making some coffee, while Duncan disappeared into the lounge with his jacket.

"Drat, the man!" she murmured, his brief absence giving her the respite she required to both compose herself, and hastily remove Hannah's enveloping apron, which she hooked onto the back of the kitchen door, "Drat! drat! drat!"

The removal of the apron and the erasing of the smut seemed to restore an amount of lost confidence, for she was now neatly dressed in a complementary shade of pastel green. — Her blouse, made of the finest Vyella, toned with the darker shade, echoed in her well-tailored, tweed mix slacks, to which she had privately complied.

She set about laying the tray, "Empty sugar bowl," she again murmured to herself and stretched up into the cupboard above her head, for the bag of sugar.

"I'll get that down," he said, startling her from somewhere behind. — And before she could move, he'd reached *up* and over her, retrieving the bag with comparative ease.

Immediately tensing at his nearness, pinned as she now was, against the work bench, with his size engulfing her, she could feel the warmth from his hard chest; — his voice, deep and vibrating, disturbingly penetrating the fabric of her blouse; — a sudden tremor ran through her as she briefly closed her eyes, as if to still the unsteady pounding of her heart. — Now aware only of her reeling senses at his nearness, she couldn't breathe and a return of the desperate struggle to withhold her emotions, assailed her, tremulously, she said, "My Lord, I know that this kitchen is very small, so small that it will hardly contain the two of us. You might find it more comfortable in the sitting room, if you would care to wait."

"I always helped, Mairie," he revealed.

"Mairie was old school, possibly unstable on her legs and welcomed the assistance in the kitchen," she retorted, firmly, "I am young and able."

"And independent," he said.

"And independent," she affirmed, and put her feelings under a false umbrella, "Pride, they call it."

"Then, I will get out of your way and leave you to it, and I shall suffer the rejection in silence," he replied, releasing her and retiring to the adjacent room, she shortly followed with the tray.

While he studiously lit his pipe, Helen poured their coffee, "Milk and sugar," she asked, smiling a gentle amused smile.

He nodded and said, "Both, - two sugars," followed by, "Your smiling, I hope that's because your happy."

She softly sighed, her eyes smiling, "Oh … it's just that everything seems so surreal, suddenly leaving my work, home and family."

"You were given two months in order to get used to the idea."

She glanced his way, "Do you believe in Deja' vu?"

"You mean, the feeling that you've done something before."

She nodded, finished her task and handed him his cup.

"I'm sure you've made coffee before," Duncan replied, smiling in an amused sort of a way as he took the proffered cup and placed it on his side of the table, and then relaxing back into the chair in order to observe Helens' graceful movements, — he studied her speculatively — she had a rosy glow about her features; — he surmised that she hadn't been awakened; — there had never been any mention of boyfriends in her letters to Mairie, but Mairie Campbell had been chary, she had only read out what she wanted her listener to hear.

Unaware of her companions' thoughts, Helen chuckled, "I didn't mean that."

"It's probably the air of change," he reiterated.

"When does the season finish?" she asked, relaxing back also with her drink.

"Mid October, in about four week's time," he replied, still gazing intently at her.

She sipped the warm liquid before replying, "The village won't seem the same," she sighed, "I've never been here in the winter."

"Then, I'll guarantee that yeel like Arrochar in the winter. — The mountain peaks are covered in snow, and the loch freezes solid enough for skating. — It's another Switzerland," he said, with some conviction.

At his words, Helen had a sudden notion, "Then, perhaps you should start another season, for winter sports."

He grinned and shifting his position, replied, "It's worth a thought." — He suddenly moved to stand and reach for his jacket, "I've been so busy, I'd almost forgotten my errand," and produced from his pocket a bundle of fading blue envelopes tied with pink ribbon. He handed them over to her.

"My letters!" she exclaimed, untying the ribbon and flicking through them.

"Mairie was always greatly excited when one arrived," he informed, while reseating himself in his armchair, feeling that it was like the old times when he had sat with Mairie, listening to her yarns, but Helen seemed more closeted. "Why didn't you ever send any photographs?" he ventured.

At this question, her face wore a puzzled frown, "But I did … I sent loads, in fact…," she said, pausing mid-sentence while sifting through the envelopes and coming to the last one, it was still sealed.

"That one arrived on the day that she died," Duncan informed, while watching her slit open the envelope to extract a photograph. — She passed it to him.

"There's me at my desk in our U.S. offices — and with me, is my colleague, Rita — she comes from Brooklyn — she's very scatty, but lots of fun and has a heart of pure gold. — I wonder where the others are?" she queried.

"They may be in her jewellery box," he suggested. "I have it in the safe at The Loch House. I'll keep it until you pay me a visit," he reached out to return the picture which she took, trying to avoid touching his electrifying fingers.

She rose to tidy the table, and then sauntered to the window to peer out, the weather was still sunny, and with Duncan's close proximity, a feeling of claustrophobia suddenly overcame her, it seemed such a waste to be indoors, "Shall we go outside?" she suggested, — he nodded and followed her through to the kitchen and out into the garden, there to saunter towards the banks of the stream.

Duncan spoke, saying, "You didn't come to the funeral. Were you too busy?"

She bent to pluck a daisy from the grass before replying, "Yes, I'm always busy. — I could have had some time off, but my parents advised otherwise. Charles said that it was a pointless exercise; — we knew that all the arrangements were in place; — I was inclined to agree with him at the time, but that was before we knew about the *will*," she shrugged and sighed. "After all, by that time, you must understand, we were *pretty* peeved with the whole situation, but it's something which I've regretted ever since. — And now, all this insistence; — you must know that I was left with no alternative, — why, why, why?" she puzzled aloud, "And right in the middle of a career crisis."

She paused in transit as Duncan came to stand behind her, so near that she instinctively wanted to lean back against him while he spoke, her imagination running away with her — She could feel his hands on her shoulders, even though they weren't there, reminding her of the sensual way in which he'd caressed her bare silky skin the previous evening while dancing, it had felt so evocative, like being bathed with liquid soap, so soft, so gentle. — And then his arms sliding around her waist and moving down to her hips, pressing her closer, so familiar was the magical process, their bodies moulded and welded together, every rounded shape had seemed to fit. — She could imagine a soft, velvety kiss on the temple, followed by warm lips trailing down the side of her arched neck, but the kiss wasn't there, and his hands were safely tucked into his pockets; — she snapped herself from her meandering thoughts, to become aware of his answer.

Duncan smiled thinly, his reply was dour, "I'll never know *why* ye lassies have the need of a career, other than the one you were created to do."

Helen chuckled, "You sound like an anti-women's libber."

"Perhaps, I have a reason," he replied, as they moved on.

Helen silently gave him a surreptitious sideways glance, giving a brief moment's thought to his remark, but she didn't want to think about Alex Craig at this precise moment, considering that his good reason must be Alex and her career stakes, but, she felt that this was an ideal opportunity to smooth the way, "I'm only on a provisional holiday," she said. "I'm duty bound to return to my full employment in six months time, to the very day."

She flinched at his touch, when he stopped and turned her round to face him, and then returned his hands to his pockets, he appeared disappointed. "You've only just arrived, why talk about leaving, and you never know, you may want to stay. — I can always do with more help, fresh ideas to develop the village, — you've suggested one already and you've somewhere to live, somewhere for your family and friends to come when they visit."

She smiled up at him, apologetically shaking her head, replying, "Mairie Campbell, for some reason, has drawn me back into the past; my life and my future are in London."

"Have you thought seriously about your future intentions for the cottage?"

"I haven't," she replied, and reassuring as if in compensation, "But I do have six months in which to decide."

"Duty bound," he murmured.

"Your duties as executor must have been an added burden."

Her colour maddeningly heightened, as he chuckled and gave her a lopsided grin, replying, "They're no great burden, Helen, I wouldn't have it any other way," he assured her. "More of a pleasure, — and I'm grateful that they won't end until you've decided what you want to do with the cottage, so don't decide too quickly, — will you?" — And suddenly appearing concerned, when he checked his watch, "I don't want to go, but duty calls," he murmured softly. "I have a confounded appointment, and on a Sunday too. I have business on the other side of the estate tomorrow, so I'll call for you on Tuesday. We'll go for a tour of the village and have lunch in the Arrochar Arms. — Also, I'll order you a phone, — then you can ring Rita, your family, the whole damned wide world, if you so wish," he chuckled in his enthusiasm and then bravado took over. — She sucked in her breath, when suddenly he bent and swiftly gave her a surprise warm kiss on the cheek, while she was guiltily thinking with relief about the phone as a lifeline to Ryder, "Welcome to Arrochar," he said.

She remarked, "You mustn't keep Miss Craig waiting," and accompanying him to the picket gate, where he surprised her again, — she laughed melodiously when he neatly and firmly leaped the gate, he turned and roguishly grinned and, raising his hand in farewell, his fingers formed a very positive circle of triumph in salute, he winked, and she waved until the car had disappeared out of sight and then sauntered back across the lawns, feeling dazed by the events of the morning. — Momentarily, she touched her tingling cheek, before thrusting her hands deeply into the pockets of her slacks, as she strolled towards the banks of the stream, to stand, staring thoughtfully at the pure crystal water, as it rippled over the dark rocks which littered the streambed. — She suddenly sighed, and raised her face to the sun, enjoying its late warmth. — It seemed that the Laird was taking charge of her life, but she gave an involuntary shrug and shelved her problem, as Arnie had shelved his film, until a later date.

Chapter 10

The Grand Tour

Just what to wear for the grand tour of the village, was a difficult decision, but Hannah advised that the Lady Eleanor, would undoubtedly wear a suit on these semi-formal occasions, which included visiting and inspecting the public buildings around the village, and which always included luncheon in the Arms Hotel, — and so suitably instructed, Helen put the finishing touches to her smart lilac linen suit, by tying the loose fitting jacket into her trim waist, and after smoothing down the short pencil skirt over her slim hips, she stepped into a matching pair of low heeled court shoes.

She hummed to herself as she pottered about her bedroom, tidying away the several discarded garments and straightening the rumpled bedcover. — She then crossed to the latched door, sighing happily as she paused to peer back at the pretty room, and further, skipped down the stairs with a definite bounce in her step, evidence of her buoyant spirits. — After Alex Craig's caustic reception of her, she wasn't too sure why she felt so buoyant, but there it was. She mistakenly felt grateful that she hadn't bitten the flying bullet, but just now, there were more pleasant things on her mind.

As she stepped into the dining room, the outer door opened, filling the room with the morning sunshine. — Duncan smiled lazily at her as he stepped inside, his immaculate navy-blue lounge suit emphasising his breadth of shoulder, he had teamed with a crisp white shirt and navy tie. — What ever he wore, he seemed to wear with a certain amount of panache that most men would envy, she thought, and noticing again that he had slipped his pipe into his breast pocket, led her to idly wonder if he ever singed his suits, — she resisted the irresistible temptation to tidy his pocket handkerchief, as the intimate action could be misconstrued.

Amiably returning his smile, she walked towards him pulling on her gloves.

"Good morning, Helen," he said, as his eyes strayed lazily over her, appraising her appearance. "You look as though you're ready to take Arrochar by storm?"

Blushing slightly, she felt the warmth of his voice, rippling and tearing through her calm reserve and hastened to caution herself that he was merely being hospitable, but despite herself, she drew on her confidence, saying as she smiled, "You look in fine fettle yourself, my Lord."

"Well, now that we've agreed upon that issue, we'll be on our way," he said, giving a mocking bow and sweeping a hand, for her to pass him, "After you, my Lady."

"And they say the age of chivalry, is long since dead," she chuckled.

"Knights in shining armour come in many guises, Miss Campbell, — we'll head for the mill first," he told her, as he settled her back into the Rover's passenger seat beside him. "It's all modernised mechanism today, but there's a small museum with the old style techniques of weaving on display, which should interest you."

The mill was only a ten-minute drive away, but Duncan decided to skirt the village, taking the long scenic route, as driving through the dramatic mountainous scenery would enable Helen to enjoy the surroundings, from its best possible vantage.

For September, there was an air of an Indian summer in the offing. The sky was a clear blue and the bright orange sun, seemed to float like a duster, polishing away the fluffy white clouds, — she squinted slightly against the bright light. — Observing her discomfort, Duncan leaned towards her to pull down the sun-visor, — for a brief moment his nearness took her breath away, but she cautioned herself to stay in control, to get a grip of her emotions, to keep her mission within her grasp.

"We're in MacFarlane country, on the Western shores of Loch Lomond. - We took our war cry from Loch Sloy, at the foot of Ben Voirlich. - We are descended from Duncan MacGilchrist, mentioned in 1296, brother of Mulduin, Earl of Lennox, — the name 'MacFarlane' came from his grandson, Bartholomew, in Gaelic it means 'Parlan'."

"You should write this all down," Helen remarked. "The tourists would love it."

"He chuckled, "You're talking yourself into a job."

"Is there more?" she smiled towards him.

He nodded. "Malcolm received the lands of Arrochar in 1395, but the male line failed and the lands were forfeited. Then, Andrew MacFarlane married the daughter of the Earl of Lennox and succeeded to the lands and title, in 1493. — Sir John MacFarlane fell on Flodden's field in 1513 and Walter MacFarlane of Talbert was killed at Pinkie in 1547. — The clan fought against Queen Mary at Langside in 1568. — The battle of Langside, a by-water of Glasgow, was a civil war; — Mary was in opposition with her brother Moray who wanted her son on the throne of Scotland, and not the good lady herself. — In the wake of all this, the MacFarlanes were stripped of their title, the 'Earls of Lennox' for various errant deeds and the title was bestowed upon Mary's husband, Lord Darnley, but that was to be short-lived, Darnley was murdered."

It was Helen's turn to chuckle, "This sounds like the plot of the film. You didn't name the daughter of the Earl of Lennox," she noted, surreptitiously glancing at him, while privately wishing that she had her notebook with her.

"I don't know her name," he admitted.

"We could christen her, and then suggest the name to Arnie," she suddenly, enthusiastically, keenly, suggested, "What do you think?"

"You choose," he replied, suggesting, "Something Scottish."

A Medieval sounding name, she thought, "Well … I like, 'The Lady Ghislaine' it's really French, but it means 'pledge or hostage', and the poor girl was a pledge *and* a hostage of her husband, — he can't have loved her with such a Machiavellian attitude." Helen remarked.

"I can't answer for him," he replied. "But I would say that he must have had plenty of 'down-to-earth' business acumen."

"How strange," Helen said, giving a small laugh, raising finely shaped eyebrows.

"What is?"

"W… ell, that's what Mr. Crawford, said of you."

"It must have come down the line," he chuckled. "Don't read too much into it, will you?"

"You must be very grateful to your ancestors."

"In many respects, I am. But owning land has many a drawback, — for one, it has to be maintained, — a thing that cannae be done single handed, — hence the sectioning into smaller croft units, which I lease on a long term basis to individual managers. — The bulks of the profits are then, in turn, ploughed back into the business. — If I drew too extensively on the revenue, then I would consequently end up landless as many neighbouring Lairds of past era's; — some of them sank to low practices in the time of the Highland clearances; — they betrayed their own people by turning them from their homes, — out into the wilds and bringing up instead, the

Northumberland sheep farmers who paid extensive rents for their lands; — the suffering was abysmal, — the tenant farmers had been loyal soldiers, who were bribed by the Lairds, with promise of land in exchange for their loyal support during battle, — they had no further use once peace had been restored, — after burning their homes, they suffered cholera, deportation, families were separated, never to see each other again; — death was sometimes merciful, it was shameful."

"They've left a legacy," she replied.

"Aye, they have that; — they haunt the bare hills, poor lost souls; wandering spirits. — I suppose it's quite relevant that you're angry about having your life disrupted; it's quite reminiscent."

"Not so turbulent." she assured.

As much as the stories he told her fascinated her, so did the man himself and no longer in the vein of a journalist, she found herself wanting to know more about him. — His facial expressions and odd inflections of voice told her much of his love and pride for his homeland, until Helen couldn't imagine him anywhere else but in Arrochar — she knew that the racy city life would stifle him.

This thought led her again to remember Alex Craig. — With Alex's titian beauty and the dark rugged looks of the man beside her, they made a volatile couple. — It wasn't impossible to imagine them married, but their lifestyles differed so tremendously, — she likened them to the butterfly and the yacht. Could Alex really adjust to life in Arrochar, she wondered? — it certainly had appeared that she was prepared to make the effort, — and certainly again, she hadn't been exactly adverse to the Laird, or him to her, which in the prevailing circumstances, Helen now admitted, was ideal; — It would take the hard core of his ancestors, in order to realise their kind of ambitions, which is to marry, — as the Laird had previously confirmed, — without love and affection. — Also, she thought, what a miserable existence for a woman to dote on her Lord and master, whom she knew didn't care a whit for her, — a real chattel in fact. In conclusion, Helen considered that it was going to be interesting to witness the outcome of the situation.

At the road's summit, Duncan steered the car into a small, 'lay-by' called 'Tor Point' a natural section, perfect for the viewing the scenery. — Within seconds of parking, he had swiftly left the car to walk around and open the passenger door, Helen lightly stepped out. — There was a fresh cool breeze blowing which playfully teased her hair, causing her to toss the glorious profusion back behind her shoulders.

"It's so perfect a day," she said, sighing and breathing in deeply to fill her lungs with the invigorating mountain air, and her nose with the fragrant smell of heather.

"Every day is perfect in Arrochar," he softly replied, while his eyes greedily absorbed the entrancing picture that she made. — Once again, taking in her pert nose and rounded pink cheek, — his eyes lingered on her moistened, pliant lips, while resisting the temptation to kiss her, for in truth, he felt desperate to know, they had come so close to it many times during the party, — the longing had troubled him ever since their meeting, his resistance was becoming low, — he would be a traitor to his cause, were he to do so, Helen was just a short term visitor, he reminded himself, but his control, momentarily slipped, "Even more so, now that you're here," he irresistibly murmured, softly aloud.

She turned to him, holding his gaze and giving a soft pleasant laugh, replied, "And I … make such a difference?"

"Oh, you're the *dream* topping," he keenly assured, with so much innuendo.

"You flatter me; — it would be such sweet vanity, were I to believe you."

"I only speak the truth," he confirmed, and taking her arm, steered her over to the waist high natural stone wall, there to lean and admire the view.

She expelled a small gasp of pleasure at the panoramic scene below her. Arrochar appeared as a model village, — so neat, so compact, and so safe enveloped by the purple mountains and low green slopes. — The sun shone brilliantly on the tiny house window-panes, turning them into a miracle of golden sheets. — And it reflected again on the loch's shimmering, translucent blue water and on the majestic castle, offering its protection to the village, as she knew that the Laird beside her extended his protection to her. — She sighed, enjoying the tranquillity, feeling her nervousness abate in the beauty of the most perfect moment.

"That mountain is nicknamed, the Cobbler," he informed her and then pointed, drawing her attention to a convoy of grouse flying against the wind and following the line of his finger, she watched fascinated, as they flew low, keeping close to the purple-patched hillside, seeming to follow the contours of the ground.

"Do you shoot them?" she asked, as they disappeared into some plantings of Scot's pine."

"Hunting season starts in August, — the glorious 12th to be precise," he informed her. "It's a national sport that I enjoy, so that others may enjoy the delicacies on their dinner table, and I hope," he hastened to add, "… that you aren't an objector, or I shall have to remind you that you enjoyed your pheasant at Jeans a few days ago."

"Oh, no, I'm not an objector. Who am I, to interfere with the matters of the countryside?" she informed him, while gazing into the blue, his finger again pointing out a lazily circling hawk.

Helen sighed again in pleasure of the view, and hearing the small, soft sound, Duncan intently studied her once more, absorbing her lovely heightened colour and clear innocent sparkle in her emerald eyes, which he knew could turn into a tempestuous sea green. "Are you now glad that you've come, Helen?" he enquired softly, sounding anxiously concerned.

She turned her head to peer up at him. — He was so disturbingly close beside her, and his obvious pleasure at sharing what he loved best, moved her greatly. — His hand strayed upwards to smooth back his hair, his eyes gentian violet in the afternoon sunshine. — There was something light-hearted and boyish-like in his mood today, she thought, — so much so, — that it didn't seem possible that he was Lord of all they surveyed, — she could not lie to him. — She smiled at him, a warm, happy, gentle smile in reassurance, answering him simply and honestly, from the heart, "I couldn't fail to be. — I cannot lie; — I feel very much a part of the Highlands, especially here, now, at this very moment," she softly underlined.

He briefly returned her smile, and then turned to gaze at the view. "Could it be that you're more Scot than English?" he suggested, with hope flourishing within him. "Your likeness to your grandmother couldn't only be skin deep."

"I didn't know her well enough to judge. — I only know that I've always had a special affection for my father's homeland." she sighed, speaking her thoughts aloud, "He was just like you, in love with his country, — he apparently was quite bereft when he moved to London, but my mother missed her friends and relations, and daddy only had Mairie, — I think it killed him to leave and be so far away, — but my grandmother hadn't tethered him, — and so it stands to reason, — I know that you love your home."

"I couldn't deny it. — Every mountain, every glen, every loch from the southern most tip of the borders to John 'O' Groats, holds a special meaning for me," he replied, with noted warmth in his voice.

"And as Mairie, you will never grow tired of your heritage," she concluded.

He sighed in resignation, "My heritage has made me a lonely man."

Something plummeted inside Helen as his reply seemed like the reason

110

for Alex's return and an answer to his problem, giving rise to the thought, 'but you won't be lonely, for very much longer' he looked thoughtfully hesitant, as she waited for him to continue.

He tentatively asked, "Helen … have you a long memory?"

"As long as anyone's, — I do forget things, but so do most people who lead busy lives. — I make notes in my notebook, to remind me of the things I have to do."

"You keep a diary," he keenly suggested.

"Only for business purposes, — why, only recently, we ran an article asking the public to write in with their life stories, because people don't write down their day to day experiences anymore, — your forebears' have created *their* chronicles on life in the Highlands, which is why you're able to tell me so much today, — do you *still* despise the press?"

"You're *still* talking yourself into a job," he chuckled.

"Perhaps, it's a job that needs finishing," she suggested laconically.

He spoke with appeal in his voice, "Then … will you finish it for me, Helen?"

She fell silent, not knowing what to say to this 'lap-of-the-gods' situation, but still feeling that she was being led into a trap of some kind, — or was it her conscience, she wondered, shaking her head, while apologetically refusing, "Duncan, I can't, — I really can't."

"Not even for the right price."

She stared at him, her face displaying the shock that she felt; she replied, indignantly, "There would *be* — no price."

"I didn't mean to offend you," he hastily replied, suddenly covering her small hand where it rested on the wall.

She looked at him earnestly - again apologetically, "Oh, I only meant that it would take too long." She suddenly sighed, a wobbly sigh as he raised her captured hand to his lips. — With his noble head bent, he didn't see the naked love that suddenly welled and shone unashamedly in her eyes, or knew about the resisted urge as she stayed her hand from reaching out to caress his dark hair. — It was over in the briefest of moments, — when he raised his head to meet her eyes; her emotions were once more veiled.

Eventually, they continued their journey at a leisurely pace coming upon Arrochar's Woollen Mill set back off the main road. — It proved to an interesting collection of buildings, built in the same grey flintstone as Bracken Cottage and heavily surrounded by neat gardens, displaying, chrysanthemums and dahlias, a glorious array of hanging baskets of begonias, petunias and geraniums with multitudes of late roses rambling over the walls.

Scotland in bloom, Helen idly thought; realising that Rory's father must be responsible for the public building displays.

As they left the car and walked toward the building, Duncan held out his hand towards her, she automatically responded by slipping her own hand into his to be held in a firm, warm grasp.

To the side of the mill, a natural flow of crystal clear spring water tumbled down a dark rock formation, feeding a small stream.

"Where does the stream lead?" she enquired.

"In Scotland, streams are called, rills or a burn, — so the rill flows through the grounds of Bracken Cottage and then on, circling the village until it disappears into the loch."

It seemed as though the staff knew that he was coming, for the manager joined them for their inspection. — He slightly inclined his head towards Duncan, "My Lord," and then turned towards Helen, "Miss Campbell, delighted to meet you, — your grandmother used to work here, many, many, years ago," he smiled and then courteously swept a hand for them to pass through the door.

They were left alone to browse. — Duncan steered her around the displays by her elbow and when stopping, stood slightly behind her shoulder, while explaining, that …

The mill was today, mechanised and required very little manpower, a vast difference to the days when her gran had worked there in her youth, — as the museum proved. — Every process had been hand operated, the raw wool cleaned and much to Helen's delight, the wool had been spun on a spinning wheel, then dipped into vats of vegetable dyes, then hung out to dry in readiness for weaving on the enormous looms, until finally made into colourful tartans, blankets or hand-knitted into jumpers. — The famous Arran was very much in evidence.

"I think I recognise these," she chuckled, when she saw the sets in the mill shop. "They remind me of a certain incident in Bracken Lane …," he didn't seem to have heard her as they were approached …

The manager addressed her, "Miss Campbell, I would like to present you with this shawl, — it is a very fine example of the Campbell Tartan, and may it keep you ever warm in winter."

Helen's colour, heightened. She slightly trembled as she accepted the gift "For me," she said, with delighted surprised, "Oh, thank you." She turned to Duncan, "Isn't this beautiful?"

112

"It's wonderful, Helen, - if you like it."

The manager then took it back from her, and with a snap of his fingers, an assistant took it away for wrapping. — He then shook Duncan's proffered hand and gave Helen a small bow before taking his leave.

She turned to follow him back outside, where she caught sight of a large man with fading reddish hair, and clinging to his arm was a small dark waspish looking woman of some fifty years. "Oh look, Duncan, — isn't that James Craig?"

The moment was mutual, — they immediately came to join them, "Duncan," he greeted, in a pleased gravely tone, while vigorously shaking the Laird's hand. Immediately turning, "Helen," he also greeted, warmly, affectionately, and kissed her on both cheeks. "You look radiant. I would hardly have recognised you, but for that wonderful profusion of hair."

"I thought it was time to change my image."

He grinned, "You mean … you've washed behind your ears."

"I thought that no-one could see them behind the hair."

James changed the subject, "Sorry to have missed your party, but I have little doubt that my daughter will have made up for the lack of us, — she manages to monopolise everything, and everyone in sight."

Helen smiled brightly, saying evasively, "I didn't see much of her."

James continued, "I can't believe that you're the same person who writes those rather spearing newspaper articles."

She sighed, hearing the all-to-familiar surprise, replying lightly, "It's just a job, James, and to use a common cliché, they do say, that the pen is mightier than the sword."

There's very little to report on in Arrochar, so it's my guess that you'll find Alex's Press Conference a blessing in disguise, — come late November. However, I wish you luck all the same, — how long are you staying?"

"Six months," she firmly underlined. "… And I don't think that it's going to be an idle six months."

"You may settle here," he suggested. "You'd be an asset to the village. — Duncan can be very persuasive."

She shook her head doubtfully, "Things change, things move on, I'm not ready to retire to the country, - just yet."

James appeared surprised, "I really had a very different opinion of you; — I remember the time when you and Rory cycled up to Craigiemhor Farm to collect goose eggs for your grandmother, — you stayed to harvest the pears, Rory climbed the trees and threw them down for you to catch in your apron, and when he came down from the tree, he gave you a piggyback, —

you were loving every minute."

At the visual memory, Helen gave a soft laugh, which ended in a sigh, "On the way home, we fell off the bicycle and broke the eggs. — Gran was so mad with us; Rory told her that we'd been waylaid by a fox and that he'd stolen the eggs."

James grinned, slightly leaning towards her, "And, she believed you?"

Helen shook her head, "My apron was covered in a slimy mess; Rory felt the raw edge of her tongue for lying."

"You mean he embroidered the truth."

"I got into trouble for siding with him."

Introductions were then made to James's companion, — a- Mrs Murray from London.

"How are you enjoying your stay?"

"I love Craigiemhor Farm," she said, sighing. "But I couldn't stand to be cooped up here for any longer than a month. — It's so isolated, and just the thought of spending a bleak winter here, is enough to freeze the blood in my veins … and sheep!" she exclaimed, raising her dark eyes aloft, "… nothing but sheep!"

Helen laughed softly; the gregarious lady seemed to be so disenchanted with life, — she unconsciously became defensive.

"Forgive me for sounding unsympathetic, Mrs Murray, but Arrochar has much to offer, if you look for it," Helen assured, knowing that she spoke honestly.

"I'm sure that it has," the disenchanted lady, replied. "But if you have to look for it, will it be worth finding, when you've found it?" she shook her head, doubtfully. "— Give me the bright lights of London, — every time."

"Well, I think we must be off," James said. "Take care of her, Duncan, she's a little treasure!" he exclaimed, as he bent to give Helen a parting kiss on her cheek.

"I'll try, if she'll let me," Duncan grinned.

"Have a wonderful life, Helen, and be *sure* that you make the right choice." he made a sound as if to stimulate some settling agreement.

"I'll try," she called in farewell. "But I can always come back."

"After lunch, we'll visit the castle," Duncan informed her, while checking his watch and leading her towards the car. — The manager was already standing beside the vehicle, waiting to hand over her parcel before closing her door.

Once on the road again, Helen glanced surreptitiously sideways, making a study of his strong profile as he concentrated on the way ahead, the movement and position of his long legs clad in the finest woollen blend, she found disturbingly attractive; — suddenly, a warm welter of affection trickled through her, a pleasurable tickly feeling of happiness inside, — Alex's threats and warnings, momentarily paled into insignificance; — she smiled towards him, sighed and relaxed. "I'm looking forward to seeing Mairie's portrait," she revealed. "What's it like?"

He suddenly looked strangely concerned and uncomfortable, saying briefly, evasively, assuring, "Yeel see."

Helen's smooth brow furrowed, the mystery deepens, she thought as they lapsed into a communal silence.

The Arms Hotel, which was situated on the north side of the village, and just a mile from the castle, proved to be a large, square, white painted Victorian pile, set off the road. — She brightly smiled and waved to Rory who was getting into his car as they approached the building. — She surmised that he'd already spent a leisurely lunchtime with his friends in the lounge bar, when she heard her companion sigh an irritated sigh, murmuring tetchily, and saying, "That man doesn't have enough to do."

"He likes his job," Helen swiftly remarked, as if in compensation and protection of her friend.

"Aye, he's like the eternal pied piper, never without a female following."

"Well, perhaps the ladies feel safe with him, he's such fun," she mistakenly remarked, and then glanced at him sideways, raising exasperated eyes when he tersely replied,

"He easily gets sidetracked; — I'd be obliged if you would *stop* encouraging him; — no woman is safe with Rory Cameron."

The rest of the journey was taken in slightly strained silence, his lips were slightly pinched and his head, leaning to one side, she felt certain that he was sulking.

"The tourists must love this." Helen commented at an attempt to be light-hearted as they entered the dining room, — scanning with admiring eyes, the MacFarlane Tartan carpeting and light oak panelled walls, covered with scenic water colours, which had been painted by a local artist and offered for sale at interesting prices. "I must have this," she said, peering at a picture of The Loch House in its non-restored state. "There's just a right place for it in the cottage."

First inclining his head towards Duncan, the waiter led them to a private alcove table near to the window, where he seated Helen and then handed Duncan the wine menu, "Mouton Rothschild," he ordered Champagne.

"You certainly do things in style," Helen observed. "Everyone shows such servility."

Duncan suddenly relaxed and chuckled, which cleared the slightly tense atmosphere, "I don't insist upon it — it just happens."

"Well, it's very impressive," she replied, gazing around at her surroundings while waiting for the waiter to return with the, al a'carte menu, when her eye came to rest on the MacFarlane Crest, "The little figure in the centre appears sinister, and not at all romantic," she commented. And reading with an exaggerated pomposity, 'This — I will Defend — Loch Sloy!"

"We're a warring clan," he reminded her. "It wouldn't do to display frailties of nature to our opponents; they could use them as weapons against us."

She studied him briefly, as he turned away when the waiter reappeared with their Champagne and the menu, — suddenly an unbidden thought then entered her head, and for some reason his informative remark had cast another shadow over the moment. — Could he regard love as a frailty of nature, she wondered? — If so, then he would most certainly adhere to bondage just for the sake of uniting his lands. — And it was feasible enough that he had inherited the hard core of his ancestors, and that - without love in mind - had waited for years, for Alex to become homesick and return to Arrochar. — Also, she decided, it must have been a heaven sent opportunity to keep Alex locally interested, by fulfilling the Film Company's request of hiring the castle, despite the fact his grandfather had refused his permission, which then led to further speculation, — what had the feud been about?.

However, she wasn't allowed to ruminate on the Laird's past or future any longer, as finishing with the waiter; he had now turned his attention back to her, smiling a warm smile, which reached his deep blue eyes, thus drawing her back from her fantasy to the present, and managing to dispel for now, her notions of him having a hard heart. — She felt him to be a curious mixture of man.

After their lunch of; - Lorraine Soup, named after The Queen of Scot's mother, 'Mary of Guise or Lorraine', as the menu informed them, followed by Lossiemouth Scampi Mornay. — But with a soft laugh of triumph, Helen declined — the Tipsy Laird trifle, rolling the accent on her tongue in order to tease him.

"Are these visions of things to come?" Duncan remarked, chuckling at the antics of his recalcitrant guest.

"My Lord, I would not tire you, — you have only to endure me for six months," she reminded him.

He chuckled again, "I'd wager a bet that Helen Campbell is here to stay, despite the loud protestations, she makes."

She leant towards him, shaking her head, "Oh no, my Lord, this humble subject, nay maiden, begs to differ," she flicked her eyes wide open while sipping at her Champagne.

"My subjects, Miss Campbell, as you have seen, — do my bidding, and I have a shrewd suspicion, that you may not."

"I exercise a free spirit, my Lord."

He gave a soft amused laugh, smiling a smile that crinkled the corners of his eyes, "Ye lassies."

The entrance to the castle was through a pair of magnificent wrought iron gates, set in a high stone wall, hardly discernible for the mass overgrowing of creeper.

Helen took pleasure at the scene as they drove slowly between the gates, across the drawbridge, over the moat and through the great stone portico, bearing the MacFarlane coats-of-arms, and then along the extensive driveway towards the imposing castle. — Driving between close mown lawns dotted with silver birch, rowan, and eared willow trees, their branches, dancing in the soft warm breeze, shadowing small attractive flower beds of exotic plants, their perfume intoxicating as it drifted through the open windows of the vehicle.

"It always reminds me of a fairy-tale palace," she commented, gazing in admiration at the well-preserved, square, grey-stone structure with its quadruple spired turrets, in the French fashion.

"An adequate fortress, nevertheless; It's served Arrochar many times over the centuries, offering sanctuary to the populace." Duncan informed her as they entered the vast open forecourt. — They drew up to a halt in front of a pair of heavy studded oak doors.

A few moments later, with the car parked, they entered the oak panelled entrance hall where Helen's heels rang on the ornate, multi-coloured tiled mosaic floor, which replicated the coats-of-arms. "Over there, is the Great Feasting Hall," he said, indicating, "It's the scene of many a MacFarlane Chieftain's revelry."

Helen gave him a sidelong glance, "What did they revel in, or would that be a leading question?"

He grinned, while softly laughing, replying, "I haven't exactly revelled myself, but my grandfather was given to the odd, *wild* moment or two."

The hall was again oak panelled, stretching the entire length of the north wing. — The walls were lined with oil paintings of gory ancient battle scenes, the sight of which stimulated a cold shudder, as did the several beautifully embossed targes with evil looking spikes protruding from their centres. Grimacing, she commented, "I'd hate to think what they did with these."

"Then, I won't explain," he replied, safeguarding the information that he and Rory had strength tested them a few times.

Intermingled amongst the display, was a collection of elaborately designed claymore, plus a collection of chain-mail, all trophies of long-ago victories. — In the centre of the hall, stood a preposterously long polished oak refectory table, and stroking it with an appreciative hand to feel the warmth of the wood, she curiously enquired, "How many can dine at one sitting?"

Duncan shrugged, "I'd say, in a civilised manner, about fifteen on either side, and four at each end."

She mischievously smiled, glancing at him sideways in amusement, saying, "And uncivilised?"

He grinned down at her, "Uncivilised, your guess is as good as mine; I would hazard a guess that a few maidens were deflowered upon this table."

She flicked him a ruminating glance, "You've tested it?"

He wryly grinned again, slightly flushing, "Ask Rory the same question."

"Right ... I will," she agreed, with a nod of the head and a satisfied grin.

He suddenly became anxious, saying hastily, "Helen, I didn't mean ..."

"It's too late," she replied. "I might even ask him to demonstrate."

Duncan felt shackled in a knot which he couldn't untie, Helen was worrying him and wobbling his confidence, she was punishing him. — He swiftly diversified, "If you look above your head," he said, pointing up at the standards, "They were captured in battle, and once belonged to the Queen of Scot's."

All this information, she had been soaking up; — she moved from his side and he watched her slow stroll over to the great-carved stone fireplace, an expression of reverie on her slightly raised face, — she had her back to him, he chuckled as she romanticised, hearing her sighing a soft groan of pleasure, — she inhaled, "Oh ... I can almost smell the 'Roasting Baron of Beef'." — She just as suddenly, swung round on her heel to face him, to see that he was leaning against the table, industriously lighting his pipe, while watching her. "And I can almost hear the laughter of the feast, while the Chieftain drinks his fill of ale or wine," she continued, raising her arm in demonstration, "... *Toasting* the victories of the day, and surrounding them ... a bevy of beautiful wenches, suffering their unmerciful, guileless *wit*," she gave a soft laugh, calling, "Do you know any wenches, Duncan?"

"Oh … you would make an adorable wench," he replied, grinning roguishly while chuckling. "They lived hard and played hard," he continued, "… and some of them, wallowed in cruelty, there was no time for sentiment."

She held his magnetic gaze for a moment across the distance, and then sauntered around the room, studying the pictures, feeling his eyes following her, thinking as she went; — 'hard, ruthless, uncaring men and he's exactly like them, his lands come first before his women, small wonder he doesn't appreciate liberation in the female sex, poor Alex a chattel. — She was quite within her rights to run away; — I would run away also, rather than play second fiddle. – Why … the man must be a complete boor' — and once more remembering his arrogance in the lane, served to confirm the very fact.

"How things have changed," she said aloud, and sauntering further, she came to an abrupt halt, in front of the painting of a Tudor woman, — she bent while peering at the gold inscription, reading: - "Mary, Queen of Scot's —Why do you have a portrait of the enemy in your household?" she called back to the Laird.

He chuckled as he came to stand beside her, "My ancestors reluctantly fought her, but despite their opposition to the crown, they still maintained an element of respect for the tragic lady, and you must admit that she adds to the castles atmosphere, — the tourists expect to see such portraits," he informed, acknowledging, "… but you're not a tourist."

"Can we see Mairie's portrait?" she asked, eagerly.

A fleeing shadow seemed to flit across his fine features, as he replied, "The portraits are on the next floor, — and there's no rush, they won't go away." Although, Duncan was privately wishing that they would, as he felt as though he was approaching his pending doom.

Despite his seeming reluctance, he led the way out of the Feasting Hall and back into the entrance hall, where their voices echoed in the hollowness of the high ceiling, as they ascended up the wide, light, airy, winding stone staircase, passing walls hung with rich tapestries. — On the slow journey to the gallery, she remarked, "You must have a ghost; you can't own a castle and not have a ghost."

Again, he chuckled, "It's said that we have, but, I've never encountered the poor, unfortunate soul. — Most Scottish ghosts are said to be Queen Mary, but she would have to be very obliging to appear everywhere it's said that she's appeared."

Eventually, they reached the subdued lighting of the upper gallery which contained only MacFarlane family portraits. — The gallery was simply furnished with a long centre strip of plush red carpet, partly covering a wood block floor. Elaborately gilded high backed chairs, upholstered with gold and red brocade, were intermittently placed opposite the paintings, backing along the window wall. — Helen stopped to admire the view from one of the many mullion windows.

"Why don't you live here anymore?" she curiously enquired. "Your family did at onetime."

"Now, you wouldn't like to live in a draughty old castle, would you, rattling around like a dry old pea on your own?"

His remark took her thoughts and assumptions back to Alex, weighing up that the Laird had possibly moved in order to accommodate the actress with better home comforts.

She sighed, remarking aloud, "Oh, I don't know, — it must have its virtues."

He grinned, "When you've seen The Loch House, yeel understand, just why, I don't live here anymore; — you're going to love it, Helen."

"I'm sure I will," she replied, smiling her assurance.

They sauntered down the gallery, pausing at each picture as they reached it, while Duncan explained carefully who they were, and where they fitted into the history of the village, until they came upon a more modern collection. — The first was of the old Laird when a young man, proudly wearing Highland dress, and, as Duncan, he wore the heavy gold-crested ring on his small finger. — A very striking man by all accounts, he was very dark haired as Duncan, but his eyes were a deep grey in colour.

Standing beside him in contrast, was his wife, — Duncan's grandmother; a sallow complexioned, fair-haired woman, buxom and heavy boned, who appeared to have strange brown eyes that didn't quite suit her other features. She was wearing of mode of dress which had been fashionable in the Edwardian period, "Angus and Alicia MacFarlane," Helen read aloud, "Your grandparents?"

"Not exactly … Alicia was my grandfather's second wife," he informed her, "Bridget Macleod, wasn't strong, she died in childbirth."

"Having your father," she murmured, enquiring, "Do you resemble your mother?"

He gave her a lopsided, almost embarrassed grin, replying, "You will have the opportunity to judge for yourself, quite soon, when you meet her."

"I shall look forward to it," again, she smiled her assurance.

He suddenly appeared quite concerned, he heavily sighed, almost in resignation, "Helen … we're nearly there — Mairie's picture is just three portraits down; — I'm so worried that it's going to make you angry."

"Why should I be angry?" she enquired, shrugging, "I'm no connoisseur of art, so I shall only see a portrait of my grandmother."

Again, he sighed in a resigned sort of a way, he was obviously very reticent, "Wait here, I'll just put the spotlights on."

She gazed after his departing back, looking perplexed as he disappeared into a small corner alcove, but ignoring his instruction, she sauntered into the darkness of the south wing, to stand in front of the picture he'd indicated. Suddenly — she sucked in her breath when the portrait became illuminated and alive, — startled and unsure of whether she felt horror, shock or pleasure, so mixed were her emotions at what she saw; — she covered her gaping mouth with her trembling hands. — The picture had real depth, it was euphoric in appearance, causing a curious sensation to flow through her veins, — a sensation that she seemed to be gazing into the depths of her own green eyes, but the eyes in the picture held a certain, soft, misty expression, which puzzled her.

The Laird came to stand slightly behind her as she gazed up at Mairie's portrait, — she felt acutely conscious of him, with his hands deeply pushed into his pockets and his dark head down, just waiting for her reaction, — and sensing his apprehension, she shook her head in disbelief as her eyes wildly trailed down the beautiful image on the canvas, softly gasping, she murmured, "No *wonder* everyone stared at me."

Mairie Campbell's hair was just like her own, dressed as it had been two nights before, held into place by the same combs. — Her green eyes smiled down from a face of exquisite, creamy, complexioned beauty. — Her dress was made in white satin, styled in the late Edwardian period, sleek at the front and trailing skirts to the rear. — The Cairngorm brooch adorned it; — even gold shoes peeked from the hemline. — Her left hand, down by her side, was ringless, her right hand was resting on the back of a chair, upon which the green cloak had been strategically draped, displaying the Cawdor Campbell lining. — There was an unmistakable 'certain incandescence' about the figure.

"The easiest thing to have done was to take it down, but I overheard Rory telling you about it, and you were bound to ask, — you're … not angry," he enquired, with stilted uncertainty.

She was trembling and breathless, her emotions were so mixed, she shook her head as she stammered an awkward reply, "I … I didn't really

take in what Rory had said, - he was flirting; - it was unimportant; - I …
don't know what I feel; how … could I be angry? She looks very beautiful."

"As all the Campbell women," he murmured, seeming to breathe a sigh
of relief.

Suddenly, feeling tremulously unstable on her legs, an overwhelming
desire swept over her, a returned longing to lean back against him, but
in her effort to resist, she must have swayed, for Duncan caught her by
the shoulders, pulling her close to him for support, "You smell like the
heather," he urgently whispered against her hair. — Spontaneously, she
lifted her hand to cover his, feeling the warmth of his skin beneath her
fingers, stirring her, as his touch had stirred her, the entire day.

The coiled spring began coiling more tightly about them; — she briefly
closed her eyes, as if to still the unsteady pounding of her heart. — Devoid
now of speech, or power of movement, aware only of her reeling senses
at Duncan's nearness, and the soft, sweet, lingering kiss which he placed
on her temple, and then repeated at close intervals down the side of her
face until reaching her arched neck. — She sighed, softly with pleasure,
unwilling to move, until he turned her within the circle of his arms to face
him, tracing the line of her jaw with gentle fingers that left a tingling trail.
— As he made avid study of her upturned face, his blue eyes searching her
every flawless feature, to momentarily linger on her inviting, softly parted
moistened, lips.

Unable to resist, Helen slid her arms about his neck as he lowered his
dark head, his lips claimed hers, gently at first, expertly coaxing and teasing
them into response. — It was a beautiful sensation, she thought, poetically,
reminding her of whispering fresh winds, blowing through the heather,
fanning sparks into flame. — She responded gladly, sighing again, — his
kiss deepening, his tongue invading the warm velvety softness of her mouth.
— And both seeming to slake a long insatiable thirst, — she clung to him
closer, feeling that she never wanted the moment to end, and softly sighing,
relaxed against him, enjoying the pleasing, sensual, caressing motion his
hands made on her back, unsure of whether she was floating or drowning
in the exquisite ecstasy of his embrace, — then Helen's burning senses
reeled anew, when Duncan again, urgently breathed her name against her
lips, and she felt his trembling hands slide down over her hips, pressing and
moulding her against his muscular thighs, of his physical need, she was in
no doubt.

From somewhere, sanity suddenly returned in the awakening remembrance
of Alex Craig and the words, *reincarnation* and *fetish* suddenly exploding

in her head and taking their toll, this is madness, she frantically told herself, wondering however this heinous situation had occurred. — Now trembling from head to foot from his lovemaking, her heart hammering in her breast, she wrenched her mouth free from his tantalising kiss, while at the same moment, sliding her hands down from his neck to push at his hard chest.

"No!" she barked brusquely, when he tried to pull her close again.— Automatically, his arms dropped, freeing her from his warm embrace — immediately, she took a step backwards, recoiling in horror, "I don't *think* that that was on the agenda, my Lord," she hotly retorted.

For one split second, his face was the picture of astonishment, — instantly, to be replaced, — his jaw hardened, his eyes steeled, "No — how right you are, it wasn't on the agenda, my Lady Helen," he replied, his voice gruff with anger, as he moved towards her. "But I didn't hear you complaining very strongly, either."

Edging further backwards, she was now pinned by her prey, — indignant, she raised her small chin, conscious at all costs that she couldn't blow her story cover, wanting more than anything to punish him for his deceit, "Well, — for your information, I do object, my Lord, — you have no *right* to take such liberties, — a liberty that you wouldn't have dared to take, had I not been … Mairie Campbell's granddaughter … or was it," she mistakenly added, maliciously, voicing, "… a vein attempt on your part, to *lay* Mairie Campbell's ghost?" while hastily dismissing the fleeting look of pain that crossed his fine features that her harsh words had evoked.

"You sound jealous," he spat in disgust, his eyes now icy glints where only a few moments ago there had been, loving kindness. "You're not fit to utter her name. — And I have no intention of discussing, or explaining anything of my friendship with your grandmother. — But just to set the record straight, remember this, Helen Campbell, — Mairie Campbell was a lady, — a lady I respected, and you have a lot of living to do, before you could even think of *stepping* into her shoes."

Unguarded now by rage, Helen stormed on, struggling once more with the temptation to strike the arrogant face above her — her voice wobbled, rasping with temper, "How *dare* you speak to me like that, — I have no wish to step into a dead woman's shoes, and who are *you* to pontificate about jealousy? I'll choose my *own* friends," she then passionately spat the vicious words, "You … you're nothing but an inherent barbarian! — Unlike your ancestors you need no sword to strike down the innocent, only your hands on the steering wheel of c … oh …," she groaned, shaking her head in disbelief and utter regret, as her voice faded lamely away.

"You're nothing but a beautiful sham, Helen, and now I hope you're feeling satisfied, that you've managed to vent an amount of vengeance upon my head, for having reduced you precious *pride* to nothing."

"You haven't even apologised," she snapped, complaining, still struggling with words, "You hadn't even the common decency to stop and ask if I'd been injured, — do you think that by ignoring the fact that you almost killed me, that … that it will go away?"

His steely eyes narrowed, and pointing his finger, accused, "You hold grudges, and you were protesting so loudly that I had no doubt that you weren't suffering any serious injury, as you are doing just now."

My Lord, she earnestly wanted to say, opening her mouth, but no reply issued forth, her mouth closed again, without uttering a word, nipping her lower lip between her teeth. — It was preferable to allow him to think as he had, rather than disclose the real reason for her sudden adverse attitude.

Not having received a reply, Duncan took it that the matter was settled, "I think … we had better cancel the rest of the tour for today," he suggested.

Feeling bruised and miserable inside, Helen reluctantly conceded, "I have no wish to trouble you any further; — I'm sure that Rory can fill in any points of interest that you may not have covered."

"As you wish," he curtly replied, his jaw hard, pointing to himself with his thumb, "But not during *my* time."

And not wishing to sit in uncomfortable strained silence, in the confined space of the car, — she had to get away, — had to be alone, "I … think, I'll walk, — it isn't far."

"Have it your own way, I'm not holding you, it would be preferable if you did," he conceded, stepping aside. — She hesitated, her lips moved soundlessly, her eyes became bright; her throat constricted, and as she choked back the threatened tears, she again shook her head in silent, remorseful disbelief, at her own treacherous behaviour.

She suddenly moved; — he stood helplessly immobilised, watching as she sped back, running lightly down the gallery until she had disappeared down the staircase. — He hesitated too long, wanting to call her back, but his voice and own pride failed him. — He suddenly let out a soft expletive, "Damn!" Knuckling the panelling, he cursed himself for choosing a wrong moment; — he had only wanted to lesson the shock. — But he had felt so sure that Helen was feeling receptive of him, her eyes had spoken volumes when they had stood on Tor Point, at exactly the same time he'd had the strangest feeling that they had stood together in the same place, in another time, another dimension, — she had stroked his bowed head with gentle

124

fingers, — was this Helen's, 'Deja' vu', he now wondered? – He'd always wanted to know what Mairie Campbell had looked like as a young woman, and just why she had commanded the adoration of almost an entire village. — Over the years, he'd tried to imagine, and it was beyond belief when they had first found the portrait, but it hadn't been satisfying enough, he tortuously ached with the desire to hold her, — he wanted to know the beauty, the gentleness, the warmth, the tenderness and the passion, and having now savoured it, he greedily wanted more of it, but he was conscious that these things were not his to hold, just a cruel, brief taste of honey. — He had been committed since birth, — cursed by family expectations, he'd had been denied freedom of choice, just a life that had been mapped out for him, and now all that faced him, was a cold, hard, empty, bitter future and a picture of dreams in remembrance, — *this* was his destiny.

He lingered a few moments longer, before swiftly walking the length of the gallery, loosening his tie and undoing the restricting neck buttons of his shirt as he went. — With hands in pockets, he just as swiftly descended the stairs which he had so recently ascended with such trepidation; — a harsh voice suddenly, rudely, broke into the silence, echoing upwards,

"Ah, Duncan darling, I thought I might find you here," Alex addressed him. "I heard raised voices, and I've just seen Helen running as though there were a pack of hounds behind her."

Five minutes later, as Duncan reached his car, he glanced back at the building, feeling concerned, — he curtly called out to Rory who was just crossing the courtyard, "Take *down* Mairie Campbell's portrait," he ordered, "Take *down* Mairie Campbell's portrait — Immediately."

Chapter 11

Beware, my Foolish Heart

Alone in the cottage, she aimlessly wandered from room to room, reflecting again on the heinous, agonising, mortifying situation. — In her little bedroom, she sighed as she sat down wearily on her bed. — Why did one stolen kiss bother her so much? — Because there's no point in becoming involved in anything emotional, — she told herself, now admitting that she wasn't so completely adverse to the Laird, — in truth, the depth of the kiss had panicked her, — had taken her breath away, — had stirred her sexual senses; — and why, of everything else in the book, had she used Mairie Campbell as her ploy? — There was no sense in what she had implied, — no truth in what she had said, and yet, — she had thoughtlessly, maliciously, maligned the memory of a much-loved lady and the character of a well-respected man, — 'Oh, Ryder', she inwardly groaned, '... you should be proud of your star pupil now' — She stared through the window onto the lane and seeing her car, she rationalized that it was a long time until the evening and that there was plenty of daylight left, — she wanted to leave the claustrophobia of the house. — Moments later, she left the cottage and drove, trying to lighten her heavy load, not seeing the countryside in all its evening glory, — the tears blinded her, and half way along Bracken Lane, drawing level with its gates, she diverted, and after parking her car, entered the graveyard of the little Kirk, with the intention of seeking solace in the tranquillity of the prayer seeped walls of the ancient Presbyterian building. — There was no-one about, but the unbearable, excruciating torment was still there, — the words *reincarnation* and *fetish* still rang in her head, and would not cease to annoy her.

Duncan's afternoon had faired no better, he felt edgy, knowing that his life seemed to have taken a U turn, his mind stirred by pensive thoughts. He was very conscious of Helen's presence; his deep desires were burning deeper into his soul since meeting her, — so like Mairie Campbell, — she was indeed a replacement. — Mairie's craftiness had been boundless when dealing with the Craigs. — He knew that Helen should be told, but how to brooch the subject was beyond him, — perhaps he should enlist Hannah's assistance in the matter; she was very good at explaining the motives behind anyone's actions.

It must have been an hour before Helen sighed and stirred, deciding to venture outside, to roam with heavy heart through the moss covered gravestones, kicking at the bounteous collection of coloured leaves. — On reaching a great shady oak tree, she bent to read the inscription on the nearby gravestone. — It bore just her name 'Mairie Campbell' with no record of her coming and none of her going. — A strange kind of epitaph of a much-loved lady, she thought, sighing softly, it was as though she had left some unfinished business and was lingering to see it completed. — Suddenly, why, she couldn't understand, she beseeched the departed, "What am I to do, Mairie Campbell? How can I right the wrong of so unjust an accusation?" she whispered. "Why do I feel so guilty? I'm just trying to stay."

For a few moments more, she stood devoid of an answer and the hopes of ever finding one, but then, with another sigh, she glanced around as if searching for inspiration. — She lifted her face, feeling an involuntary smile break into her now tired features, just as somewhere above her, loud and clear, a songbird burst into shrill tune, filling her soul with an instant feeling of lightness and release.

Glancing around further, her eye came to rest on another nearby grave, that of the MacFarlanes, bearing its last sad message of: - Alicia, Angus and Robert.

Hearing a soft footfall, she turned sharply to come face to face with Hannah. Her arms were full of flowers for the Kirk, "Och! Lass, I didnae mean to disturb you."

"That's okay, Hannah." She gave a watery smile, feeling more uplifted at the sight of the housekeeper's beaming face, "Want some help with the flowers?" she asked.

Hannah glanced at her sideways, as they made their way along a narrow pathway between the ancient tombstones. Her expression turned to one of kindly concern, "You look tired, lass, she commented, noticing the tell tale dark shadows beneath her moist eyes.

"It's been a strenuous week," she brushed. "I'm okay."

"I hear you're going to help young Rory," she sighed. "That's nice, it's what we need, plenty of entertainment."

She raised a finger to her lips, "Hush! It's supposed to be a secret Hannah, don't go telling the Laird."

"No, I won't lass, I promise. He'll be fair tickled pink; — I'm just a trifle concerned that Alex Craig will get wind of your plans."

Helen sounded surprised, her voice rose in a questioning way, "She's organised a gathering herself to launch her film?"

"It's out of character," Hannah scoffed, glancing sideways at her companion, "She wouldnae do anything that didn't benefit herself, the village isn't lavish enough for her; she's just making a show."

Helen thinly smiled, "She would be hard put to compete with, Jean."

"It nay Jean she's competing with — you mark my words. — Nay, it's far different nowadays, from the old Laird's day, when I was a wee lassie. Alicia MacFarlane, didnae have a clue how to enjoy herself."

"I've just seen her inscription," Helen remarked, as they entered the Kirk, where she took the flowers from the housekeeper, before following her down to the Vestry to find vases. "What was she like?" she asked eagerly.

For a few anxious moments, she wondered if Hannah had heard her, engrossed as she now was with her head inside a large cupboard. — Then, as if no time had elapsed since Helen's question, she reappeared with the glass vessels to set them on the large oak refectory table in the centre of the room, answering with disparagement, "Pah, that one — very self-assured with all the condescending airs and graces, — just like Miss Alex."

Helen poised in her task of placing a flower in a vase, looking thoughtfully puzzled, "Alex … you mean, Alex Craig?" she questioned.

"The one and only," Hannah replied. "Alicia was her great aunt, or rather step aunt. — She was a disagreeable old sour face, fancied herself as a second Victoria," she said, with a shake of her grey head and further distaste in her tone, her voice wobbled, "Heaving up her bosom's; — there was no doubt, nobody were allowed to enjoy themselves in Alicia MacFarlane's day. — Your gran and she were always arguing the toss; — 'twere a pastime with them; — they kept the whole village entertained." Hannah suddenly grinned, "Alicia tried to ignore her, but Mairie had the upper hand. — Your gran used to scuttle out into the garden and wait by the picket gate, just as Alicia's carriage passed by, but Mairie knew that the coachman had to wait until he could safely turn into the High Street, and 'twere then, that she'd let 'Bruce' her little terrier dog out, perfectly timed, it were. He'd yap around the horses' hooves, startling them, — 'twere such a ruckus."

Despite herself, Helen gave a soft laugh at the very descriptive vision, which so fitted the former, haughty, Lady MacFarlane. "Did Angus marry her for land?" she asked.

"According to folk law, he did, but it all went amiss; Alicia was an only child. — Shortly after old Angus and she were wed, her mother very inconveniently died, and it wasn't but two years later when her father married again, a young woman from the Isles. She bore him a son."

"James Craig," Helen guessed.

"Aye, Lass, you're right, James Craig. You're very quick on the uptake," Hannah acknowledged, impressed.

Helen chuckled, "Oh, its only genealogy. I've done part of my own family," she sighed as she stood back to admire her display. "The Laird told me that his real grandmother was Bridget MacCleod, where is she buried, obviously, not in the family plot?"

"Her plot is on the north side, she selected it herself by all accounts. A real lady, they say."

After all this talk, she had to ask, "And ... did she have lands, Hannah?"

"The rich all had lands," the housekeeper replied.

"Oh ...," she nodded, feeling a distinct plummet, while feeling a curious, personal welter of disappointment and sadness, pushed into a cold, empty aloneness, a desertion, but knew she had received the expected, obvious answer, she had non of these riches, only the small comfortable wealth of a job. She despaired, and diversified. "I'll give you a lift home," she offered, a while later, after they'd finished their task and cleared away the debris.

On their short journey, Helen enquired, curiously, "Hannah, what happened to Mairie's wedding dress?"

"She were buried in it, or what was said to be her wedding dress, but I'm nay so sure; it was small loss, it suffered an accident of some kind; it was covered in red wine stains and quite ruined. — 'Twere in a trunk with a few other oddments, including the cape, she told me where it was and what to do with it; I hadn't seen it before."

"And, where was it, — the trunk, I mean?"

The housekeeper seemed surprised at the question, "'Twere in Bracken Cottage, just in a trunk, in the loft."

The gossip had calmed her, lightened her spirit, and had increased her knowledge. — With the close connections of this community, there was every possibility of intermarriage; it must have been hard to find a little fresh blood, she concluded.

But the dimming shadows of the evening brought a fresh burst of anguish; her thoughts were feverish, not even playing her favourite classics could soothe her. — She sat on her sofa, hugging her knees, just gazing into the fire. — The unbelievable pain in her stomach just would not go away, she heavily sighed, 'Is this what it's like, being in love' she wondered, giving a low groan as the truth suddenly smote her? — Someone had once said that it only took a moment, 'I must get a grip on myself,' she thought, determined to stay focussed.

But her night faired no better, and with the coming of the dawn, the nagging aching pain had increased and the words *reincarnation* and *fetish* still troubled her, feeling that Alex Craig had indeed invaded her life. — The only comfort was, that Alex was not aware, or was she — she further ruminated, — she was such a determined woman.

Rising early the following morning, after spending a restless night, her spirits were now as dreary as the overcast weather, and judging by the grey collection of clouds hanging low over the mountains, they were in for quite a downpour of rain. — So much for the promised fine spell, she thought dejectedly.

After dressing casually, she made her way downstairs just as the postman knocked on the door to deliver several letters, exchanging comments on the weather with him as she accompanied him to the gate, with the intention of collecting her milk.

It was as she turned at the gate, intending to return to the cottage, when she realised that something had radically changed, "Oh!" she gasped aloud, clapping her freehand to her mouth, as she stared in bewilderment around the now neatly mown lawns. — Doing her arithmetic, she realised that the castle had been closed, so it should have been Rory's day off, and Duncan had warned that he would have to make up for lost time. — So this had been his punishment, and in the misery of her return yesterday, she hadn't noticed. — Poor Rory, she commiserated, she alone was to blame, making ridiculous excuses on his behalf.

On hearing an approaching car, she turned back to see who the newcomer was, and the subject of her sympathy suddenly screeched to a halt outside of her gate. — Still holding the bottle of milk, she went to meet him as he left the estate's Land Rover.

"I see I'm in time for tea," he said, cheekily.

Helen's spirits rose a little at Rory's cheerfulness, she grinned at him as she replied, "its small reward for the mowing, thanks Rory, I think I owe you an apology."

He slung a brotherly arm about her shoulders as they walked down the path towards the cottage, "Think nothing of it, Helen, actually, it didn't take that long. I brought the power mower down from the castle."

Helen appeared concerned, "Shouldn't you be there today?"

"Yes," he replied. "But it's early yet; — the Laird wants me to deliver some new equipment to the Top Farm before the castle opens. — Old Brooks, the manager, is laid low with influenza, and can't get out for the collection."

Helen felt her treacherous heart quiver at the mention of the Laird, as still feeling raw from their overheated argument, she didn't want to risk any conversation about him, and prayed that Rory wouldn't ask any leading questions about the previous day. — But within a few minutes, he gave a sudden gasp, and giving a hasty apology as he checked his watch, he downed his tea and had departed, after remembering that he'd first, — to collect the equipment from the station.

Alone again, Helen remembered her unread mail. — After pouring herself a second cup of tea, she gathered up the letters, and went to settle herself in her sitting room beside the blazing fire to read them, just as the first raindrops started to pitter-patter on the window panes.

The first letter proved to be from her parents, and was full of news of concerts they had recently attended, plus several programmes that she may find of interest; — the second was from Giles inviting her to some promenade concerts, these revelations only served to increase her frustrations and irritations; her free adventures into the cultures had been cruelly curtailed. — The third was addressed in Rita's untidy scrawl, the news it contained astonished her. — Apparently, after she had left London, a dishy new photographer had joined the Daily News, and according to Rita, they had 'clicked' immediately, he had wasted no time and had moved into the flat with her; — they were now engaged, planning a spring wedding, a whirlwind romance in fact. — Helen smiled to herself, noting the postscript, 'as you will be home by the spring, I expect you to be a bridesmaid; there just isn't anyone else, who will do'. — The final letter was from Ryder, demanding his ideal in articles and reminding her of their bargain, from which he expected an adequate return for favours. — She sighed, as she returned the missive to its envelope.

While browsing through one of the programmes from her parents, she heard the rattle of the door latch, followed by a cheery, "Hello Helen," from Jean. — Jumping up, she hurried through into the dining room to meet her friend, and judging by her very wet appearance, it had begun to rain heavily, "Oh, I do hate these wet spells," she grumbled, as Helen led the way through into the kitchen to make more tea, while Jean hung her bright blue raincoat onto the rear of the kitchen door, her umbrella, she strategically placed in the sink to drain off.

Instinct told Helen, that Jean would ask about the tour, but still feeling reluctant to discuss the Laird, she braced herself to be reserved. — After all, Jean didn't know that he had kissed her, or anything about the results of that kiss, and she didn't want her friend guessing at her innermost thoughts, "A cup of tea will warm you," she sensibly, evasively said, as she set about the task.

Once settled in the living room, Jean warmed her hands by the fire as Helen chatted on about the contents of her letters, particularly discussing concert programmes at great length, anything in fact, barring Ryder's missive, which would keep off the subject of the tour. — But knowing full-well that she was only delaying the topic, until eventually, Jean's polite patience gave way, as she suddenly leaned foreword to ask the inevitable.

"Did you enjoy yourself, yesterday?"

Immediately, Helen's eyes clouded, and her voice shook with the supreme effort to reply, "Y...yesterday — Oh, yesterday ... yes, yes, I did, it was extremely interesting," and volunteering nothing further, she hastily sipped at her tea.

A puzzled, thoughtful expression flit across Jean's features, she hadn't received the enthusiasm that she had expected from Helen, and wondered why, also, she lacked her usual sparkle and was unusually pensive, she noted.— Cautiously, she tried again, "What did you think of The Loch House? You were dying to see it, Hannah told me so."

Helen looked surprised at the unexpected question; she fumbled for words, "The Loch House," she echoed. "We ... didn't go to The Loch House. I ... there wasn't time," she finished, lapsing once more into silence, conscious that she was making a poor job of being reserved, in desperation, she groaned, "Jean ... please ...," she begged.

Jean, in her wisdom, sat back in her seat, deciding not to pursue the subject any further, on recognising Helen's obvious reluctance to discuss her day out with Duncan, — but it was strange, she thought, that he hadn't shown Helen his beautiful home. — Although not usually a boastful man, he was proud of the restorations made to The Loch House, and knew he wouldn't be averse to showing it to Helen, the granddaughter of a great family friend. — Of course, she thought on, Helen was a very attractive girl, perhaps he had chanced his luck, she secretly surmised, and had been shown the door.

Glancing at Helen, who was now pensively gazing into the fire, her face was becoming pink from the warmth, she changed the subject, "How would you like to come on a shopping spree in Edinburgh — the week after next; I love a little jaunt, whenever the season finishes."

Helen drew her eyes away from the bright orange and blue, mesmerising, dancing flames, and her thoughts away from the previous day to eagerly answer Jean's well-timed offer. "Yes, yes, thanks, I would love to come."

"Good." Jean replied, stirred into her favourite hobby of planning. "Then, I'll book us into a hotel. There's small point in going for only one day, it would be very laborious."

Jean stayed chatting about the arrangements for their coming outing and the various aspects for the Christmas festivities, for some time, with the hope of enlivening Helen's obviously dulled spirits a little more, but eventually, time became pressing and she had to leave, grateful to accept Helen's offer of a lift as it was still pelting with rain. — Once settled in the car, their conversation went thus …

"I would be grateful if you could help me serve up some cream teas, and organise games of croquette for the American visitors, they just love them."

"The Laird is a lucky man to have you, Jean," she underlined with a sigh.

"I think he would consider his fortunes tenfold, were you to stay."

"It isn't a pressing fact," she irritably replied, as she changed gear and slowed down, as they entered between Talberts' open gates to make steady progress along the drive. "I'm grateful that everyone seems to have taken me into their hearts, but I've only just arrived." She sighed, her tone changed to one of more apologetic tolerance, "I'm still very confused as to why; Mairie Campbell brought me here in the first place."

"Have you asked, Duncan? — He may know."

"If he does, he's not saying. — It's for me to work out the riddle, for myself."

The weekend came and went without any sight or sound of the Laird, a fact which Helen didn't find altogether surprising, but renewing the knowledge that Arrochar was only a small village, it was more than just a possibility that she would encounter him eventually, an event which she didn't particularly relish. — He was never far from her mind however, his presence ever haunting her, and any effort to banish the utter misery that she felt, had failed, and equally as upsetting, Hannah hadn't called either. — According to Rory, she had gone to visit a sick relative in Aberdeen, but would be home very soon, and her thoughtful message to Helen, was to be sure to care for herself in her absence.

During the following week, the weather faired again, enabling Helen to help Jean with the cream teas and the games of croquette, which she first had to learn, amid many gales of laughter, and Jean was delighted with the idea, of Helen demonstrating the Spinet to her transatlantic customers. — It made an attractive tableaux in the house, along with the many artefacts, which had belonged to the previous generations of the MacFarlanes'.

Rory called several times to help with her garden, but of Duncan, she saw nothing and nobody spoke of him in her presence. — It seemed that she was being spared further torment.

Her evenings were spent playing bridge or organising social events with the entertainment's committee. — Friday evenings, as promised, she spent with Rory at the Youth Club, — the disco mad teenagers had welcomed her enthusiastically into their circle, — they had decided to keep their separate arrangements a secret and Rory was true to form, she discovered, as Duncan had indicated, he had quite a following of female admirers; — the handsome young man was quite unabashed by their open adoration of him. — She soon realised that he was brimful of prestige, and so an excellent choice for a Youth Leader, Duncan had certainly recognised his Gillies attributes.

All this did little to alleviate the nagging ache, which continued to knaw at her stomach. — And there were private moments, when she was so rapt in thought, having to be gently startled back into reality.

Her telephone had been duly installed, but she had been so pre-occupied that she hadn't phoned Harry Ryder, and anyway, why should she, she was on the pretext of a holiday, she deceived herself, and Alex's conference was over two months away. — Alex Craig appeared on the horizon only once, but Helen did have the impromptu thought that she was doubtless seeing Duncan, and to her studious mind, Alex's ploy had worked, but how to turn the trick, momentarily evaded her, she was so weakened by her emotions.

Chapter 12

Insurgence

Drawing towards another weekend, she still hadn't sent Ryder any articles and was very well aware that if she didn't produce something very soon, he would cut her salary. But one idea had formulated in her mind, and she looked forward with eagerness to Hannah's expected return, as she intended making good use of the unrestricted clause she'd had inserted into her contract, and having already sampled many of the housekeepers' culinary delights, Highland style, 'Hannah's Highland Kitchen' was born, she explained to Jean one day while helping to arrange flowers in the little Gothic Kirk.

"Hannah's recipes are sacrosanct; you will have to do a lot of crafty wheedling to get her to part with them."

"Well, I can try," Helen returned with a grin. "Perhaps we can produce cookery books and sell them in the local shops."

Jean glanced up from her task of arranging some large dahlia blooms to study Helen's face, now concentrated on her own vase of flowers. She began ruminating — there were definite shadows under her eyes that hadn't been there a week ago, and her lovely eyes themselves still lacked their usual lustre, revealing the possible evidence that she wasn't sleeping adequately, she sometimes seemed to be on the brink of tears.

Again, she couldn't help wondering if it had something to do with Duncan, knowing that Helen hadn't seen him for over a week now, and he'd been decidedly tetchy, the last time he had visited the surgery on some business or other, and it certainly hadn't been ill-health that had made him so — curious, she thought.

After finishing the flowers, Jean had to collect a special parcel for Iain from the Post Office — being flu vaccine; it required a signature; Helen obligingly drove her into the village. — After parking the car, they walked along the bustling High Street. — The Post Office was centrally situated, neatly positioned between an empty premise and a gift shop, where Helen decided to browse while Jean collected her parcel.

She was in the process of admiring a selection of Celtic jewellery displayed in the window, when a tall redhead in the familiar shape of the immaculately clad figure of Alex, poised on the opposite pavement kerb facing the shop, preparing to cross the road. — Suddenly, Helen's stomach lurched and knotted, her heart jerkily skipped a beat as Alex was joined by Duncan's tall broad shouldered figure; equally as immaculate in a well-tailored dark suit, they stood talking for a few moments. — Alex smiled up into his face, her every feature lit with interest while sharing some intimacy.

Feeling no envy or pity at the sight of them, her unselfish heart, gladdened, realising that they could come to terms with themselves in such a way, that they were prepared to make a successful marriage for the sake of uniting the land, which was so important to both of them.

Helen touched her lips with shaking fingers; his warm kiss still lingered, as if haunting her. — It had seemed so natural, so right, to be in his arms, he hadn't forced her, she now admitted, she had been an equal party to it, the wine had flowed, she had felt light headed, she had flirted with him, and she had been wrong to place the blame entirely on him, as she had, and fervently wished that she could enjoy the same ease and contact that Mairie Campbell would have found in his company. — She saw him glance across to where she stood, and although hidden by the display, it was almost as if he had heard her silent plea.

She stirred suddenly, as a hand lightly touched her arm, drawing her out of her reverie.

"Helen, are you ready to leave?" Jean said kindly, noting the girl's pallor and the watery brightness of her eyes, and then following her gaze through the display window, across the street. — Her brow furrowed slightly as her eyes rested on Duncan and Alex, but she said nothing, withholding her court.

"Oh … yes," she said, trying to swallow the emotion that shook her. "I … think … I'll buy this brooch, its pretty; — don't you think?"

"It's lovely Helen — heather gemstones, and such a pretty setting," she replied kindly, taking in Helen's cold trembling hand, holding the jewel."

Between the time Helen had made her purchase, and leaving the shop, both Duncan and Alex had disappeared, much to the silent, shared relief of both women. — After further shopping, they eventually returned to the car. Helen then drove Jean back to the surgery, only to be greeted by the sleek lines of the Rover, standing empty in front of the house. Jean glanced from the car and then back to Helen's strained features, and wasn't surprised by her refusal to share a pot of tea.

"Thanks Jean, another time," she said, only wanting to escape. "I'm going up to the castle, I haven't seen the dungeons, Rory tells me there's a new tableaux on display," they bade each other a farewell.

"Jean, was that Helen you were with?" Duncan enquired, as he met her in the hallway.

"It was, but she's gone; you've missed her, she's very upset and she's obviously avoiding you," she sighed. "I could murder a brandy… join me."

"Thanks!" he said, following her into the salon, where moments later he stood broodily gazing out, staring sightlessly, but thoughtfully into the gardens towards the spiny and the fountains, his dark head slightly lowered, glass tightly clenched in his hand; his jaw muscles moving, as if he was controlling his deepest, most painful emotions.

Jean felt that he was suffering rejection, "Duncan, I don't want to interfere, but I know that there's something wrong between you two …"

"It was just a little misunderstanding, it will all work out," he tersely replied, and raising his glass to his lips, downed the golden liquid in one.

"You seem very certain of that," she appealed, frowning, "Is she going to understand just *why* you've taken down Mairie Campbell's portrait; — it will surely stir up more rebellion? I've kept her away from the castle for as long as I can; — use the phone, there's still time; Rory can hang it back."

"It's gone for cleaning," he replied.

"I've known you for a very long time, and I hate to say it, but you're a poor liar, Duncan MacFarlane, the portrait was cleaned soon after it was found, in July."

"You're prying, Jean," he replied, as a soft warning.

Jean sighed, knowing that it would be tempting fate to pursue the topic, "I speak as a friend, so, on your own head, be it," she said cagily.

"Mr Cameron is very enlightening," was his reply, "… and he'd better make it good."

Jean gave him a sidelong glance, realising that he had placed Rory in the firing line. "I'm taking Helen into Edinburgh for a couple of days; perhaps you should see her before we go."

He half-turned towards her as she approached to take his empty glass, his eyes narrowing, he replied, "Perhaps, I feel that she should come to see me."

"And, your word is law," Jean commented, taking back the glass and hovering for a brief moment, before re-crossing the room for a refill, — she spoke softly, pleading; "Would it be so difficult to bend a little, on this occasion?"

He chuckled, while shaking his head, "And show frailties of nature, Jean. Nay, this will not do, Miss Campbell will soon come to her senses."

"Oh, she will, — will she? Can you be certain of that?" Jean replied, giving a sceptical nod of her head, "You may be the mighty Laird of Arrochar, but Helen has strengths and weaknesses, as do we all, and I don't think that she's going to 'cow tow' to a domineering male, my Lord. — We all bend to your will, Duncan, but after all, Helen's your guest, *not* an employee."

"You're scolding me, Jean."

"You need scolding," she smiled, fondly, "… and someone who *dares* to say *no* to you, now and again."

"I'll never take *no* for an answer," he replied stubbornly. "Miss Campbell, will soon beg my forgiveness, she will be keenly forthcoming, just you wait and see."

"And, I think, your calculations are incorrect, for whatever cardinal sin she has committed, she has Mairie's stubborn, rather perverse spirit. Angus could never make her bend to his will, and he died a broken man. — Helen thinks that you know the reason for the rather tight restrictions on the *will.*"

"Then, you can safely *tell* Miss Campbell, that I do not have my finger prints on the *will.*"

"Tell her yourself, Duncan."

"The things men have to do, to win a maiden's favour," he sighed, shaking his head while complaining in disbelief.

"Should we just fall into your unsuspecting arms, and have our most private emotions tampered with," Jean replied, giving a smile. "I think you are fast becoming a womaniser, Duncan MacFarlane, just how many women do you need in your Harem?"

He briefly grinned, his answer flippant, "Oh, a couple would do; — one for mid week, another for the weekend."

"And, you think Helen should be agreeable to this?"

"She would soften Alex as a blow; Mairie softened Alicia for my grandfather — made her more tolerable."

"Helen does have a forgiving nature, but you're getting yourself into a very compromising situation."

Duncan nodded. "But I can't help my feelings."

"You're in love with her." she suggested, "Or do just fancy her?"

Duncan just wryly grinned.

"Matters of the heart," she said, knowingly, "This, I will Defend."

He raised his glass, "Loch Sloy!"

"Another battle, another trophy…. Loch Sloy, my Lord."

"Ye Lassies," he briefly smiled, "Yer try a man."

Helen arrived at the castle, to be met by Rory at the gates, "I want to see the picture," she demanded.

Rory appeared to be distinctly uncomfortable, "The gallery is closed today."

She peered down the driveway ahead of her; it was a hive of activity, "That isn't very good for business," she observed, feeling suspicious, she narrowed her eyes, "You mean … it's closed to me."

Rory's curly head went down, he silently, slightly raised his eyes; he could not speak a lie. — Helen read his expression which spoke volumes, her anger rose, instantly she revved her car engine into life, Rory immediately leapt onto the car's running board as she grated the vehicle into gear, stepped onto the accelerator and roared along the driveway, honking impatiently when stuck behind a coach load of tourists. — After coming to a scrunching halt outside the great oak doors, she leapt out to enter the building and darted through the hallway, weaving her way through groups of astonished tourists, who were trying to listen to the commentaries of the tour operators.

"Helen!" Rory yelled after her, "Helen wait!" but she was already half-way up the stairs and heading towards the gallery.

Ignoring him, she speeded her step, and when reaching the top, raced along the gallery towards the south wing. — She stopped at the point where she had viewed the picture, she was panting, and looking up, realised that it had gone, and had been replaced by another, "No!" she cried out in her trembling anguish, "This is to punish me."

"Punish you … punish you for what?" Rory echoed, in perplexed frustration, "What are you blithering about, woman?"

Her breasts heaved as she replied, "You wouldn't understand."

Rory gaped at her, not knowing what to do with a woman in an emotional, distraught state; he had no idea, for what reason his employer had instructed him as he had. It had been inevitable that Helen would find out, rather sooner than later, "Helen, please laugh," he pleaded, struggling to find a plausible explanation, "It was put away for safe keeping," he came up with.

She suddenly felt angry, although she wanted to cry with frustration, "It was safe enough where it was," she blurted and moaned, "Oh, how could he do this?"

"The Laird can do anything," Rory needlessly replied.

"Where is it?" she tersely demanded. "Can I see it?"

"No, it's locked away in the vaults."

"Back in the dark?" she cried.

"Helen … the day I took the painting down, Miss Craig was here, I thought that … maybe she'd instigated it, she seems to be able to twist the Laird's arm somewhat."

"Alex?" Helen questioned, exclaimed.

"She complained that the portrait of Mairie Campbell overwhelmed the portrait of her great aunt. — After all, Alicia MacFarlane wasn't all that photogenic, and the artist, who had captured both the ladies, must have had a warmer feeling for Mairie as his subject, the brushstrokes are finer, her cheeks have more bloom."

"I didn't notice the signature," she informed.

"The signature is hard to decipher; it looks like 'A. Parlan', like this one, which is quite clear," he indicated Alicia's, "… but who knows?" he paused before asking, "Can I take you out tonight, you look as though you need cheering up?"

"I could do with a bucketful of cheer," she said, enthusiastically. "Where shall we go?"

"There's a barn dance on in the next village," he informed her. "I'll call for you at seven."

Later that evening, Rory called on time, to the minute. — She peered through the window when she heard the clopping of snorting horses' hooves and the sound of rolling wheels on the stone road, mingled with loud singing outside her door. — The old hay wagon was laden down with excited party revellers, the beer had already been freely flowing; it was a fun and sensible way to travel under these conditions. — She was already at her door when Rory called to her. — She ran out, everyone of Rorys' friends greeted her with gusto; he immediately lifted her from the waist and many hands hauled her onto the cart. — Rory was in the driving seat, he covered her denim clad legs with a tartan blanket, and then rolled the wagon through the High Street towards the station, passing The Loch House as they went; it was in darkness.

The journey to the village of Carrick was taken along country roads, under the most perfect, clear, dark, starlit sky, it was a night for lovers and their passengers were making the most of it.

The noise from the farm could be heard echoing over the rolling valley between the mountains, the lights and music were enticing, thrilling and inviting. — Their passengers were soon unloaded and everyone joined in the colourful affray, — the music was played by a- fiddle and piano accordion band, their zest was spent on reels, dance circles and set squares, the food in the interval, included Aberdeen Angus burgers served with buns, sauces and hot spiced steaks or sausages, cooked over a barbeque, the harvest was in, — in Carrick.

During the interval, their host approached Rory, and the message that he related to Helen, was a request for them to play a piano duet, — the Boogie-Woogie, Peter Dundas was also in attendance. — It was at this point when they communally set eyes on some newly arriving guests, Duncan with Alex, Arnie and the Widow Calhoun, they had a small entourage of strangers, Helen's traitorous heart skipped a beat, but she soon had it back in tune.

"He's such a- stuffed-shirt," Rory remarked. "They were made for each other."

It was the first time that Rory had made any derogatory remark about his employer, and she felt that it was for her benefit that he made it; there was an element of frustrated jealousy in the remark.

"Well, I don't know, he's wearing jeans," she observed. "Has he ever worn jeans before? And his leather bomber jacket is the height of fashion and so is his Indiana Jones hat, very trendy, they suit him."

"It's a first," was Rory's laconic, disgruntled reply. "We're always competin' on some matter or another, but it's the first time that it's ever been a woman; — he's frustrated because he's hands tied."

"Miss Craig looks most uncomfortable, wearing a denim skirt. — They haven't seen us; we'll keep out heads down behind the piano; let's see what they can do; — make it *eight* to the bar."

Rorys' eyes opened wide, "Are you trying to kill them?"

Helen chuckled, "Let's go — you can't beat a bit of rhythm."

It must have been the sun shining so brilliantly through the sprig curtains, or was it the delicious aroma of grilling kippers, drifting through the open window? Whatever it was, caused Helen to stir from her nights slumber, for she had slept fairly fitfully, her mind being not quite as tormented as it had been. — Enjoying Rory's easy, 'devil-may-care' company the previous evening, had seen to that.

A little more awake, Helen stretched luxuriously and then sniffed, inhaling the smell that tantalised her appetite. — Suddenly, fully awake, she realised that it was coming from her own kitchen, "Hannah!" she called out gleefully, and hastily leaped from her bed to drag on her blue negligee, while pushing her feet into fluffy blue mules. — Within moments, she had sped lightly downstairs, not even pausing to brush out the heavy tangled profusion of hair, about her head, "Hannah! Hannah!" she called out again, only stopping to survey the laden breakfast table.

"Is there a fire?" questioned Hannah drolly, as she walked through from the kitchen carrying a bowl of steaming creamy porridge.

Helen stared at her for a moment, while she placed the bowl onto the table, then suddenly feeling a warm welter of love, as if sixteen again, she stepped forward to throw her arms about Hannah's neck in welcome, "Oh, Hannah! I've missed you," she said, warmly, enthusiastic, "And I'm *so* glad that you're back. How is your cousin in Aberdeen?" she ended breathlessly.

"Och, Lass, give an old woman some air," she said, with good humour, and then surveyed Helen at arms length, giving a sigh and a disapproving shake of the head as she absorbed the sight of Helen's pale features. "Sit you down, deere," she said kindly. "You look as though you've entered the winning stakes for a diet. — Haven't you been eating properly?"

"I've been off my food, for a couple of days."

"Couldn't be bothered to cook, more than like," Hannah suspected.

"Oh, no, no, no," she denied. "I've been busy helping Jean; she wouldn't allow me to starve, anymore than you would. "No, I'm just off my food."

Hannah shook her grey head, and frowning quizzically, softly murmured, "Strange … Mr Duncan's off his food as well." She raised her voice full with firm authority, deciding, "Well, there's nay going to be any arguments this morning, you need feeding up and we'll start right now, with a good old fashioned Highland breakfast. — Porridge to start, followed by kippers with rowies, and then oatmeal baps spread with some of my home-made preserves, so tuck in, and that's an order, then, I'll be sure, you're glad I'm back." She sighed as she continued with her sermon, muttering, "I don't know *why* people with artistic talents insist on starving themselves, it must be some-kind of a- conscience."

"You mean, the 'Artists Garrett' stuff," Helen replied, as she dutifully sat and began to eat, when Hannah finally answered her question.

"My cousin is none the worse for wear. A touch of flu, which was all that ailed her, but she's well enough now."

"I'm so glad," Helen replied, again meeting Hannah's smile with her own as she cut open, and then spread lashings of butter on the warm oatmeal bap, — her appetite suddenly wasn't so lacking.

While waiting for Helen to complete her breakfast, the Housekeeper sat with her chatting and enjoying a cup of tea, gratefully noting a return of some colour to the girls' cheeks, "You look a mite better already, lass," she commented. And suddenly, thoughtfully, plunged her hand into her apron pocket, withdrawing from its confines, a familiar looking grey envelope, which she then placed on the table in front of her, "It's a note from Mr. Duncan," she needlessly informed her.

"I wonder what *he* wants?" she murmured, while at the sight of the missive, a fleeting shadow crossed Helen's features; — she swallowed convulsively, feeling a return of the cold inner trembling that had shaken her ever since her argument with its author, — his bitter words, she felt, were branded into her soul for all time, — were these now more of them, she wondered, or was he apologising, for his harshness?" — The latter, she instantly dismissed as impossible, for if there was any apologising to be done, then it was her place to do it, not his, she privately admitted, and possibly, he'd been waiting for her to do just that, and had now become intolerant of waiting. — She sighed softly, and then became all too conscious of the enigma written on Hannah's face, and knew that her hesitation was arousing her curiosity. "I'll open it later," she told her, giving a brief grin.

"Aye, yeel no doubt be seeing him later yousel' to give him any replies," Hannah replied, in a suggestive, knowing way.

Suddenly, fearing a misunderstanding, Helen hurried a stumbled reply, "Oh … oh, no, no, I won't be seeing the Laird today," she said with finality.

Hannah glanced at her over the rim of her teacup, and then placed it thoughtfully back onto its saucer, — standing, she proceed to clear the table, "I'll wash the dishes, lass," she wisely informed.

Helen helped her to load the tray and when alone, her eyes wandered back to the envelope, still lying like a beast of prey on the table. — Making a sudden decision, she hastily picked it up and ripped it open with shakily cool fingers, with the thought that, delaying the opening wasn't going to alter the contents. — It contained only a few, brief curt words.

Helen,
It is my intention to call on you this evening. I have a matter of mutual interest to discuss. Duncan.

It didn't need reading again. With shaking fingers, she replaced the missive back into its envelope, while making a supreme effort to maintain her cool head. She thought positively, — 'oh, no, my Lord, if you think that all you have to do, is *snap* your fingers and I'll come a-running, then you have another think coming' and he could have telephoned, instead he chose the coward's way out, well, if that's the way he wanted it, then, so be it. — Tonight she wouldn't be at home to the Laird, and the following day was the planned shopping trip into Edinburgh. — She would see him in a few more days, she decided, when she felt perfectly ready to do so. — And with this thought, she stepped over to the writing bureau to seat herself in readiness to compose a reply, on her own powder blue paper.

Duncan, my Lord,
 I regret, but I have another engagement this evening.
Helen C.

Brevity was all that was required. It was absolutely true; she had another engagement. — It wasn't impossible to break, she knew, because Rory wouldn't mind if she missed a part of their rehearsals, especially as they were extra rehearsals called at short notice. — But she wasn't going let the Youth Club down, she told herself, and anyway, she was looking forward to drinks with Rory in the Arms Hotel, where the fishing fraternity of the village congregated, along with their wives and friends from the arts, during the fishing season. — The talk in the bar and at dinner was all fishing talk, and if anyone was lucky enough to have a big catch or to land a thirty-pounder, the news sped around the village, in no time.

Hastily, before she could change her mind, she folded the note and slipped it into an envelope, sealed it, and then addressed it to Mr. D. MacFarlane, after which, she hurried into the kitchen to hand it to Hannah. "Thanks, Hannah," she laconically said to the surprised housekeeper, and picking up the tea towel began to busily dry the dishes.

"Are you no going to ring him, then?" she asked, bemused by all the letter writing.

Helen shook her head, "No, just give him that, please."

Hannah chuckled, shaking her grey head while muttering, "Ye lassies, you just love giving a man the run around."

"I'm stepping out with Rory, Hannah," she replied firmly.

Hannah surreptitiously glanced at her sideways, taking in her renewed heightened colour and congratulating herself that her hearty meal had been a success. — Warming and revitalising, that was what Helen needed, none of these sandwich bar meals or takeaway MacDonald's, which the young seemed to survive on in the cities. — Wholesome sustenance is what she requires, in order to maintain her beauty, and Helen certainly had that. — She had unquestionably inherited Mairies' good looks, she acknowledged, and the Campbell women had that unerring quality of being unaware of it.

"What again?" she exclaimed, aloud. "Word had it that you were out with Rory last evening."

"It was Saturday night and we boogied until dawn, — by the last dance, we even had Alex Craig boogying; one of her crowd was a dance coach, she never travels without one," Helen's gleeful mirth ended in a sigh. "She'll be spending the whole of Sunday, soaking in a hot bathtub — she'll resemble a prune by the end of it."

"So, that's why you look like the morning after the night before," Hannah smiled. "… and here I was, feeling sorry for you."

"It was a great evening, Hannah; even the Minister was wearing his jeans," she keenly remarked.

Her companion grunted and then asked a fortuitous question, "How are you finding work?" she asked.

It was at this point when Helen broached the subject of the cookery articles; "They would be perfect for the women's feature page, Hannah. And I can follow it up with an article on 'Life in a Highland Village', city dwellers seem to have such a warped view of country life," she said, recalling her meeting with Mrs Murray at the Woollen Mill.

"Och, it doesn't suit everyone, lass," Hannah replied. "But, while you're away in Edinburgh, I'll think about the recipes. You never can tell; I might just be feeling in the mood to oblige."

Helen made no comment to this; she just glowed with anticipation, and was left with a feeling of hardly daring to breathe, even though she knew that Hannah wouldn't let her down.

Duncan returned to The Loch House in the early evening, to read Helen's note, he immediately, frantically, reached for the phone, "Jean, she's refused to see me."

"Well, surprise, surprise," Jean chuckled. "… perhaps she saw enough of you last night. I hear tell that you lost your temper with Rory again, and slammed down the piano lid, — that was very unsociable of you. I'd have been there myself had I known that Helen was going to let her hair down."

"But …what do I do, now?"

"Nothing," she replied. "Take heed, Duncan, don't badger her, you will push her even further away."

But, compelled as he was, Duncan flouted her advice.

Chapter 13

Duncan's Olive Branch

The alarm clock suddenly rang at 8am. She would be picking Jean up from Talbert within the hour, for their planned trip into Edinburgh. It was Hannah's day off; she was not expected. — After hastily showering and dressing in a bronze coloured trouser suit, and downing a light breakfast of croissants and coffee, she began clearing and washing the few dishes that she had used and was stowing them away, when she heard a light tap on the window pane, "Come in," she called, half expecting to see Rory, she startled, and suffered an uncomfortable rise from her stomach into her chest, when the subject of her many disturbed nights, stepped into the kitchen. — Colour immediately suffused her face, as his lazy blue gaze scaled her appearance from the top of her shining volumed hair, to the tip of her leather shoes.

His penetrating, scrutinising, teasing appraisal made her feel undressed, "Oh, I … didn't expect to see you, my Lord." she managed to say.

"You've been avoiding me," he remarked, softly accusing.

"I wasn't aware that I had to report to you each day," she stiffly replied, her nerve ends jangling at the unexpected intrusion, it was a painful effort to speak, "And anyway, our last meeting didn't exactly end on a very friendly note."

"You're going away with Jean," he said, frowning with concern. "When do you expect to return?"

Her nostril's flared, "Are you so afraid that I won't come back? Is that why you've come, to check up on me, or are you suffering from pangs of guilt?" she finished caustically.

"I asked the first question?" he reminded her.

She sighed, "In a few days, no set time."

"I wanted to see you before you left, to … perhaps apologise for taking

146

undue advantage; I … err … misread the signs," he explained, as he watched her half-fold the damp tea towel and hang it over the edge of the sink, with slightly jerky movements.

"That's very magnanimous of you, my Lord, I'm sure that it must have taken a great amount soul searching on your part, to reduce yourself into making an apology to a mere minion."

"I thought that we may be able to salvage the situation, — to at least … live in harmony."

"This whole situation is so humiliating, — not only do I look like her, but I was dressed like her, — no wonder Miss Craig had a field day," she said vehemently.

"It was hardly my fault," he pointed out, "It was a coincidence."

"*That* was no coincidence." she snapped, tartly.

He tried again, "Then, Hannah chose the dress in all innocence."

"This situation is impossible." she breathed.

Duncan frowned, querying, "Impossible?"

She nodded, "You've removed Mairie's portrait."

"You know about that?" he said, appearing all innocent. "Well, you can't have it both ways, it was offensive to you."

She ignored his latter remark, saying, "You know full-well that I know," she retorted caustically, giving him a sideways glance, and then turned around to lean against the workbench with her arms folded, facing him, — she was challenging, "You know everything that goes on in this village; — I visited the castle, I wanted to see it again, I thought at first that you'd taken it down for spite. …"

He nodded once as he appealed for her to continue, "But then …?"

She swallowed and sighed, as she met his gentle gaze with veiled eyes, saying softly, "But then … I decided that you wouldn't spite Mairie Campbell, so your reasons went far deeper."

He sighed and murmured, sorrowfully, "Deeper than you know."

She nodded and turned again to face the window, positioned so that he could not see her full face, feeling desperate to ask, her nervy fingers toyed with the cloth, "Duncan …," she paused, nipping her lower lip between her teeth, finding the words difficult to say.

"Ye … s," he encouraged, while listening intently, waiting patiently, until she tentatively asked.

"Duncan, were you … in love … with Mairie Campbell?"

"Is it so important to know?" he asked, gently evasive.

"Please, answer me," she pleaded, softly, tremulously, "You hung her picture like … like some holy grail to be worshipped and adored."

He sighed, continuing to be evasive, answering with caution, "Helen, everyone loved Mairie Campbell. — My grandfather … the people of the village … and you've got to remember, that we weren't sure what you looked like, Hannah was just as surprised …,"

She changed the subject to what was uppermost in her mind, "Duncan ... you could *buy* the cottage from me."

He sighed again, "I cannae do that, Helen … may I remind you, that you signed a very legal and binding contract, saying that the cottage may not be sold for financial gain, so if you think that you've found an easy way out, then you haven't found one."

"I'm surprised," she said, her small chin spiritedly rising, "… but it does come to mind, that owning land, no matter how small the portion, is of prime importance to a '*Land Baron*' such as yourself. — It seems that Mairie Campbell has made a prisoner of me, and you my gaoler."

He chuckled roguishly, pulling at his collar while stretching out his chin, "It could be a very pleasant pastime."

She turned her slightly lowered head towards him, while speaking in a determined manner, "This *matter* isn't flippant; I'm not going to be, someone's toy, someone's pastime, or anyone's dalliance; — do you understand? There's small point in holiday flirtations, they're just passing fancies; the people concerned only end up hurt and disillusioned, — anyway, you'll forget me, once I've returned to London."

He raised his eyebrows, drawing a soft intake of breath, while sliding his hands into his trouser pockets, "Oh … is that what this is all about; — well, if you ever change your mind, I'm open to offers."

"It isn't *about* anything," she snapped irritably, saying firmly, "The only thing that I was asked to do, was to live in the cottage for six months, and if I wanted your help, I could ask for it, but I haven't found the need to ask for your help, and until I do, I would very much appreciate, if you would just leave me alone to get on with it; — there were no other conditions; — and, I don't think that it was very nice of you, to … to position Rory as you did, and while we're on the subject, I don't appreciate public displays of temper either, — Carrick Glen is *out* of your domain and Rory was *in* his *own* time; — you were an embarrassment. — Now, I must go," she said firmly. "Jean will be waiting."

He took a step towards her, reaching out his arms with the intention of pulling her into them, "Helen, come here."

"Duncan, no —!" she said, more sharply than she had intended, immediately feeling panic at his touch, and a return of the intense aura which constantly surrounded them. — She struggled with her innermost feelings, she desperately wanted him, and she couldn't deny it, she wanted to feel his gentle hands on her body, caressing the most intimate places, his skilled touch like a tantalising whisper of silk. — But no, she decided, daylight and reality had brought back the shattering memory of Alex Craig and her warnings, "Kissing you, is a very dangerous pastime, now, I must go, and I daresay that Alex will be delighted to keep you company, she may need your help in *rearranging* a few more pictures," she breathed, hastily moving into the dining room to pick up her coat and small suitcase, and called back as she headed for the front door. "Lock up for me," and was gone.

"Helen, wait!" he shouted, speeding after her and seeing her stepping into her car and starting up, "Helen, wait!"

"I'll see you when I get back," she called, and sped away with her heart hammering in her breast, choking back the unbidden tears, — and as he watched over the widening distance, he ran a frustrated hand down the back of his head.

They journeyed from Arrochar to Alexandria and then onto the Lomond road, heading towards Stirling, and then further on to Grangemouth, across Kincardine Bridge to Crombie and then Rosyth, towards the famous Forth Road Bridge, which started a topic of conversation on films, — one of Jeans' hobbies, "It was filmed in 'The 39 Steps',"

"Who starred in that," Helen enquired.

"Oh, they've done it three times, Robert Donat in the 1930's, Kenneth More in 1959 and lately, Robert Powell."

"I think I saw that one," Helen chuckled, "Robert Powells' eyes are as blue as Duncan's," she mused.

Jean cast her a surreptitious sideways glance, smiling secretly to herself as they finally hit the Queensferry Road, and then entered Edinburgh itself, considering that Helen wasn't as adverse towards Duncan as she made out, "So that's settled," she observed, aloud.

"I think … I'll have my hair cut," Helen threatened. "I've never had short hair."

At this suggestion, Jean was aghast, "Don't you dare!" She warned. "It just needs a little trim on the ends, and that's all."

Helen gave a- soft, tinkling laugh.

They did a 'shop 'til they dropped' scenario, returning to their hotel, laden down with dress boxes, "I hope they all fit into the car," Helen commented.

Saturday evening, they sat in the hotel's cocktail lounge, sipping at Martinis and nibbling at small hors d'oeuvres. "How did you meet Iain?" Helen enquired.

"I was a nurse on the rescue helicopter, the one that came out for Duncan's father, we air lifted him off the Crag and back onto the flat, Iain was waiting, but it was too late, he pronounced him dead — a broken neck. The ironical thing was … that the rescued sheep was prancing all around us. Rory was so upset, that he took aim and shot the animal dead on the spot. The Lady Eleanor had to be told the news — Iain asked me to do the telling. She didn't want her husband's body taken away from the village, and so we took him home, and then had to wait a day for the autopsy to take place, and the Lady Eleanor asked me to stay with her until Duncan arrived, — we worked so well together, that after the funeral, Iain asked me to stay — I suppose, I seemed stable — it met with approval."

"And Duncan; how was he?"

"He was collectively calm — the women of the village went to the castle to lay out his father's body, he watched every single detail, — the embalming, the dressing with kilt was a- meticulous operation, and I think he cried on that day. He deserves to be loved Helen, but he just isn't, Alex Craig is a bitter pill to swallow."

"But, it's his choice to swallow it, and I think their well suited, neither of them are exactly, 'love's young dream,'" she remarked, a trifle sharply, and then regretted, she softly, remorsefully, apologised, ascertaining, "I'm sorry, but I stand by my original opinion, — he's so smug, boorish, self-righteous; he has the makings of a control freak."

"I suppose that comes under the heading of 'dull and pompous'," Jean underlined. "He's just a young man, Helen, he makes mistakes."

"I don't know *why*… we're even discussing him."

"You started the conversation," Jean indignantly reminded her. "And he's obviously made an impression on you, or you wouldn't be talking about him."

"It's just a woman's curiosity," she mused. "I can't help wondering what makes him tick. — He's eight years older than me, practically the next generation."

Jean gave a soft, mirthful laugh, "Only almost, you're obviously not kindred sprits."

Helen chuckled, "The only spirit hanging around is Mairie Campbell's, and she's blighting me."

Jean glanced around the room, "Here comes the bell-hop, I wonder what he wants?"

The following day they journeyed home, leisurely stopping at various villages en-route and taking in the breathtaking scenery. — The weekend had been a refreshing change for them both, but still had not allayed Helen's physical discomfort. — By the time they had reached Arrochar, she knew, without a doubt, that her visit to The Loch House could not be postponed any further, but how to find a reason, the courage to go, without misguiding Duncan with her actions. — She dropped Jean on the doorstep of Talbert and then drove down Bracken Lane. — The phone rang as she entered the cottage, she tentatively lifted the receiver, it was Rory, and his first words were rather inane, to say the least, "You're home at last."

"I've just arrived, is something wrong?" she frowned.

"Can you come up to the castle?" he asked.

For some reason, she felt wary, "Are you alone?"

"Except for my father, — there's something that I want you to see."

"What is it?" she asked, hedging, "Can't it wait until the morning?"

"It's a surprise; you have to come now."

"Ten minutes," she said.

"I'll be waitin'," and then he rang off.

Rory's surprise was the answer to a maiden's prayer, the relief that flooded through her, would have filled the loch; they spent the evening in the Lounge Bar of the Arms Hotel, in celebration.

Chapter 14

Joy and Splendour

Monday morning arrived with Hannah enthusiastically greeting her, and needing to admire her new purchases. "It's becoming a question of ... what shall I wear today, Hannah? My wardrobe is groaning at the seams. I've gone from three garments to owning a shop-full," she softly laughed.

"Wear your new trouser suit; — the navy-blue one and wear your hair down, it's more casual. — I've placed some pretty ribbon in the drawer; you may like to use it, it will match your outfit. — Now, I must go, or I will be late for work," she paused, turning at the door before leaving, calling back, "Remember the Campbell slogan ... be mindful, lass."

Helen nodded, understanding.

She took her time, enjoying an exhilarating shower, stretching her limbs and opening her mouth to devour the soft mountain stream water. Her skin felt silky, soft to touch, and her hair had increased in volume, having benefited from its treatment in Edinburgh.

Donning a towelling robe, she descended downstairs for a coffee before dressing, knowing that she was just delaying an agonising task.

She dressed slowly, in a snowy white crepe blouse with billowy Bishops sleeves, navy trousers and a little waistcoat made in the Cawdor Campbell plaid. Her shoes were red, low heeled, and comfortable for walking. Being still warm, she decided to carry her jacket; she discarded thoughts of a bag.

It was a twenty-minute stroll through the village to The Loch House, a journey, which she elongated by dropping into the Farriers for a chat with Scottie the Blacksmith, and to pet the horses and trekking ponies, which had been stabled there to rest after a long summer of being hired to the tourists. Many people cheerily called out and waved to her on her journey. — Mr Monroe, the butcher, young Callum, a very talented trumpeter from the Youth Club came riding by on his bicycle, and Deidre, the Widow

Calhoun, passing by, gave her an affectionate gleeful bear hug. — But eventually, the entrance to the beech-tree lined drive appeared, and if the pain of apprehension had ever tormented anyone, it did Helen Campbell at that very moment.

Nervously, she entered the drive, gazing above and about her, at the rustling bronze and yellows of the autumn shaded leaves, and despite her discomfort, was charmed and refreshed as she inhaled the balmy smell of mossy undergrowth. — A slight breeze suddenly evidenced itself, cooling and drying the glistening moisture on her nose. — All was silent, other than the musical songbirds calling; the sound of lapping water at the loch's edge, enhancing the beauty that she behoved.

She switched her slung jacket from one shoulder to the other, slid her spare hand into her trouser pocket, stopped again to admire the purple mountainous backdrop and then she was there. — Sighing, she raised and cast studious eyes across the white painted irregularities of the stalwart, wooden and granite stone structure, and the spreading proportions of the building, rambling with quintessential 'old-world-charm'. The old mill wheel sat silent now, lying dormant as the water had long ago ceased its driving flood, she sighed with pleasure; it seemed unbelievable that only a few short years ago, these same buildings had been a shambling ruin, and remembered that Rory and she had clambered about them, — had swum in the loch, not heeding the warnings of their elders until she had fallen and cut her knee. She had cried bitterly while her gran had bathed the wound, but not so much from pain, but from the chastisement they had each received.

Hannah suddenly appeared on the front, dusting down the doorstep, she was obviously startled, "Och! I didn't expect to see you, lass," she said, seeming surprised. "You never mentioned."

"Oh, I just thought I'd take a walk on such a lovely morning," she casually remarked and sighed, her heart was welling over with happiness. "Is the Laird about, Hannah, I need to see him."

"Nay Lass, he's gone up to Top Farm and will be away all day. — Old Brooks still has the after effects of influenza; he took it very bad. — There's a problem with some cattle to be dealt with, — I think it's a vet's job, but come in; I'll make you a cup of coffee, I daresay it will be welcome, after your morning exercise."

Helen appeared disappointed, but her expression was short lived.

"There seems to be an epidemic of influenza," Helen remarked, as she followed the housekeeper into the house, giving out an unexpected soft gasp of pleasure at the unfamiliar surroundings.

"Iain's been very busy these last few days, giving inoculations. I've had mine, the Lairds had his, and you must have yours."

"I feel well enough," she murmured.

"Sit you down," Hannah invited, taking her jacket from her.

"I don't think I want to sit down," she said, gazing about her with pleasure. "And I think I'm glad that the Laird isn't here, I'd be accused of being nosy or some such thing," she chuckled. "It's so wonderful and so tasteful, a little masculine perhaps; — it needs a woman's touch."

And smiling with pleasure, her sparkling eyes followed natural lines, starting with the upper gallery of the room, trailing down the oak-wood stairs, and then returning to the gallery, encircling the enormous light, airy room and forming the upper story of the house. — With its beamed ceiling and accessories, it reminded her of a hunting lodge.

The walls were of simply exposed, reddish-brown brick. The floor, composed of highly polished parquet, was scattered with large, heavily piled sheepskin rugs. — The deeply buttoned comfortable, black-hide chesterfield couches, were placed either side of the fireplace, which had a heavy tapering stove of hammered copper, and displayed a shine which evidenced Hannah's caring attention.

As she cast her eyes even further, they glanced off expensive elm furniture and came to rest, staring at the far end of the room, which was on a slightly higher level. — She sucked in her breath, as the midday sun streamed through a complete wall of window, richly hung with drapes of cream, now drawn completely back, so as to allow breathtaking views of the loch and purple mountains beyond. — The expanse of water was clearer now, with yachts gliding peacefully and silently in the distance. — But the most pleasant surprise of them all, directly before the window, stood a white 'Steinway' grand piano."

She heard the housekeeper return with her drink, "I didn't know that the Laird played, Hannah," she remarked, sounding surprised.

"I didn't either, lass, but there you are." came the dour reply. "And if you keep turning around like that, ye'll get giddy."

She gave a soft laugh as Hannah watched her for a moment, strolling across to the window, where she stood to gaze out in awed wonderment, at the spreading view.

From where they were motivated, Helen couldn't tell, but she again gasped in awe as the great windows began to slowly push outwards. — She followed them onto the granite verandah, and gazed thoughtfully at the scene for inspiration, "There simply *must* be a piece of music to fit this," she called.

"If there is, no doubt yeel think of it," Hannah replied, smiling and noting the girl's heightened colouring, and a certain effervescence and excitement that seemed to be exuding from her, it was infectious.

"Joy and Splendour," Helen murmured, measuring her mood, suddenly snapping her fingers. "There couldn't be anything else."

Moving to the low backed stool, she sat at first sideways and tested the piano chords picking out a melody — it was concert pitch. — The whole piece then flooded into her head, and shifting her position, began to play, softly at first, a Rachmaninov Concerto, "Come on strings," she whispered, "… do your best," — Love drove her, as the piano pounded and the great reverberating, crashing, crescendo's rose and fell. — She smiled as the melody elated and exhilarated her whole being, flooding the notes from her skilful fingers. — Faster and faster, — softer and softer now she played, until the two final softest chords brought the piece to a peaceful end, and she rested, heart thudding from adrenaline — silence reigned.

Suddenly, a small, almost indiscernible air sound reached her ears, and a sensation of nearness, irked her, she moved her head slightly, listening to the silence.

"Hannah?" she cautiously called, and suddenly, shrieked, gasping, startled, as a male voice answered,

"Hannah's in the kitchen, — she can't hear you."

With heart pounding, she turned to face him; — he was dressed casually in a pristine white cotton shirt with the sleeves rolled up, revealing muscular tanned arms, and the front open, revealing an equally tanned muscular chest, as if he had hastily pulled the shirt on, and had tucked it into his closely fitting blue-denim jeans. — His blue-tinged, raven-black hair glistened damply; — he looked and smelt freshly showered. "Duncan … you frightened me," she accused, while holding her hand to her thumping breast. "Hannah said that you weren't here."

"I followed you up the driveway."

"I don't think so, my Lord, you look rather wet and it isn't raining," she murmured, under his scrutinising blue gaze. He crossed the room to join her and leant on the piano as she continued tinkling at the keys while they spoke.

He merely grinned in a lopsided way, "To what … do I owe the pleasure of this visit? — You aren't going to tell me that you've seen the error of your ways in your absence, and have come to apologise, or — has Jean advised you accordingly."

"I hate to dissolution you, my Lord, but why should we waste a perfectly pleasant shopping spree, talking about such trivial matters," she replied, with certainty. "I want to make it perfectly plain, that I'm not bending to your will, I'm just a person of my word. But my enforced, condescending mission this morning, is to thank you for returning Mairie's portrait to the gallery."

He nodded in acknowledgement, and then changed the subject, he stiltedly asked, "Helen … have you ever been in love?"

"That's a very impertinent question, and a very nosy one," she replied, but answered, "I suffered all the schoolgirl agonies about the boys in the school next door to mine; — I would have much preferred to have attended a mixed school, instead of a ladies seminary, — I've had my admirers. — Does that answer your question?" she smiled.

He returned her smile and then sighed, relaxing, casually he revealed, — "Hannah's preparing some lunch for us."

At this revelation, Helen chuckled, "You were expecting me, another one of your dark, manipulative plots into which I have fallen, — I might have known."

"I don't like being at loggerheads with my guests," he admitted. "I thought that if I put the portrait back, — you might think more kindly towards me."

Helen nodded, "Then, I shall graciously accept your olive branch, and … I would love to share lunch with you, providing … you behave yourself."

"You ask impossible things, is this, misbehaving?" he replied, as he leant towards her with one hand resting on the piano, and the other resting on the back of the stool, upon which she was sitting, and, instead of averting her head, she shyly raised her lips to receive a light, soft kiss, — she quivered, as he temptingly lingered, studying her with misty, questioning eyes, but for a moment in time. — Her breath quickened, her own questioning eyes searched his face, "Welcome to The Loch House … Miss Campbell," he said softly.

She gazed up at him, softly, apologetically appealing, "Duncan. …?" she murmured, "I … I didn't mean …,

"I know." He grinned, whimsically replying, "I'm glad that the history of the MacFarlane's has such a dynamic effect. — It was *very* impressive. I must file it for future reference."

Helen's face turned an all-telling crimson, which didn't pass Duncan's notice, he diversified. "We can sit on the verandah, but ye'll have to suffer the midges."

Despite the fact that she had cautioned him, she felt disappointed that he didn't further the kiss, possibly a risk that he chose not to take. "Insect repellent," Helen suggested.

"This calls for a celebration," he said, strolling towards the sideboard and snatching up a bottle of Champagne.

"Oh, it's a little early for Champagne," she remarked, fearing a repercussion.

"Nonsense," he replied, "… it's almost twelve thirty, and it goes down well with the oysters."

"That's a trick I've never mastered," she chuckled, as they strolled out onto the verandah where they seated themselves around the patio suite.

"I'll show you, — you have to hold your head well back and let the oyster slide down your throat — it's easy, — like this," he demonstrated.

Helen grimaced, balking at the idea, "I think I'll save this until later," she said evasively. "I'll just make do with Champagne … Loch Sloy, my Lord!"

Duncan raised an impressed eyebrow, acknowledging, "You're learning, we'll make a Highlander of you yet."

They paused in their conversation when Hannah bustled into sight, pushing a trolley laden with mixed salads, and waited until she had finished laying the table.

"This looks delicious," Helen commented. "I think I'll have to steal you away from the Laird and take you back to London with me, — in my suitcase."

"I'd fair no better than your grandmother, lass," she replied, casting Duncan an affectionate, motherly smile which displayed her obvious pleasure at being able to spoil him. — To Hannah, there was none to equal the Laird, she had an honest loyalty towards the MacFarlanes, but it crossed Helen's mind that she would find Alex something of an interloper when she married Duncan. — This thought led to further speculation, — would Alex be contented to live in The Loch House? It somehow didn't seem her style. — Hannah said before she departed, "Bon appetite."

They ate their lunch, savouring and discussing every one of the delicacies, and when finished, "I didn't know that you played," she said, referring to the piano.

"You didn't ask," he laconically replied, continuing with a change of topic, "Helen, I wanted to discuss something with you."

"And what could that be, I wonder?"

He lazily relaxed back into his chair, while he thoughtfully raked her appearance for a moment, and then reached for his pipe lying in the onyx ashtray; — she smiled as she watched, fascinated, as he began his methodical preparation to smoke it, "I suppose, I shouldn't do this while you're around."

"Do what?" she questioned.

"Smoke, I was told that you suffered from chesty complaints, pneumonia wasn't it?" he shook out the burning match, the smell of sulphur and Virginia tobacco wafted into the atmosphere.

Helen sighed, and tutted in exasperated annoyance, "Oh…my mother… she exaggerates everything to suit herself. — I caught a heavy cold, because I was run down after my father died, it resulted in a cough, and because she was anxious to be away on holiday in Switzerland, and so as not to change her plans, and so as not be encumbered by a sick child, and to protect her own health, she placed me in a Swiss Clinic, while she swanned-off to do her thing. — My father was my best parent, and as you might have gleaned, I left home at the age of eighteen, and went to live in France while I studied, but I couldn't settle. I felt irritated and out of reach of something … I don't know what, — now, what is it that you want to ask, because I have a shrewd idea, that it's a renewal of your former request, for me to chronicle the history of the MacFarlanes?"

"How did you guess?"

She shook her head and chuckled, raising her eyes; "I don't know *how* this village has ever managed without me."

"I don't want it to manage without you, I want to make you feel indispensable," he replied. "Alex, couldn't do these things, she wouldn't know where to begin."

"There *is* no indispensable man," she said firmly. "And, was that a comparison or a compliment?" she enquired. "Enlighten me."

"I wish that you would tell your editor, that there is no indispensable man."

"Touché," she called.

Duncan merely grinned in acknowledgement and continued, "So far, we've only dabbled in the tourist trade, I want to open a complete Tourist Centre, we need advertising material in the shape of maps, books, pamphlets and of course, your skilled publicity techniques. — You can set this up for me, using your prowess with your newspaper, for obtaining single page spreads to launch the scheme in the New Year."

Helen thought for a moment, considering the latter part of his explanation. To write the brochures, she would need to know all the information which was locked up inside his head, which would mean spending a lot of time with him. The deadline for the newspaper spread presented no problem; that could be done for the right fee; — her industrious mind ran on, they would need a photographer to photograph all the places of main interest, and plenty of knowledgeable guides. — And if they introduced winter sporting, they would need experienced instructors, she sighed suddenly, and sipped at her Champagne, conscious now of Duncan's expectant, waiting gaze, "I'll think about it," she said.

He condescended, "I'll give you until the weekend; when I hope that you're free. — My parents will be paying me a visit, and I know that my mother in particular, is anxious to meet you," he informed her.

"I haven't got anything planned."

Having reached this quiescence, she sighed and turned her head to absorb the idyllic view, she opened her mouth to comment, when suddenly, simultaneously, the door bell rang, followed by a scrunching squeal of brakes, announcing Rory's pending arrival, to take Hannah back into the village. — The housekeeper duly answered the demanding door chimes, and Alex swept in, immediately filling the air with her expensive heady perfume and the room with her evocative presence. — Her cream velvet trouser suit fitted her to absolute perfection, setting off the contours of her sensuous figure; — her black brimmed trilby, she had set at a rakish angle over one eye, and she oozed with her usual confidence. — Casting Helen a raking stare, deliberately making her feel awkward and embarrassed, she nodded a silent acknowledgement, and then as if dismissing her, she lithely moved across the room to Duncan, whose greeting was nothing but cool. The relaxed atmosphere immediately became charged with tension.

I came earlier," she said, caustically accusing. "Hannah told me that you were away all day, — a slight exaggeration, I would suspect."

"We were just about to have coffee, Alex; would you care to join us?"

With her usual poise, she ignored his question and kissed his cheek as she replied, "Darling, we're expecting you for dinner this evening, that awful Mrs Murray is leaving tomorrow for London and she's invited father to her home, on a return visit. — I can't imagine why he would want to go when he has me here, but there you are. ... I shall be a permanent fixture before very long and taken very much for granted, — just as Aunt Alicia was — a mere pattern on the wallpaper." she sighed in a resigned way, it was obvious that she was going to stay — she was creating a territorial atmosphere, which made Helen feel very much in the way.

"I ... err ... I think, I had better go, Duncan, I have some shopping to do in the village."

He didn't get a chance to reply as Alex answered, "That's very diplomatic of you, Helen. — I have some private business to discuss with Duncan," she glanced affectionately at the Laird whose expression was one of granite. "You don't mind ... *do* you, darling?" she glanced towards the open window at the view, saying acidly, "I hope ... I haven't interrupted anything; it seems that you were having a nice little tete a' tete."

"Just a little business lunch," Helen murmured, feeling suffocatingly uncomfortable, and rather than worsen the situation, she said a little sharply, "Duncan, I really do have some shopping to do, I can cadge a lift with Rory. Would you fetch my jacket for me ... please?" she earnestly entreated.

He hesitated, seeming reluctant to leave, "Please, Duncan," she implored again, and without a murmur, just a sigh, he left the two women alone.

"This is so good of you, Helen; I knew that you would understand. Duncan and I have plenty to catch up on, but it sometimes feels as though I've never been away, — we just slipped into old shoes." She sighed affectedly again, followed by some almost inaudible murmured words of annoyance, "So much *wasted* time."

Helen frowned, remarking suspiciously, "I find it very hard to understand just why — you would give up your career in order to settle down and have children."

"Seeing ... is, believing," Alex sharply replied. "Duncan is tired of waiting — he's madly keen to get his hands on Craigiemhor Farm, — my father has adamantly refused to sell, and he has said, — that the only way he will get Craigiemhor is to marry me — there's no alternative. — Of course, I shall also bring an extensive dowry; — it will help with the running of the estates."

Helen appeared quizzically thoughtful at this aspect, "I hadn't noticed that the village was lacking in funds, more lacking in heart, drive and enthusiasm ...."

"Mairie Campbells' relations were left-over from the Highland clearances," she superciliously bitched. "What could she afford?"

"She was a woman of the earth!" came, the defensive sharp reply.

At this remark, Alex reared up, snorting spitefully, saying, "I didn't expect some little *chit* from London to be taking me on."

"I was born in Edinburgh, Miss Craig. It just happened to be a misfortune that my young life was spent mostly in the South. You have deserted, and now wish to ... reinstate, yourself." she suggested. — Helen glanced past Alex's shoulder to see Duncan mercifully descending the stairs, with her

160

jacket over his arm and a box in his hand. "Then, I wish you luck," she said in finality, watching as her adversary wandered onto the verandah.

Duncan approached, saying, "I said that I would keep Mairie's jewellery box, until you were here to receive it, Helen, this is what I was instructed to do."

Helen smiled warmly as she received the box, knowing what it contained, just a collection of costume jewellery, which she had played with as a child.

She smiled affectionately, "I shall look forward to renewing my acquaintance with this." And while lightly holding his arm, a current ran through them as she leant forward and kissed his cheek, he responded, briefly pressing his lips onto her own soft cheek, closely, momentarily, catching his eye as she slowly pulled away, a private, intimate, hesitant glance that spoke volumes, — communal minds were at work, she whispered, "thank you, my Lord."

"Hannah and Rory are waiting; — I'll walk with you, to the car."

"Goodbye, Alex," she called, but the actress ignored her.

"I wish you would stay," Duncan anxiously said, as he accompanied her outside.

"I think that The Loch House is just a trifle overcrowded, my Lord."

He bent to open the passenger door of Rory's car, and again anxiously waited while she stepped in, "Consider what I have said, — won't you, Helen?"

She smiled and nodded, "I try never to break a promise."

"It's necessary to make a start before the snows," he informed her.

"Goodbye," she called. "And thanks for this," she said positively, referring to the jewellery box.

"Until the weekend, it will be a small informal party in the evening."

She nodded as Rory leaned forward to start the car, and Duncan closed the door. — He waited and waved until they had entered the drive, and then disappeared through the open doorway of the house.

She accompanied Hannah into the village, where the housekeeper spotted her friend, Mrs Duniclieff, through the window of the little bakers shop; — she was frantically gesticulating for them to join her, "This must be Helen," she remarked, all agog. "I've been longing to meet you, lass, welcome to the village. — Of course, you won't remember me, but I am the one who runs the village sewing circle, your granny and I went back many years, further back than Mrs McPhee, in fact."

"The quilt circle," she managed to say before …

Hannah bristled, "No-one goes back further than I, Mrs Duniclieff, and if you're going to tell us that Alexandra Craig has ordered monogrammed sheets and pillowcases, then, — I already know."

Helen's newly rejuvenated spirit rapidly plummeted as the conversation continued, there was no chance for intervention.

"Oh, of the very finest quality linen and they're to have the MacFarlane Crest with an entwined A and D — to be ready by the spring, of course, and a matching whitework bedcover. 'Tis a very large one, to fit a modern bed and the lace maker has been commissioned to make the thistle and heather flounces." Mrs Duniclieff, then redirected her conversation, "T'would be a pity were you to miss the wedding, Helen, 'twill be such an extravaganza, and I overheard the baker say that he's been commissioned to make the wedding cake,— four tiers, I understand — isn't that right, Mr MacCready?" she called to the baker, nearby."

"That's right, Mrs Duniclieff, the phone call came from Craigiemhor, not long since."

Mrs Duniclieff's eyes sparkled triumphantly, and puffing out her chest, continued … "You see, you're not always first with the gossip, Mrs McPhee, — now, what have you got to say to that?"

Hannah answered tightly, "That you're very fine at embroidering the truth, Mrs Duniclieff."

The whole village was rife with the latest chapter of events surrounding Duncan and Alex's relationship. — As she jotted further notes into her reporter's book, the words, her own words, seemed to shriek up at her from the page, her joy had been short-lived.

Chapter 15

Mrs Eleanor Graham and the Madison Case

Rory kept Helen busy during the following week with their evening Youth Club sessions, and an exhilarating day sailing on the loch. But in private moments, with The Loch House in the corner of her eye, she thought about Duncan whom she considered was inevitably busy, keeping Alex occupied during her vacation. Interwoven into her thoughts, was the mulling over of his Project idea, the concern here – was that Alex would also inevitably become a diversion. This was something that she wished to avoid at all costs, her run-ins with the actress were distasteful to all concerned, — her one goal in this field was the conference, and she was saving all thoughts and energies of that, —paintings were still on her mind, however, she enquired of Rory, "How did you know that the portrait was Mairie Campbell, it isn't labelled?"

He shrugged, answering, "Just a few days before Mairie died, she summoned my father, she gave him a description of the painting; we found it, and took it to show her, it was very dirty."

"Did she say anything?"

"Only: *'the coast is clear'*."

Duncan was in an irritable, restless mood when his mother, along with her husband, Henry Graham arrived.

Mrs Eleanor Graham, was one of the Edinburgh ladies who frequented Jenner's, the Harrods of the North, she was unquestionably a handsome woman, with coifed, silvering grey hair, and at the age of sixty-five, still had a slender figure, which today was immaculately clad in a suit of the most flattering shade of hyacinth-blue, a colour which complimented her eyes perfectly, and so startlingly resembled those of the Laird.

"I expected Helen to be here," Eleanor admonished; her tone was one of annoyance.

"I hardly ever see Helen, she's always otherwise engaged with Rory Cameron."

"Past custom and practice," she murmured. "Can't you, un-engage her?"

"A fat chance I'd have of doing that, with Alex full of her plans, Helen won't come near me, I'm even afraid that she won't appear this evening."

"Not even the piano tempted her?" she questioned.

"She prefers the Spinet at the surgery, its safer territory," he replied.

Eleanor continued to be annoyed; she spoke firmly, "Duncan, you're *supposed* to be in charge of Mairie Campbells' affairs, why don't you *ring* her?"

"I have been ringing her, — all week, I've been ringing her; I never know where she is."

Eleanor tutted, "In this village, how can anyone ever get lost, in this village? And if that's the case, find you're Ghillie and then you will find Helen, — you're far too soft, Duncan."

"I know someone who I wish would get lost," he murmured.

"Duncan!" Eleanor exclaimed, sounding shocked.

"Och, I didnae mean you."

Eleanor looked thoughtful as she checked her watch, "Now, I think it's high time I called in on James," she said. "With all this talk of weddings in the air, I feel the need to get involved with all the pre-nuptial arrangements, as soon as possible."

Later that same afternoon, Helen swung her car into the driveway of Talbert, she was returning from a flying visit to Paisley on behalf of Jean, a journey that was a matter of forty-five minutes. — She drew up alongside the unfamiliar, ruby-red Mercedes, which heralded a warning that Jean had guests.

Jean saw her arrival through the window, and, followed by her guests, hastened from the lounge into the hallway just as Millie, her maid, answered Helen's demanding ring.

"How exquisitely charming," Eleanor softly exclaimed, when Helen appeared in full view.

Helen felt a distinct rise in glowing colour, tinge her cheeks as she met Duncan's lazy smile, and tried to still her slightly trembling hand, as she reached out to greet, 'The Lady Eleanor MacFarlane'.

"Lady Eleanor," she nodded. "I remember you presented the prizes for the cake making and vegetables competitions, on the village open fete day."

"Not strictly accurate, my dear, a short while before my husband died, I did the cakes, and he did the vegetables, — the annoying fact about judging competitions is that you can never compete in them yourself."

Helen smiled in agreement, "no, I suppose not."

Jean spoke, "I think we'll retire into the lounge, Millie can bring another pot of tea, — you'll stay, Helen."

"Of course, Helen will stay," Eleanor indignantly answered. "I shall be very disappointed if she didn't, after I have come all this way, especially to meet her."

"Where've you been all week? I've been trying to get hold of you." Duncan enquired, arresting her as she went to pass him.

"Enjoying myself, which is exactly what you told me to do?"

"Where have you been today?"

"Paisley," she replied, a trifle annoyed.

"Why Paisley?"

Helen suddenly felt on her mettle, "Is this to be another third degree?" she asked a trifle hotly, and then answered sarcastically, "To see how far it was."

Eleanor tutted and muttered, "No wonder Helen stays away from you, Duncan, and it wasn't so very hard to find her."

With some surprise, Helen glanced back at Duncan and then stared, she felt certain that he'd winked at her; — she drew herself up to her full measure, squeezed her eyes and shook her head in a disgruntled, huffy way.

He merely shrugged, and watched her turn her attention to his mother.

Eleanor patted the cushions on the sofa beside her as an invitation, "Come … sit here beside me, I want to have a good look at you."

Helen obediently did as asked, catching Duncan's derisive glance as she seated herself opposite him, and holding her head thoughtfully to one side, wondered what was going through the canyons of his mind. — Eleanor spoke again as she studied Helens' features, she sighed as if in pleasure, "Your attributes to your grandmother are so clearly defined, and well-captured in Mairie's portrait."

"You pay me a great compliment, Lady MacFarlane," she said. "But it would be difficult, if not impossible to possess equal qualities to those contained in the portrait. — Mairie Campbell's features hold a soft wistfulness, an almost undetectable rapture."

Duncan raised an eyebrow, interjecting, scoffing, "You surprise me, only a romantic would recognise such a quality, not a hard and fast gossip columnist."

"Duncan, you're being very perverse, even the most liberated young females have soft, romantic hearts, whatever their calling."

"A few hours ago, you accused me of being too soft," he grunted.

"Well, I would prefer it, if you would go away and practice on someone else."

"I'm staying," he said, adamantly.

Helen replied, "Please, don't concern yourself on my behalf, Lady MacFarlane, the Laird as extraordinarily old fashioned points of view on the modern woman, — like blades on *ice*, he skates only across the surface."

"If it's only for the sake of *fashion* that a woman hides her intrinsic qualities behind its façade, then she hasn't the right to complain when a man refuses to seek below the surface, — you've made your choice, Helen, and now you must abide by it," he said.

"I have no regrets," she replied, firmly and indignantly defending herself. "But why should you accuse me of failing to recognise finer, deeper feelings?"

"You reports on the Madison Case."

"The Madison case!" she echoed, wide eyed with surprise. "And I *suppose* that you've been discussing this with Alex, and that she's vindicated, Roland Barrett."

"She might have done," he said evasively, veiling his eyes.

Eleanor chipped in, "I've read Helen's reports on the Madison case, and I thought that they displayed a large amount of enterprise, — why, she saved Mr. Madison from being swindled by her exposures."

"I don't think that you could have followed the situation from beginning to end," he remarked, and then glanced towards Helen who considered his current tirade was the result of more piqued pride.

"Then, enlighten us," she invited. "I always welcome *public* opinion, — be my guest." She redirected, "Lady Eleanor," she appealed, "… the Madison wedding was my very first solo assignment …"

Duncan suddenly, caustically spouted, accusing, "But … instead of sticking to a simple report on the ceremony, Helen decided to launch herself into her chosen profession by sowing seeds of doubt into the happy couples' minds."

Helen sighed, her smooth brow creased into a frown, arguing, indignantly denying, "I did *no* such thing."

At which, he raised an arresting hand, ordering, "Don't interrupt, I'm accepting your invitation — with the obvious intention of announcing her arrival as a journalist to the world, and then not content, she periodically hounded the Madisons, hoping to discover a chink in their marriage, and then, gave herself a congratulatory pat on the back, when she thought she had found just that."

Eleanor interrupted again, saying, "Duncan … where is this all leading; Helen only did what she thought was right?"

"Alex has been busy," Helen retorted, feeling fraught with anger. "Please continue Duncan, I want to hear this all-damning evidence, which is an obvious attempt to demoralise and embarrass me in front of your mother."

Eleanor barracked for her, "If it's any consolation, Helen, my son isn't succeeding."

"Then, pray continue, Duncan and I'll help you out," she again invited.

He merely grunted.

Jean joined in by saying, "Tell us yourself, Helen, better it comes from the horse's mouth."

She shrugged, before relating, "Well, Clarissa Madison denied having an association with her former fiancé, Roland Barrett, and Madison had been prepared to accept his wife's word, dismissing my reports as preposterous nonsense …."

"And they were." Duncan injected.

Helen cast him a glowering stare, saying, "Have you no conscience, my Lord?"

His pointing finger flicked up, he grinned as he spoke, "Oops! Never ask a question during an argument, yeel never win."

"Duncan … could you *just* listen?"

"I'm sitting on the very edge of my seat – carry on."

She appeared thoughtful, "Now, where was I before I was so rudely interrupted?"

"Preposterous nonsense." Duncan reminded her, and laughing, suddenly ducked when she launched a folded newspaper at him.

Eleanor demanded, firmly commanding, "Duncan … I would *like* to hear the story."

"So would I," Jean championed. "If our witty noble host would allow us."

Helen stiltedly continued, — but it then came to my ears that Clarissa Madison was pregnant, and that Barrett was openly boasting that he was the father of the child, — another report followed which led Madison to seek a divorce. — Under oath, Clarissa still denied having had an affair and emphatically maintained that the child she was carrying was Madison's. — Barrett also stuck to *his* story, saying that he was willing to marry Clarissa when she was free; — the divorce was granted to Madison." She sighed, continuing; - "And then, after the hearing, Clarissa became inconsolable, and a few days later the trauma seemed to have taken its toll, she had a miscarriage."

Duncan interjected, "And then again, very mysteriously, Barrett left the country."

Helen continued, "Yes, that's correct; — it was after that, that Madison sent me an invitation to a small press gathering. — He said that he had certain statements to make which would interest me, and when I arrived at the Madison mansion, I was as surprised as anyone to find Clarissa happily back in residence, and it was clear that she had resolved her differences with her husband."

"And so the following day, Helen was able to make a report of a very different nature," Jean added. "The Madisons had cancelled their decree."

"Then, I have missed something, I'm longing to hear the end," Eleanor exclaimed, while taking a sip of tea.

"Well, originally, Clarissa had jilted Barrett in favour of Madison, and consequently, Barrett was a very bitter man. — On the evening that I saw them in Claridges, he had met her by pure chance and was in fact pestering her, with little or no result. — Then, the following day, he read my report, which gave him an idea and the ability to reap some revenge. — He had lied about Clarissa and the baby," Helen concluded, "But when she had a miscarriage, his conscience tormented him, and so he went to Madison and confessed. — Madison had him removed by his own methods and then became reconciled with Clarissa."

Eleanor smiled, "A happy ending."

"After a lot of needless suffering and none of it would have occurred, had Miss Campbell kept her court," Duncan concluded, while leaning to tap out his pipe into the burning, crackling fire grate.

Helen, thoughtfully bit on her lips anticipating her next move, — without a doubt Duncan had deliberately shown her in the worst possible light to his mother, — should she vindicate herself, she questioned? — She was well able to do so, but then she thought not, — if this is what she represented to the world, then, along with success goes the consequences, and he must think whatever he will; Alex had done her damned best. Aloud, Helen retorted, "I hope that you're happy with yourself, my Lord."

Eleanor suddenly patted her hand, and Helen turned her serious gaze into a smile which would have warmed the coldest of hearts, "I have my own views, and if that picture I was looking at only half-an-hour since, is anything to go by …,"

Helen commented, "When that portrait was painted, Mairie Campbell was obviously in love, you must agree, there is soft warmth in her eyes, almost as though she was looking at the object of her love."

"Yes, Angus captured her emotion very well; it lies deep within her eyes."

"Angus?" Helen affirmed, with some surprise. "There must have been someone standing behind him."

"It apparently caused quite a stir." Eleanor related, "Mairie told me that Alicia was so jealous of the portrait that Angus had painted of her, that she forced him to paint one of herself, the results you have seen, one very flattering and the other … well … they offended her so much that Alicia had Mairie's picture taken down from the gallery, in order that comparison's could not be made, — it kept the whole village entertained," she chuckled. "I suppose, Duncan, that you've attempted the impossible and re-hung them in order to strike a balance between your two guests."

"I did *no* such thing, and if there are anymore arguments, both pictures will disappear into oblivion, — forever, — do you understand?"

For the following half-hour, the conversation entailed only general chit-chat, mostly between the ladies. — The Laird seemed to be quite content to grumpily absorb himself in the copy of the 'London Daily News', and Helen gratefully acknowledged that it wasn't the copy containing her Highland Recipe article, as she considered that he would only find more cryptic remarks to throw.

As they were all leaving Talbert, Duncan helped his mother into her car, which he was driving. — Helen suspected that he hadn't used his own vehicle, in case it heralded his presence and she turned tail and ran, — she had been cornered, yet again.

"I'll call for you later this evening," he informed her, "… just in case you change your mind."

"I promised," she reminded him.

He raised his hand and disturbingly stroked the satin softness of her cheek with his knuckle, while saying, softly, "I wish you would look upon me, in the same way that Mairie looked upon Angus."

"Well, I'll try to practice," she said, raising a hand also, to remove his disturbing one away, while smiling a farewell. "The only emotion that you arouse in me at the moment, Duncan MacFarlane, is one of *pure* contempt; — it wouldn't look very good on canvas. — I'll see you later, as arranged."

When later came, Helen had dressed herself in a silver grey silken two piece dress, a self-coloured tambour flower motif stretched from the right shoulder to her neat breast. The soft fabric felt cool and luxurious against her skin, as she wrapped the crossover bodice around her, tying it snugly into her trim waist, the gently flaring skirt emphasised her still tanned, well shaped legs. And to complete the pretty picture, she stepped into a pair of strappy grey sandals, which made attractive compliments to her slim ankles. — Thus attired, she dabbed Dior perfume behind her ears and onto her wrists, flicked back her shining nut brown hair behind her shoulders, and considered herself ready for the evening.

Duncan called for her promptly at the allotted time, and barely casting his companion a second glance, he settled her into the Rover's passenger seat beside him and drove in almost complete silence, passing just the scantiest of pleasantries, which surprised her, as she thought that he would be anxious to secure her decision. — It was an awkward journey.

When arriving at The Loch House, there appeared to be no-one else about, "Leave your coat in the library," he said gruffly, indicating towards one of the doors which led off the main room - it was ajar. "I'll make us a drink, and then you can tell me of your decision."

She nodded and moved, passing through the door. — Immediately, a newspaper on the roll top desk caught her attention, she meandered over to absently drape her coat onto the chair. — Upon inspection, the paper proved to be an Edinburgh paper, dated some weeks before, and picking it up, read the headlines; -

'Court Wrangle over Madison Shares'

Roland Barrett, the onetime fiancé of Clarissa Madison, has returned from his enforced exile to face charges of fraud. — He confessed to having made several attempts at obtaining certain shares in Madison Holdings by illegal means. — The shares in question are the property of Clarissa Madison, left to her by her late father.

Barrett has declared that during the course of their courtship, the shares were promised as part of their marriage contract, but owing to the fact that it was Clarissa who had ended their relationship, he felt that the shares should be his by right. — His attempts at blackmail were, — earlier this year,— blown 'sky-high', as his actions were fortuitously misconstrued by the press as a renewal of their friendship.

This revelation gave Madison the incentive to adopt elaborate techniques, whereby he fell foul to numerous gossip column articles, the actions of which, were designed by Madison for the purpose, and were played out by Madison and his wife like practised troupers, right into the divorce courts and beyond.

It was revealed that the Madisons' had gone so far to protect their interests, into faking a pregnancy and an eventual miscarriage…

Madison had been no fool, she had discovered. — He had used the press to his own advantage, and afterwards, when he and Clarissa had called their Press Conference to announce their reconciliation, they had congratulated her for her efficient coverage of their affairs, and thanked her, for she had unwittingly saved Madison from loosing a sizeable portion of his company.

Helen irritatingly tapped the now furled paper into the palm of her hand, just as Duncan suddenly appeared in the open doorway, to see her gaped expression, "You knew," she accused, indignantly, "And you expect me to …,"

"Helen, I can explain …," a soft tap suddenly came on the door. "Damn!" he breathed, both looking up as it opened to see Eleanor Graham pop her head into the room, at what seemed an ill-timed moment.

"Ah, there you are my dears. I hope that you aren't going to discuss business all evening." She smiled as she walked further into the room, very suitably dressed in pale peach silk, — her ensemble had a distinctive forties styling, but softer, more subtly designed than the originals. "You look very beautiful this evening, Helen, your dress looks like one of the latest Versace models, so youthful.

"Thank you, Lady MacFarlane, and, may I return the compliment."

"I hope you will call me Eleanor, Helen, it's so starchy to be formal these days," Helen acknowledged her invitation with a slight incline of her head. "Ah, I see you're discussing your article, — I knew that I had kept it, and found it earlier this evening, *just* to point out the error of Duncan's ways. — He is so like his dear father, puritanical, contentious and difficult at times, but very loveable, all the same," she smiled fondly towards her son, and sighed. "Now, with that settled, I would love one of your Martinis, Duncan."

Chapter 16

Revelations

The evening had humid warmth about it, for mid-October, tempting her out onto the verandah with Jean. "I wonder what has kept Alex," Helen said, curiously, glancing at her watch. "There are very few people to affect an entrance for this evening," she continued, while admiring the darkening shades of the navy-blue sky.

"You're learning," Jean replied. "Alex is a creature of sudden decisions and soon becomes bored with little to do. — She's accompanied her father on his trip to London," she revealed.

"I would have thought that learning her film script would have kept her busy," replied Helen, showing mild surprise.

"She has the added asset of having a photographic memory, and so needs to spend the minimum time studying. — Alex strives for nothing," Jean concluded, with a sigh.

"Lucky Alex," Helen murmured a trifle sarcastically. "Does that also include men?"

Their conversation ended when Eleanor came to join them for a moment, distracting Jean's attention. — Iain Roach and Henry Graham appeared to be in deep conversation about a game of golf, they had shared that afternoon.

The room, so infinitely restful now, with soft wall lighting casting a warm glow over the scene; — the relaxed contentment seemed to be shared by all, except for Duncan who was staring broodily thoughtful, into his brandy glass, he heavily sighed; — her first thought was that he was already missing Alex, but she preferred her second, that he still hadn't received her answer about the Project, it possibly still irked him.

Well, it can irk him for a while longer, she thought, before Eleanor spoke to her, rousing her from her private thoughts.

"Helen, could I ask a small favour?"

She smiled at the older woman, warming to her all over again, for she regarded Eleanor Graham as a gentlewoman of the old school, a rare find in today's modern society of anything goes. — She felt anxious to please, "Anything, if it's within my power," she replied.

"You may refuse this one, my dear," she said, looking a little sceptical.

Helen's brow creased slightly, wondering what could be so difficult to ask, and then the dawning comprehension was clearly shown on her face as Eleanor continued, "Would you play for us, Helen. I would so dearly like to hear what others have enjoyed."

"My pleasure," she replied. "Have you a favourite?"

"You choose," Eleanor smiled. "You know your repertoire, something soothing …," she paused thoughtfully, and then glanced across the room towards her son, "unless … the 'Dark Island?' one of my secret favourites and very romantic."

"For you," she said, laconically addressing Eleanor. — Stepping away from the group, she crossed the room and seated herself at the piano, flexed her trembling fingers and then tinkled out the melody, while watching Duncan move from his seat to cross the room and enter the verandah. — She wondered what his stirring reminiscences were, realising that it must be something so deep, that it made him appear so moodily melancholy; — staring, as he was, so wistful and pensively alone, across the loch, into the impenetrable far reaches of darkness.

He turned towards her, wallowing in the luxury of scrutinising her entrancing face as she began to smoothly play the soft peaceful piece with sway. — Slowly, he walked toward her to lean on the end of the piano, listening to the enrapturing, mellowing tune; his mood had changed, suddenly smiling his endearing smile that always seemed to envelop her, and still her quaking nerves. She returned his smile, as with gentle flowing movements, her hands rose and fell, - he spoke …

"The island of dreams, the island of longing, the island of romance, we all have one tucked away somewhere in our hearts, this is one such island. — No-one tells us where it is, or even if it is on the map – maybe … just in case, it may become *too* crowded," he informed her.

"I think you've just made that up."

"It's so beautiful, so wistful," Jean dreamily remarked, swelling Helen's confidence. "I don't know how you managed to fail your exams."

"I asked her the very same question, but she refused to answer. — Your father knew best, Helen," Duncan said, quietly.

Feeling annoyed that he knew so much of her life, when she knew so little of his, she paused in her task, now able to level her eyes at him, retorting, "Had my father lived, he had enough of the realist in him to acknowledge the changing face of society, and would recognise small social hang ups, like that of earning a living."

"In truth, you protect your career too adamantly, and I would say, that having failed to fulfil your fathers' wishes, you're feeling guilty and have to constantly reassure yourself that he would have placed his blessing on your current lifestyle."

"Goad me if you must," she said, dividing her attention between her persecutor and the resifting of the sheet music, "… but nothing, or no-one will divert me from my ambition of gaining that column," she said, stubbornly.

"I wouldn't be too sure on that score," he replied, straightening to his full height, and then enquired, "Another drink, — you must be thirsty after your *unexpected* performance."

Reeling from his sarcasm, Helen stared after his retreating back, renewing her resolution to stand firm with her decisions, made since arriving in Arrochar.

She then lapsed into a Highland Medley, which included a rendition of 'Mairie's wedding' while Hannah brought forth a small buffet of delicacies.

"An apt piece," Eleanor commented. "Bravo," she called the accolade, laughing with everyone else, as the final chords were played.

"You still haven't given me your answer," Duncan softly urged, as he sat beside her.

"Why should I answer favourably?" she asked. "I might have done the deed in repayment for past disloyalties, but this afternoon, you took your own revenge."

"I deliberately left the paper for you to see," he sighed, a deep sigh.

Helen appeared thoughtful, "I fear, my Lord, that my answer won't be favourable."

"Do you ever immediately say 'yes' to anything," he grumbled.

"I'm not an animal of snap decisions. I say 'yes' more times than I say 'no', but on this occasion, I've reached a compromise."

"Which is?" he asked more eagerly.

"I'll do all the ground work and set up the centre, as you suggested. A lot can be achieved by March, after that you could employ a manager."

He sighed, exasperated, his expression and mood downcast, "Is there nothing, I can do to alter your mind?"

She stopped tinkling at the keys, and turned to meet his eyes, "Tomorrow," she echoed her agreement, softly continuing, assuring, "And Duncan … I

174

will look forward it."

"Then, I'll pour us a drink, I think this calls for a toast," he said lightly, while giving a relieved, satisfied grin.

Jean also felt secretly relieved at seeing Helens' rejuvenated spirits and noticed that Duncan was in a more tolerable mood also, due to the fact, she supposed, that he would now be able to commence with his long term plans for developing Arrochar, and Helens' business contacts would come in very useful to him. — He must have used some shrewd tact, she thought, to have accomplished acquiring her time away from her career, but then, she assumed, he would make anything possible, if he could create a more settling environment for Alex's benefit.

The rest of the evening passed by in pleasant conversation; — it was after midnight when the Grahams decided to retire for the night, and soon after the Roaches made their departure, leaving Duncan and Helen alone. — But oblivious of time, Duncan made more coffee, and they sat beside each other discussing, 'The Project,' as it had become known, — during which Helen informed him of her ideas. — They were good ideas, to which he keenly listened, but she was unaware of the sparkling enthusiasm that she was now exuding. — It was agreed that the furthest, uncharted reaches, they would explore on horseback.

"I don't want you to write anything of a personal nature, until I give you the go ahead, until I've settled my future plans."

"Of course, but I don't know how my derriere will clime to riding," Helen softly laughed. "I haven't ridden a horse, since I was a child."

"It's easy; like falling off a bike and remounting. — Scottie has a small docile mare that you should be able to ride quite easily."

Without realising, they talked on tirelessly into the early hours, it seemed as though the past weeks of unpleasantness had never existed, both content with the others company until Duncan suddenly, reluctantly, looked at his watch and remarked …

I think that I'd better take you home, or you will never be fit to hike the hills on the morrow."

She hadn't argued the toss about driving herself that evening, as it had elongated her time with him, admitting to herself that parting was becoming a sweet sorrow.

Ten minutes later, he walked her to the cottage door; — her low light was on, as was now her custom.

"Goodnight, my Lord," she said, softly hesitant, "I'll see you bright and early."

He leant forward and kissed her lightly on the lips, which she automatically received, this he took to be an invitation, for he moved to tighten the embrace, but she swiftly raised a preventative hand to gently cover his lips, "No complications," she murmured, authoritatively. "Goodnight, my Lord."

"Until the morrow," he replied, sighing, reluctantly hesitant, before he departed and she watched him walk swiftly towards the car, only a shadow in the dark; — she waited until the drone of the engine had faded away into the distance.

With a sigh of her own, she entered the cottage, wandered up to her bedroom, slipped out of her evening clothes and into bed. — For a few hours her dreams were haunting, misty and disturbed, as she wandered on the shores of the Dark Island.

Despite the fact that she'd only had a few hours sleep, Helen awoke early, feeling excited at the new prospects ahead of her and two weeks alone with Duncan, now realising that he had had very little chance to be alone with her. — It seemed that he was always in demand, always surrounded by people wherever he went; — any private life seemed out of the question, but most of all, there was no Alex to intrude.

She had barely finished her breakfast when she heard a car pull up outside, followed by hurried steps on the gravel path, and finally a sharp rap on the door as it opened to admit the subject of her restless thoughts. — He was comfortably and sensibly dressed for their first days outing, wearing an oatmeal coloured jumper with leather shoulder and elbow patches, a maroon cravat at his throat, his well tailored slacks were of tough twill, and his shoes, highly polished, stout, dark tan leather Ghillie brogues. Helen suspected that he dressed similarly when he spent a day, hunting grouse.

He smiled at her, his eyes twinkling mischievously, appraising her, "I've seen you in that outfit before," he remarked, " but it was a trifle muddy."

"You're not precisely accurate," she replied, smiling with him. "On closer inspection, my jeans were beyond repair, and so I replaced them with these," she indicated her mulberry coloured, cord slacks.

"You should have told me, I would have replaced them for you," he said, having the grace to acknowledge a loss.

"Charles doesn't approve of women in jeans, so their passing won't be mourned."

"Up to a point, I'm in agreement with Charles, but I can bow to the fact that it's necessary to dress accordingly. — In fact, I hope that your boots are as sensible, we don't want any re-occurring accidents."

176

Helen laughed softly, "I've opted for walking boots; — flat, sensible, lace-ups," she said, swinging her feet from beneath the table and holding up her legs for an inspection.

Duncan sat on a chair near to her and bade her to lift her legs again, she rested them across his knees, "I'll re-lace them," he said, untying and taking off one shoe, explaining: - "The herringbone show isn't practical, so you do it like this, so that the lace is in a straight line across the shoe, then if you're unfortunate enough to get a foot trapped, then the only thing your rescuer has to do, is to slice through the lace and your foot will slip out of your shoe, - another lesson of the countryside." She watched him deftly retie the laces, enjoying the small cautionary act. "Not too tight?" he enquired, after a few more minutes and then stood up together.

"No, they're fine," she assured him while looking down at her feet, and then raised her head, — green eyes met blue and locked for one passionate, searching, electrifying moment, "My L ..."

But suddenly, the moment was broken as Rory burst into the cottage; — for once they hadn't heard his impending arrival. — Duncan let out a quiet expletive at the intrusion.

"Phew! Just in time," Rory exclaimed, rubbing the back of his hand across his brow.

"In time!" the Laird echoed, curtly surprised. "If you're ever in time for anything, it would be for the first time in your life."

Rory shuffled his feet as he spoke, "I'm sorry, my Lord, but Mrs Brooks rang to remind you, that you and Helen are expected at Top Farm for lunch."

Listening to the exchanges, Helen doubted the servility, it was only surface, — she had seen them together in the Arms Hotel lounge bar one evening, after a game of billiards, testing their strengths in hand-wrestling; — neither knew she had been watching them.

"You may return Mrs Brooks call, and confirm our arrival for noon, and then I expect some work out of you today. Good Morning ... Mr. Cameron," Duncan said firmly, in dismissal.

Hastily, Rory turned on his heel in flight, and was just moving through the doorway when he paused to call back to Helen, with an after-thought, "Don't forget our date, later in the week," he called, cautiously referring to the Youth Club rehearsals.

Helen smiled, waved in acknowledgement, and then caught Duncan glowering down at her; — she shrugged, flippantly remarking, "I lead a very busy life."

"Shall we begin the Project, Helen?" he suggested, grunting with controlled impatience.

For the ensuing two weeks, they enthusiastically worked for long hours together, Duncan relating all the facts, while Helen took down, in note form, all the history which belonged to Arrochar and the MacFarlane family. — They walked or rode on horseback for miles, treading the banks and braes, tirelessly planning the best aspects of the lesser known walks for hikers, considered the placing of public notices, noted the ancient battlefield scenes. — They did everything that would be done by the tourists, loving every minute of the companionship, they now had. — Helen refreshingly glowed, not only with healthy fresh air and exercise, but also from their elongated, lazy stays beside the riverbanks to eat Hannahs' packed lunches.

"I could eat a horse," Helen, once commented.

"I could devour you, Helen Campbell," he replied.

"That's cannibalism," she accused, with a laugh.

"I know," he chuckled, "But at least, I'd know I'd always have you with me, and you wouldn't be escaping to London at every next excuse."

"You would still be complaining, because you couldn't see me," she pointed out.

"I'll see you, as I've always seen you, in my heart."

"You say the nicest of things," she sighed.

"But, I don't just want to see you in my heart; I want to see you, touch you, feel you, smell you and be with you every day, just like this."

"It's a strange place to find a hut," she said, evasively, acknowledging a crumbling building on the opposite bank of the river, in the middle of nowhere.

"It just looks like a hut," he informed her. "It's called a 'Shieling' the shepherds used to take shelter and light their peat fires; — I think more went on out here with the lassies, than ever met the Laird's eye."

"I think, my Lord has eyes in the back of his head," she laughed.

He replied, "I wish I did have eyes in the back of my head, and then I would know what you were doing with Rory Cameron."

She glanced surreptitiously sideways, and with a secretive, mischievous smile, answered, "It's none of your business."

Still not satisfied, they considered the winter sporting possibilities of skiing, curling and ice-skating on the loch, also the possibilities of extending the Arms Hotel, and the introduction of private boarding facilities. — The Agency Centre itself was to be opened in the vacant premise, next door to the Post Office.

At the end of a fortnight, Duncan made the suggestion that they accompany the Grahams on their return journey to Edinburgh, visiting for a few days and making use of the opportunity to call in on Crawford to register the Tourist Centre as a business. Also, they planned to select a printers in readiness for the printing of the brochures and posters, as soon as Helen had them completed in there typewritten format.

Mr Crawford met them at the door, "I see you've found her, Duncan," he said, vigorously shaking his hand and then Helen's.

Helen glanced at Duncan, curiously, "Found me?" she echoed, puzzled, "I wasn't aware that I was ever lost."

"I'll explain, later," Duncan hastily replied.

Mr. Crawford cleared his throat, realising that he may have said the wrong thing, "Yes, — it was quite extraordinary, you both missing each other like that, — but now, matters in hand," he brushed, changing the subject. "I'm glad that you've come together, we can kill two birds with one stone, but before we begin with, the Project matter, I was on the verge of sending you this," he said, while handing Helen a package. "I was instructed to withhold it, until now."

Helen frowned, "Whatever's this?" and when she broke its seal with trembling fingers, revealed, "The missing photographs!" she exclaimed, surprised, and flicking through them while laughing softly, "I think I'll save these 'til later."

Crawford studied her for a moment, privately thinking that Helen looked prettier than she had two months previous, her eyes were glowing with happiness and she had obviously struck up a very good rapport with Duncan, noticing that they were very familiar with one another. But strong news had reached his ears that Duncan had made arrangements to marry his latent love, a Miss Alex Craig, whom had chanced to call in on him, not two months earlier.

With their business completed, they spent a few minutes chatting sociably to the Solicitor, who was pleased that all seemed to be going according to plan. Helen took this golden opportunity to ask, "Mr. Crawford, perhaps you could tell us ... just what it is, that is going according to plan?"

The Solicitor shrugged, "Why, the terms of the *will* ... of course."

"Just ... how was the *will* constructed; was anyone else with you?"

"No-one," he informed. "Mairie Campbell must have felt that the end was nigh in May of this year, Duncan can confirm this. — She called me to attend her, she had the outline plans for the *will* written out on several sheets of paper, each one numbered and dated several months apart, — there were twelve of them, she called two friends from nearby Carrick to bear witness, solely to her signature, only, they have since passed away." Mr. Crawford was apologetic, but could shed no further light on the matter.

"That's very inconvenient of them," Helen facetiously remarked.

Later, while seated in the nearby café, "Duncan, what did Mr. Crawford mean; — Mairie gave him twelve instruction sheets?"

"He didn't say that she gave them to him; I would think that she dictated the content. — She instructed me by word of mouth what I was expected to do and when, also Jean, — the party was to be given in your honour, the music was Mairie's selection, Marjorie Kennedy Frazers' renditions of Hebridian music from the 1920's, they probably held fond memories for her."

Helen chuckled, "She only had a scratchy old phonograph, I heard her playing it once, but she very quickly turned it off when she realised that I was watching her."

Duncan smiled, there was amused laughter in the depths of his eyes, "She loved dancing; — I obliged her once or twice, in private, — there must have been some significance; — she told me that to dance with someone, was one sure way of finding out if you had a rapport with a young lady; I think she was right."

"Rory has two left feet." she revealed, "So, no competition there."

Duncan grunted, "I think we can do without Mr Cameron's input."

The Grahams refused to join them on a midnight walk in the Waverly Gardens, but despite it being chilly, Helen wanted to see the floral clock and Edinburgh Castle floodlit again, before they returned to Arrochar.

"We'll have to install floodlighting in the Castle Drumbrae, next year," she unconsciously, romantically, suggested. "If Edinburgh Castle is any example, the effects will enhance its fairy-tale appearance, no end," she remarked, while familiarly tucking her hand through Duncan's crooked arm. — Automatically, he warmly grasped her fingers with his free hand, his thumb rhythmically caressing the silky surface of her skin, as they strolled on.

"Next year, you will be back in London with Arrochar only a memory," he reminded her. "It seems absurd to work so hard, never to enjoy what has been accomplished."

"Oh, but I shall enjoy it, Duncan, in a small way. I intend to spend my holidays in Arrochar."

He glanced, sideways, "I understood that holidays were a thing of the past with you. Has something happened to change your mind?" he coolly, enquired.

"No, nothing has changed my mind," she denied, "but there are a few scattered occasions when I feel the need of a retreat, and the cottage would be ideal."

"You have it all worked out."

"As near as I can, for now. — My current concern is to settle with Ryder for an extension of my contract, before it runs out next Mon…," her voice trailed away, she bit on her lip in annoyance, realising that she had revealed more than she had intended, but her frail hopes that he hadn't noticed were immediately shattered.

Duncan paused momentarily to look down at her, she could feel his rising anger, "So that's it, you're stalling for time, you led me to believe that your contract was settled for the full period of six months."

With sinking heart, she swiftly replied, "Ryder wouldn't agree, not immediately, he … made certain conditions, I had to settle for the best that he was prepared to offer."

"So, Alex was right," he said bitterly, his mouth now a straight line. "You told lies, Helen."

She frantically shook her head, trying to think of a swift reply, "No, no, I haven't told lies, Duncan, I … I just didn't say."

"That's lying by omission."

"No … it isn't like that," she replied in denial.

"Then, *what* is it like, Helen?" he tersely demanded, lightly gripping her shoulders.

"I don't have to explain myself to you," she replied, hotly evasive. "It's not your problem."

"The conditions of Mairie's Campbell's *will*, *are* my problem," he said, releasing her. And then turning away, ran his hand down the back of his rippling hair in sheer frustration.

"You behave as if you own me, Duncan. A few meaningless kisses and few soft words …,"

"Is that all it means to you," he snapped, gruffly complaining. "You won't even let me kiss you, not properly anyway, — a peck here and a peck there, but your mightily content to lay your head on my shoulder while we're dancing, and allow me to stroke your hair; — you blow hot and cold; what are you afraid of, or do you have an aversion to *men*?"

"That's a gross exaggeration, and that's a stupid question; the desire to kiss someone has to be both ways; we're just friends," she hastily underlined, once again, struggling for words, "… put into the position of carrying out the final wishes of a dear departed lady. — Ryder only requires articles in return for my time in Arrochar, and I have already managed to provide him with a few. — With Alex's Press Conference and the holiday advertising campaign, I think he must feel obliged to renew my contract."

"For how long will Ryder be prepared to accept your rather tame womens' page articles, and our advertising features, I fear he will find rather dry? — Ryder is a businessman, paying you high fees for which he will eventually demand a satisfactory return. — Without a doubt, he's waiting for the outcome of Alex's conference, before committing himself to an extension of your contract, and the contents of *that* article aren't going to be very *awe inspiring*, - are they, Helen?"

Ryder was unaware of the identity of Alex's fiancée, and even if he knew, he was no threat to her cover, but then, that situation would expose Duncan to ridicule and scorn, something which she wasn't prepared to allow, the idea somehow, left a sour taste in her mouth. — For the latter part of his remark, he was so near to the truth, and too near for comfort, but how to answer him, she wondered.

"I … if you're correct in your assumptions, then it would seem that I have no alternative, but to make the most of Alex's Press Conference by producing the kind of article that would clinch the deal."

"No!" he snapped firmly. "To publicise the film is the sole purpose of the conference; — you will *not* sink your poisonous reporter's pen into Alex, is that clear, Helen? — and if you feel the need of using your blood ridden tactics in which to buy time, then …"

"Then … then what?" Helen demanded, stubbornly.

"Then … I shall have no alternative, but to insist that you remain in Arrochar without the stability of a contract."

Helen then panicked, "Duncan, I …,"

"That's my final word; — the subject is closed, Helen," he said, putting up an arresting hand, finally cutting the conversation.

She stared after him as he walked on alone for a few paces, then he paused long enough for her to catch up with him; — she grasped his outstretched hand. Subject closed, she thought miserably as they strolled on, the subject won't be closed to Ryder, he expects power packed articles for his Gossip Column, she reiterated, and nothing less. 'I'm sorry, Duncan,' she silently apologised to the man at her side. 'I can't throw away my career, not even for you, but at least Mairie Campbells' last wishes will be fulfilled.

He had left her with a curt goodnight, before she ascended to the dormitory rooms in the roof of the house, while he disappeared into the dining room, without an invitation to join him, there to brood alone over a last brandy, before retiring. — This act had left her feeling frustrated and needful of bending to his will, — he had such a way with him, and she had piqued his pride, yet again, but this fact, she brushed aside.

The following morning, still feeling weary after her turbulent nights sleep, Helen rose early making a firm resolution to be bright and sparkling at breakfast, by carefully applying her make-up, in an effort to conceal any tell-tale shadows under her eyes, but Eleanor's keen eye penetrated her mask. "Did you sleep well? Helen deere; you still look a little tired. I hope that Duncan isn't working you too hard, — not enough beauty sleep." she suggested.

False colour tinged Helens' pale cheeks when Duncan entered the dining room, having overheard his mother's remark; he spoke irritably, almost growling in his agitation, "Helen is a liberated female, mother," he reminded her. "Your sympathies are wasted on her, she doesn't appreciate the old traditions of consideration from the opposite sex; — she is well able to conduct a *jam* session, 'til dawn."

"You weren't doing so badly, yourself," Helen reiterated. "You cut quite a rug with Molly Henderson."

"Molly Henderson doesn't have your stubborn disposition, — and thank goodness that Peter Dundas has left town."

"Duncan … if you are so disillusioned with me, then *don't* come knocking on my door."

Eleanor appeared quite amused at their exchanging retorts.

"Lady Eleanor, I appeal to you ..."

"You're doing quite well, Helen, you don't need a champion."

Helens' resolutions of being bright were fast fading, Duncan in a bad mood wasn't entirely new to her, but if he intended being boorish this morning, then she would ignore him, she decided, but his morose mood continued to dog him throughout the day.

En-route to Arrochar, Duncan's black mood lifted enough to at least resume a slightly business-like relationship, and so it was arranged that Helen should start work on the typing of the brochures, using the office in The Loch House.

Monday morning, being a glutton for work, she presented herself at an early hour, knowing that Duncan kept similar hours. — However, upon her arrival at The Loch House, she stared in dismay to see the silver Cadillac parked in the drive. — So Alex has returned, she thought, and as Alex was known to dislike early morning rising, this was out of character; — Duncan obviously had a breakfast visitor. — Unprepared to face the reality of seeing him so soon in Alex's company, and knowing that her presence would only be an embarrassing intrusion between the lovers, — miserably, Helen acknowledged that Duncan would now be, otherwise engaged.

Sighing dejectedly, she slowly turned the car and drove back down the drive. With heart aching, and mind tormented, she drove blindly on, blaming her own stupidity for having allowed herself the luxury of deeper feelings. — Why did I have to fall in love, where there can only be heartache, — she asked herself, — for now I am committed to making a study of Duncan's intimate relationship with Alex?. — I should have been stronger, — she reproved, murmuring aloud to some passing wild goats, and honking her horn in agitation, when a small flock of sheep annoyingly roamed across the road in front of her.

Nearly an hour later, she turned along the coast road, following the road signs which led into Oban, a popular tourist town, briefly stopping for a time to admire the tiny harbour and colourful yachts and fishing smacks moored along the sea wall. — The water appeared calm and peaceful, even though the day was cold; it tempted her into taking a ferry crossing over to Mull and Iona where she was able to wander about at leisure, content to be alone, pretending that she was unconcerned about Duncan and Alex. — She even allowed herself to wonder if the latter was the Island from whence Alex's grandfather had found his second bride, anything was possible. — She sighed, trying to shift the pain that had settled within the boundaries of her heart. — Aimlessly, she walked along the seashore, with her hands thrust deeply into her coat pockets, kicking at the white sand, oblivious of the scenery and feeling no interest in exploring the Priory which the island boasted. — Oblivious also, as to the time, giving no consideration to the fact that her absence could cause concern; she loitered for hours, delaying her return to the mainland.

Dark was descending when she finally drove into Bracken Lane. — A terrible, foreboding, crashing reality, smote her at the sight of the Rover parked outside the cottage gate, and beyond it, stood Rory's car. — With sinking heart, she parked her Mini, trembling with the knowledge that Duncan was going to be furious with her, for suddenly changing their arrangements without telling him, but bracing herself for the inimical outcome, she decided that she didn't really care.

Lifting the door latch, she swallowed, immediately greeted by his menacing, icy stare, his jaw set granite, ridged in anger; — he was propped, legs crossed, against the dining table, with his arms folded across his waist, his size engulfing the room, momentarily swaying her confidence. — Rory rose from his seat at the table behind the Laird to cross the room, and as he met her at the door, he patted her shoulder in passing, silent reassurance, leaving through the still open door, closing it softly behind him.

The tension between the two was electric, — nervously, Helen plucked up the courage to speak, "Good evening," she said, as firmly as she could.

"It isn't a- good evening, Helen," he replied, between stiffened lips, "Where in damnation have you been all day?"

She walked further into the room, slipping off her coat, avoiding his accusing expression, "I … I went to the islands," was her stammered reply.

"Alone!" he bellowed angrily. "I would have taken you, had you taken the trouble to ask."

With a show of controlled impatience, she kept her voice infuriatingly low, replying, "Duncan, I'm sorry if I've been the cause of any concern, but your company wasn't required to …" she didn't finish her sentence before he butted in.

"Do you realise, Helen that we've had half the population of Arrochar out looking for you? Rory saw you take the mountain road out of the village, and as you failed to turn up at The Loch House as arranged this morning, what were we to think? There are plenty of dangerous crags in the mountains; — you could have fallen over any one of them."

She stood in front of him like a disobedient child with shifting feet, head bowed, sickened at the trouble she had unwittingly caused. — But the aching pain of remembering why she had left the village was still in her mind. "No, I didn't realise," she answered, shaking her head, her eyes bright with the anger that threatened, suppressed only by the knowledge that his anger was caused by a misplaced responsibility, "Duncan, again, I apologise, I had no intention, or any idea that my movements could cause so much trouble."

"He suddenly changed the subject, still angry, his tone still terse, "Did you learn anything about the islands?"

She looked surprised, "Well, no, no, I didn't, but we did pass Lismore."

"Then, why did you go?"

"I … just … fancied a boat trip."

"A boat trip?" he echoed, "… a boat trip in the middle of all of our plans."

Really angry now at his insistent impertinence, she drew herself up to her full height, tossing her hair, balling her hands into small fists at her sides; — she levelled eyes which flashed, from amber to green, and keeping her voice low, breathed the emphatic words, "Duncan, I'm tired of this constant battle; **You** ... are *not* my keeper." She moved towards the kitchen, and not having eaten all day, the pangs of hunger were gnawing at her stomach, — her tormentor followed and overtook.

"I'm responsible for you."

"Then ... I relinquish you of all your responsibilities."

As she went to pass him, he snapped a hold on her upper arm, his biting fingers bruising and pinching her soft flesh, "I'll expect to see you at The Loch House, on the morrow," he ordered.

Her eyes blazed, she trembled with rage, her voice rasped as she emphatically replied, "Don't ... *touch* me, Duncan, I don't know where your hands have been, or for that matter ... anything else ... I *am not* coming."

He stared at her meaningful expression for a moment, then roughly releasing her arm, he straightened and strode to the door, "Goodnight, Helen," he said firmly, while wrenching it open, leaving without a backward glance and slamming the door shut behind him.

For a moment, she stood staring at the closed door, listening to the opening and the slammed closing of the Rover's door, hearing the angry roar of the engine as it spurted into life, followed by the skidding turn into the High Street, until it faded into the distance. — And finally, still feeling the bruising pressure left by his hand, not bothering to eat, Helen wearily climbed her stairs, numb now at the violent change once more, in her relationship with the Laird.

For a while, she lay fully clothed on her bed until a light sleep overtook her. — Awaking in the early hours, cold and with a dull thudding headache, she undressed, slipped into her night-clothes, buttoned herself into a rose pink satin quilted housecoat and then made her way downstairs. — Presently, with a hot milky drink, a sandwich and an aspirin inside of her, she returned to her bed for a few short hours of oblivion, before awaking again, with the aching realisation that she had a migraine, and previous experience told her, that it would last for days.

She groaned, partly with pain and partly because it was obvious that she was in no fit state to continue with the pamphlets. — After yesterday, Duncan would never believe her reason for not calling at The Loch House, was anything but sheer stubbornness. — But fortunately, Hannah came like an administering angel on her usual morning visit, and laying cool expert fingers on Helen's fevered brow, realised that the girl was in need of more than just aspirin. — Clutching at Hannah's arm, she vainly tried to lift her leaden head from the pillow.

"Hannah, please would you give the Laird a message?" she begged.

"Och, Lass, don't you fret now, I brought a note with me from Mr. Duncan, I think it very likely, that it's telling you he's been called back into Edinburgh, urgently."

Sinking back onto the pillows, her head began to thud more than ever at the news of Duncan's departure, but she managed to ask, "I hope that it isn't bad news?"

"Och, there's no telling, Lass, I think Miss Craig has maybe gone with him, probably some legal stuff or another," Hannah replied. "He's been like a bear with a sore head, this last day or so."

Helen wasn't surprised, and with a painful sigh, made a statement, "He's always bad tempered."

"Nay, lass, not always; something is worrying him, I'll be bound, and when he's sorted it out, he'll be his old self again, yeel see. — Now, I'm away to fetch Dr. Roach and I daresay that Jean will arrive with him, so lay still, I'll see you later. It's rest you need lass, plenty of rest."

Within three days, Helen's migraine had lifted, thanks to the injected painkillers that Ian had administered, plus the kindly care of Hannah and Jean. In the main, her migraine had been caused by her day of fasting, aided by the trauma inside of her, which she kept secretly to herself, locked away from prying eyes, — with Alex's return, she knew that she would have to hand Duncan back, relinquish him.

Chapter 17

Bogles

Feeling reasonably fit again by the weekend, and having missed her Friday evening with the Youth Club, Helen apprehensively agreed to celebrate 'The Festival of Samhain' or Halloween as the Sassenachs call it, by joining in a ghost hunt to be held at the castle. — Apprehensive, because she wasn't too sure whether the still absent Laird would approve of the idea, but Rory assured her that it was a popular annual event, celebrated in the same way for many years and explained the Celtic origins.

"Samhain, is considered a time to eliminate weaknesses — our Celtic ancestors slaughtered weak animals that were not likely to survive the winter, and their meat was salted and stored for the dark months, this has evolved into the custom of writing your own weaknesses onto a piece of paper, and then burning them."

To say that organising this popular event became a trifle bizarre, is a mild explanation …

"Rory, I look ridiculous! She exclaimed, irritably. "Like … like some medieval, vestal virgin, about to be offered in bondage. — And, why white, and it's *so* clingy?"

"Awe heck, Helen it's authentic to wear white. You look more like a phantom, so that the departed spirits won't feel afraid to show themselves."

Helen raised her eyes heavenwards; "Did the hire shop have another colour?"

"Only orange and you don't wear orange."

"Then, white it will have to be. — Oh, why couldn't I be a witch, a black fairy or even a vampire or … or, even 'Dracula's Bride'," she continued complaining.

"Couldn't you *pretend* to be Dracula's Bride," he suggested. "That would solve the problem, and anyway, this material does have a bluish tinge."

"Oh, alright," she agreed condescendingly. "But I'm not wearing this cone hat."

"Well, why not plait your hair at the sides, and draw it back like this, then you could wear a daisy chain, like a coronet."

"I don't like daisies, and I didn't know that you'd taken up hairdressing," she snapped, agitatedly.

"Och Helen, be a sport?" he grumbled, mildly. "But you *do* like heather," he keenly suggested, in compensation, brightening at the idea. "We can pick some on our way to the castle. — Helen, we're going to be late, Hannah and Mrs Roach won't be best pleased if we spoil their eats. — There are pumpkin pies, hot tatties, and toffee apples on the go, and the game of apple bobbin, please. …," he begged.

It was dark by the time they'd reached the castle; the only lighting was in the medieval tent containing the refreshments. — Helen stepped in to greet Jean and Hannah, dressed as witches, stirring a cauldron of broth.

"My …," Jean commented, "Your dress is very luminescent in the dark. — You looked like a ghost as you floated across the courtyard."

"Oh, it was Rory's idea, Jean, and I'm very worried about it."

"Well, I think it's very pretty … and seen as Duncan's not here …," she shrugged.

"That's what I'm worried about."

"What the eye doesn't see; the heart won't grieve over."

"Helen!" Rory called her from the castle door. — She ran to join him, "Everyone has been allotted a specific room," he informed her, "I'm sorry, but you've drawn the short straw, "You have the Feasting Hall."

"It's just as well I'm a sceptic," She grumbled. "Oh, Lead on MacDuff."

"If you're scared, shout loudly," he patted her on the shoulder as if in confidence.

"Rory, this is the most ridiculous thing I've ever done in my whole life," she whispered, "And why are the lights down?"

"Ambience, ghosts don't appear in the light. — Here's your shawl, you may feel cold."

"But it's hot in here," she continued, whispering, "And it all looks so eerie with all this green light."

"It's supposed to be eerie," he argued, indignantly. "The dungeons are even more eerie; be thankful that you aren't down there."

"Rory, I don't know about this," she hedged. "I wish I'd had that orange dress. Why did I let you talk me into this 'glow in the dark' number?"

"Helen, … you said you'd be a sport."

"I *am* being a sport, and why are we whispering?"

"You started it; anyway, shout loudly if you feel afraid, otherwise, I'll see you in about half-an-hour." And he left, closing the great oak doors behind him. With trepidation sinking in; she took a tentative step forward, and was tempted to call him back. "Oh," she grumbled to herself.

With heart thudding, almost heaving in her breast, she suddenly, with a spasm of bravado, spun round on her heel to face the hall, and leaned for a moment with her back against the door, trying to find the courage to move.

The hall really looked menacing, and her luminescent dress shrieked her presence, as she took her first faltering step, and then with more bravado, began to saunter her way around, to peer at the portraits. — With pounding heart, she began humming softly to herself, reminiscing 'The Dark Island' in a vain attempt to subside her rising panic, 'If only Duncan were here' came the unbidden, wishful thought.

Reaching the portrait of the *Bloody Mary*, she gave an involuntary shudder, sucking in her breath as the air in the hall had seemingly become more chill, causing her to pull her shawl more closely about her, to cloak her icy flesh, "I'm ... not afraid," she whispered, trying to convince herself that her legs were not shaking, as she continued her sauntering, her nervy fingers trailing the edge of the table as she circumnavigated.

She peered about her, suddenly standing still to strain her ears; she frowned, listening, to hear a faint sound, again, — and suddenly gasping in fright as the lights dimmed even further, — the faint sound becoming louder, like the eerie plaintiff wail of pipe chanters.

"It isn't happening, it cannot be, I'm dreaming," she tried convincing herself, her panic rising to a crescendo, "Please, Please, Rory, don't mess about," she cried, but her pleading voice fell only on the deaf ears of the portraits.

Somewhere, she'd dropped her shawl and stood trembling with cold in front of the open fireplace, the music of the chanters growing deafeningly louder and louder in her ears, when a musty smell suddenly filled her nostrils, — like that of damp clothing, "I'm not afraid," she murmured, adamantly refusing to acknowledge the fact.

Her feet seemed fixed to the floor, rooted on the spot where she was, peering into the eerie green darkness of the hall. — She sensed that she was no longer alone, her eyes straining to see into the now pitch-blackness, coming to rest on a shaft of pale watery moonlight, beaming from a window onto the floor. Startled, she drew back while sucking in her breath; her cold trembling hand flew to her mouth while staring at the tall shadowy figure, standing in the circle of light. She could see that it was a man in full Highland costume, a long feather attached to the side of his bonnet; frills of white were at his throat and wrists. He was wearing what she knew to be a velvet doublet, partly concealed by a fly plaid, matching his kilt. — His features, she couldn't determine in the shadows, but the light glinted on the Dirk pushed into his stocking.

As she stared, a sense of peace transcended on the atmosphere, 'I'll close my eyes and think beautiful thoughts,' she decided, 'he's only in my imagination.' With eyes closed, Helen waited, conscious of the mustiness growing stronger. Trembling, she sensed someone or something that wasn't menacing, close to her. She swallowed convulsively in an attempt to clear her throat, "I'm going to speak to you," she softly, tremulously, said. "To prove to you that I'm not afraid; I have my eyes closed, but I know that you're here in front of me, so close that I can almost feel you. — I sense that you are young, and it saddens me that you could not have had a very long life. — I don't blame you for wanting to haunt the Castle Drumbrae; it's so beautiful, tranquil, and full of love. — The world is a beautiful place when shared with others; full of sweet smelling roses and fresh purple heather clad hills. — There are none in the city; I know you would hate the city as much as I do."

She ceased to speak then, heart pounding, to stand as relaxed as possible, perfectly, perfectly still, feeling a coolness fan her cheek, a light caressing sensation on her hair, she shuddered despite her outward bravado, "I'm not afraid," she whispered, trying to convince herself, while again feeling the feathery lightness near her lips. — Sighing softly, she lifted her head, slightly arching her neck, her breath quickened as it continued down to the pulse beating at the base of her neck, then moving into the small hollow of her throat, until finally, returning to her lips. — She felt herself to be held lightly, unable to move her feet and with no desire to, she slid her arms upwards, it was the strangest phenomena to be in the embrace of a ghost. — The caressing sensation of gentle loving hands on her back seemed almost real, sliding to her waist and then smoothing down her slim rounded hips. — She wasn't too sure to what she was clinging so wantonly, but she gave herself up to the pleasure of the moment as her lips were parted by the ethereal sensation. — Gradually, she responded again as the velvet pressure on her lips increased slightly. — Then there came a breeze, followed by a faint smell of heather, a feeling of freedom, and then a shattering sense of loss, and Helen knew herself to be alone again.

When she opened her eyes and gazed around, the Great Feasting Hall was exactly as it had been when she had entered it. — The lights were on; it was warm and silent as before, empty but for herself and the portraits.

She stood for a moment longer, taking in her situation. — Her face felt warm and flushed; her lips, she touched, still retaining the sweet tingling sensation of loving lips. — She had all the hallmarks of a young woman who had been thoroughly kissed, and yet, it had left her feeling strangely incomplete. —Suddenly shaking herself from her reverie, she murmured, "Talk about laying ghosts," she chuckled.

She double skipped towards the door as it opened, to admit Rory, "Did you see anything, Helen?" he called.

"Well, you didn't hear me call, did you?"

Rory frowned in a dubiously perplexed way, convinced that he was losing his touch.

Leaving the hall after a disappointed Rory, she turned and pulled at the great double doors, "Goodnight," she whispered. "Rest in peace, and I'll see you in my dreams," and blew a kiss to the room, before sealing it off.

The night was warm, the sky a deep navy-blue, sprinkled with stars which glittered like tiny diamonds, and over the full moon, drifted a light sailing of dark cloud, occasionally misting its face as the evening drew to a close, a perfect Samhain night.

"Goodnight Rory, Helen called cheerfully, as later, the inmates of the Arms Hotel spilled out from its doors. "I'll see you on Sunday for lunch," she called.

"I'll look forward to it," he waved as she walked towards her car, jangling her keys.

"Have you got your torch?"

"At the ready," she called back.

After a five-minute drive, which brought her into Bracken Lane, she parked the car outside of the cottage where she'd left on some low friendly lighting. Only the sound of the rippling water in the burn seemed to disturb the peace; then an owl hooted from a nearby tree, startling her. — A wood pigeon then joined the chorus and suddenly there was a soft rustle from the hedgerow, chilling her to gooseflesh. — Giving a soft nervous laugh, she decided that it was possibly a hedgehog, and was rewarded when she saw the animal scurry across the lawns to disappear into a dark bush. — Shaking her head in the darkness, she then realised why Duncan had been so insistent on seeing her home on the night of Jean's party, — the cottage was quite isolated, despite being quite close to the High Street, and with the lack of street lighting, this corner of the village, being surrounded by woodland, appeared quite menacing at night. — With heart pounding, and nervy fingers fumbling with the lock, she finally, with relief, entered the dim confines of the cottage, to stand leaning with her back against the closed door, only to be met by a dripping tap in the kitchen, and the sound of a ticking mantle clock in the living room, disturbing the virtual silence. — It was warm, but a little oppressive inside the cottage, she thought, and shrugging, she then moved to cross the room towards the kitchen without raising the lighting, the fire embers glowed in the half darkness.

She hummed while filling the kettle in order to make a night-cap, startling when she heard a soft sound, "I must be dreaming," she murmured aloud, while turning to flick on an overhead light, but as she did, the electric in the cottage fused, the bubbling water in the kettle fizzled to a standstill. — She groaned, letting out a soft expletive, realising that she had left her torch in the car, and then remembered that Hannah had shown her where the candles were stored. She groped, sightlessly in a low cupboard, "Oh, Mairie Campbell! Why don't you go away?" she whispered. "Go and haunt someone else, I'm sure that the Laird would love a visit," then her searching fingers found her goal. — Some matches, she found in a nearby drawer, she struck one, but immediately the tiny flame went out, blown by the cool breeze from the open fanlight window.

She then stood perfectly still in the darkness, straining her ears to some far off distant sounds, echoing on the atmosphere. — Multitudes of franticly raised voices shouting commands; neighing, snorting, terrified horses' hooves rose and pounded, cries of pain, clashes of steel, heavy thuds on armour and shields. — She sucked in her breath as the oppressive atmosphere in the cottage increased, stifling, and the smell of acrid burning torches scorched her nostrils. She closed her eyes as the sounds continued and the rising panic smote her, her chest heaved with atmospheric pressure; her breath, came in short panicky puffs, "Duncan! Duncan Macgilchrist!" she suddenly cried aloud. "My Lord, take care … come back to me … come back to me!" she finally whispered, her head lowered as the sounds began to recede.

"Lady Ghislaine …," she heard the plaintive words in answer, and tightly hugged herself, feeling the frustration of eternal, aching longing, the feeling of hopelessly unsatisfied desire burning in her loins; — it was an area of void which desperately needed filling, her breasts rapidly rose and fell as the torture increased, "My Lord, I know that you're here, your wretched subject awaits you, and I can feel your noble presence," she whispered and groaned as she swayed, was caught, and drawn backwards, feeling a feathery lightness resting on her shoulders, she raised a hand to cover what was not there. — She arched her neck, feeling an imaginary tingling trail of soft kisses as they journeyed down, into the hollow base of her throat; — tantalising, phantom hands slid up and inside her sweater, she thrilled, her head rolling from side to side, moaning her pleasure, her passion rising as they cupped and caressed her breasts until her nipples grew hard with sweet desire. — And when she was slowly turned, she lifted her arms to fill the embrace, her lips were covered and gently coaxed apart, her mouth invaded, her hips gently pressed, caressed and moulded around his naked desire.

She was gasping and groaning with the tortuous desire of her own, when her loins desperately opened in age old supremacy, her urgency increasing. — She felt herself lifted by strong arms and carried towards the stairs, drifting upwards until Mairie's bedroom door opened, and she was laid on the bed, her clothes slid away leaving her unashamedly naked. — She knew that he was above her, his knees either side of her hips, still using his stimulating hand, but she felt no fear, only the need for the continuing, exquisite, ecstasy. — Soft, feathery lips and gentle fingers again plied their stimulating trade, until a desperate, greedy longing for unity and her throbbing burning ache to be fulfilled. — He kept her waiting, writhing, and the waiting for the invasion was sheer pained torture; —she slid her hand down her centrefold and dipped her fingers, feeling herself moist and ready, "My liege Lord, I beseech thee," she whispered, begging, as she raised her hips for the union, while hearing the faint words coming from so distantly far away, as if from another dimension …

"I cleave only unto you, my Lady," the hollow voice announced, as he went into her; — immediately, the thrusts were rapid, hard, splitting and hot, the pain was sweet, erotic desire; — she was crying and moaning, straining against him, begging for the ultimate release, and when it came, the heat of his passionate release, scorched into her like a branding iron, — she was fulfilled, he jerked until he'd finished, but only moments later, her desire arose again to a pinnacle, the agony of her need was sheer torture, she desperately reached out, grasping until his hardness once more filled her aching loins, 'Uh!' she panted, over and over again, the beating thrusts were ceaseless, there was no drained energy, he came again into her, their bodies released in synchronised union …

Helen awoke with a start in Mairie's bed at dawn; she switched on the bedside light to frantically peer down the covers to see her body dressed in a white, filmy silk, night top and French panties. And leaning down to peer at the floor, she saw her discarded clothes in a heap. She lay back on the pillows, in a state of euphoric confusion, thinking and trying to fathom out the happenings of the night. — Exactly when had she gone to bed, when had reality ceased and when had the dream begun? — There had seemed no line, no division between the ghosts of yesteryear, and the solid life form of the present, and yet her body felt awakened, fulfilled and more experienced in the ways of the world; it was strangely exhilarated, satisfied for now.

She rolled onto her side, to pull the empty pillow beside her into her arms to hug its warmth, nestling her head, smiling dreamily, as a cat with cream, purring deliciously when inhaling the faint male aroma; — her shouts had not been timorous, but ones of ecstatic elation, or was that also in her imagination, "Oh, my Lord Lennox," she sighed. "If this is what it's like, being a wench … then, Mmm, it's more comfortable than a table," were her murmurings as she drifted off into further, dreamless slumbering.

The following morning, she felt strangely happier and more resigned to Duncan's commitment with Alex. — It seemed stupid to think of it as a commitment, she thought, humming to herself as she potted about her bedroom, and then skipped downstairs to enter the kitchen, and began tidying away her breakfast dishes. — It was a sunny morning, she noticed, but what should she do until her lunchtime appointment, decisions … decisions … decisions.

The rhapsody continued to beset her, making her feel almost exhilarated, but she suddenly stopped singing to listen, she frowned; the temperature in the cottage had dropped. — Was that a breeze, she questioned, when suddenly shuddering. — There was no noise; all was silent but for the ticking clock, then she shrugged, "Mairie Campbell, away with you," she murmured softly, "Haven't you've caused me enough trouble?" and considered that she was still suffering from the after effects of the Samhain.

She continued to tidy for a moment more, but suddenly had the feeling that she wasn't alone. — Leaving the kitchen, she slowly, curiously, peered into each room. — What was she looking for, she wondered? — Still the feeling would not leave her, — shrugging, she returned to the lounge, deciding that she was imaging things again, and headed for the front door.

She suddenly stopped in the centre of the room, standing perfectly still. — She waited for a moment longer. A soft smile flit across her features as she spoke out loud, "My Lord Lennox, you're a minute late." and suddenly shrieked with laughter when a chuckle came from behind her.

"You know me so well," he acknowledged. "I hope that all this happiness that you are displaying, is a celebration of my return."

"I've decided that I'm not going to allow you to terrorise me, anyway, the revenge may come later," she smiled.

"Then, I had no need to bring you a peace offering," he remarked, indicating the bouquet of red roses.

Eyes sparkling, she unwrapped the blooms, ever conscious of him watching her, their perfume intoxicatingly filling the room, "Rory's father is the most amazing gardener," she commented, as she buried her face in them, inhaling, while lifting her sparkling emerald eyes to meet his fond, searching gaze, "They're beautiful, thank you Duncan, it's very sweet of you," she said, raising her face to kiss his cheek; — she briefly laid her head in the hollow of his shoulder; and silently, his arms closed around her, creating a haven, — it was a needful, poignant moment, she clung to his sleeve, and while holding her head, he buried his face into the thickness of her hair, inhaling her freshness and intoxicating femininity. – His gentle fingers teased at her hairline; the sway was such warm comfort, then her guilty mind tortured her, 'Judas' it whispered, knowing that in just a thrice of weeks, she would betray him, she swallowed a well of tears before she gently released herself.

"Is that the best, you can do?" he softly remarked, releasing a heavy sigh.

"For now," she laconically replied, and then her eyes clouded and she became awkward. "I'll … just put the flowers in water," and adjourned to the kitchen where she suddenly thought of the previous evening, 'Sweet smelling roses?' that's what she'd said to the ghost. — She thought for a moment longer, and then shook her head, murmuring, querying, 'Duncan … impossible' and pushed the thought aside.

"I'm having lunch at Top Farm Helen, why not come with me?" he called.

"I'm already booked up," she replied, not daring to say who with.

Duncan was propped on the table with his legs casually crossed, looking somewhat dejected, an unfamiliar mood to Helen. "Can't you change your plans?"

She carried the flowers, now beautifully arranged, to stand on the table.

"Not at such short notice," she informed him, and then offered some compensation, "Jean's invited me for tea this afternoon, why don't you come and join us?"

With baited breath, Helen waited for his reply, which, when it came …, "I'm expected at Craigiemhor Farm this evening; — I'll see you on the morrow. — We've plenty of work to catch up on: there's been enough time wasted this week."

"Of course," she murmured laconically, her spirit plummeting, while thinking miserably, that he would be anxious to be with Alex again.

"Do you need a lift anywhere?" he offered.

"I'm okay, thanks."

I'll see you then," he said, reluctantly shifting and moving towards the door.

She nodded, "Thank you for bringing my shawl," she called across the room.

He turned at the door and nodded in acknowledgement, saying, "I dropped into the castle on my way here, I realised that it was yours, good-day."

"Good-day, Duncan," she replied softly.

"Good-day," he said again, as he left.

For a moment she stared apprehensively at the closed door, hesitating, wanting to call him back, but instead she picked up the shawl and cradled it's softness to her cheek.

Hours later…

"Duncan should return this evening," Jean announced, with a sigh.

Helen frowned, perplexed, "But … I saw him this morning."

Jean shook her head, "You must be mistaken, he was with the Lady Eleanor in Edinburgh when she phoned at lunchtime; — I heard him in the background."

Helen was insistent, "Jean … I was talking to him, he was as close as we are now; he brought flowers. …"

Jean was doubtful, "Well, if he brought flowers, they will still be in the cottage when you go back." she said sensibly.

Helen said very little else during her visit to Talbert, only managing to pick at the delicious meal.

And, noticing her returning lack of appetite, Jean reminded her with genuine concern that her migraine had been caused by her lack of nourishment.

"I must have eaten too much at lunchtime," she replied.

"I doubt that" said Jean, glancing at her shrewdly. "Young Rory hasn't Hannah's tendency to notice what anyone else eats, he's too busy pumping iron, so he can toss a good caber in the field events."

Helen chuckled, despite herself, saying, "Hannah thinks my appetite is equivalent to Duncan's, just one of her meals a day are enough."

Hannah cares for those she loves, she loves Duncan, and she loves you, and would never forgive herself if either of you became ill for lack of care. — In fact Helen, we all love you and Duncan, and we wish that would seriously consider staying permanently, — why you even have a job, if you want it," she said, her voice rising enthusiastically.

Patiently, Helen replied, "Jean, staying is out of the question, but during my limited time here, I shall help Duncan all that I can with his Tourist Project."

"It isn't only Duncan's Project, it's *your* Project as well, Helen," Jean chastised. "The thing won't run with only half its resources."

"But it won't come to that," Helen argued. "I suggested that Duncan hire a manager. — There are plenty of tour operators to be found who would jump at the chance of living in Arrochar. — It would be an ideal situation, as there's adequate living accommodation above the shop."

Trying not to show impatience, Jean continued, desperately, earnestly, "Helen, you have thought about this only as a regard to leaving. — Didn't Duncan explain that to hire a manager from the outside would immediately commercialise the whole concern? — Arrochar is totally run on a strictly private family basis. — Although the business and the farms are independently run, only generations of the same families have run them," she finished, her voice softening, "Don't you see, if you leave, Helen, you will take the heart of Arrochar with you. — Think about it again, won't you? Study every aspect, every angle, please," Jean begged.

"I have thought about it, until my head aches," she tersely replied, "I've thought about it, and while everyone keeps badgering me, I'm determined, *not* to be swayed. — Duncan knew when he accepted my conditions that the work I did on the Project, would only be on a temporary basis. — If he doesn't employ an experienced tour operator, then he must have someone from Arrochar trained in the methods of running the agency.

"Helen, all his hopes, dreams and aspirations are centred on you."

"That's a very big responsibility. — I have my *own* plans, for my *own* future and Arrochar has only a fleeting interest in those plans, this village needs fresh blood, but not *my* blood."

Saddened by her friend's reply, Jean fell silent on the subject.

The evening came, and upon returning home, she frantically searched everywhere, every nook and cranny, but there was no evidence of flowers anywhere in the cottage, the vases were still stored in their usual cupboard and her shawl seemed to have disappeared as well.

Tentatively, she picked up the phone — moments later, "Rory, did you find my shawl in the castle?"

"I have it here, I meant to give it to you lunchtime, but I forgot. — Are you missing it?"

"Tomorrow will do, thanks."

She put the incident down to a figment of the imagination, mere wishful dreams.

Chapter 18

Conflict

During the course of the following three weeks, Helen achieved miracles. For love of Duncan and her subject, it became easy, and so they were soon able to send the first batch of pamphlets off to the printers; — work had commenced on the renovations to the agency shop, of Alex, Helen saw very little, for the actress was now deep in the throes of rehearsals and costume fittings, but when she did appear, she wore a distinctly adverse air. — Acknowledging Alex's dislike of her presence, she didn't treat these occasions as important, feeling herself to be of no personal threat towards the intended couple's future.

Duncan, in his rejuvenated mood, returned to The Loch House at varying intervals during each day, so much so, that Hannah complained bitterly that his irregular visits to his own home was a distraction and disrupted her routine. This chastisement, he met with good humour, and his reward, a hearty meal. His appetite, boosted by the open air was insatiable, but not one ounce of copious flesh appeared on his muscular physique.

It was two days before the film muster party, when Helen met the postman at the cottage gate with a great amount of alacrity. Her collection of mail proved to be variable, containing an invitation to Alex's Press Conference for the following evening, and a letter from Rita announcing her pending arrival with her photographer fiancée the following day. Ryder had sent her with the intention of assisting with the coverage of the conference.

The thought of seeing Rita again increased her already recharged buoyancy with a small amount of guilt, as it was her intention of eventually employing Rita's fiancée to photograph the vantage points of Arrochar's locations for inclusion in her glossy brochure. The third piece of her mail caused her to swiftly untie Hannah's enveloping apron, protecting a pair of well-tailored, brown velvet culottes, topped with an attractively styled peach coloured cashmere cardigan, casually open at the neck; — she swiftly sped upstairs to slip into her fox fur jacket, and within the space of minutes, she had driven to The Loch House with her prize. — Skidding to a scrunching halt, she leaped from the Mini, taking into account that the Rover was still parked in the drive, evidence that Duncan hadn't left for his days work, she gratefully acknowledged. With silent relief, she entered The Loch House, calling out his name several times, but feeling disappointment at not receiving a reply, "He must be somewhere," she murmured aloud. — Hurrying around to the outside of the house and down the towpath to the waters edge, her glance encompassed the cold brilliance of the loch, where she spotted him in the distance, fishing.

Waving to him frantically and calling his name, Helen ran along the towpath, with her precious cargo clutched in her hand.

Duncan heard her call, and alerted as to her speed and her obvious joy as she neared, he swiftly positioned his fishing rod, calling and waving back, he broadly grinned, anticipating the inevitable, a moment that he'd been waiting for, a moment for which he prepared.

She was warm and breathless, her cheeks glowed from the exhilarating exercise, and her jade green eyes sparkled brilliantly with the excitement, which she felt. — Infectiously laughing on reaching him, unconscious of her enthusiasm, without thought, she immediately leaped up and he caught her in his arms, swinging her around twice until he set her back upon her feet, immediately again, with his dark head lowered, he claimed her responsive lips with his own, a brief moment of mutual, unadulterated joy.

Moments later, oblivious of what she had done, she pulled him to sit down on an old fallen tree trunk.

Duncan gazed at her, and a lazy pleased smiled flit across his rugged features, Helen looked so beautiful in her innocent excitement, he thought, while taking the pamphlets from her. — They sat, heads close together, studying them, agreeing that they were good samples, "They're a fine job, Helen," he confirmed gently, watching her, feeling heartened, while she replaced them into their envelope. Her eyes still sparkling, she told him,

"Then, I'll order a *whole* batch of each."

"As many as you wish," he replied, "Enough to distribute among the various local hotels and the city tourist shops."

She surreptitiously glanced at him from beneath long lashes. — With his dark hair unruly from the blowing wind, his strong determined jaw relaxed, and his vivid blue eyes free from strain, Duncan looked today as he had on that fateful day before reaching the castle, a day which now seemed so very long ago. — At this moment, Helen loved him even more, her treacherous, pounding heart betrayed her, it was at this very moment, her eyes locked with his, searching his face, soft with undisputed love, "Duncan, hold me." — It seemed that in one electrifying moment, a love that had lain dormant for centuries had surged to the surface in a desperate longing.

Reaching out, he smoothed back the hair from her temple, "Helen," he breathed her name, his voice rough with emotion as he pulled her into his arms. She sighed, suddenly relaxing, and reaching up rested her trembling hand on his nape, where her fingers rhythmically teased the soft curling hairs, stirring his ardour. — His desire rising to a pinnacle, he shuddered, groaning her name over and over again and when moving away the restricting collars from her neck, his gentle fingers deftly slipped another button on her cardigan. . — Another tremor shook her at his touch, she moved to ease the much needed route; — blissfully, she raised her chin, thrilling to the sensation as his lips left another delicious burning trail of kisses, which led down from the corner of her mouth. She swallowed as they reached the hollow base of her pulsing throat, further down to the roundness of her breast, and then returning with equal ardour and deliberation, to claim her parted lips again, there to continue their deep, sensuous motion.

"My Lord," she breathed, stroking his head, while drinking from a cup brimful of longing, a cup that he continued to replenish, she wanted him, with every fibre of her body, as she knew that he wanted her. — This was no dream, this was reality, and this was what she had stopped that day in the castle, a love that had come too late. — too late ... with this sudden thought, another reality rose it's ugly head, in a few short hours, she was going to betray him; and as she pulled away, her eyes were bright with threatened tears, her trembling hand covered her mouth, her voice wobbled as she spoke, "Duncan, I must go ... I must go, I can't do this," she cried, standing and turning on her heel, she ran back down the towpath.

Duncan let out an expletive as he too rose and began running after her, "Helen ... come back!" but despite Helen's gazelle lightness, he soon caught up with her, gripping her savagely by the shoulders, she wrestled with him.

"Duncan, let me go ... please, let me go." she earnestly begged.

"Why?" he asked angrily, "Tell me why? — I love you Helen, and I could have sworn that you felt the same. — You've been so happy, and the pamphlets ... I thought you'd changed your mind and would stay."

Helen struggled frantically to fight off the aching longing to be back in his arms, — she tried vainly pulling away again, sobbing, "No, you're wrong Duncan, I can't stay in the village … it's impossible."

A shaking anger now swept through the man as he grit his teeth, the muscles of his jaw bunching, his eyes ice cold slits, — he lost his last vestige of calm, "Why impossible, Helen? I hadn't noticed that you were suffering from home sickness, or have I managed to fill your life with the kind of boring, mundane simplicities which you were only prepared to put up with, because of your enforced time here, is Arrochar such a prison?"

"Yes, yes, you're right," she lied. "I didn't promise anything, nothing at all, in fact. — You know I have a career, and you can't expect me to throw it all up for … for …," she struggled for the words, "for the sake of whims and fancies."

"The whims and fancies are *my* life," he rasped.

"But they're *not* mine," she sobbed.

The deep pain in his eyes tore at her like grasping vixens as he replied …

"You're even shallower than I first thought," he said, thrusting her from him. "Is this the stored up vengeance?" he spat viciously. "You and your precious career are made for each other."

"No … no, Duncan, I've never … Oh, what's the good?" she ended, hopelessly, "Think whatever you will."

He suddenly seemed to soften, and reaching out held her arms again, pleading, "Helen listen …,"

"No! Go away … just go away and leave me alone," She cried, wrenching herself free yet again, and turning, ran from the towpath, closing her ears to his demanding call.

There had been two witnesses to this scene, one pained and heartfelt, and one leering, gloating and sadistic. Rory had been fishing with a pack of anglers further around the towpath and Alex Craig, who Helen had driven past on her forward journey, and who had turned around on seeing her and having arrived unannounced, had deliberately parked her car, hidden away on the opposite side of the road and had walked the short distance to The Loch House, until within earshot of Helen's overheated conversation with Duncan.

After a frantic drive, Helen reached the blessed sanctuary of the cottage, hastily leaving her car, she ran inside, upstairs, to her bedroom where throwing herself onto her bed, she sobbed away her pent up emotions, until finally falling into an exhaustive sleep.

Sleeping until mid-afternoon, awaking with a dry mouth and a dull thudding headache, Helen rolled onto her back, awaking also to the reality, that crying had never solved anyone's' problems, least of all, Helen

203

Campbell's, but time and logic had.

Taking herself to task, she rallied enough of her spent spirits to take a refreshing shower and to shampoo her hair; — it was during this operation that the impossible situation of remaining in Arrochar, shrieked at her. There was only one solution, — tomorrow night's conference, she would have to wave the extension of contract and return to London, immediately. For the sake of decency, Mairie Campbell, she felt sure would forgive her. Her further regret was, that Alex Craig had seemingly won, yet another round.

That evening, Helen called in on Jean.

"The tension is building," she explained. "I always become hyper-sensitive, before a conference."

"You've enjoyed, leisurely, unhurried work and peace and quiet for the last twelve weeks."

She chuckled, despite herself, "I think I've worked harder in Arrochar than I ever did in London."

"I don't think so," Jean replied. "You've just wound down and now you have to wind up again, you're overwrought, suffering from an adrenaline spill. You look rather peaky, Iain has prescribed something to calm your nerves," she raised her eyebrows, "And, I mean, good grief, life is hard enough without being forced against your will, into some strange environment. It's like taking a kicking child to the dentist."

The phone suddenly rang shrilly.

"Oh, hello Duncan," she said brightly, smiling and turning to face Helen, who silently shook her head, indicating a warning to Jean, to say nothing of her presence. Jean put up her thumb in acknowledgement.

"Jean, have you seen Helen, today?"

"Have you two had another row?"

"Just a tiff," he replied.

"Then, if it was just a tiff, why don't you just apologise, you've managed it before, but you make light of things; it's more than a tiff, - isn't it?"

"She won't talk to me."

"Then, leave her, until she comes around," she suggested.

Jean covered the mouthpiece with her hand; Duncan's reply was muffled.

At that point, Helen whispered, "Jean ... I'm going."

As Helen left the house, Jean ended her conversation with Duncan, "You're going to have to accept the inevitable; there just isn't enough to keep her here, — she's back in harness, my Lord; Arrochar will just have to manage without a Campbell."

After a short drive, Helen arrived at the castle gates which were still standing open, allowing admittance to the film crew. — She wandered into the Feasting Hall where lines of chairs were now positioned in preparation for the following evening. And then a rare sighting, Arnie hailed her from a distance, "I was coming to see you, Helen," he called, hurrying to meet her in the entrance.

"Arnie, how nice to see you," she greeted.

"I need a favour," he replied.

"So ... what can I do for you?"

"I would be very pleased, if you would play the musical score for the film."

"Oh, I couldn't possibly appear in a film," she ascertained.

"You don't have to, - it's the theme music. We just record in a studio with full orchestration; - there is a fee," he added, as a sprat.

"Oh, what are the pieces?" she enquired with interest.

"The main theme is 'Rhapsody on a Theme, by Paganini, - 18th variation.

"Joy and Splendour," she ascertained.

"There's another piece," he informed her, proffering the score.

"The Rustle of Spring," she read, followed by a sigh. "They're both pieces that I know."

"Then, you will?" Arnie questioned hopefully.

"I'll think about it, and let you know on the morrow."

"I don't think you'll let me down," Arnie remarked. And suddenly stepping forward, gave her a big hug, revealing, "I heard you play years ago - in Paris. You were just a kid, and I thought, this kid's got talent, a little rough around the edges, maybe. ..."

Helen frowned, puzzled, "You saw me in Paris; was Miss Craig with you?"

Arnie nodded, "It was just after we met, we stopped off to do a bit of sightseeing; you were in a competition, Alex insisted that we attend; we had box seats near the stage, a really good view, the music seemed to make you cry."

It had swiftly registered that Alex had recognised her from many years ago; she had known who she was from the onset.

Helen sighed, painfully, "It was the last time that I played in public. — That morning, I had received a letter from my grandmother, she had refused my last request to visit her, — I was playing, 'The legend of the Glass Mountain' memories of Switzerland, and dreams of here," she revealed.

Arnie nodded. "The Laird's upstairs," he informed her, as he began to retreat into the Feasting Hall. "I take it that you're looking for him."

Her heart jerkily skipped a beat at the news, she had supposed him to be at home when he rang Talbert, but he must have rung from the castle's library, "Oh no, thanks anyway. — I'll see you tomorrow evening at the conference," and then began to make a hasty escape, but she hadn't heard Duncan come down from the gallery.

"Helen," he softly alerted her.

She stopped in her tracks, she was feeling bristled, having wanted to spend a few quiet moments with Mairie Campbell in order to ask forgiveness for her changed plans, it now seemed that Duncan had wanted to do the same thing.

"Mairie Campbell seems to be the healer of all hearts," she painfully sighed in acknowledgement, only half-turning towards him so that he could not see her face. — He appeared jaded; the jacket of his grey lounge suit was unbuttoned to reveal his white silk shirt, which was open at the neck; his hands were thrust into his trouser pockets, his dark head down, his soft voice was gruff.

"You heard what I said, then."

"I heard," she replied, assuring him. "I am honoured, but I cannot return your love, Duncan."

"Is there nothing I can do, Helen, to persuade you, nothing I can say?"

"You could let me go home and let me get on with my life, that's something that you could do; I would rather go with your permission, than without it, my Lord."

His throat moved convulsively as he tried to swallow the searing pain, to keep it from entering his eyes, "I cannae stop you, Helen, but I would remind you that it is honour and duty that binds us, could you live with yourself if you break the ties?"

"I shall have to learn to do so." She again sighed, "I *still* think that you know more about this situation than you're letting on."

"That's for you to decide, I could say the same of you, but for some reason, best known to yourself, you're in denial," he softly accused.

"I deny nothing," she said, evasively.

"I had occasion to visit Alex Craig in the week …,"

"Is that supposed to worry me?" she replied, caustically. "It isn't such an unusual event, I'm quite sure that Alex would do anything to hold onto her precious heritage, — she has you fettered, hand and foot," she replied, scornfully. "Now is *not* the time to discuss Alex Craig, and if you don't mind, I had better go," she turned away but he further detained her by earnestly saying …

"Helen, I beg of you, don't do this interview, you have no need."

Her reply was swift, defensive and stubborn, her voice wobbled with passion, "I grant that it's your job to carry out the wishes of Mairie Campbell's *will*, but it's *my* job to sell newspapers, and sell them, I will, at whatever the cost."

His tone became scathing, "Beware the stealthy, beautiful snake who carries an inkwell of poison, ready to inject into its unsuspecting prey."

She hesitated for a moment, his words had hit the mark, her eyes were flashing green fires when she raised them, and then she found her voice, which wobbled through her pained throat and came out in a soft, determined rasp, "You *dare* to pontificate to me about venom, my Lord, when, by your own volition, your village houses a bigger snake in the grass than I, but you do not *stamp* on it," she spat the final words, vehemently.

"I hope that you're not telling me *how* I should handle *my* job, my Lady."

"I'm quite sure that no-one would ever *dare* to suggest how you should do your job, my Lord."

"You could be right," he replied, with a sigh. "No-one has ever tried, but then who would want my job."

"You love your job," she firmly said.

"I would love it even more, if you were to stay…,"

"Duncan, this is getting us nowhere, we just keep going around in ever decreasing circles," she firmly said, cutting the conversation. "Now, if you would please excuse me, I have a heavy day tomorrow and would like to retire early … Goodnight, my Lord."

He stepped forward, reaching out a hand, every nerve and sinew reluctant to let her go, but then resignedly, dropped it again, saying, "Another time, my Lady Helen."

She bit on her trembling lip, before murmuring, "Goodbye, Duncan."

Chapter 19

Dilemma

The alarm woke her at eight, with the sound of songbirds and sunshine streaming through the lattice window; she lay back on her pillows, smiling at the ceiling, "My Lord," she whispered, "I should have told you that I love you so. — Yet again, I feel regretful that I have once more, to let you go, without this urgent message to comfort you in your toils of war. — Live, my Lord Lennox and I will await thee with impatience, until you come again."

That afternoon, Helen drove with Rory to the station to meet the press train, reporters and photographers galore poured from the train onto the platform. Nearly everyone, she knew, greeted her, with a great amount of alacrity, shaking her hand, kissing her cheek or giving her a friendly pat on the back, showing their camaraderie. Rory was trying to keep up with her through the pushing throng, he cheerfully questioned, "Who don't yer know?"

"If they're not here, then, they're not worth knowing," she jovially shouted her answer, while searching for Rita's shock of carrot red hair.

"Does that mean, Ryders here amongst this bunch," he yelled back.

"No," she called, "I'm Ryder's scapegoat."

Rory frowned in puzzlement at her reply, but having missed the point he merely shrugged, reapplying his energy into following her. — They found Rita with her new fiancée knee deep in luggage at the far end of the platform.

"Kidda!" she yelled over to Helen.

At the sound of her old affectionate nickname, she waved, and on reaching Rita, she was immediately enveloped in a warm embrace, amidst plenty of girlish shrieks.

Returning to some semblance of calm, Rita observed, "You've got an accent already."

Helen grinned; she made her introductions to Rory, and immediately, warmed to the young man known as Gary Redmond, a photographer, to whose arm Rita now proudly clung.

She cast knowing glances in Rory's direction and Helen falsely laughed, shaking her head in denial of any romantic attachments. Rita looked very crestfallen, her main ambition to pair Helen off seemed never to be realised, she casually mentioned ...

"Giles sends his regards."

She nodded, without committal.

Driving towards the village, they became ensnared in a steady stream of traffic pouring from the station. Arrochar's taxi service had been swollen on this particular occasion by private enterprise, and Helen's sore heart suffered to see Duncan's Rover in the distance, ahead of her. Rory saw it also, and commented.

"The Laird must have been at the station, Helen."

Rita became curious and quizzed, "Would that be the MacFarlane chap you spoke of, Helen; I'd love to meet him, - any chances?"

"We'll discuss it later," she evasively said, feeling relieved on reaching The Loch House turning, where he changed direction, releasing from Helen an indiscernible sigh.

Later that evening, she dressed in the most becoming sleek lines of an electric blue suit and toning French heeled shoes, and after many a re-do, succumbed to wearing her back hair long, with the front and side hair caught back to form a curly, bouncing pony-tail, with softening tendrils to frame her face, Rita commented that she had worn it thus, when she had first met her some years previous. — Feeling confident and businesslike, she headed for the Arms Hotel, for a relaxing hour of cocktails with Gary and Rita prior to the Press Conference.

A polite while later, Gary made his apologies and departed from the girl talk to join their colleagues in the public rooms.

"Now, you'd better go through this problem you have with Miss Craig," Rita suggested.

Helen related all the information to date, ending, "She's trying to blackmail me. If I openly attack her, then Duncan's name will come out into the open, and well, — I wouldn't like to be me, — anyway, Ryder will be expecting me after tonight, I haven't written anything of any substance for the last three months."

"I had sorta noticed," Rita winced. "What are you going to do about it;

tonight is your last chance?"

"I suppose, eating humble pie is in order," she replied, sipping her drink.

"Why don't you just *tell* Duncan about your contract?"

"I *have* told him, I blurted it out by accident, it went down like a lead balloon; he seemed to know, anyway. — Alex Craig is such a bitch; I just don't believe that Chester Maxwell would have betrayed me, anyway, he denied it when I confronted him at the onset, he's too good a friend; — Ms Craig unwittingly fabricated a truth."

"Then, what are you so worried about?" Rita asked, with some surprise.

"Does she know that you've told him?"

She shrugged, "It's the principle of the thing; I accepted a challenge."

"She openly challenged you, and you will lose face if you don't carry it through."

Helen nodded. "Duncan said, that he didn't want any of his private life publicised, until he gave me the go-ahead."

"And, he hasn't given you the go-ahead. It sounds as though she dealt you an early trump card and now, she's using you; — she's loaded the gun and got you to fire the bullets."

"I seem to be in her way," Helen continued morosely, "but I'm not sure why."

"She's trying to get rid of you, and you're going to let her — what's the matter with you; surely Mairie Campbells' wishes are more important than Alex Craig or Ryder? ... or *is* there, something else that you haven't been telling me?"

"What else could there be, either way she's going to win, and Duncan seems so determinedly on her side. — Mairie Campbell has placed us in this ambiguous situation; we've carried out eleven of her instructions, and there *still* seems to be neither rhyme nor reason for any of it. — The welcoming party was the order of the day, there's a display cabinet in Talbert with an arrangement of trinkets, lace hankies and gloves, a menu card and dance cards; the invitation card that I received was an exact replica of the one in the cabinet, and so was the menu on the night of my party. When I first saw the cabinet there was a space; I immediately thought of the aigrette and the combs, which are still in my drawer in the cottage."

"Were the items labelled?"

"They were purportedly worn by Alicia Craig at her wedding to Angus MacFarlane."

"What else is missing?" Rita enquired.

Helen appeared ponderous; "He should have met me at the station; I feel that the station has some relevance, that it was the most crucial clue."

"Well, it's a bit late to do an action replay, - what happened?"

"The high and mighty, Miss Alex Craig took the precedence; she always takes the precedence," she grumbled.

"I suppose she has to, if he's going to marry her."

"It's strange," she frowned. "In all the time that I've spent with him; he's never mentioned it."

"Well, I think you would be the last person he would open up to, with your reputation; — you've always got your pen poised, ready for action.

Helen winced, "You mean; he doesn't trust me?"

"It's possible, and that's the reason he's been so evasive, but let's see what we can find out. — Come on, we'll act our socks off, Alex Craig isn't going to be the only one to win an Oscar."

Alex never did anything in a small way, and as this was going to be her last film for an undecided period of time, she had made the most of this opportunity. With cameras flashing, — she within their focus, Alex made her favourite grand entrance into the Feasting Hall. — For the occasion, she had chosen to wear a clinging, silver lame evening dress, which left little to the imagination, the diamond and safire ring was conspicuously flashing. Rita whispered in Helen's ear in reference to the dress, "Is that thing kept on by willpower? Or is she hoping the make the headlines, by loosing it?"

Helen facetiously replied, "Don't so be bitchy Rita, you know Miss Craig's modesty is at stake in more ways than one, this evening."

Rita just stared at her, incredulously exclaiming, "Modesty! Helen, she lost that year's ago, along with her virginity."

"Hush," she replied, sharply, "I'm not interested in Alex Craigs' intimate details," still dogged by her private thoughts, and wanting fervently to dismiss any thoughts of Alex in compromising situations, which she may have shared with Duncan. — In fact, her whole reason for being there suddenly sickened her, she couldn't do it ... she couldn't expose his private life to the unmerciful press. He would hate it; hate her for doing it, if indeed he did now love her as he had declared, unless, he had only said it in a rash moment, to encourage her to stay, the same rash moment on her part also, when she had yielded to her feelings, thus betraying herself.

Rita's brow furrowed as glancing at her companion sideways, she whispered, "Are you going soft? You won't earn that column by being sentimental. Ryder expects great things from this conference, and you're the only one in this room, who has inside information on Alex Craig. — Scoop the story, Helen; you may never have another opportunity like this."

Suddenly, the whole revealing truth sank into Helen, she passionately blurted, "Then Ryder is going to be a very, very disappointed man. I don't care one jot about the column anymore, Harry Ryder, Alex Craig or her celluloid image."

Rita openly gawped at her reply, her friend sounded sincere with her declaration.

A female voice suddenly alerted them by firing a leading question, "We understand that you may be retiring to enter the marriage stakes, Miss Craig, are there to be any announcements of a pending wedding this evening, and who is the lucky man?"

Helen lifted her head and stared, heart pounding in anticipation of Alex's reply, but her answer was suitably cagey, suggesting that she was still prepared to protect herself and the Laird from public scrutiny.

"I'm sorry to disappoint you, Ladies and Gentlemen, but if the film topic isn't sufficiently scintillating for you to whet your readers' appetites, then they most assuredly, will find my private life, — even more dull. The only comment that I am prepared to make on the subject this evening, is … that I *will* be marrying … eventually."

"Would you get that?" Rita exclaimed.

At her meaningful, non-revealing words, Helen's head shot further up to meet Alex's supercilious grin, with eyes that reflected her horror. — The invisible coil was tightening; it now had a stranglehold on her emotions, damning her with the dawning knowledge, that she was faced with a horrifying, larger than life dilemma. A yawning, tempting, inviting, open doorway faced her, bearing a notice which read, - enter if you dare!

"Now, Helen," Rita frantically urged, "what are you waiting for, — say it now?"

Hesitantly, she glanced about her; taking in the hushed whispers and puzzled expressions, until, "I … I can't," she whispered, "I'm damned if I do, and I'm damned if I don't," and biting gently on her lower lip, she lowered her head, hesitating further, deepening the mounting tension. — A breathtaking, pin dropping, tense silence reigned, until …

"We're waiting … Miss Campbell," Alex called.

Rita urgently whispered, "Scoop the story, Helen, if that's what you want to do — it's your last chance, but do you really want to be a traitor to Mairie Campbell and your new friends. — There'll be other opportunities in London if you want them, Ryder would be insane to hedge his bets on this one assignment. If anyone is blackmailing you, Ryder is, he's testing your loyalty."

She hesitated a moment longer, "You could be right," and suddenly became aware of Duncan's presence; his whole demeanour shrieked a warning, "There's no alternative, I've got to back down." She heavily sighed in resignation, deciding, "There's only one thing that I can do, so here goes," and drawing in her breath, through frozen lips, she called back the time tested reply, "No comment … Miss Craig," her reply, sending a gasp of astonishment around the room.

Alex visibly gloated at her moment of triumph, inclining her head, acknowledging, "Miss Campbell."

Helen's head bowed as she choked back the threatened tears, her earnest desire was to leave the room, but it was cram packed to the doorway.

Within half-an-hour the conference had ended. They were preparing to leave, waiting until the worst of the crowd had shifted, when Rita's attention became riveted towards the entrance, "Who's that dish-of-a-man by the door? The dark haired one, the one dressed in the navy-blue suit with his hands shoved into his pockets, he looks a bit ruffled; He's intently staring at you."

Helen's heart sank, feeling a warm flush of colour rise to her cheeks; she said casually, "Oh, that's Duncan."

Rita was suddenly doing her arithmetic; taking in Helen's heightened colour. — Her eyes moved from Helen to Duncan, and in a flash, it smote her, she was aghast, "So that's it … you're in love," she accurately deduced. "This is what you are running away from, and he's in love with you, but he's going to …,"

Helen swiftly, tersely announced with some concern, "He doesn't know how I feel — no-one knows how I feel, the situation is impossible; there isn't room enough in this village, for both of us."

"Then, *make* room," Rita exclaimed, sounding astonished.

Never mind about that, Rita," she hastily replied. "This is our trump card — if he escorts Alex from the room, the whole *damned* world will know that he's going to marry her, and Alex Craig will have won, yet another round."

"Then, I'll block her," Rita swiftly, elatedly said, "until everyone has left."

Duncan cast her one last glance before leaving the hall, without Alex. — Rita's ruse had blessedly worked; Alex left the hall with Arnie. Helen sighed with relief.

Alone now, except for a few film technicians unloading cameras and equipment, from large vans which had recently arrived from the States,

Helen wended her way upstairs into the gallery, pausing only to switch on the lights. After which, she sauntered down the centre carpet strip, turning occasionally to glance about her. — Reaching Mairie's portrait, she sank down on the gilded chair opposite, to pensively gaze up at the beautiful image, which had caused her so much trouble, and it was about to cause her, some more …

"Good evening, again! Helen," a sudden, female voice addressed her.

Helen gave a start, shaken from her reverie, — she turned towards the owner of the voice who was meandering along the gallery, "Oh, good evening, Alex!" she exclaimed, with some surprise, mingled with trepidation. "I didn't realise that you were still here, I thought I saw you leave."

She was obviously gloating, her whole demeanour was weighted with it, "I did once, but as you can see, I've come back; — Arnie wanted to check on some equipment, — quite an advantage finding you up here, like this."

"You have something more to say," Helen suggested. "I thought that you and Duncan would be celebrating."

"The celebrating can wait; we have the rest of our lives to celebrate. – No, just tidying up a few loose ends; small matters of mutual interest, before you left."

"Perhaps … I'm not leaving."

Alex flashed a contemptuous glance, her air was haughty, she continued, "Oh, you'll be leaving, Helen, just mark my words. — Quite a turn of events; I'm amazed that you didn't verbally slaughter me this evening, a heaven sent opportunity, one that I gave you, one that I knew you needed."

"How condescending of you," she replied. "Why me, Alex, there were plenty of others to pit your wits against this evening?, — you've had your knife in me ever since you laid eyes on me; — you've achieved your goal, what you set out to do; you've just come up here to gloat about your triumph."

"Ye … s," she trawled the word, taunting, sneering, "but you, the pride of Fleet Street, kept silent, and I have to confess to feeling a certain amount of disappointment; I had so looked forward to your *challenging,* manipulation of phrase."

"It wasn't necessary," she replied. "I feel that I have sufficient information to write an article without the pressures of a conference, I know most things about you, some of them quite distasteful."

Alex's eyes narrowed cruelly, distorting her harsh beauty even further in her determination, "But not quite enough, it seems. — I wasn't sure until this evening's … shall we say … little fiasco; but I now know for certain that you're in love with Duncan, and you love him far too deeply to expose his personal life to the press, which is the reason you didn't take up the challenge, — your protecting him." Helen's head snapped up to meet Alex's cruel grin, but she remained silent as the actress continued, "Oh, no need to worry, he doesn't know and I promise you faithfully, that I won't be telling him, you can rest assured upon that matter. The situation, shall we say, is far more preferable the way that it stands, and we can't have history repeating itself, - now can we?"

Feeling puzzled by her latter remark, Helen realised that Alex must be in possession of some past knowledge, of which she herself was unaware.

"You must forgive me, Alex, I don't understand; — if you have something to say; then say it, and then we can *all* go about our business, whatever that business may be. — You should be satisfied that you've manipulated the situation, as you call it, to suit yourself; — your spiteful, meaningful ways are designed to hurt, but most of all, you're hurting Duncan, and you will go on hurting Duncan, until you destroy him; and you're using me as your instrument. I would rather go than torture him anymore, but you don't care, - do you?"

"Not a tosh," she replied.

"Explain yourself," Helen demanded. "It's what you're endeavouring to do."

"Very well, if you insist," she agreed, while moving over to Mairie's portrait, "It's a harsh reality; — I know that you're familiar with the events surrounding the discovery of this painting. — Very obviously, it belonged to the old Laird, Angus MacFarlane. — Understandably, he had to hide it, but feeling that he owed something to Mairie Campbell, Duncan had it hung in here amongst the family portraits ...," she paused, interrupted by her companion.

"There's nothing devious in what you have said, Alex, the whole of Arrochar is aware that Mairie Campbell was friendly with Angus, and I'm fully aware that there lay a certain amount of animosity between Mairie and Alicia, just as there seems to be, between you and me; — it is of your own creation."

"You're very naïve, and not very well informed," she continued. "Angus gave Mairie Campbell that cottage in return for favours, you do understand, - don't you?"

Taking in her innuendoes, Helen rapidly replied, "The cottage was paid for, Alex. I have the title deeds, and Mairies' favours were her contributions to the Woollen Mill."

Alex's face evilly contorted, she scoffed, "Come now … Mairie paid a token price of one shilling for Bracken Cottage. Having lost Alistair Campbell's protection by his premature death, it satisfied the gossips at the time. Mairie and the old Laird were more than just friends, they were lovers; she was his secret mistress for many years, even while engaged to Alicia. — She knew that he would never marry her, and so settled for an alternative, and the cottage provided, a nice, cosy, respectable, little love nest. — Why, he only had to ride down the lane in the dark — you surely must have noticed that Bracken Cottage is very secluded."

This revelation rendered Helen breathless, a chard of ice cold pain surged its way through her stomach, she visibly paled as it seared up into her chest, "It isn't true!" she exclaimed, gasping at the unexpected weapon.

"You must now realise, Helen," Alex continued sneering, "That there's a distinct possibility that your father was Angus MacFarlane's bastard son, or why did he feel so duty bound to rear him alongside his own son, and finally pay high fees for his schooling? It wasn't from pity; — you and Duncan are closely related, — why, you're virtually his sister," she scoffed and taunted. "So now tell me, how does it feel, owing your middle class upbringing to the MacFarlanes?"

Helen suddenly found her pride, "That's slander, Alex. It isn't true, none of it is true," she refuted. "My father was undoubtedly Alistair Campbell's son and a commercially self-made man. If he was in anyway indebted to the MacFarlanes, then he more than repaid his debt by being successful in his chosen field."

"I don't think that Duncan considers the debt paid."

Helen was further perplexed, "What … just what do you mean, Alex?"

"Oh, it's quite simple." She continued, sneering, "Duncan has worked hard to involve you in the village community by giving you this Project of his to do. He could have done it without you, Helen, but it didn't suit him to tell you about the recordings that his father had made, some ten years ago. — He's made a fool of you; the finish was only the polish, his ploy was enticement, you fell for the bait, and now you're on the verge of throwing up your hard-earned career in London, to stay here and live in what will eventually become - your love nest, also. I'm fairly certain that Duncan has already made advances towards you, he's swayed you that far, I tried to warn you, but you wouldn't listen."

"You're … just guessing," Helen cautiously replied, flushing.

"Am I?" Alex retorted, raising an eyebrow, noting her tell tale rise in colour.

"I've seen him, he can hardly keep his hands off you, — I'll leave it to you to know how far your relationship has gone, — incest is still illegal, which brings me to the reason for this little *chat* now. — I just want to remind you that Duncan wants Craigiemhor Farm very badly, and is unlikely to be swayed from his lifetime's ambition for sentimental reasons. — As for me, I am not going to tolerate living with the same situation as Aunt Alicia, and so thought it best to sort out the matter - *right now*, before it goes any further."

Distressed, enraged, Helen replied through ice stiffened lips, "Then, you've made your point needlessly; — your destructive, Alex, and yes, I gave in, — but I would never consider living in the shadow of such a hypocrisy as you have just suggested. — If you and Duncan wish to live out your lives in cold, calculated indifference, then that's your affair, but for me, only the warmer climes of an open, honest love will do, and if you don't understand the alien word of love, then take a closer look at Arnie the next time you meet, and recognise, a different kind of reality."

"My, my," Alex continued, with raised eyebrows, "… quite a pretty speech, Helen, but under the prevailing circumstances, — shall we play it safe? — That chirpy little redhead who was with you, asked for my autograph, she said that you'd lost your job because of this evening's little fiasco. — Without a job, you'll need money; — you'll need money in London, Helen. May I remind you, that I'm prepared to pay?"

Sickened, Helen replied, "Rita exaggerated; I still have my job. I lost my promotion, plus my extension of leave, — the latter should suit you very well," she vehemently said, secretly coveting Arnie's well-timed proposal.

"So long as we both know where we stand, I'll leave you in peace, but I don't think that you will find Duncan so eager to let you go. Angus would never allow Mairie to roam far from the village, but again," she sighed, "you'll find me a friend if you feel the need of one. — Goodnight, Helen Campbell," she said in finality, inclining her head towards her before casting a last glance at Mairie's portrait. "I'll send you a wedding invitation, next year. - Sleep well."

Helen's eyes followed Alex's path until she turned at the door to raise a hand in final farewell, before she disappeared from view.

For some time, she sat, with eyes raised, staring at the portrait, feeling numb with shock, a cold emptiness chilling her heart, as she thought that Alex's story seemed incredible, but, she realised, not impossible. — With good reason, Duncan had kept the truth from her, his own reasons. — Remembering the catch phrase, 'you'll find a welcome' contained in

Mairie's letter, made her wonder, did Mairie send her here for Duncan's purpose, and she'd almost succumbed, but only almost.

The feeling that Duncan knew far more about the situation, had always irked her, — had Mairie made some kind of a bargain with him, — his instructions had been verbal; there was no evidence of any conversations made in private? — History repeating itself, the thought echoed, remembering Alex's words; — had Mairie loved so deeply that she had accepted a hole in the corner affair, even married another, living a lie, all to enable the MacFarlanes to glean land? — Why should the Lairds so selfishly, ambitiously, own everything to the exclusion of respectability? — "I find it hard to believe that you were a kept woman, Mairie Campbell," she whispered, while the welling tears of defeat slid down her cheeks. "You were ensnared by trickery and deception, as I nearly have been, but your fate, shall not be mine, Mairie Campbell."

Chapter 20

Farewell, My Gentle Lover

Helen sighed at the thick white carpet of snow that had fallen during the night, even though the sight of it was familiar, — she had watched the first fluffy flakes descend shortly before midnight, to steadily increase and deepen by the dawn. — Sleep had evaded her tortured mind, which reeled again and again with the events of the past two days. — The ache in her heart was even more painful than the growing ache in her body. — She felt grateful now that she had been evasive, hurt because Duncan's declared love had proven to be overshadowed and dishonest, he was as she had first suspected, hard in heart, uncaring in nature, and ruthless in actions. — Tired and dispirited, she turned from the window, feeling unable to arouse any enthusiasm for the muster party that evening.

Later in the morning, Rory drove up outside of the cottage, bringing Hannah with him, his intention to clear the snow from the cottage path, a task upon which Helen was about to embark, and one that she was grateful to hand over.

In the kitchen, Hannah took one look at her pale face with the dark shadows beneath her eyes, evidencing her fatigue — a sight which caused a look of deep concern to cross her homely features.

"Are you no sleeping, lass?" she asked kindly.

Helen gave the housekeeper, a thin, weary smile, "It was all the tension of the Press Conference, one minute the adrenaline's up and the next it's down. ..."

Hannah patted her hand sympathetically, "And I expect seeing all of your friends again, made you feel homesick."

"It was good to see them again, but I didn't feel homesick," she replied honestly. "In fact, most of them envied me living here. Had it been the summer, I would have had a deluge of holiday visitors on my hands."

"Will you stay, do you think; after your six months, - I mean?"

"That's the eternal question," she sighed, bending her head to study her neatly manicured nails, wondering whether to confide in Hannah. "It depends on a lot of things, a part of me wants to stay, but logic and my career are dragging me back to London."

"Ye lassies' of today and your careers," Hannah admonished, shaking her wise old head. "Its small wonder that the population ever increases at all. You should be married lass, and raising bairns."

"There's no-one that I particularly want to marry," Helen replied, denying her deep-seated feelings.

"You could have fooled me, lass," Hannah returned knowingly, while patting her companion's hand.

Helen felt a slight rise in her colour, but remained silent as she busied herself by carrying the now laden tea tray through to the adjoining sitting room, where Rory joined them, while rubbing his hands together to restore his lost circulation.

"I hope you're ready for tonight, Helen," he said. "Arnie's delighted that you've agreed to play your recital, he swore me to secrecy, even the Laird doesn't know.

"I think Arnie was a bit chary about telling him," she sighed. "He should be grateful that we have so many of his best interests at heart."

"You're a good sport, Helen," he grinned roguishly before dropping a casual kiss on her lips, his face was cold.

"Aye, she is that," Hannah chipped in. "And I hope you appreciate how lucky you are, in escorting Helen to this affair, for your nay deserving of the honour."

Rory chuckled wickedly for Hannah's benefit, placing a hand over his heart, he said, "I promise faithfully, Aunt Hannah, that I will be the perfect gentleman."

"Mmm," Hannah grunted doubtfully.

Later, having failed to restore either warmth or enthusiasm, Helen dressed lethargically for the evening, finally brushing her shining chestnut hair into a tumbling profusion of waves behind her slim shoulders, — she sighed, softly, dejectedly thinking of Duncan. — She and Rory would be in the Laird's party that evening, and it was a daunting prospect to have to face him with this new, silent resentment — but I don't resent him, her aching heart cried — he's trapped as Angus must have been trapped, by family traditions — but I won't be a party to them, — she newly resolved, while staring momentarily at her silver backed hairbrush, and then replacing it to the polished surface, picked up her white heather aigrette which she pinned to her side hair. — Suddenly, she was shaken from her reverie by a shout,

"Helen! Helen! Are you ready?" Rory called enthusiastically from the foot of the stairs.

"Hush! …." came Hannah's commanding voice. "Do you want to waken the dead?"

Helen smiled to herself, knowing that with all Hannah's scolding, Rory adored her. "I'm nearly ready, Hannah," she announced, as the housekeeper entered her bedroom.

She stood up and away from the dressing table, dressed in a strapless powder-blue 'Balenciaga' gown. — The rustling, many layered, netted skirts were encrusted with tiny Swarovsky crystal beads, which shimmered as she moved. It was echoed on the nip-waisted bodice, the whole, creating certain incandescence about her pale features.

"Now, just your plaid over your shoulder and your Cairngorm pin, we don't want you catching cold - there. — Oh, Lass, you do look a picture, just like one of those French models."

She looked down at herself, remarking, "Thanks, but I hope that I'm not as flat chested."

With a sweeping glance, Hannah amended, "Och! Nay Lass, on second thoughts you have a far better figure." Helen nodded while picking up the full length, deep-blue velvet cape from the bed and slipped it around her shoulders with Hannah's assistance, "I can't understand why Mr Duncan isn't taking you to this affair," she remarked.

Helen's smooth brow furrowed, perplexed, she queried Hannah's meaning, "But … he's escorting, Miss Craig?"

"Pah! Miss Craig indeed, it was a sorry day for everyone, when that one came back, she's just a thorn in the side."

Helen turned towards her, earnestly appealing, "But, there's nothing to be done, Hannah, - is there?" she implored.

The housekeeper brushed away a stray tear, replying, "Och, I know lass, I know." And sighing, "Come now, see how handsome that young rake Rory looks in his tartan; A real Cameron Highlander, he is."

And it was true — Rory had shed his blue-denim image, replaced by tradition — he looked a real heart-stopper in full Highland dress, — his tartan, red in colour with a green inset check and a yellow line.

"Now, be sure to be a gentleman," his aunt reminded him.

Rory could only drive slowly on their journey to the castle; — he was in good up-lifting spirits, chuckling and joking, remarking en-route, "We could have done with a sled, I should have thought of that before — now, that would have been an entrance to behold."

"I see you've gritted the lane," she in turn remarked, noting that the car was holding the road.

"Oh, Aye, the Laird had me out in the early hours." He glanced at her sideways, "Haven't you seen him today?"

She shook her head, "I had no expectancy of seeing him, we have own separate arrangements."

It was almost as if they had communal thoughts as the conversation continued …

"I must say, that Alex Craig isn't what I thought she'd be like. She's thrown plenty of tantrums already," he remarked, sounding disillusioned.

"Actresses do these things," Helen laconically replied.

The castle - as they approached - was ablaze with light, looking entrancing beneath a sable starry, winter sky. — Music reached their ears, growing louder as they neared; — Rory drew to a soft halt on the driveway. — A lackey took over the car, driving it away for parking, leaving them to enter into the entrance hall where a second lackey took their cloaks. — And true to his promise to Hannah, Rory offered his arm as a gentleman. — Helen placed a- light hand a-top of Rory's, in the best tradition of entrances, the formality brought a sparkle to her eyes. "What ever happens, I'm not going to leave you," he said. "Now, head up, in the best, proud, Campbell fashion, and we're going to do this thing - in style."

Helen began to smile, despite her inner turmoil, — Rory was so right; no-one was going to detect her inner feelings. — She wished with all her might that she had Rory's resilience towards Duncan's boorish attitude; — her defences had weakened in the face of adversity, she had bowed to his dominance and done his bidding, the conniving of the wiles of women had failed.

They reached the great oak doors, and as they entered the Feasting Hall, they paused for a moment, to steady nerves and to gaze around them at the scene.

The hall was filled with a mixture of people, some very American, others, obviously more local. — The men had all donned Highland Dress, adding a special elegance to the occasion. — Very suddenly, Rory spoke to her, and despite herself, she grinned at his words.

"Now, take a deep breath," he instructed. "And nod and smile a greeting to everyone, as we *slowly* pass through the crowd. — You know how to do it, like the Princess that you are." And moments later, "I think, we've arrived."

Helen unconsciously gripped Rory's arm, she felt his fingers tighten over hers, giving the much needed moral support, as the Laird, plus Iain, Arnie and Henry Graham rose to greet them, leaving the ladies seated.

Acknowledging each in turn, they gave a slight incline of the head, leaving Duncan 'til last, to whom, she coolly inclined her head, before dropping into a deep curtsey, addressing, "My Lord," and rising, veiled her eyes. — But as handsome as Rory looked tonight, hadn't prepared her for the sight of Duncan in full Highland Dress; proud and resplendent in his muted cranberry tartan, although, unlike Rory, and most of the men who had opted for a white frilled shirt and velvet doublet, Duncan wore the Prince Charlie evening jacket with a simple white silk shirt and black bow tie. — His sporran of white seal, hung around his hips, supported on a silver chain, his kilt pin was an eagle's claw, set again with silver. — She wanted to say how magnificent he looked, but refrained from saying anything else.

"Miss Campbell," he acknowledged, stiffly polite.

Tremulously, Helen momentarily held his steady gaze, and then forced her eyes away to greet the ladies, grateful to remove herself from his darkly angry gaze. — Pinkly conscious that his eyes never left her, while Rory seated her between Eleanor and Jean, and then, as the other gentlemen, attentively stood behind her chair. — From somewhere, a perfectly mixed Martini appeared. The tension lay heavily on the atmosphere.

"Good evening, Helen," Alex greeted, with a supercilious grin. "We meet again, and so soon."

"Arrochar is very small, Miss Craig, it's nigh on impossible to avoid meeting ones' friends … or … ones' enemies."

And then turned to listen to Eleanor, while sipping her cool iced drink, to soothe her dry throat, enough to answer Eleanor's question, "We've missed you at The Loch House, Helen, — don't allow Alex's conference report to take up all of your time - will you?"

"The report is on its way to London, carried by my aide, Rita. — It should be in the morning edition of the Daily News," she said, feeling acutely conscious of the Laird now standing behind her rival. "It should make good reading."

Alex replied, "I shall look forward with anticipation to reading the reports. — I have a copy of every newspaper, ever printed, after a Press Conference."

Helen thoughtfully ran a finger around the rim of her glass before replying, "The report in my case will be a report to suit the occasion, Alex."

"I have every faith in you," the actress replied. And hearing the band strike up, dismissed her by raising her eyes above Helen's head, and glancing up at Duncan, who had moved to speak to Rory, never missing an opportunity, she addressed the Laird, in a voice which was falsely warm and adoring, appealing, "Duncan, my darling, you're not going to refuse me the first dance, - are you?"

"My pleasure, Alex."

The actress patronised the company with a smile as she stood to leave, — immediately, Helen began to feel the tension relax, as they moved away onto the dance floor. — The Grahams followed suit and took their partners' for the Gay Gordons.

Arnie leaned towards her, "Ready in half-an-hour, Helen."

She nodded in silent acknowledgement.

Jean leaned towards her, showing kindly concern, "You look rather peaky, Helen, is there anything ailing you? I think you should consult Iain, you look as though you're coming down with something; there are plenty of germs about."

"I'm fine, thanks," she replied with a sigh, trying hard not to stare at the Laird and Alex, tremulously biting on her lip when she caught sight of them engrossed in some intimate conversation.

"Where's James this evening?" she enquired.

Jean replied, while glancing around the colourful throng, "He's around somewhere, — there's going to be a family announcement this evening, he wouldn't want to miss it."

Helen chilled even further at these loaded words, and felt grateful when the music changed to the haunting strains of a song, a duet sung by a man and a woman of the village, a popular Scottish melody which was traditionally sung at most Highland gatherings, a song entitled, 'Farewell, my Gentle Lover'. — She suddenly felt Rory's hand on her shoulder, "Let's dance, Princess," he suggested, and she rose, taking her leave of the company. — Closing her eyes, she nestled her head into his shoulder, if she couldn't see the couple, then they wouldn't disturb her, she decided.

"You look so beautiful," Rory whispered. "I wish I were the keeper of your heart."

"I love you as a brother," she sighed. "We've had such fun together; I sometimes wish that we were children again, it was much less painful, much less complicated."

"It doesn't have to stop. I'd ask you to marry me, but then you'd have to stay in the village, and I know how determined you are to leave."

. Helen shook her head, "You should court Fiona Drummond, now that

224

she's passed her teacher's degree and has come home. — I had heard that there's a vacancy at the school, a word in the Laird's ear wouldn't go amiss."

Rory nodded in agreement, but changed the subject, "You can't make up your mind what to do, - can you?" He asked.

"No, but I have a few things to sort out, and so I'm going to try and get the Laird to let me go back home — there, I may see things differently. But there are other issues pending before I leave," She confessed.

"Helen, he *won't* let yer go, whatever he has said, - be warned," and sighing, continued, "The terms of the *will* are far too stringent; I hoped and prayed that I was in Mairie's plans. She knew that I loved you. I had my instructions. …"

Helen appeared stunned, further perplexed, she incredulously gasped, "She *asked yer* to propose to me."

He appeared a trifle embarrassed, "On this very day," he revealed.

"Does the Laird know?"

Rory silently shook his head, and suddenly glancing up, caught sight of Duncan's stern expression as he approached, he whispered a warning, "The Laird's coming over; I think I'm going to have to go. — Now, keep your pecker up, I'll see you in a while," he said, squeezing her hand.

She then felt herself gathered closely into such a familiar territory. His Givenchy after-shave began stirring her senses, as she surreptitiously glanced up at him through her lashes; his hand felt warm encompassing her cold one, resting on his shoulder. — She felt a light tingling sensation where he touched her centre back, and as always, his touch against her skin was sensual, disturbing and awakening, ever lowering her resistance. — He spoke curtly, "What was Rory saying to you?"

Helen sighed, "It's none of your business," she snapped irritably.

"May I remind you, that while you're in my village, you are my business, Helen, and while we're on the subject, when's this grand departure taking place, or has the weather held up your plans?"

She just stared up at him, her eyes raking his features, feeling speechless," You're … letting me go?"

"As I said, I cannae keep you here if you don't want to stay, our lives must go on, either *with* or without each other, so, I'm making up your mind for you, and now that you've got me around to your way of thinking, I'll guarantee, it won't be what yer want. Anyway, the weather is too rough to drive."

"I can go back on the train, on the morrow, the sooner the better," she answered a little too eagerly.

He stiffly informed her, "The tracks are frozen."

Undaunted, she replied, "Then, I'll get there somehow."

His voice was softly entreating, pleading, questioning, "Helen, we've enjoyed ourselves, you cannae deny it?"

She shook her head, "I must go," she replied. "Ryder ...,"

She didn't see his concerned, frustrated frown, as he earnestly, gruffly replied, speedily interjecting, "You're running away from yourself."

Her voice wobbled as she stammered a nervous reply, "I ... I'm not running away."

"Liar, Helen Campbell," he gently replied. She lifted her head to meet his eyes; there was none of the expected derision, only a deeply warm searching expression, he was pleading with her. — She longed to unveil her own eyes, thus revealing the overwhelming yearning, she felt for him. — He knows, she silently considered, as everyone else, I'm sure that he knows. — Duncan spoke again, "The last time that we danced together was in Edinburgh. Do you remember, Helen? You laid your head on my shoulder, and I stroked your hair as we danced."

Helen bent her head towards his chest, closing her eyes while she wrestled with her deep seated emotions, trying to stave off the acute feeling of panic rising up inside her, — if he kept on reminiscing in this way, he would break down her already fragile barriers, rendering her incapable to resist. He knew her weaknesses also, and would play on them until she yielded, — the song continued, — the words so hauntingly perfect ...

"Farewell my love, the time has come for you to say, farewell to me
You leave me now, in this fair land, where once we met so tenderly.

I bless the days, we were together; I know that parting is forever
Remember me when you recall, the hills of Caledonia.

My dearest heart, we always knew, before you held me close to you
that stolen moments in your arms, must end in tears of destiny.

So fare-you-well, my gentle lover, I know you're promised to another,
we'll meet again in dreams, my love, in dreams of Caledonia.

"Duncan, please ... don't speak to me in this way. I have no intention of changing my mind," she replied, firmly, "I'm leaving for London, on the morrow."

"If you feel no allegiance to Mairie Campbell, the least you can do, is to stay and finish the Project."

She felt a sudden spasm of vehemence; — her voice shook as she remonstrated, "Oh, I had it from a very good authority, that you could cope with the Project very well, and on your own," and immediately the words were out, bit on her lip in the knowledge that she had revealed too much.

"Whose authority?" he demanded roughly. — Abruptly, they stopped dancing, conscious that everyone was now staring at them, Helen turned to move away, but he had other ideas, restraining her by gripping her slender wrist, "Who's authority?" he demanded again, with jaw set hard. "I'm the only authority in this village."

Quietly, but firmly, Helen replied, "I *am not* going to tell you, — now, you're hurting my wrist, please let me go?"

The song finished with a repeat of the final chorus, and with the singers voices trailing away, the music stopped playing. — For a moment longer he detained her, determinedly staring at her until he read the softening plea in her eyes. — Resignedly, he let her go, saying, "As yer please, Miss Campbell," he replied curtly, now looking down at her. "I hear that Arnie has asked you to do an *unexpected,* farewell performance. — Have you had a change of heart about your reporting career, and are now opting to fulfil your fathers wishes?"

"It wasn't my fault that I failed my exams," she flashed.

"You lost your concentration, for reasons best known to yourself," he tersely said. "Or perhaps, you failed on purpose, *because* you *wanted* to *be,* somewhere else."

Her voice accusingly wobbled with passion, while her darting eyes took in his granite features, "Or perhaps … I was distracted, which one is it, Duncan?"

But, before he could reply, "Here comes Arnie, they must be ready for you and you're *all* on your own, Miss Campbell," he announced.

"I can manage," she brushed curtly. "I shall ask Rory to champion me. I really have no wish to openly divide your attentions and embarrass you any further, my Lord Lennox," she inclined her head, before leaving him.

Aching inside, with Rory following her, it was a very thoughtful Helen who walked onto the rostrum, but she shook herself from her reverie, to concentrate on the matters in hand. — If that's the way he wants it, then that's the way, he can have it, she decided.

The twelve-piece orchestra saluted her by tapping their instruments, as she arrived to seat herself on the stool, spreading her skirts. — She waited with baited breath while Arnie made his announcement, her lovely head lowered; she chewed gently on her glistening, moistened lips. — Afraid, she didn't want to meet Duncan's eyes knowing that as ever, he was watching her, devouring her, with his fathomless deep blue gaze.

"My Lord, Ladies and Gentlemen ...
I am very proud to present, Miss Helen Campbell. — She has agreed to play the backing score for the film, tonight. — The first piece, I think Helen regards as her signature tune - Rhapsody on a theme by Paganini - 18th variation – a piece she has nick-named, Joy and Splendour, followed by a piece played in sole honour of the village, its people and her love of the countryside which has been so personally engraved upon her heart, - Sinding's Rustle of Spring, - I give you, — Miss Helen Campbell."

She allowed the applause to subside before she began to play, she concentrated; — the concerto was so startlingly different, and feeling as though she could hear a pin drop, her hand lifted, creating the first chords, that were soft and gentle, then the deeper and deeper notes, reverberated. — She reached and downed, absorbing the drama, the orchestra joined her in the crescendos, and then she came to the 'come on strings' and smiling, felt the joy and elation. Her skilful fingers were confidently riding the crests, until the last two, final soft chords. — She sat, feeling breathless, her chest heaving with the exhilarating flow of adrenaline; — she then took an intake of breath while the orchestra played the link to the Sinding, and then she joined in, remembering the days that she'd spent with Duncan, — remembering their pleasure as they had roamed the countryside. — Breathless days, joyful days, heady and playful days, their days, — 'the swallow' she mouthed, 'the lambs', love, and a land of poetry, history and romance, — all these things flowed from her. — The centre notes were so tinkley and joyful, deep notes rising with the orchestra, a short rest and then the melody again, lower notes then the great crescendos. — Her hands zipped and rivered across the keys, knowing that whatever the future held, no living soul could take this sweet past away from her. — Note followed note, the performance was perfect; her love had made it so, until the final rousing finale.

She sat still, panting from the exhilarating exercise, waiting for the last chords to die, tears of emotion glistened on her lashes, then the tumultuous applause broke, with the whole hall rising up to its feet, shouting and calling, Bravo! Bravo! the orchestra seemed to tap ceaselessly on their instruments in accolade.

Arnie came to bring her a bouquet of red roses. — She stood beside him bowing and inclining her head, and then standing back to give credence to the orchestra. — They called for an encore, everyone called for an encore. — She chanced a glance towards Duncan, who had remained seated and wasn't applauding, neither was Alex Craig; she saw her touch his arm, and he turned his head away, 'mistress in the art of distraction' Helen thought.

And so she seated herself again and replayed, 'The Rustle of Spring', she again played out her rapture and her love, knowing that she had caused some distraction of her own.

The tumultuous applaud came again, only dying when Arnie and Rory helped her down from the Rostrum. — She was immediately surrounded, Rory became lost in the crowd and Arnie had to pave a very difficult pathway, through to the great oak doors and blessed freedom, "It's going to be a winner," he said. "It's recorded."

"You don't need a studio?" she questioned, surprised.

He shook his head, "It was better that you weren't aware, the acoustics are perfect in the castle. — Thanks Helen; that was great. You'll get a nice fat cheque and we hope to use you again."

Moments later, Arnie returned to the Feasting Hall, giving Helen time to draw new breath. — She read the card with her flowers, it said simply 'Duncan' she pulled out one bloom, and then placed the bunch onto a nearby table, 'what was he thinking' she wondered, had he guessed by her performance how she really felt about him? 'Oh fool, Helen Campbell, she thought, to put your heart on display'.

She suddenly startled, "Quite a farewell performance Helen, and a very rendering one," Alex scoffed. "I must congratulate you."

"How can you be so sure that I'm leaving," she replied, dully.

"It's written all over you, that music tore the heart out of you. — It was a good idea of mine to get Arnie to pay you for tonight's performance. Here's your cheque," she said, proffering the piece of paper. "And there's a little bonus from me."

Helen drew herself up proudly, saying, "I don't want it, Alex; nothing would induce me to take money from you."

Alex looked at the refused cheque, raised her eyebrows and then shrugging; slowly tore it up. "Very well - have it your own way. — We'll meet again, Helen Campbell," she said, turning to leave.

"I doubt that, Alex," she replied in finality, as Alex returned to the Feasting Hall.

Trembling, and now choked with tears, she sped upstairs to the quiet stillness, which she knew she would find in the gallery.

The gallery, — only dimly lit this evening, — had originally been intended for daily exercise, it hadn't always contained windows which had been an added feature only about a century before. But still — as Duncan had explained — it was cold and draughty in the winter. — With a feeling of peace and solitude settling on her, refraining from switching on more lighting, she sauntered, occasionally stopping to peer into the darkness outside. — The lights from the Feasting Hall immediately below, shone brilliantly onto the snow, and the faint drum of music and high-pitched voices carried upwards, disturbing the silence.

Swallowing, in an attempt to remove the uncomfortable ache in her throat, she sank wearily down onto a nearby chair, and leaning her head back against the wall, tears trickled from beneath her closed lids. — It became completely silent in the gallery; all sound seemed to be sucked away into a vacuum, leaving a hollow void, until suddenly, beginning to feel the chill atmosphere penetrate her flimsy gown, she shivered. — The drop in temperature caused her to re-open her eyes; — she strained to see into the dimness, knowing that she was no longer alone.

Helen stood then, cast in a shaft of pale moonlight, a shimmering apparition herself with the musk and the heather aroma growing stronger, and hearing faintly playing bagpipes, the sound gradually filling the gallery as she moved across to its centre. — A space of several feet separated her from the spectre, although she could see him clearly.

I'm not afraid," she whispered, I believe that you're in my imagination, but if you are not, then you could only be Angus, his young spirit seeking Mairie. —I am not Mairie Campbell, my Lord, I am Helen … her granddaughter, merely a carbon copy, and I feel so sad, so very sad, that you both lived with such impropriety, but I condone you both, for I know that there is no easy measure to resist." — And closing her eyes, she shut out the vision, calling softly, finally, "Goodnight, goodbye, my own dear love." The atmosphere steadily became oppressive, a soft feathery lightness touched her brow, then the air clarified and the party beneath, became audible again.

Remaining where she stood, her legs suddenly became weak, unable to support her. A clammy, undulatory giddiness swept over her, followed by a sickening, engulfing blackness, she sank to the floor, overcome at last by the fatigue and the trauma of the last few days.

How long she had lain there on the floor, she never knew, but she became vaguely aware of herself being lifted by strong arms, she felt too tired to even open her eyes to comprehend. — Faint shadows flit beneath her closed lids, soft caring voices touched her ears, and a soothing warm hand stoked back the hair from her brow, she sighed in contentment and then sank back into oblivion.

Opening her eyes drowsily to a bright sun-filled room, she blinked and stretched luxuriously, then lay still, steadily becoming aware of a sweet perfume filling the room. — Raising her eyes, she frowned, and then propping herself up onto one elbow, she reached up to touch one of the red blooms neatly arranged in a vase beside her bed. — Suddenly, a realisation smote her, now fully alert to her surroundings, she looked down at herself properly dressed, in a lacy pink nightgown, when her memory came flooding back. — She had fainted, of that there was no doubt, but not at the sight of the ghost. — Forcing her mind back, she thought, I don't remember anything after that, so how did I get home? And the worst thought of all; — who had put her to bed? — Flinging back the bedclothes, she sat up, glanced at the alarm clock and immediately expelled a groan, realising that it was afternoon, also, supposedly the day of her departure. A soft, sharp tap came on her door.

"Come in," she called, expecting her visitor to be Hannah. She pulled her pink satin robe about her as the door opened to admit, not Hannah, but Jean.

"Ah! Helen, you're awake at last. I hope that you're feeling better for the rest," she said, exchanging smiles with her as she moved towards the bed. "You had us all so worried, fainting as you did. It was Hannah, who told us this morning that you hadn't slept the previous night, and then the tension of your recital must have been too much for you."

Sighing despondently, Helen agreed with her that they could have been the possible causes, while feeling a strong reluctance to discuss the real reason for her lowered state of health. — She wondered if Jean could be familiar with her grandmother's past, but then she doubted it, as it would be a subject treated with the utmost delicacy, a skeleton in the MacFarlane's cupboard and now one in her own.

Jean seated herself beside her on the bed, she spoke kindly concerned, she studied her speculatively, feeling that Helen needed her friendship, "Do you feel well enough to venture downstairs?" she asked.

Although feeling shaky, Helen hated being an invalid, she replied a trifle too brightly, almost keenly, "O … Oh, I feel fine; I really do, thanks."

"Good, then I'll make a pot of tea, plus a little something for us to eat while you dress." — Standing, she then walked towards the door, turning to smile brightly once more, before leaving the room.

After spending sometime in the bathroom, Helen dressed casually and comfortably in navy-blue slacks and a winter-white blouse. — Feeling refreshed, she was on the point of leaving the room when her eyes came to rest on the roses, realising that they must be from the bouquet that Duncan had given her the previous evening. — Re-crossing the room, she selected a flower, holding it near to her face to inhale the heady fragrance. — Immediately, she felt a warm welter of love, she whispered, "Oh, I do love you Duncan, my Lord Lennox, if only you were free to love me," her treacherous heart cried. "But it cannot be," she groaned and sighed in final resignation, casting away her deep-seated emotions.

Moments later, she had made her way downstairs to join Jean, who had been reading the morning edition of the 'Daily News', Jean enquired ...

"Do you wish to read your conference reports?"

Helen glanced at her, she again sighed, showing disinterest, her voice, lack-lustre, "No, I know what they say; I'll read them later."

For a moment, Jean's eyes lingered on Helens' still pale features, and then onto her fingers nervously toying with the stem of the rose, she was clearly troubled about something, she realised. Her newspaper reports had reflected none of her original journalistic capabilities. — In fact, on the whole Alex Craig issue, she had barely touched, causing her to fleetingly wonder how her Editor had received her report. — She desperately wished that Helen would confide in her ... proud, stubborn, Campbell spirit, she thought.

Suddenly, Helen sighed, before thoughtfully sipping at her tea, before making the startling announcement, "Jean, I've decided, I'm returning to London. I ... I can't stay any longer."

Jean carefully, thoughtfully, replaced her cup onto its saucer, trying to choose her words with equal care, "Will you tell Duncan of your decision? I feel that your news will be unwelcome."

She spoke flippantly, leaving some doubt in her companion's mind, "Oh, he shouldn't be surprised; I spoke to him last night and mentioned that I might be leaving today."

Jean raised her eyebrows in surprise, "Today ... when?" she questioned.

She sounded desperately anxious, answering, "As soon as possible." She earnestly cried, "Oh Jean, its imperative that I see Ryder, I ... I ...,"

"You're not well enough to travel," she hastily replied, in the hope of dissuading her.

They both suddenly startled, and immediately stood to face the direction of the gruff, shaky voice, firmly ordering from the kitchen doorway, "Ye'll no be going anywhere, Helen."

"Duncan …," Jean's tone was arresting, pleading, as she stared concerned at the sight of his angry features; the set white line of his lips and hardened line of his jaw; — she desperately wanted him to listen to her, but she knew that it would be to no avail. — Helen had been squeezed by all and sundry about staying in the village, and she felt that he was about to loose the last vestige, from his rapidly emptying, cask of hope.

"I'll go where I please," Helen said, firmly, stubbornly determined.

"Jean … would you excuse us," Duncan sharply ordered, still staring at Helen evocatively.

"Duncan … I beg of you." she tried again, anxiously concerned to stop something that she knew he was going to regret.

Irritated, arresting, he snapped the order again, "Jean … could you *please* leave us."

Reluctantly, Jean collected up her coat, "Goodbye, Helen," she called. Gently, with resignation, as she passed Duncan, she shook her head in despair.

"Goodbye Jean, I'll write to you," Helen called as her friend opened the door and left the cottage, closing the door softly behind her.

Once outside the door, Jean hesitated, torn between leaving and returning as a deterrent — suddenly, an idea smote her and she hurried away to find Eleanor Graham.

Duncan's voice sounded wobbly, gruff and passionate, his breathing laboured as he spoke, "Ye'll no be leaving, Helen, if yer go back to London, ye'll no come back, and I'm in no mind to risk that possibility."

"You can't stop me," she snapped, with more assertion than she felt.

"As executor of Mairie Campbell's *will*, I can, and I *will* stop you, I have every right to stop you, and by any methods that I see fit," the words were coming through a throat that was as pained and constricted as the day that his father had died, — he desperately needed to hold onto what he loved, he just didn't seem to know how do it, "I know what you enjoy, Helen, try to deny it."

She shook her head, her voice tremulously wobbled as she replied, "I did as you asked, Duncan; you must now reap the consequences."

He earnestly pleaded, "Helen, you *must* listen to reason."

He looked so tired and drawn, she thought; he was unshaven, the fine lines about his eyes seemed to be etched even deeper, and at the sight of

233

them, she felt a renewed longing to smooth them away with gentle fingers; to have his arms fold about her, his strong but gentle hands pressing her close, so that she could feel his deep seated need of her. — She desperately wanted him, and all she had to do was take one step towards him and she would be in his arms, with the earnest desire of his body, soothing away the tired ache in her own, as she knew that he alone could do, but she had to deny herself, deny him.

"I don't want to hear your reason."

"I love you, Helen," he softly pleaded. "I can't stress the fact more fervently, but last night, when you played … I'm the only one you've toured the area with, and not only was Arnie's introduction revealing, but the music tore the very heart out of you. You feel something for me, I swear."

She turned away from him, her breasts heaving, passionately, strongly denying, "No, you're wrong, you're wrong." — He moved to stand behind her, treacherously close, she tensed when he placed his hands on her upper arms, with the intention of turning her to face him.

"Was it for Rory that you played so tortuously? You were so cosily content when wrapped in his arms, while dancing with him."

She turned to face him, she was trapped between the wall and her predator, she placed her hands onto his hard chest in an effort to push him away, but he gripped her wrists, "No!" Helen frantically denied, as Duncan's grip tightened, she just as frantically wrestled with him, trying to free herself, realising his intention when he forced against the wall. — Her breasts heaved, she averted her head, but there was to be no escape from his hard, cruel, demanding lips now imprisoning her own, "Duncan, *please*, don't do this," she pleaded, when she had managed to wrench her mouth free from his bruising kiss.

"Is Rory's love making more welcome than mine — is it?" he gruffly, angrily, demanded, his jealousy more flagrant. "I promised myself this moment, and I will have it. — Your branded, your mine, no-one else is going to spoil you, Helen Campbell … all the way and every day, until you beg for my body, every hour."

"But … can't you understand, I don't want you, Duncan," she suddenly sobbed, shaking her head. "I don't want *you*," she lied, "You're contemptuous."

He stared wildly at her, then angrily, roughly, released her, expelling a grunt of disgust before moving towards the door, and pointing his index finger at her, "Yeel no be leaving," he warned, "If you do, on Mairie

Campbell's grave, I so promise … I'll destroy you," he threatened.

She took a step towards him, earnestly intending to protest, but he had gone, left the cottage, and the last that she heard of him was the fading angry roar of the Rover's engine as he left the lane.

"No," she sobbed, tremulously murmured, as she stood listening to the deathly silence for some minutes. — His threat had hardly penetrated, there remained only cold numbness and one thought in her mind, she had to escape.

Within half-an-hour, she had packed a few essential items from her wardrobe into her suitcase, and abandoning the idea of the train, eventually, with trepidation, transferring them to her car. — Undaunted by the weather, she planned to travel to Gretna, staying overnight in a hotel, to continue her journey via Westmorland to London on the morrow.

On leaving the boundaries of Arrochar, she glanced back in her rear view mirror, saddened by the knowledge that not only was she leaving involuntarily, but she was letting down so many people — Jean and the winter entertainment programme, Rory and the Youth Club, Duncan and his Project, but most of all — if she stayed — the morals of Helen Campbell, she couldn't trust herself to remain aloof to Duncan's advances for all time. — She needed him, wanted him as much as he seemed to want her. — But he didn't need her, she reminded herself, he had Alex, and the sooner she put some distance between them, the better it would be, for all.

Chapter 21

Downfall

"No longer required!" Helen exclaimed, aghast at the news which Ryder had just conveyed, "Why … tell me … why?" she frantically demanded.

Ryder had the grace to shake his head apologetically, "After having received this letter from an associate of yours, I engaged the services of an older, wiser, more experienced columnist, someone who wouldn't back down at the eleventh hour. — And, quite frankly, Helen, your report on the Alex Craig Press Conference was pathetic, — to quote, 'Miss Alex Craig, glamorous Hollywood star, is to make a film in her home town of Arrochar, Scotland' unquote. — This chap MacFarlane, I understand, was present at the conference; he enlightened me, as to the fact that you didn't even bother to respond to an open invitation from Miss Craig to interview her. And quite frankly again, Helen, when you knew that you alone had a scoop, I could only conclude that the paper was no longer of any importance to you, — can't have my Reporter's falling down on the job, by allowing sentiment to stand in the way of headline news, - we're the laughing stock of Fleet Street."

"MacFarlane … Duncan, he told you what happened at the conference?" she replied, feeling choked with humiliation.

"He did," Ryder confirmed, while pulling at his crumpled tie which seemed to be forever at half-mast.

"Can I see this letter?" Ryder nodded and handed her the missive, typewritten on the estate's crested notepaper: -

Sir, she read …

With reference to the Craig/Browning Press Conference

I wish to take this opportunity to convey to you my congratulations for employing such an astutely sympathetic young lady, such as - Miss Helen Campbell.

Miss Craig is a relation of mine, and is of an impetuous nature, therefore, I had correctly surmised that she would be vulnerable under Miss Campbell's slick interviewing techniques. Knowing of her aptitude at cross-questioning, I requested of her to forsake interviewing Miss Craig on the personal level which she had intended.

I might add, in her defence, that she acted throughout the last several months like the determined professional she appears on the surface, but in reality, her true personality, that of a humanitarian, came to the surface at the conference, and it was heartening to witness, that in the face of Miss Craig's innocently open invitation, Miss Campbell resisted and complied with my wishes. Please convey my thanks to her. Regards — Duncan R. MacFarlane

Innocent, impetuous, vulnerable — the three unbelievable words blazed up at her, three words that in no-way described Alex Craig — aghast — Helen stared at the letter until it became a blur, — Duncan is the astute one - she thought - he knew exactly how Ryder would react to what appeared to be an innocently made acclaim. And without a doubt, he had deliberately, truthfully, given Ryder the reason for her failure to produce the expected standard of article. — Then she remembered his warning that she would stay and complete her six months in Arrochar, with or without the stability of a contract. — But, if he expected her to run back into his lair now that she was without ties, then he was very much mistaken. — He had done as he had threatened, destroyed her career, in one simple blow.

Sadly, Helen returned the letter to the Editor's desk, choking back the tears of disappointment which threatened — tremulously, she said, "I'll try another paper."

Again, Ryder shook his grey head, "No chance, too many were witness to your downfall."

"Then, I'll freelance," she stubbornly replied.

"You can try, but that racket is a long, hard haul."

She wearily, resignedly, stood — it had taken her three days to return home under impossible weather conditions and a burst tyre. — Suddenly, she shuddered with cold despite the overwhelming central heating — with an effort, she turned on quivering legs, wondering if they would carry her to the door, while at the same moment, feeling a return of a familiar stabbing pain in the region of her chest, — a pain, which she had been trying to ignore for days. — She hesitated, conscious that Ryder had dismissed her to answer the telephone, and when she glanced back, he absently raised a hand in farewell.

In the building foyer, Helen became wracked by a fit of coughing, the spasmodic pains increased tenfold, leaving a dull ache when the fit has subsided — she shivered again, expelling a groan when the pain caught her once more unawares. Eventually, she managed to find her way outside and into her car.

"I can't understand it!" Glynis exclaimed, later, "Arrochar should have been the perfect climate to ward off chest complaints, but instead, here you are, in much the same condition as you were six years ago. — I do wish that the doctor would hurry up," she continued worriedly, while straightening the pink silk eiderdown on Helen's bed.

Charles sat beside the bed, holding her hand, staring with concern at Helens' pale but still lovely features. — She had a frail delicacy about her; he had seen it before when her father had died. — She was fretting about something that must have happened in Arrochar, of that he felt certain, but she was too ill to question at the moment.

She opened, large, frightened eyes, dull with fatigue and pain, — she gripped his hand surprisingly tighter, frantically saying with difficulty, "Charles, I beg of you, I don't want to see anyone, or for anyone to know of this — promise me."

Suddenly, she became wracked with yet another fit of coughing. — He tenderly raised her head, reached for the glass of water beside him and held it to her lips for her to sip.

He nodded. "It's Switzerland for you, my girl; I've had enough of this career nonsense to last a lifetime."

It was confirmed, without a doubt, that Helen had a return of her old enemy, pneumonia, which she adamantly argued, that she was merely struck down by a bout of the flu, which had been sweeping the village. — Her arguments fell on deaf ears, for immediately, Charles arranged for her to be booked into a Swiss clinic with the highest possible reputation for medical care. — She was denied all papers, which bore any resemblance to news of the outside world.

In her fevered state, she tossed, turned and struggled with her tortuous un-rested mind …

*"The arrangements **are** that you travel to Edinburgh by **train** in ten days*

time, where I've booked you into a hotel for one night."

Helen did look a trifle perplexed; she sat up pert, echoing, "train, train, train ..."

.

"Can't we airlift her?"
"And risk spreading the infection?"

"Dull and pompous ... no ...no."

"He had a fetish for Mairie Campbell ... a fetish ... a fetish ...."
"You are her replacement ... replacement ... replacement ...."

"Helen." he spoke her name quietly detaining her, and then pausing as if he couldn't find the words which he wanted to say, while looking down at the now unlit torch between his hands. — His face in the shadows, she couldn't determine, realising that for the second time that evening, he had something to say — and yet — there he was stumbling for words again, — Alex had prevented him earlier, so what prevented him now, she wondered while waiting for him to continue?— He heavily sighed, almost in resignation, "I'll see you on the morrow, I have some things which Mairie left you," he said. "Sleep well," and lifting her hand, raised it to his lips to kiss before hastily turning to leave. — She hesitated, sucking in her breath, wanting to call him back, the words dying on her own lips as she watched him departing, before disappearing into the darkness of the lane, there to become a mere shadow. — Moments later, she heard the car spurt into soft purring action, — whatever he had wanted to say, had once more, been, left unsaid, — and pondering further, wondered what it was that he found so difficult, for he wasn't at a loss for words; these bouts of shyness seemed alien to him.

Unable to resist, she slid her arms about his neck as he lowered his dark head, his lips claimed hers, gently at first, expertly coaxing and teasing them into response. — It was a beautiful sensation, she thought, poetically, reminding her of whispering fresh winds, blowing through the heather, fanning sparks into flame. — She responded gladly, sighing again, his kiss deepening, his tongue invading the warm velvety softness of her mouth. — And both seeming to slake a long insatiable thirst, she clung to him closer, feeling that she never wanted the moment to end, and softly sighing, relaxed against him, enjoying the pleasing caressing motion his

239

hands made on her back, unsure of whether she was floating or drowning in the exquisite ecstasy of his embrace, — then Helen's burning senses reeled anew, when Duncan urgently murmured her name against her lips, and she felt his hands slide down over her hips pressing and moulding her against his muscular thighs, of his physical need, she was in no doubt.

Later that evening, she was preparing to retire early, but as she lowered the lights, she suddenly sucked in her breath as an unexpected, rumble of thunder sounded in the distance; she shivered with the sudden drop in temperature,

"Duncan! Duncan MacGilchrist!" she murmured his name, and then tensed, as a whispering sound, as if on the howling wind, came to her ears, 'Lady Ghislaine; Mairie Campbell' she heard, the hardly audible, echoing, whispering voices, followed by the nearing of the threatened storm.

"My Lord, I beseech thee, finish your quest and quiet this maiden's desperate need of you."

The softest voice from afar whispered, "You are no longer a maiden, you are the wife of the noble Lord Lennox, and I am honoured to serve thee with my body, my Lady... I love only you, until the sands of time run out, and we can be eternally, together."

"Please ...," she tremulously whispered.

"I know you called me last night," he revealed, "which is why I've come this morning ... you needed me, deny it if you dare."

"I don't need you ... I don't need anyone." she earnestly denied.

Helen moaned, hearing soft voices from afar, and seeing a misty crowd of faces above her.

"We daren't move her until her temperatures down."

"How long?" the laconic reply questioned.

"There's no telling, it could take hours; it could take days."

"Fight, Helen," a determinedly firm voice pleaded.

"Excuse me, miss," the bell hop said, as he approached, "Are you, Miss Helen Campbell?"

"I am."

"Well, it's like this," he said, while nervously shifting his feet, "I believe you stayed here about a month ago."

Helen nodded, while Jean sat bemused.

"A gentleman left this envelope for you, but somehow ... it didn't get delivered and seen as you're here now," he proffered the envelope, "Well, here it is."

Helen took it from him and then let out a gasp, staring at the object, recognising, "Jean, its Duncan's crest!" she tipped the bellhop, and then with trembling hands, swiftly ripped open her mail reading ...

September 11th

Miss Campbell,

Please will you wait in the Hotel's foyer? I will look forward to meeting you directly at 14.00 hours.

Yours faithfully - Duncan R MacFarlane

"This is very strange," Helen frowned, "In accordance with the will; he was supposed to be meeting me at Talbert station."

" Jean replied, "Well, obviously, all did not go according to plan and he was trying to kill two birds with one stone, by meeting both you and Alex."

"Then, why didn't I get this?

"Bad service," Jean suggested, chuckling. "Perhaps you shouldn't have tipped the bellhop." She read the envelope, "It says that it was handed in at 12.45pm."

Helen looked thoughtful; "I left the hotel shortly before 12am to keep my appointment with Crawford, but I was an hour early, I then went into a nearby café; I wonder what happened to him."

"That's no mystery, he was just tied up, he was like a 'bear with a sore head' when he arrived back in the village with Alex and Arnie," Jean informed, again chuckling, "And after your little fracas in Bracken Lane, he was like a man demented."

"I bumped into him, bumped into him, in Edinburgh, I bumped into him."

Deep in thought, she crossed the square and rounding the corner, she suddenly startled, sucking in her breath as she collided with a well-dressed young man in a tearing hurry, "I beg your pardon," he apologised, gripping *her shoulders to steady her on her feet.*

"I ... its okay, you startled me ... that's all," she said, breathlessly, though her bag had fallen to the pavement. — Both bent to retrieve it, and then her coat slid from her shoulders, and gripping the errant garment, saved it from dropping onto the pavement also. "I don't think, I'm winning," she chuckled.

"Yours, I think," he said, proffering her bag. "I'm sorry, I must dash," he apologised, hovering for barely a moment.

"Oh, thanks, don't let me detain you," she smiled.

He returned her smile and then was gone.

For a moment, Helen watched his hastily departing back, he must be late for a lunch appointment, she considered, and shrugging, brushed the brief incident aside.

"Helen fight, you must fight,"

"Noooo," she groaned.

She turned at the sound of the door opening, and smiled as Duncan entered carrying two steaming cups of coffee which he placed onto the side tables, either side of the desk, he then stood behind, leaning close to read what she had written, the radar from his cheek, so warm and disturbingly close to hers, took her breath away, and rosied up her complexion, evidencing her emotions — her heart thumped noisily in her breast – so noisily that she was afraid that he could hear, "Helen, the word Talbert, should be, a- Tarbet."

"Oh, I ... was thinking of Talbert House. – Remind me what a Tarbet is?"

"You know about the Viking King Hakon from the Shetlands, and when he decided to attack the MacFarlanes, — the piece of land they rolled the boats over is called a- Tarbet — it's a stretch of land between two lochs, in this case — Loch Long and Loch Lomond."

With the coffee forgotten, he glanced at her sideways, increasing her discomfort at his close proximity, his lips so close to hers that it felt as though he was willing her to turn her head and blend her lips into his, — the willing continued, — heart still pounding, she began trembling as the irresistible, magnetic, age-old attraction increased, — she silently gasped as his cheek brushed hers, and then indeed, she slowly turned her head until their lips met, — he pulled her up in front of him, a moment when the torture of long spent denial could easily turn into the sweetness of a fully-

242

satisfied union, — he coaxed, understanding her fear, "No-one is going to come, Helen – no-one will know," he earnestly breathed.

As his lips plied their trade, searching, heady and devouring, she felt his shaking, desperate urgency, "Come and share a shower," he tempted.

She spoke against his lips, "Duncan, you promised to behave yourself if I agreed to work in the Loch House, – and what are you doing home — you've only been gone an hour?"

"I can't work knowing you're here – it's like a dream, I had to make sure that it wasn't. ..." he murmured, as his stealthy hand slid between them. ...

Mr Crawford met them at the door, "I see you finally found her, Duncan," he said, vigorously shaking his hand and then, Helen's.

Helen glanced at Duncan, curiously, "Found her?" she echoed, puzzled, "I wasn't aware that I was lost."

"I'll explain, later," Duncan hastily replied.

Mr. Crawford cleared his throat, realising that he may have said the wrong thing, "Yes — it was quite extraordinary, you both missing each other like that. — but now, matters in hand," he brushed, changing the subject. "I'm glad that you've come together, we can kill two birds with one stone, but before we begin with the Project matter, I was on the point of sending you this," he said, while handing Helen a package. "I was instructed to withhold it, until now."

Helen frowned, "Whatever's this?" and when she broke its seal with trembling fingers, revealed, "The missing photographs!" she exclaimed, surprised, and flicking through them while laughing softly, continued, "I think I'll save these 'til later.

Crawford studied her for a moment, privately thinking that Helen looked prettier than she had two months, previously, her eyes were glowing with happiness and she had obviously struck up a very good rapport with Duncan, noticing that they were very familiar with one another.

Found ... found ... found ...

"I could eat a horse," she commented.

"I could devour you, Helen Campbell," he replied.

"That's cannibalism," she accused, with a laugh.

"I know," he chuckled, "But at least, I'd know I'd always have you with me, and you wouldn't be escaping to London at every next excuse."

"You would still be complaining, because you couldn't see me," she pointed out.

"I'll see you, as I've always seen you, in my heart."

"You say the nicest of things," she sighed.

"But I don't just want to see you in my heart; I want to see you, touch you, feel you, smell you, and be with you every day, just like this."

"It's a strange place to find a hut," she said, evasively, acknowledging a crumbling building on the opposite bank of the river, in the middle of nowhere.

"It just looks like a hut," he informed her, "It's called a 'Shieling' the shepherds used to take shelter and light their peat fires. I think more went on out here with the lassies, than ever met the Laird's eye."

"I think, my Lord has eyes in the back of his head," she laughed.

He replied, "I wish I did have eyes in the back of my head, and then I would know what you were doing with, Rory Cameron."

She glanced surreptitiously sideways, and with a secretive, mischievous smile, answered, "It's none of your business."

"I've told you before, you are my business."

"Can we go and look? We can cross the river by the bridge, it isn't far — I'll race you."

"Helen wait!" he called, and started running after her, soon to overtake, heading for the little stone parapet bridge, where he barred her way. — She was panting and laughing as she darted this way and that trying to pass him, but he was swifter with his movements, "I thought you were going for a paddle," he grinned.

"The water's too cold."

"The waters never cold, you should go for a swim." She turned away as if she had lost interest, when he suddenly lunged and grabbed her from behind by the waters edge, where he began to tickle her. — She tussled with him, trying to escape, but he had a restraining arm across her front shoulders; his hand clutching her breast; — she shrieked and giggled, he suddenly let go, she stumbled, loosing her footing and her balance, she wildly reached out and grabbed his arm, but it was too late — they both fell floundering into the stream, "I said you should go for a swim," he laughed, panting, as the water swirled around them.

"Duncan, you did that on purpose," she accused, also panting with excitement while splashing him with hands full of water. — He grabbed her and pulled her to her feet, his shirt was unbuttoned to the waist; the button on his jeans had snapped off and his zip had slid partially down,

exposing his tantalising, flat, muscular belly and a dark fringe of hair, — he hadn't realised his state of undress until he saw her studying him, — she was stirred at the sight, she was aching, burning with desire for him; the moment became insane — in a trice she was in his arms, his lips found hers and passionately welded — in a frenzy they tore off their soaking clothes; he had watched her bouncing derriere on the horse, and had quietly envied the animal for being between her thighs, - that, plus the shape of her naked breasts and moulded peeked nipples beneath her close fitting tee-shirt, which had been disturbing him all morning, "now there's nothing between us," he breathed, hoarsely.

Her loins were throbbing with excited, expectant desire, she was desperate to receive him; he edged her back onto the riverbank where they sank down together, Duncan swiftly rolled her onto her back where he knew, his dominating thrusts were more forceful, more powerful, more satisfying. - with the same desperate urgency, he went inside her; immediately his thrusts were strong and determined, hitting the gee spot every time, her hips wildly gyrated in unison with his, she frantically clung to him, he knew that she was climaxing, she panted urgently, "Duncan, don't stop; it's coming again."

"Christ!" he muttered, and with all his might, he exercised control, his powerful young limbs supporting him, suddenly, she strained against him; he loudly groaned in release, for the second time, shooting out his passionate royal ecstasy.

Moments later, Duncan grinned; he was somewhat out of breath while petting her as they lay locked in rest, "If the need was that great, my Lady, why you didn't you tell me sooner; - is it always like this?"

She chuckled, teasing, "I could blame it on riding the horse."

"You're winding me up; you haven't been on the horse for hours."

He put his hand down between them, in an effort to gently withdraw, and as he did, she gasped, while frantically clutching at his wrist; she wanted him back again. ...

"I love you, Helen, love ... love ... love."
"No, you can't ... you mustn't ... mustn't ... mustn't."

"The dress was quite ruined ... ruined... ruined."

Charles felt angry inside, mostly with himself; he felt that he'd failed in his duty to care for Helen's welfare. — He had been weak in allowing

245

her to go against her fathers' wishes as he had, wrong — in suggesting a career with Ryder, knowing that he was a ruthless, hard bitten businessman without sentiment. For one thing that Helen had conveyed to him before her departure with her mother, was of Ryder's refusal to renew her contract, a visit to Ryder told him why, thus throwing him into a rage. — His reasons were feeble, Charles considered, and accused him of taking advantage of an eager young girl, but at least he felt he had the answer to Helen's lowered state of health. — Loyal to her wishes, her parents met any enquiries as to her whereabouts with the scant reply that she was holidaying abroad and didn't want to be disturbed.

Leaning her head against the frame of the open French window in the Swiss hotel, Helen surveyed the splendid snowy scene before her. — She sighed as she had sighed for many months while gazing at the same scene, haunted by echoed words, "It's another Switzerland," Duncan had said it again and again, and as so many times before, she yearned to be back in Arrochar. — She hadn't uttered one word about her experiences there, and her parents hadn't questioned her beyond the loss of her job. — Gratefully to Helen, Duncan's letter to Ryder had seemed beyond reproach, feeling no hatred for him; she contented herself to let it remain so.

They would be married by now, Alex and Duncan, and unselfishly, Helen hoped that Alex wouldn't make him wait too long before she had his child, for Duncan needed an heir. — A son, she thought, with a soft wistful smile, a son with smiling blue eyes, a not such a handsome face, but with hair so dark ...

"Are you packed and ready to leave, Helen?" came, her mother's enquiry. "Charles will be meeting us at Heathrow, unless of course, you wish to change your mind and go via Paris. — Monsieur Muchet assures us that he is still prepared to continue with your piano studies."

Helen half-turned from the window, she sighed again, shaking her head refusing, "No, I haven't the heart or the will to play the piano. To accept your offer would be a criminal waste of the Maestro's time and daddy's money." But to herself, she knew that without the spirit of Duncan's love, her playing would not be of any consequence.

He alone had been her inspiration, the missing essence for which she had so long sought to complete both her talent, and her life, but because of circumstances, she was forced to remain incomplete, — and yet, she had discovered a feeling of strong kindred spirit with Duncan, as though they had met before in another dimension, — or perhaps it was a perception of things to come in a later life, — or perhaps again, mere wistful thinking on her part, as had been the ghost, of the Castle Drumbrae. "Perhaps, I am

Mairie Campbell and he Angus," she whispered aloud.

"What did you say, dear?" Glynis called, along with a perplexing frown.

"O ... Oh, nothing," she hastily replied.

Chapter 22

The Rustle of Spring

A stroll in St. James Park on a Sunday afternoon in the spring was a pleasurable event. It was the day after Rita and Gary's wedding, they were honeymooning in some secret place abroad, but Helen gave no thought to the fact as she gazed about her, finding pleasure in the fresh green leaves on the trees, in the early May blossoms, in the young ducklings paddling so laboriously to keep pace with their proud mother duck on the river, and again in the daffodils scattered so bravely amongst the grass, their yellow heads dancing in the soft breeze. — The scene struck her as always, incredible, that only a short distance away laid the bustling city centre, which she hated. — It would be lambing time in Arrochar, she suddenly thought, so Duncan would be very busy, he would be busy with other things also, it was Easter, the tourist trade would be booming now. — Silently, she wished him success with it, perhaps Alex would be of assistance; she hoped so.

She ceased walking to lean over the parapet of a small bridge, where water lazily flowed beneath, looking refreshingly cool. It reminded her of another bridge, her bridge in Arrochar, and then she wondered, — not for the first time, what arrangements Duncan had made for the cottage. Charles had never bothered her with any details, and she had felt reluctant to ask, fearing that she would hear something of an adverse nature.

Absently, she turned from the parapet intending to continue with her stroll, when she collided with a woman, "O ... Oh, I beg your pardon, please forgive me," she said, feeling very embarrassed.

"Why, it's Helen Campbell!" the Lady suddenly exclaimed. "I only met you the once, but I would know you anywhere."

Collecting her wits, Helen looked more closely at her unexpected companion, "Mrs Murray!" Helen also exclaimed, in surprise.

"Not anymore," she said, smiling with glee, as she glanced beyond Helen's shoulder, "... and to prove it, here comes my husband, now." Helen turned to face the newcomer, unprepared, followed by pleasurable surprise, filling her every feature, as she waited for the familiar figure of James Craig, as he neared his approach, "Look who I've found, James!" Connie excitedly exclaimed, while holding Helen's arm.

He greeted her pleasantly, enthusiastically shaking her hand, "Helen, how the devil are you? We were surprised that you left Arrochar so prematurely." He kissed her proffered cheek,

"Well, it seems that congratulations are in order James, are you holidaying in London?"

"Gracious, no," replied the new Mrs Craig. "We live here, in Kensington, to be exact."

"But ... who is caring for Craigiemhor Farm?" she stiltedly enquired, confused.

James sounded surprised at her question, he replied, "Duncan ... until he finds a suitable manager?"

"Oh, of course, the arrangement; how silly of me."

James continued, "Yes, I sold the property to him last year, I thought you might have been aware of it."

Helen stared up at the large man, her face clearly blanched with shock; accompanied by a lurching stomach. — She shook her reeling head, clamouring to absorb the enormity of his words, her voice faltered as she spoke, "You ... *sold* Craigiemhor Farm." she exclaimed in incredulous disbelief.

He nodded; he frowned, as it was becoming obvious that his news had been disturbing, and that he would have to choose his words with care, "Yes, that's right."

"I ... I have to confess that your news has come as a shock," she said, quietly forcing the stammered words through trembling lips, "I ... I understood that Alex had returned home to keep certain promises that she had made to Duncan, some years ago."

James forehead again creased in a perplexing frown, he shook his head, not seeming to understand; his hesitant reply was blank, "I ... don't know what you mean, lass."

Fearful now of what she may hear, Helen replied, "Alex indicated, that the only way Duncan could acquire Craigiemhor, was to marry her."

James eyes held an amused expression, but taking in Helen's pale anxious face and her fingers now nervously plucking at her fine leather gloves, held between her cold shaking hands, he realised the consternation his news had evoked; — he became serious with wondering, he took hold of her elbow while urgently scanning the area for a seat.

"We'll go home," Constance suggested, immediately reading his mind. "It's only around the corner, Helen looks as though she could manage a good hot, cup of tea."

Helen felt too overwrought to notice much of her surroundings, but the Craig's flat appeared comfortably, expensively furnished as befitting a Kensington flat.

Constance disappeared to prepare the much-needed tea, while James sat talking to Helen, "I owe you an apology for finding what you said amusing, Helen, but the truth is … that Duncan wouldn't marry Alex, even if his very life depended upon it, and seen as it's never likely too …" he shrugged.

"But Alex seemed so positive?" Helen queried, obviously still confused.

James shook his head in despair, pleading, "Forget that I'm Alex's father, and tell me *exactly* what she told you."

Slowly, stiltedly, she relayed the conversations, which had taken place between her and Alex, both at the party and in the castle gallery, managing to withhold her true feelings for Duncan and the part on history repeating itself. But made it abundantly clear, how she was told that Duncan and Alex would be marrying to unite the lands, also, she included her grandmother's association with the old Laird. — As the story unfolded, a steady disgust for his daughter spread across James Craigs' features. The man shook his head, "I should have dealt with her years ago," he murmured sadly. "I only hope that I can repair some of the damage she has done, by urging you, to go and see Eleanor Graham. She and she alone, will tell you the truth about your grandmother, better it comes from her."

"You said that you were married in January, is that when Duncan purchased Craigiemhor?" Helen enquired, feeling agitated, trying to content herself, for in reality, she felt like catching the next train, plane or anything that would carry her back to where she belonged, but she was also eager to hear what was to be said, she keenly listened to what followed …

"Before that, Helen, in fact we completed the contract on the very same day that you arrived in Arrochar. — Duncan was impulsive, I felt that it something that he was going to regret, although his plan seemed quite straightforward at the time, — the idea was to meet you at Crawford's office, and sign the papers, which we knew were ready and in order, thus transferring Craigiemhor over to the estates, but there was no chance of pre-warning Crawford of our impending arrival in Edinburgh, and unfortunately, Alex arrived on the very same day. Thinking that we had plenty of time, I mistakenly persuaded Duncan to accompany me to the Airport in the morning; it was difficult, as he was reluctant to change his plans. — It was apparent that he felt anxious to meet you, and when Alex realised this, she delayed him even further by acting out some ridiculous scene from one of her films. — She snatched his car keys from him, leaped into the Rover and drove off at break-neck speed. We caught up with her at South Queensferry, some miles outside of Edinburgh. — Duncan has been angry before, but I never want to see him in such a murderous mood again. — Alex laughed scornfully, and commented that it had been a pity that the cameras hadn't been rolling."

Helen suddenly chuckled, feeling on cloud nine, and pink for the first time in months, she sat forward on her seat, asking eagerly, "And what happened, then?"

James smiled shrewdly, noticing Helen's renewed heightened condition, she was actually laughing, but he didn't continue until Constance has served the tea and had settled with them.

"When we finally got back into Edinburgh, it was lunchtime, Duncan knew that your appointment with Crawford was at 1pm, but you had been and gone before he'd got there. — Crawford couldn't see us immediately, so Duncan then went over to your hotel and left a note asking you to wait until we had completed our business with Crawford, — just after 2.30pm, when we returned to the hotel, his note to you remained unopened, still in the pigeon-hole behind the reception desk," he smiled. "Needless to say, the clerk suffered the raw edge of Duncan's tongue."

Helen gave a soft laugh, "He's a much tried man," she remarked.

James continued, regretfully, although his voice held a slight unbelievable chuckle, "More than you know, Helen. He dashed into the Waverly Station, to see your train leaving, and having missed you by minutes, he decided to stay in Edinburgh overnight, but that single night was doomed to be extended into two. Alex discovered that she would be living in the Arms Hotel during her stay. She complained bitterly, until Duncan agreed to lease Craigiemhor to her, so that involved returning to Crawford and waiting until he had drawn up the lease agreement. — Against my better judgement, I allowed Alex to talk us into extending our stay in Arrochar. She hadn't been home for some years, and it didn't seem decent to leave the minute she had arrived, but it did help Duncan, we did our share of diverting her away from him. — And when we did leave last October, in order to make the arrangements to marry in London," continued James, "Alex showed reluctance to accompany us, but then, — the Lady Eleanor finally managed to shame her into it."

"Duncan had had enough of her, even then," Constance added.

"James nodded his agreement, and then downed his remaining tea, "I wasn't surprised to find that he'd cancelled the filming."

"Cancelled the filming," Helen echoed, showing incredulous surprise.

"You're very out of touch for a reporter," Constance remarked.

"Oh, I'm not a reporter anymore. I've been abroad; I haven't bothered with newspapers."

"Somewhere nice?" questioned Constance, with a hopeful suggestion in her voice.

"Switzerland," Helen truthfully replied, for now she was home, it seemed unnecessary to avoid the issue.

"If you're not employed, why not return to Arrochar?" James suggested, indicating that he would like to enjoy a cigar.

"Carry on," Helen smiled. "I could never stop Duncan from smoking, it so suited him."

He began to light up and between puffs, informed, "Duncan could do with your help, this Tourist Project idea that he was so keen to start, seems to have fizzled out, among a lot of other things. I don't think the village is going to boom as well this year, as in the past."

Helen's smooth brow furrowed; she appeared perplexed, "He had such plans for the village and a lot of support from the villagers. Why should he neglect his interests?"

The older couple glanced at each other helplessly, "We're not sure, Helen," Constance replied, "The hearts gone out of him."

Helen's brain suddenly clamoured, trying to remember something, which at the time had hardly registered. Echoed words spoken by Jean, 'If you leave, you will take the heart of Arrochar with you' she had earnestly tried to warn, trying without so many words to tell of the depth of Duncan's feelings, "Oh, I've been so blind," she groaned aloud, regretfully remembering her stubbornness at the time.

Constance patted her hand sympathetically, as if she understood, "Not your fault," she said.

"I must go," Helen urgently exclaimed, suddenly standing, knowing at once where she should be.

James stood also, grasping her by the shoulders, "Helen, lass, heed me, you belong in Arrochar as much as Mairie Campbell, but before you leave London, go and see your Editor. — Before Alex returned to the States, she let slip that she had made some sort of an arrangement with him, involving you. — I'm sorry, lass, it seems that my daughter really had her knife in you. I have a shrewd suspicion why, but only when you have seen Eleanor Graham, will you fully understand the substance of Arrochar."

Charles insisted on accompanying her for her interview with Ryder, in fact, Charles had become something of a mother hen since her recent return from Switzerland, hardly allowing her to be alone, but on this occasion, she was afterwards to feel grateful for his moral support.

They invaded Ryder's office unannounced; Charles sternly demanded to be told of the arrangements that had been made with Alex Craig. — At first, Ryder refused to comply, until the conversation which followed, became overheated …

"I'll sue you, Ryder, for breach of contract and unfair dismissal, if you don't comply," Charles said angrily, hammering his fist on the news desk. Ryder dropped his large frame wearily into his chair. He had been working all night to get the morning edition of the Daily News onto the streets, and now, to cope with this situation with Charles Petrie and Helen, was becoming overbearing. He scratched thoughtfully at the dark morning stubble, covering his chin, then sighing, raked a weary hand through his dishevelled hair, "Well, Ryder," Charles snapped, irritated by the long silence, "What is it to be?"

Ryder shrugged, raising his hand slightly in resignation and then stiltedly began, "I lied to you, Helen," he admitted, "I didn't meet Alex Craig at Heathrow. She had in fact already arrived in Edinburgh. You sounded so confident that you had a sensational story, that I thought it worth the time and effort to follow it through by flying north with the intention of waylaying Miss Craig, which I did, with a large amount of success, as having been delayed, I found her staying in an Edinburgh Hotel."

Perplexed, incredulous, Helen queried, "You went yourself; you didn't send Chester Maxwell. Why go to all that trouble?"

"I still had my doubts on your ability to carry that column single handed. True, you're a crack reporter, Helen, but you're not cut out for the game. You're too sentimental, true … you helped Madison with your ideas, so I thought on this occasion, I'd find out what you were letting yourself in for, and as it turned out, nothing. — Alex Craig, found it amusing when I asked her if she intended staying in Britain to marry a local man, she said, and I quote, 'Oh, that old story' unquote, and then she wanted to know how I knew about her life before she became famous. I explained that one of my top reporters was at present staying in Arrochar and that you were in fact, a relative of one of the locals. She became interested, and asked who you were; on hearing your name, she said that she knew you, that you were an old childhood friend. Well, one thing led to another," he shrugged. "I explained about my indecision of whom to hand over the column to, and why, she seemed sympathetic and wanted to help. She came up with the idea that she would act as though she still had an interest in the man, plus dropping the occasional little hint, so that by the time of her conference, you would have plenty of facts on which to base your interview."

Sadly, Helen shook her head in sickened disbelief; she felt a dull, miserable ache inside, realising that she had been set up, "So Rita was right, a test," she said, "which I failed."

Again, Ryder shrugged, replying laconically, "Something, like that."

"There was nothing to win, I would have made a fool of myself, either way," she reiterated.

"What did you pay this woman?" Charles angrily demanded. "She didn't do it for nothing, I'll be bound."

"Money never entered into it," Ryder denied. "She said, she would relish the challenge of a little acting on the side, plus the chance to publicly outwit a skilful interviewer, and that she would do anything for the applause."

"Public humiliation," Helen murmured.

"Some friend," Charles grunted in disgust.

"I've heard enough, Charles," Helen announced, trembling with anger while gathering her bag and gloves together as she hastily stood to leave.

"You can have your job back, Helen, — if you want it," Ryder casually dropped.

She stared at him with angry disbelief, before shakily, passionately, vehemently, replying between taut lips, disgust showing on her face, "Is that meant to be some kind of a joke? You sicken me Ryder, there's only one thing that you understand, and that is — the way to destroy lives."

A few minutes later, Helen sat in deep thought, sipping at the brandy which Charles had poured for her; the spirit was warming and settling. He sat watching her pondering, from across his desk, frowning, feeling helpless knowing that Helen's pale wistful face contained the evidence of the hurt that she was suffering, but how deep was that hurt, he wondered?

"Who is man in this situation?" he tentatively questioned.

"Duncan MacFarlane," she softly replied, while studying the golden liquid.

Charles chanced a cautious, furtive soft question, "Are you … in love with him, Helen; you know, loosing someone that you love, is the same as a bereavement, and that's what you've been suffering - isn't it?"

Helen sighed, feeling the weight of her pain, "Should I admit that, Charles?" she said evasively.

"You're running away from the truth," he said, shifting his position. — Still studying her, he carefully continued, revealing, "While you were away, he called on me about the cottage, he said he would leave the matter pending for a while, when I told him you were on holiday, but of course, that was months ago; probably changed his mind by now. — I must say, that I find it hard to believe that he would be a party to a façade like this, fine upstanding young man, I thought, proud to have met him."

Helen suddenly became livelier, smiling with incredulous disbelief, "You've met Duncan?" she said, eagerly surprised, trying to imagine Duncan in London. It was impossible, she thought, while feeling a return of some happiness, knowing that Charles had approved of him, but then she couldn't imagine anyone not approving of Duncan, — her expression warmly softened, immediately feeling a well of gratitude that he had talked her out of her interview with Alex. — Better the private humiliation she had suffered, than the public one planned, she underlined. "I have to say, that you're quite right, — Duncan wouldn't have had anything to do with it."

"Fasten your seat belts, please," smiled the stewardess. Helen complied to the request, then giving a soft sigh; she relaxed into her seat ready for the flight.

Charles had expressed surprise, followed by a show of paternal concern when she had stressed her desire to visit Eleanor Graham. — She had carefully side-stepped, giving the real reason for her visit, but she had indicated that she would possibly extend her stay to include Arrochar, in an effort to discover exactly what Duncan's intentions were regarding Bracken Cottage. — To have rescinded the cottage, Duncan would have only to furnish proof that she had failed to fully comply with Mairie Campbells' wishes, and he already had that proof. — Her absence from the country on his visit to Charles was proof enough.

Charles had suggested that a phone call or a visit to Crawford would clear the matter up, once and for all, but she had decried the idea, telling him that she had a moral obligation to discuss the matter with the Laird himself. And that it was the least she could do, in apology to Mairie Campbell for having failed her.

She sighed again, suddenly shifting to a more comfortable position, thinking that whatever happened on this visit; she at least would see Duncan again, even if it were for the last time.

Within only a short space of time, she would be in the Graham's large, luxurious, bungalow set in Corstorphine on the outskirts of Edinburgh. Eleanor had expressed pleasurable surprise when she had telephoned her two days previously, to announce her intended visit, and that she was anxious to see her on a matter concerning her grandmother. — There had been no question of where to stay, Eleanor had insisted that it must be with them, also, it had been arranged that they would meet her at the airport to save hiring a taxi.

She fleetingly wondered if she would inform Duncan of her pending arrival, but even if she did, there seemed only faint hope that he would travel into Edinburgh to meet her himself. — After all, she thought, sighing once more, the last time that they had met they had argued bitterly, she had frantically told him that she didn't want him, didn't want his love. — Usually, when a man such as Duncan had been humiliated, then he was bound to remain so, and she had had so many chances. Had she killed that love, she wondered?

The plane veered, changing course, sweeping over the bustling city centre, descending in readiness to land. — She renewed her lipstick and settled her pink brimmed hat onto her head, partly covering her upswept hairstyle. — She was smartly dressed in a stylish navy-blue suit, the colour of her hat, echoed in her blouse; an outfit that Glynis had exclaimed was the perfect choice for the time of year, but had insisted on her carrying a matching coat of lightweight wool, as a precaution against any change in climate, "The north, —" she had renewed the information, — "is very unpredictable with its weather, and it's early yet, Helen, far too early to be discarding clothes in readiness for the summer, besides, my dear, we can't have you ill again, - can we?" Helen had felt too weary to argue.

On leaving the plane, she entered the terminal lounge, anxiously scanning the crowd for familiar faces. She caught sight of Henry Graham's tall imposing figure, and the Eleanor's slighter one as they approached, smiling a welcome. She swallowed her disappointment on realising that they were alone.

At the sight of Eleanor, she couldn't control the emotion which suddenly welled up inside of her to evidence itself in glistening tears on her lashes. The sight of Eleanors' eyes, so like Duncan's tugged at her heart strings, "Oh, Eleanor," she softly sighed, emotionally, "It's so good to see you again."

"Helen, my child, welcome," she replied, with equal emotion, immediately embracing her. "You should never have left as you did, but I'm not going to scold you, — you followed your heart, and did what you thought was right," she continued, sensibly composing herself. "Now … we have a lot to talk about, and we can't do it here, standing in the airport."

During the drive, Helen anxiously requested news of Hannah, Rory and the Roaches. She stressed her sorrow for not having written to them, but offered no explanations, as she felt reticent to use her illness as an excuse, it would only evoke unnecessary concern and sympathy where she felt that none should be given. For now she knew, that she had needlessly deserted them, an instance whereby she would deserve their derision, and definitely Duncan's anger.

"You will have every opportunity to make your peace with them," Eleanor informed.

"I will," Helen replied feeling surprised at Eleanor's statement, for she hadn't confided her intention of visiting Arrochar.

"Of course, my dear, you can't possibly travel all this way without calling to see old friends. — Two days spent in Arrochar would put your mind at rest, and then you will be able to return to London to pick up the threads of your old life, in peace."

Helen's stomach plummeted at Eleanors' latter words, "O…Oh, yes, of course, Eleanor. — In fact, I had toyed with the idea, but I wondered if … if … oh …," she nervously trailed off, appealing for help.

"You wondered how the idea would appeal to Duncan," she said, questioningly while glancing at Helen's pale, anxious face, while thinking that Helen didn't have the appearance of a young woman who had recently returned from a refreshing holiday abroad. — She lacked that Campbell sparkle, in fact, she thought on, Helen had seemed unreasonably tired when she had last seen her at the muster party, but she had unwisely, dismissed it at the time.

"Yes, yes, I did wonder."

"He's angry, Helen. Did you expect him to be anything else?"

"No," she softly replied, and haltingly asked the question uppermost in her mind, "How is he Eleanor, in himself?"

"He's quite well, health-wise, probably growling at some poor fish or another, this very minute," — Eleanors' words brought a gentle wistful smile to Helen's face, remembering sweet, happy days spent with Duncan, golden days from which her musical joy had stemmed, — he had proved to be a master stone skimmer, equal to Rory, and she doubted Eleanors' statements, for she had been fishing with Duncan on more than one occasion, and he'd always impressed upon her, never to fish if you're angry, the fish are sensitive and refuse the bait, he had told her. She had laughed at the time, not taking him seriously, and as a punishment, he had attempted to tip her into the stream. – it was that day, the day that the universe had changed forever, while gripping a hold of his sleeve to still her balance, she had pulled him with her, both tumbling into a laughing wet heap into the water, and of course, he could not behave himself for very long, the playful kiss had turned into an erotic blissful dream, and now she came to think about it, Duncan had always managed to steal a kiss and he always went one further, as if it was his right …

She was tinkling at the piano one rainy afternoon, and despite the weather they were both in a light-hearted happy mood, Duncan stood leaning against the sideboard, just gazing at her from across the room,

"If you stare at me for very much longer, my Lord …

"I want to remember every moment with you, every move," He started to walk towards her and as he did so, he raised his hands to make a circle with his fingers and peered through.

Helen chuckled, "What are you doing?"

"I am the lens of a camera, photographing a face of exquisite beauty."

"Duncan … you're crazy," she said softly as he pulled her up in front of him and she slid her arms about his neck, his eyes caressing, wooing, urging, "Why do you keep kissing me? You complained about Rory taking undue advantage."

"Rory is just a game – I am the real thing, you're attracting me with your body chemistry; we are like magnets and should be together, always and forever, whatever the circumstances. And I like kissing eyes that are so alluring and lips that are so tempting and suppliant, — lips which stir the senses, mind and body. …"

"And I suppose that you have the answer to what two people should do on a rainy Sunday afternoon."

He Roguishly grinned and flicked up knowing eyebrows, before deepening their embrace.

All that seemed such a world away, she thought, and then became aware of Eleanor speaking.

"We'll phone him this evening, use all the feminine wiles that you can muster. If he's still under the impression that you're so completely liberated, then you're bound to take him by surprise."

Helen felt her stomach nervously churn, as a slight amount of panic beset her. — Phoning Duncan hadn't occurred to her, nor had announcing her arrival. — She had merely imagined travelling to Arrochar, quietly booking into the Arms Hotel, and later contacting him by sending him a note, asking if he would see her in reference to the cottage. — A coward's way, she thought and a stupid one. — But aloud, she said, "I don't think that Duncan would appreciate the use of feminine wiles, Eleanor, not in this instance, I'm quite sure that he's tired of them. Duncan would much prefer a direct business-like approach."

"Eleanor smiled in approval, and patted her hand as they drew up to the bungalow's gate. "That … was exactly the answer for which I had hoped."

Chapter 23

Mairie my Beloved

Helen stood gazing at the breathtaking view spread out before her, a view of the Pentland and Moorfoot Hills, as seen through the panoramic living room window. — So near and yet so far away was the focal point in her mind, just a short journey over those hills and she could be there, where she belonged.

She heaved a nervous shaky sigh, before turning into the room and smiling, on hearing Eleanor return with the replenished coffee percolator, and then began the process of pouring the steaming liquid into prettily flowered bone china tea cups, when the telephone rang shrilly. — She made the familiar inane remark of, "Now, I wonder who that can be? It certainly isn't Henry; he won't have arrived at his club yet." As she replaced the percolator on the tray, she rose to leave the room, closing the door behind her.

Helen finished filling the cups, and then with a half-contented sigh, sat back into a Victorian button-back chair, feeling happier now that she was in Eleanor's, sensible, caring company. Her down to earth approach had managed to dispel some of her inner turmoil, making the past few months seem unreal. Eleanor, had in fact, instilled an amount of hope into her without actually promising anything. — Suddenly, the door re-opened, Eleanor smiled in reassurance, "It's Duncan, Helen; he wishes to speak to you."

Her stomach nervously somersaulted as she tremulously reached out to replace her cup onto the coffee table, while stiltedly answering, "I ... I don't know what to say to him."

"Then, leave it to, Duncan," her companion suggested, kindly smiling, "Come now, get it over with, you only have to do it, the once."

With a feeling of trepidation, Helen stood to cross the room, she moved through the doorway with a hesitant step while her heart rapidly pounded in her breast. She crossed the wide expanse of hall, and reaching out a cool, trembling hand, lifted the receiver from the table from where it lay in wait for her, "Take a grip, girl," she self admonished, for she had never felt fear of Duncan before, even during his worst fury. — But her self-imposed rebuke hadn't helped, as she raised the receiver to her ear, "Hello, Duncan," she managed to keep her voice level and light.

He didn't answer immediately, but when he did, his voice came over the line in cool, curt tones, "I hear that you're planning on a visit to Arrochar. I shall expect you on the morrow, Helen, — on the noon train. I've a few, long overdue, loose ends to settle with you, so don't let it enter your pretty little head to suddenly … change your plans."

"I … was planning on staying with Eleanor for a few more days."

"Yeel do as I say, and be in Arrochar on the morrow," he ordered with authority. "Once I've received a signature from you, you can return to Edinburgh or even the damned earth's core, if you so wish."

Helen's throat ached with a- suppressed sob, as she momentarily covered the mouth piece, until she could reasonably compose herself enough to reply, "It seems that I have no alternative, but to do as you say." She quietly continued, "But, I wish to warn you that you don't hold all the aces, Duncan."

"I'll see you on the morrow, Helen," he said, before the line finally clicked and became dormant.

She stood holding the silent receiver for several seconds, before slowly replacing it onto the instrument. — Beaten into submission, she had her answer, her welcome in Arrochar's heart was no more, 'Oh, you simple, dreamy fool' she thought, — 'you should never have come; you should have left well alone'—. Saddened once more, Helen returned to the sitting room and Eleanor's company. "He insists that I be in village by tomorrow," she informed Eleanor, dully.

"Oh dear," she sighed, at the vision of Helen's unhappy countenance, saying kindly, "Come and sit down. I've poured you a brandy in the hopes that it may settle you. Duncan can be such a brute at times."

Helen sadly shook her head in disagreement, "No, he isn't Eleanor. — His anger is coupled with frustration and disappointment, I think he expected me to be a replacement for Mairie Campbell, and because of the …," she sought for the right words, "circumstances, I let him down."

"The circumstances being your job, you mean," she replied. "But I feel that you're quite wrong about Mairie Campbell. I agree that Duncan had a strong regard for her, but it was a very healthy regard, and I feel that she hid your photographs to avoid all this confusion, and after Alicia died, she asked Angus to hide the portrait from view, it just surfaced again at precisely the wrong moment."

Helen sighed, she spoke softly, "Eleanor, it's all such a muddle, there was an occasion … when I think that Duncan was prepared to discuss Mairie Campbell's past with me, but something happened, and after that he refused to broach the subject. — So many things happened ... things got started and never seemed to get finished."

"Oh, I see," said Eleanor in surprised interest. "So you know nothing?"

Helen shook her head, replying, "No — only that after her Press Conference, Alex waylaid me in the castle gallery and spun me some yarn about Mairie Campbell's past."

And so once more, Helen carefully related her story, in the same way in which she had relayed it to James Craig. But this time, adding her meeting with the Craig's in London, and the results of her eventual interview with Ryder, which included her own assignment, but omitted his offer of a job.

"I'm beginning to understand," said Eleanor. "But, I feel very sad and just a tad annoyed with you, but more so with Duncan. I had given him credit for having more sense in allowing such a bizarre situation to arise."

"Duncan was hardly to blame, Eleanor," Helen replied, between sips of brandy.

"What man is, between two women?" Eleanor smiled, but silently she forgave her son, knowing that there were none as blind as those in love, and seeing Helen now with her peach-bloom beauty, she could fully understand why Duncan had adored her so. — She had seen it in his face on the night of the muster party, — when they had found her in the gallery; he had cared for her so tenderly, refused all offers of help. She then remembered that Helen has sighed contentedly as he had lifted her, turning her face into his shoulder as if in her dreamy sub-conscious, she had known that she was safe in the arms which held her. At the time, it caused her to wonder, even to hope, but she herself could be forgiven for being wrong, she sighed. "It's a sad kind of pleasure that you have given me, Helen, but at least, when I have related certain facts to you from Mairie Campbell's young life, a lot of things will make sense to you, especially, Alex's overbearing malice towards you. — If only you had come to me sooner," she sighed again, and began relaying their story…

"Mairie and Angus were childhood sweethearts; their love blossomed in and around the village, but fate or circumstances, — whichever you may want to call it, — prevailed upon them in the shape of: - greed for land."

Angus's father, Walter MacFarlane, desperately wanted Craigiemhor Farm to complete the estates; in fact, he was prepared to stop at nothing to get what he wanted, even to the ruination of his son's life. — He made arrangements with the Craigs, that as soon as Angus attained the age of twenty-one, he would marry their only child, Alicia, thus solving the problem, as their marriage would ensure eventual unity of the lands.

Unfortunately, it hadn't entered Walter's head that Angus would defy his wishes, and so when he told his father that he was in love with Mairie Campbell, and intended to marry no-one but her, Walter became enraged, consequently, there followed strife, between father and son, but Angus remained stubborn …

"I want to wed, Mairie Campbell."

"A mill girl," Walter shouted, "… a servant, a forester's daughter, a simpleton."

Angus argued, "She has the bearings of a great lady, and she's scholarly."

*Walter's voice was angry, low and gruff as he replied, "Pah! The only education that Mairie Campbell has had is from the village school of which I am the benefactor. — It seems that it's dangerous to educate **peasants**, it gives them airs and graces and grandeur, far beyond their station. — I'll remind you again, that your life is mapped out for you, and that it has been since birth, — one day, yeel be a titled Lord."*

"Are you planning your own death, then?"

*"My life expectancy has nothing to do with this; you will marry Alicia Craig, — and **that's** final."*

"I'll not lay with her," he warned.

With irritated hands, Walter snatched his cigar from his mouth to speak, "Then, keep Mairie Campbell on one side and lay with her, it's about all she's good for."

Angus blazed, "You insult the girl that I love, Mairie is sweet and kind, gentle and loving, — she doesnae deserve to be used in such a manner."

"Nothing will have changed." Walter continued, "The gentry have always kept mistresses, they're useful in times when wives refuse to be forthcoming, — good wives always turn a blind eye to these sorts of things."

*"I'll nay impregnate Mairie unless she's my wife —You're mad keen to keep the Campbells in the village, — why; Yer fancied her mother and she wouldnae have yer, — would she, — not for **any** price?"*

"Yeel do as I say, or I'll cut Mairie's wage."

"She's poor enough as it is," Angus angrily replied.

"She isn't so poor that she cannae afford, silk dresses," Walter had observed.

"I bought it for her," Angus revealed, rashly admitted. "She made a wonderful artists model."

*"You bought it?" Walter echoed his son's words, his tone of voice was again passionately angry, questioning. "You bought that dress, so that she could be the subject of an **oil** painting, then it seems that I'm paying you too much as well."*

"Eventually, in desperation, Walter enlisted the aid of the Craigs in the matter, for they had as much, if not more to gain by their daughters union with Angus. Between the two families, they lifted the pressure from Angus onto Mairie; they took the opposite view, and suggested offering her substantial bribes to deny her love for Angus. — Those bribes, she wouldn't accept, so they used other, more devious methods by informing her that Angus would be completely disinherited if she persisted with her stubborn refusals to comply."

*"I'll **never** stop loving Angus, **never,**" she emphatically, passionately, underlined.*

"And loving Angus as she did, and knowing that Arrochar meant so much to him, she felt unable to destroy him, and so she unselfishly left the village."

"But what happened then?" Helen enquired, while sitting on the edge of her seat.

Eleanor sipped her drink before continuing with the heart rendering story …

"Angus, was of course, distraught, broken hearted when he found Mairie gone, — it didn't take him long to discover what his parents had done. So he defied them again, by going in search of her. — He searched for over a year, without success, and then the cruellest blow of all came, when he received a letter, which seemed genuine enough, informing him that Mairie Campbell had died from consumption."

Helen was beginning to understand, sadly, she added her own punctuation, "And then years later gran returned to Arrochar. It must have been a great shock to Angus."

"Yes, it was, but a greater shock on his part, to find that she'd married

Alistair Campbell, and they already had your father, David; — and very obviously, Alistair's son, — you see, Mairie and Angus realised that they were still very much in love."

He squeezed her tightly, she felt his anguish, his voice wobbled coming stiltedly, gruff, "Mairie, no, no, my own dear love, he kissed her moist wet face feverishly, "I cannae bear this life without you, I thought you dead, I thought you gone from my life and my being. — Mairie, I stand a man, demented and broken by love. I have nay pride, nay stubbornness, and nay tricks. I am naked, and as so, I bend on one knee to my Lady Mairie," and kissing her fingers, continued," I am, at last your humble servant," his eyes were bright with unashamed, anguished tears. "Why, is it always — too late?"

Mairie replied, "I'll never leave you again, my own darling, deere one. I will remain close and work alongside of you until the day that I die."

"But, she remained loyal to Alistair, he was a good man, and so realising that Angus was going to have none of it, his parents allowed him to marry Bridget Macleod. — She had his son, Duncan's father, but she wasn't strong, — in the end, he did marry Alicia, but only because Robert needed a mother, but he made pretty sure that that no Craig blood ran in his children's veins."

She answered, "I'll marry you, within the year, but only for the farm, I have no intention of being rendered homeless. It will be in name only."

"If you desire to remain infertile, it would suit me very well."

"I abhor the ways of men." was her reply.

"Then, my grandfather, Alistair died, leaving Mairie a widow 'til the bitter end."

"Yes — that's it. And so far as we know, Angus remained loyal to Alicia, even though she was barren, and as the only male heir, Craigiemhor was handed down to James Craig."

"If Alicia died first, why didn't Angus and Mairie marry?"

"It was thought that they had, but there were no records found, that was their secret, — we believe that they went through a ceremony without licence, just before he died, — a vow of loyalty to the end."

Helen shook her head, concluding, "And so Duncan and I are not related."

"Not a jot." Eleanor confirmed. "James realised too late, the damage he did in doting on Alex, many parents make similar mistakes, by overcompensating."

Helen enquired: - "He indicated that Duncan would never consider a marriage with Alex, so the rumours must have originated from somewhere; — Alex must have been aware of his feelings."

"She was made fully aware of Duncan's feelings, years ago. She started the rumours herself. — Originally, because they had grown up together, Alex took it into her head that one day Duncan would marry her, and she received plenty of encouragement from old Alicia. — You see … Alicia felt bitter at having been forced into a loveless marriage, and when she realised that Angus still had a great regard for Mairie, she understandably resented her. — It critically added to the situation, when she was forced to accept the glaringly obvious fact, that Duncan's affections were far greater for Mairie than for herself, — the woman who had reared his father. — So the bitterness, plus the jealousy, strengthened Alicia's resolve. — It was she who concocted the tales about Mairie and Angus, and over the years, she fed them to Alex, impressing them into her theatrical mind. — Alicia was well aware that if her niece and step-grandson were to marry, then James, having no male issue of his own, would have no alternative but to leave Craigiemhor to Duncan and Alex, thus making her own marriage to Angus seem less pointless. She was on her deathbed when she summoned for James, and he poor man, in his distress, promised that he would see to it that the marriage took place."

"Did Angus agree to this?" Helen asked in surprise.

Eleanor sighed, before replying, "Angus knew nothing of it, and neither did anyone else, including Duncan, until well after Alicia had died. Duncan had always taken his forthcoming responsibilities seriously, and was at the time, knee deep in his agricultural studies when it all came to light. — The thoughts of marriage hadn't even entered his head, but Alex, left with only Alicia's lies and last wishes, became impatient to be married. — James then approached Duncan's father on the subject, and I must admit that for a time, he had felt keen on the idea, but needless to say, Duncan's fury at having his life arranged for him, knew no bounds, — he didn't want Alex, and he wasn't interested in the Farm. — Angus and Mairie then backed Duncan's argument by revealing the true facts of their own lives. — Quite naturally, they had no wish to witness the ruination of yet another life. — Robbie immediately withdrew his support from James, but then, after a brief recourse, James also realised that it would be a grave mistake, which left Alex feeling a much spurned woman, especially as they had begged James to send her away; — it was a very difficult time for him, deciding."

"James has always been so kind."

Eleanor nodded in agreement, "But then, Alex met Arnie, in fact quite a few people met Arnie, including Mairie Campbell, who had become a shrewd manipulator, and, like you, very good at planting ideas, — and suddenly, Arnie took Alex off to the States, making it appear as though she were the injured party, as indeed, she was."

"The feud," Helen concluded, smiling.

"I believe that is what the MacFarlane v Craig mystery became known as," Eleanor smiled. "And I must admit perfect material for your gossip column."

Helen sat in deep thought for a few moments, her coffee and brandy forgotten, "I think it's painfully obvious that when Alex heard of my pending arrival, she recognised it as an opportunity to reap some revenge on Duncan. Had I interviewed her at the Press Conference, she would have been in a position to publicly humiliate him and reduce any regard that he had for me, to nothing."

"Yes," Eleanor agreed, "And I should think that she was a very disappointed woman when you opted out of the interview, hence, her later invasion on you in the castle gallery, — up to that point, you *had* won, Helen," she assured.

Helen's usually smooth brow, furrowed in puzzlement, "It was Duncan who stopped me from interviewing her. At the time, I considered his reason was to protect his and Alex's privacy, but now I'm mystified as to why he stopped me, as he couldn't have known of the situation between Alex and me."

"I think I do, Helen," Eleanor smiled. "He and Alex are old sparring partners, he would have been aware of a possible crisis in dealing with her, and by preventing you from interviewing her, he not only attempted to protect you and Mairie Campbell's name, but himself also. His mistake was in not telling you of Mairie Campbell's past. — It rather gave Alex, carte blanche," she frowned, "I wonder why she was so confident, that you didn't know; — Duncan would never have discussed you as a topic."

Helen smiled, "He really had nothing to discuss, I would think that her own observances made her realise how distanced I was from the situation, — it was all very ambiguous, we made a pact for very different reasons. I didn't want anything from Duncan, and someone who suffers from avaricious greed, would never understand those kinds of traits in another. "

"She took undue advantage."

Lady Eleanor, how did Mairie Campbell really die?"

Eleanor sighed, "Angus died directly after your last visit with your father, — an aneurysm, it was unexpected and virtually undetectable, but very quick, and so a- shock to all concerned, as was Robbie's death. For the first year after Angus's demise, Mairie continued well, but then she suffered a series of mild strokes which rendered her to a wheelchair. — Over the years, she steadily deteriorated, — each time I saw her, a little bit more had gone. She seemed to slowly disappear, as if Angus was willing her to join him; — she said it was her mind."

"Duncan made light of it, and so did Mr. Crawford."

"It was what she wanted, Helen, — your father's death just added to her grief, — she instructed that you should not be told, as you were ill yourself."

"I thought the worst,"

"It was natural, we guessed as much."

The early part of her journey to Arrochar, she spent as the previous night, in wistful thought. The same thoughts assailed her, — realisation that Alex had succeeded in her effort to cause a repeat of history. Mairie Campbell had loved and lost, just as she had loved and lost Duncan, only she hadn't experienced the true, free joy of sharing that love with him. — There must be a way, she told herself, — a way in which to tell him what a fool she had been to allow others to influence her, as she had. — If only she had listened to him that day by the loch instead of flying into a tangent and lying to him. He would have told her Mairie Campbell's story while holding her gently in the circle of his arms and kissing her, just occasionally. He would have told her while he caressed her hair back from her temple, as she knew he had done for an uncertain length of time after she had fainted at the muster party. He would have told her again, that he loved her, shared his innermost thoughts with her, as she would have joyfully shared hers with him. — If only, she thought on, — if only she hadn't been so busy drumming up business for Ryder. — If only she hadn't taken advantage of Hannah and Jean's innocently relayed snippets of gossip, and then woven them into a dramatic scandal. The realisation had smote her only last evening while listening to Eleanor that she had been the sole reason for Duncan's unrest, — but, she realised that Eleanor had forgiven her.

She became suddenly aware of the landscape rushing past the window of the train. — As it became more familiar, she became alert to the decrease in the train's speed, — journey's end, — she realised, standing and then reaching up for her hand luggage to retrieve it from the rack above her head. The train shunted to a halt, followed by the porter calling out the name of the station, 'Talbert for Arrochar', she mindfully echoed, smiling wistfully to herself. — Moments later, she stepped from the train.

"Welcome back, Miss Campbell. — Grand day," said the Porter, doffing his cap. — She smiled in acknowledgement and then eagerly glanced past him at the sound of a car. — A slight disappointment ensued when she recognised Rory's battered blue vehicle. He came towards her, whistling cheerfully.

"Hello, Princess," he broadly smiled, automatically giving her a brief kiss in welcome. "Not many suitcases this time, I see."

She returned his smile, "No, I left a fair amount of clothes behind in the cottage."

"You've been missed, Helen," he said seriously, and bent to lift the two suitcases.

As he moved from blocking her view, something drew her attention to the little white picket gate. It seemed as though her vision had become impaired, for she could just see two shadowy figures, she blinked, but her eyes refused to focus. — The smaller figure raised a hand, Helen automatically half-raised one of her own in acknowledgement and then blinked again, in a further attempt to see the taller figure, but in that instant, they had gone. There was no-one, nothing by the gate. She asked, "Rory, have you ever had the feeling that you've done something before?"

"Often," he replied, giving an amused chuckle. — "Meeting you from the station is one of them."

Brushing the incident aside, she laughed, but immediately became serious again, although making an attempt at flippancy, "Where's the Laird, Rory?" she tentatively asked.

"He's at the Top Farm. Brooks had a fire in his barn last night. They're trying to assess the extent of the damage. I've orders to join them as soon as I've deposited you with Jean at the cottage."

They drove past The Loch House, glowingly white in the spring sunshine. The painters were still hard at work freshening, the paint. She caught sight of Rory's father in the garden, — tending to the bursts of daffodils and tulips, which colourfully filled the beds, and glancing beyond, the groups of trees with fresh young fronds of green leaves gently blowing in the soft spring breeze, and further beyond, the crisp, cool, crystal azure waters of the loch, dazzling, shimmering against the dark green slopes.

The village, as they drove through it, appeared the same. The villagers' and shop owners' were industriously painting their shop fronts, or house window frames and doors in readiness for the summer season. Rory pointed out a bright new photographer's shop, advertising film developing within the hour, but nothing seemed neglected as James Craig had indicated, — only the Tourist Agency had a dark, foreboding look about it. However, a slight puzzlement beset her as they turned into Bracken Lane.

"I expected to be staying at the Arms Hotel."

"The Hotel has closed its doors."

"For ... re-decorating?" she hesitantly, fearfully, asked.

"No permanently," he replied. "The Laird has dispensed with the idea of expanding the Tourist Trade."

"But ... he can't do that!" she cried, exclaiming, protesting in horror.

Rory slightly leaned towards her, as he stopped the car. "But he **can**, and he **has**, Helen. There's to be no special encouragement given to the tourists this year, and next year, the castle will also close its doors for the last time."

"It will become a neglected ruin," she groaned sadly.

"A neglected ruin," Rory echoed, lugubriously. "A proud fortress, no more. It's the Laird's final decision, — nothing can be done."

Nothing to be done, she thought, they were familiar words. — But there's always something that one can do, she thought on, — there must be an answer. She stepped from the car anxiously surveying the cottage; — it was also unchanged. The gardens gave every promise of a magnificent display of roses, and for the first time, Helen decided that it was incorrectly named, for 'Rose Cottage' seemed a more apt description than 'Bracken'. — Jean came to the door as she approached; — Helen thought that she appeared changed somehow. — It was an emotional meeting.

"Helen," she warmly smiled and then a trifle tearfully, kissed her cheek, "I'm so pleased to welcome you once again."

Anxiously frowning, she scanned her face for signs of derision, "Jean, I ... I ... Oh, please forgive me for ..." her voice trailed away.

"For leaving so suddenly," she replied kindly, finishing the sentence, "Forget it, Helen, you're here now and that's all that matters; — the tea's brewing. — Are you staying, Rory?" she invited brightly, peering past Helen's shoulder.

"No," he replied. "I'm away to the Top Farm," and then turned to address Helen, "I'll call for you in about an hour. Yeel be lunching with the Laird at The Loch House; — Hannah will see you there."

"Oh ... oh, I see," she said, nervously thinking of meeting Duncan again, "Thanks for the lift once again, Rory."

"See you later," he called, waving from the gate, and then Helen followed Jean inside.

"You've lost weight," Jean commented.

"And you've gained some," Helen smiled, avoiding herself as a topic. She then realised that Jean looked particularly radiant, "A bairn!" she exclaimed.

"Aye, I'm to have a bairn in early August," Jean smiled.

Helen moved to embrace her friend, sharing her quiet pleasure, "Oh, it's such wonderful news," she said, tearfully excited and then became sadly composed, realising that she would miss the event. "You will write to me, Jean and let me know which you have; a little lad or wee lass."

"Are you nay intending to stay, then?" Jean asked frowning, after Helen had turned her back, seeing her slowly move towards the kitchen while nervously twisting her hands together. She paused in the doorway, half-turning when Jean continued, "There's still a vacancy in this village for a leading lady, why don't you pluck up the courage and apply for it."

Her reply was hasty, "No ... I ... I can't. — Didn't Duncan tell you, two days? And that's all; long enough to sign over the cottage to the estates?"

"Still your career, Helen?" Jean replied, softly, questioning.

"Still my career," she agreed, smiling thinly and then continued further into the kitchen to gather up the prepared tea tray, silently asking forgiveness for her white lie.

They chatted for a time, relaxing in the pretty sitting room while sipping their tea. The main topic of conversation was Jean's coming bairn, and news of the village. — Helen insisted on knowing everything that had recently occurred.

Jean was cautiously being evasive, watching, until Helen became pensive. "You're longing to know what happened after you left, — aren't you."

Helen nodded.

"It wasn't a pretty scene," she related ..."

Jean's journey through the lanes had been a precarious one; the tires of the Shooting Brake hadn't gripped the gritted tracks, as on that fateful evening, she had headed towards Talbert where the Grahams' had been her guests.

The journey had taken twenty minutes instead of the usual ten, — the driveway to the house had mercifully been cleared, since she had left earlier that morning; — she had swiftly parked, and had run to the door which had been opened by Iain ...

"Where's the Lady Eleanor?" she earnestly panted.

271

"Try the lounge," he suggested.

Jean swiftly passed him to run across the hall, frantically calling: - "Lady Eleanor! Lady Eleanor!"

On hearing the distraught tone, Eleanor put down her book. "Jean, whatever is the matter?"

"It's Duncan; he's in great emotional pain; he's lost control from sheer frustration. — I've tried, but he won't listen to reason; — he's desperately in love with Helen, and I'm sure that she loves him, but she won't tell him, I think she's afraid to tell him."

Eleanor looked alarmed, "What *has* been going on?"

"The gossip was rife in the village that Duncan was going to marry Alex. For a while, I believed it myself, and so I asked him outright …

"Should we just fall into your unsuspecting arms and have our most private emotions tampered with," Jean replied, along with a smile. "I think you are fast becoming a womaniser, Duncan MacFarlane, just how many women do you need in your Harem?"

He briefly grinned, flippantly replying, "Oh, a couple would do; — one for mid-week, another for the weekend."

"And you think Helen should be agreeable to this?"

"She would soften Alex as a blow; Mairie softened Alicia for my grandfather; — made her more tolerable."

"Helen does have a forgiving nature, but you're getting yourself into a very compromising situation."

Duncan nodded in agreement, "But, I can't help my feelings."

"You're in love with her." she suggested. "Or do you just fancy her?"

Duncan just wryly grinned.

"Matters of the heart," she said, knowingly. "This, I will Defend."

He raised his glass, "Loch Sloy!"

"Another battle, another trophy…. Loch Sloy, my Lord."

"Ye Lassies," he briefly smiled, "Yer try a man."

"It was a neat trick you played; the twelve roses, I mean."

"Just carrying on the traditions of my grandfather; — every week, without fail, Mairie would get her favourite flowers."

Jean grinned, "It was like coals to Newcastle with that garden; — it was just something else to wind-up Alicia Craig," she sighed. "Is the gossip true — that you're to marry Alex?"

"Not one word of it."

"You should tell Helen." Jean thoughtfully advised. "It might help your

situation."

"The gossip will die down soon enough, when everyone realises that nothing is happening in that direction."

"Is that a- wise decision? You're too trusting, Duncan, — take some advice, don't bury your head in the sand; — it won't just go away."

After an anxious brief explanation: -

"We must go to the cottage," Eleanor said, hastily. It took a frustrating few minutes to fetch her coat.

Reaching the cottage, they saw Duncan's Rover standing outside. On entering the cottage, they found him alone, "Where's Helen?" Eleanor demanded; — her tone held fear.

Helen's gone," he firmly announced. "I'm sorry, Jean, I went for a drive to cool down and then came back; I was determined to sort out this damned mess, once and for all."

"Jean has something to say," Eleanor urgently informed him.

Jean explained with frantic, apologetic concern, "It was two nights ago, after the conference, I saw Alex heading for the gallery; she was following Helen and as she mounted the stairs, she peered back to see that no-one was watching her; she then ran quickly up-the-stairs. I waited until she had disappeared and then followed her, but I only heard part of the conversation, it was very detrimental towards Mairie Campbell. Helen told her that she only knew how to inflict pain. I overheard her again, last night; it was something about money." She was all earnestly encompassing, "Lady Eleanor, I felt that it was none of my business, and that Helen would ask Duncan if it were true, but she was weakened by illness; I blame myself."

Duncan's face was granite, he cursed; he had momentarily let Alex off the leash. "Follow me," he angrily, huskily, commanded and swiftly turning, he headed for the open outside door, — moments later he leaped into the Rover and loudly revving the engine, he swung the vehicle around until it faced the way of the castle. — Ten minutes later, on entering the Feasting Hall … "Where's Alex?" He demanded of a surprised Arnie.

"She's up in the north gallery bedroom."

Duncan took the stairs two at a time, but Alex wasn't in a bedroom, she was in the gallery about to climb a ladder, — and she had a can of red spray paint in her hand.

"What are you doing, Alex?" Duncan arrested, shouted the short, sharp question. — Her hand immediately went behind her back; her breasts heaved as she wildly stared in terror towards her assailants. "I'll take that," he demanded, while Jean and the Lady Eleanor rounded on her, blocking her escape route. "Helen's gone. Yer drove her away. What did you say to her?"

The atmosphere was tense as she aimed the paint spray at the picture, her lip curled, and her voice raucous through her throat as she passionately threatened, "Come near me, and it will be the *end* of Mairie Campbell's precious portrait; — I'll ruin this face."

"And what will that achieve?"

"I hate you, Duncan." she vehemently spat.

"The feeling is mutual," he fiercely returned. "I'll ask again — just what did you say, to Helen?"

She began screaming, her voice still raucous, "I told her, I told her what a *slut* and a *whore* Mairie Campbell was. — Angus held her hand in full view of everyone; she cosily danced with him at Alicia's wedding, — they were defiant to the last."

Suddenly, there came an intervention in the shape of Arnie, Rory and James Craig. — Duncan put out an arresting hand as James moved towards her, but ..., "Alex!" Arnie yelled, as he hurried along the gallery, "Destroy that portrait and I'll destroy you. — I had to learn what warmth was within a relationship, now I know. — No-one wants you, Alex; I'm cancelling your contract, I only kept it open because I *mistakenly* thought that I was in love with you."

She addressed James, "It's my right, my heritage, and you've sold it," she passionately accused.

James angrily, gruffly spoke, "You have no heritage in this village, I cast you out once, and now I'm casting you out again. — Duncan marries whom he chooses, if ... she will have him, and it obviously isn't you. — You make people say things and use them in your favour. Helen makes people say things, but she is a saviour to the soul; — and if she wasn't, Roland Barrett would be where he belongs — behind bars."

"Iain had phoned James to alert him, Rory followed his boss; Alex had nowhere to run. Duncan distracted her long enough until Rory managed to lunge and floor her with her hands behind her back, the paint can just rolled away; — a bit of team work, it happened very quickly. James took her back to Craigiemhor, Duncan saw her once more, what happened to her after that, remains to be seen."

"The reason Duncan took down Mairie Campbell's painting."

"The very reason," Jean confirmed. — "Duncan was dead set on following you, but we didn't know which route you would have taken to avoid some of the weather, but then it began to snow again, the village was somewhat cut off, just a few bits of Christmas mail trickled out by helicopter; the copter couldn't land, they winched the sack up; Duncan had an idea to follow, but it was too dangerous, the helicopters' blades were in danger of freezing, and anyway, he couldn't desert the village, — for ten frustrating days, the population of the village worked tirelessly with snow ploughs and anything which would shovel away the snow, — Carrick Glen was entirely cut off."

"Duncan had it all organised."

"Aye, it's very necessary to be ready in such emergencies."

"What happened to Arnie?" she tentatively asked.

She then revealed further astonishing information, "Arnie and Deirdre Calhoun were married last Valentines Day; they fell in love while she was giving him dancing lessons; they had a four tier wedding cake, and Deirdre kept the sewing circle busy by ordering plenty of monogrammed linen. The gossips simply got it wrong with the A and the D; she was a former MacFarlane, hence the coats-of-arms. They will be returning from their honeymoon in the States in a month or so, when Arnie will start to re-caste the film."

Helen's hand flew to her mouth; her eyes were full of mirth at her own foolishness, but her eyes soon clouded again as Jean continued, pleading softly, earnestly, "He needs you by his side, Helen; end his pain and your own; its imperative. — He was so afraid that you would die, and that he would never know either way, if you loved him, — he would have risked his life to bring you back, — now, … are you going to tell him, for if you don't, then Mairie Campbell has gone to an awful lot of bother for nothing?"

Helen shook her head; her reply was evasive, "you once said that he wasn't loved, but he has a *whole* village of love."

She covered the hand that was lying on the table, saying gently, "But *yours* is more special." Jean lengthened her stay to accompany her upstairs, with the intention of helping to unpack her suitcases. "You have such lovely clothes," she sighed, gazing just a trifle enviously at Helen's latest evening dress.

Helen held up the froths of pastel pink, shading down to maroon, for Jean's closer inspection. She particularly admired the crust of tiny seed pearls entwined into intricate embroidery, which formed the wide belt and enhanced the sweeping hemline. "My parents brought it back, after a recent trip to France. I think Charles had high hopes that it may inspire me to take up my music once again; — it's the style of dress most suitable for concerts."

Jean suddenly looked thoughtfully inspired, "You could wear it this evening," she suggested enthusiastically. "There's to be an engagement party at the castle, — everyone is attending, and I understand that the couple involved will be formally asking for the Laird's permission to marry. — Of course, it's only a tradition; the law was officially nullified at the turn of the century."

"I'd like to see the ceremony," she said, eagerly at first. "But … would anyone mind my attending? I … err … don't exactly have a place in the village any longer."

"You're a Campbell?" was Jean's firm reply, as if the reason were enough.

"Who's the happy couple?"

"Some friends of Duncan's, you haven't met them. They're to marry in the Kirk, tomorrow."

"Short engagement," Helen commented, while heaping more clothes onto the bed.

"Aye," said Jean, "… but when you're as much in love as they seem to be, — why wait?"

"Why indeed?" Helen returned with a sigh, while in the process of opening her wardrobe expecting to see it full of clothes, but her face filled with puzzled surprise when she realised, "It's empty!" she exclaimed.

Hastily, Jean informed her, "Oh, I meant to tell you, Duncan had all of your clothes packed and stored with me at Talbert, until we had received your instructions as to what to do with them. There was no time in which to unpack them again as news of your visit came only this morning, and we considered that you would bring sufficient with you to tide you over, but … as you don't intend to stay any longer than two days, then it would have seemed a pointless exercise, anyway, — unless … there was something that you particularly … wanted."

"Oh … oh no, there wasn't anything in particular," she replied, shrugging, but silently thought that it was another show of Duncan's disapproval, and a strong hint that she was no longer welcome. — Having hung several garments away, she crossed the room to the dressing table where she neatly arranged her cosmetics in the small drawers, and having further completed her task, her eyes rested on the dressing-brushes and matching mirror, "I never did ask Duncan about these brushes. I'm sure that they were gran's but the initials are mine."

"Duncan is very down to earth. When Mairie died, everything went with her, except for her memories. — There seemed small point in you possessing brushes bearing the initials 'MC' so he took the trouble of having them changed. — You see, in his eyes, you *are* Helen Campbell, no matter what past issues or what resemblance you may have to your grandmother. — I found him many times over the last few months, just staring at Mairie's portrait — I asked him why – to this he replied ..."

I don't see Mairie, I see Helen, — standing, as she was, on the bottom of the stairs at the Talbert party, the pose was identical."

Helen began to ponder further on the events of the past. James Craig had indicated very strongly, Duncan's anxiety to meet her when she had originally arrived; it had been obvious to everyone, even to Alex, so much so, that it stirred her into taking revenge on Duncan. — She had even been placed at Jean's table as though she had been his companion, courtesies, she had thought at the time, but if Duncan had taken so much trouble to maintain her individuality by having simple initials changed on a set of brushes, then his reasons went far deeper. — She had never met him before, of that fact, she felt certain. — The first time she had met him had been in the lane, except for their brief encounter in Edinburgh, and yet, despite her close resemblance to Mairie Campbell, he still, apparently, hadn't recognised her.

Jean interrupted her thoughts, "You left some personal papers behind," she informed, while proffering an envelope. "They were tucked in the back of a drawer. I took the liberty of keeping them in the safe at Talbert, away from prying eyes."

"Thanks," she said gratefully, and immediately slit open the envelope, it contained her letters from Ryder and her diary from the previous year, also her notebooks. "I must change for lunch," she suddenly, hastily announced, glancing at her watch.

"Wear the pale green crepe dress," Jean suggested, "... the one with the jabot. There's nothing like a few frills to enhance ones feminine charm."

It seemed that in no time at all, Rory appeared again to drive her to The Loch House. "See you tonight," Jean cheerfully called out, before waving them a goodbye.

Her remark, led Helen into explaining to Rory, that she was intending to attend the evening party. The young man immediately suggested that he escorted her, and Helen saw no sane reason to refuse.

Chapter 24

The Return of the Prodigal

The day being fine and The Loch House's driveway only a few minutes walk in length; Helen insisted that Rory hadn't the need to enter the gates. But to herself, she admitted, that no matter how much she wanted to see Duncan, she was in fact delaying the moment.

She stepped lightly from the car, waved her brightest farewell to Rory, and then with a nervous sigh began her stroll, trying to ignore her fluttering stomach and noisily pounding heart, by absorbing the beloved rolling purple slopes beyond the house, and delighting in the well-kept gardens. She tossed her heavy nut-brown hair behind her shoulders, and then stood still to listen to the song of the birds. It seemed as though nothing else disturbed the peace. A gentle smile played about the corners of her mouth, at this so familiar scene, as she sighted a red squirrel playing in the branches of a tree. — Switzerland had its beauty, she thought, but it has none of this. — She stirred slightly at the sound of a soft footfall on the gravel behind her.

"Don't move," came, the quiet command, in a well-loved accented voice. Helen quivered, she heavily sighed, but she did as Duncan bade, "The squirrel has a mate, on the grass, beneath the tree."

He stood close behind her, his nearness disturbing, beginning to weave its old beguiling magic. Her hair stirred on the crown of her head, but she felt unsure of whether it was from his breath from which it stirred, or from a fleeting soft breeze. — She trembled again, conscious of the overwhelming longing for him sweeping over her, if only he would draw her into his arms, she thought; hold her, just for a moment. — She swallowed, while briefly closing her eyes and when she opened them again, the squirrel had gone, but not so Duncan. — She had to move to say something, anything to break the tension. Her lips formed sweet silent words, which she wanted to savour, 'I love you' they said. But despite Jean's advice, she felt that they weren't the words that he wanted to hear, — the situation became daunting. — She heard him move to the side of her, wondering now from where he had appeared, "I … I didn't see you," she said, nervously, still not daring to meet his eyes, knowing that her cheeks were tinged with pink.

"Lunch is ready, Helen," he curtly informed. "I saw you taking your time in arriving and decided to spur your step. — Hannah has prepared a special meal in honour of your arrival, so it wouldn't do to let it spoil, although, I fail to understand the welcoming of the prodigal."

— Immediately, her face flamed in anger, her head snapped upwards to meet his cold, blue, steely eyes, fraught with mockery. — But no, she suddenly thought, staying the rising emotion, "It's a grand day, Duncan; let's not spoil it by bickering. I only came because you insisted on mere legal technicalities, which could have been dealt with through the post."

He gave a small, knowing, whimsical shrug, "You stressed to my mother that you wanted to visit Arrochar, but you were feeling too cowardly to pick up the phone and arrange it, for yourself."

"I wanted to make my peace with my friends, with that done; I shall go on my way."

He pointed to himself with his thumb, "And *I* am a friend," he replied, raising a dark eyebrow in surprise.

Helen tolerantly sighed, "As I said, a moment ago, you insisted that I came."

"I did!" he agreed, "… and as you've accepted my invitation, then … I'm obliged to play the host. — After you, my Lady Helen," he invited, with a half-mocking bow and a sweep of the hand.

Hannah then saved any further difficulties, by appearing in the doorway of The Loch House, wiping her hands on her apron. And with a smile of welcome on her homely face, she stretched out her plump arms, as Helen ran the last few yards to be enfolded into her motherly warmth, "Oh lass," she cried, tearfully, "You had us all so worried, going away as you did."

Helen glanced at Duncan, noting the derision written on his face, but despite her own self, a stray tear glistened on her lashes, she turned back to Hannah, saying with false brightness, "The Laird tells me that you've prepared a special lunch, Hannah."

"Aye, I have that lass, and by the looks of you, you need feeding up." In despair, she sadly shook her wise old head, remarking, "You're just a shadow of your former self."

Moments later, they entered the house. Helen followed Hannah into the kitchen with the intention of helping to put the final touches to their lunch, while Duncan mixed their drinks. "Mmm! Smells delicious," she remarked, lifting the lids from the boiling saucepans, "What are you wetting our appetites with today?"

"Tweed Kettle, it's a salmon dish, very popular in the nineteenth century; Mr Duncan loves it. If you were back in my care lass, you'd be eating plenty of Kail Brose, it would toughen up that chest of yours," she admonished. "Your gran ate it regularly, keeps away all the winter scourges." Helen made no comment to this, as Hannah suddenly appeared worried, she hastily advised, "Helen lass, pay the Laird no heed. He's not himself today."

"I … know, Hannah," Helen sighed. "But he'll feel better when I've gone, I've been nothing but a trouble to him."

Hannah echoed a sigh in resignation, "you'd better go, lass, I'll see you later."

She smiled in agreement and then left the kitchen to join Duncan, feeling that their luncheon was going to be a strained, difficult affair.

The main room, as she entered, felt cool after the warm confines of the kitchen, she shivered slightly with the drop in temperature, and retrieved a shawl which was draped over the back of a settle to wrap it around her shoulders. — One sweeping glance told her that Duncan was nowhere in sight, she strolled over to the piano with the thought of playing the instrument, as it could ease the tension between them, but the lid was shut tight, and it didn't give when she attempted to lift it.

"It's locked," Duncan brusquely, bluntly informed, startling her as he + from the doorway of the library. — The tension hung on the atmosphere, their conversation was stilted.

"Have you the key?"

"It needs tuning."

She raised a surprised eyebrow, suspiciously saying, "That isn't like you, you're usually so pedantic about such things."

"It's a painful piece of history," he replied, caustically.

Helen recognised these words as some of her own, "Oh, I see," she said laconically, and moved to stand and gaze sightlessly at the scene beyond the window, nervously twisting her hands. — He joined her, handing her a glass, but it wasn't the usual Martini, instead, he had poured two brandies. She surreptitiously glanced at him sideways. He hadn't altered during the past months, still, a tall, proud man, casually dressed, his well pressed navy slacks beneath a blue checked shirt open at the neck, with the cuffs folded back over his wrist, but there was something different about him," she thought quizzically, unable to pinpoint the change. "I understand that you met Charles, — did you like him?" she eagerly enquired.

"Yes —" he sharply replied, "I had an occasion to visit London on some other business, and so I decided to drop in on him to discuss the matter of the cottage. — I was surprised to learn that you had gone abroad, but had left no address. — Charles didn't strike me as a man who would avoid his responsibilities, by loosing track of his stepdaughter."

"He's an honest man. He wouldn't divulge a confidence."

He raised an eyebrow, "Oh … so you mean that it was your express wish, that you should disappear without trace?" he remarked, clarifying the situation.

"It was," she replied

"Did you enlighten Charles, as to how Ryder came to dismiss you?"

"No — he's under the impression that Ryder dismissed me for failing to meet my contract. — But while we're on the subject, it was a very subtle move on your part. You left me with no bargaining power," she rebuked, glancing at him.

His jaw hardened, and his lips drew into a thin straight line, evidencing his anger as he studied the golden liquid in his glass, his voice was gruff, "I warned you what would happen," he said, and then hastily downed the brandy in one, "Where did you go, or is that still, a state secret?" Helen drew in her breath to reply, but the telephone suddenly rang in the library, taking Duncan away to answer it.

During lunch, their conversation continued to be stiffly polite, a fact which saddened her even more as she remembered the many meals which they had shared. The conversation then had been light-hearted happy banter, full of fun from Duncan's teasing. He didn't pursue the unanswered question, and so Helen decided that it was of little or no consequence to him where she had been, she heavily sighed, nervously trying to break down the barriers.

"Is the damage to Brooke's barn serious?" she enquired.

"Why should *you* be concerned with Brooke's barn?" he asked, gruffly.

"Perhaps, it was just something to say," she tersely replied, lapsing into silence.

With their meal finished, she first noticed the absence of a familiar habit. She followed him into the living room, quietly observing his movements. He renewed their brandies while Hannah wheeled in the coffee with a selection of mint sweets and almond biscuits on a trolley, and then unloaded onto the low table in front of the unlit fire. Helen crossed the room to fill the cups as she had always done, keeping him within her range of vision. He joined her, but seated himself at a comfortable distance on the opposite couch, first placing her brandy on the table, his own he held lightly cupped in the palm of his right hand. Helen frowned slightly, seeing him thoughtfully study the liquid. She glanced at his empty shirt pocket, and then raised her eyes to the shelf beside the mantel where all of his four pipes, were neatly in place. A certain indication as to the depth of his restlessness; she felt disturbed, "Have you given up smoking?"

"You're hardly a subject to be smoking around," he barked, "Ye'll be coughing in no time."

"That's very magnanimous of you," she replied. "You've never worried before."

"Perhaps, I never felt the need, you made light of your illness, and so I continued with what I had always done."

She changed the subject, "The inscription on the headstone; why was it never completed?"

"It was in accordance with Mairies' wishes; I would think that she cherished some privacy over her age."

"I've found Mairie's birth certificate," she revealed. "It was in the jewellery box; I would like the inscription completed."

"I will attend to it, in due course," he assured her.

Helen changed the subject again, "I … err … feel, that it is only polite to warn you that I have accepted an invitation to this evening's party."

He looked up sharply, immediately veiling his eyes, his words were caustic, he demanded, "And, who invited you?"

"Jean, but, there's no problem, Rory has offered to escort me."

"Thank God, for Rory Cameron as small mercies," he muttered as he lowered his eyes again to the glass, "I have no objection to a combined engagement, come farewell party," again, downing his drink in one.

"It will be a Highland evening, Duncan; I wouldn't want to miss it."

Oh, yeel no miss it, Helen, of that fact I'm certain," he said, his accent thickening. — Suddenly, he placed his glass on the table and standing, asked, "Are you ready to sign these papers that Crawford has prepared?" she nodded, and then standing herself, followed him across the room into the library, "They're on the desk. Sign the bottom half," he brusquely demanded.

She had the pen poised in her trembling hand, this was the moment, "No!" she barked sharply, seeing his head snap up, "I am not going to be dictated to, you can't do this Duncan, and I'm surprised that Mr. Crawford has been a party to it."

"You've broken the terms of the *will*," he argued. "The cottage is now, rightfully mine."

She shook her head, procrastinating, "It's mine — until I've signed this document. — Duncan, there is still time," she pleaded, arguing, "It is *still* within the year of her death."

"But there isn't enough time left," he swiftly replied, revealing, "And anyway, I've promised the lease to Fiona Drummond, the cottage is near enough to the school, she's due to move in next week. — Now, you wouldn't want to be letting her down, would you, seen as it was your idea that she took over the school?"

She could feel the pressure of his growing force, "You have an answer to everything, don't you, Duncan?"

"Everything … now just sign the papers and our business will be finished."

Feeling choked, she hesitated a moment longer and then hastily scribbled her signature, for the quicker the deed was done, the less thought would have to be given to it.

Are you … no going to read them?"

"No, I'm sure that they're in order; you have a tidy mind," she replied, just wanting to escape.

"You're very trusting towards someone who deliberately lost you your job."

She smiled thinly, replying with a sigh, "Mairie Campbells' wishes are dear to you, Helen Campbell's, are not."

"I'll take you home," he suddenly announced.

But not wishing to elongate the discomfiture, "No, thank you, but no, on such a grand day, I'll walk. — Please thank Hannah for her delicious lunch; I will no doubt be seeing her, this evening."

"Until this evening, Helen, on the point of dusk," he called, after her departing back.

She half-turned before leaving, and with a soft voice, replied, "'til this evening … my Lord," she left, stiffly proud, but …

Once more in the open, she let her calm, controlled, exterior drop; a sob tore from her. — Home, she thought, speeding her step and brushing away a tear, I've just signed away the rights to my home. — She left the driveway, turning into the main road and walking with a brisk step, she soon came to the outskirts of the village where she felt a sudden whim to visit the Kirk. A few minutes in the Kirk-yard with Mairie Campbell wouldn't go amiss, she decided, and crossed the road to continue her walk at a more leisurely pace, along another branch of Bracken Lane, despite the fact that she knew it to be a longer route. A few minutes later, Rory drew up alongside her in the estate's Land Rover. He seemed surprised to see her.

"Hop in, I'll give you a lift home," he said.

"Oh, I'm not going home," she replied. "I'm going to the Kirk."

He grinned, "It's a grand day for a drive, if you're in no great hurry, we can go for a tour, via Top Farm and end at the Kirk." And being in no particular hurry, she accepted his invitation and climbed in beside him, settling back in the passenger seat, "Did you enjoy your lunch?"

"I always enjoy Hannah's cooking," she replied, staring blankly ahead.

Rory glanced at her surreptitiously from the corner of his eyes, she looked cold and pale despite the sun's warmth, he thought, feeling concerned, her walk should have put some vital colour back into her cheeks. Then he frowned, puzzled, "Why were you walking alone? Didn't the Laird offer you a lift?"

She sighed, "Yes, as a matter of fact, he did, but I refused. I signed over Bracken cottage to the estates, and by doing that, it freed the Laird from any further obligations towards me. I … I've been such a trouble to him, Rory," she said anxiously, "I just wanted to escape."

"Cheer up, Princess," he encouraged, cheerfully, "We have a big date this evening."

In Rory's cheerful company, she soon roused herself from her melancholy mood, enough to enjoy the scenery. — To waste precious time in what could be her last visit to the Highlands, seemed to be a sin, and if Duncan wanted to be disagreeable, then he could be disagreeable alone, and it wasn't for her to worry about, at least this was how she tried to console herself.

Hours later, she lay luxuriating in a perfumed bath, her low sprits now rekindled by the afternoon drive. — After his visit to the Top Farm, where he showed her the fire damage, Rory had taken her on a tour of the estates. She was able to meet many of her old acquaintances, but she bade no-one a farewell, for it seemed too final, especially as at each farm they stopped, the women greeted her with large bunches of seasonal flowers and heather in welcome. It had caused gales of laughter as the Land Rover had become steadily more laden down. — Continuing the drive, they had touched on many points around the countryside, where she and Duncan had spent time on their plans for the Tourist Brochures, until her own music restored itself in her soul. — More than ever, she had felt a growing regret at having to leave Arrochar, yet again. She didn't want the village to die, and it surely would if Duncan remained firm with his plan to allow the Tourist Trade to dwindle. — However, there was one faint chance, she thought, if only she could find the courage to ask him.

As on a certain previous occasion, Hannah accompanied Rory when he arrived to take her to the party, he again wore his tartan with pride; this evening wearing the ancient blue Cameron of Erracht. "You look stunning, Helen," he gruffly, warmly, affectionately said, heavily sighing while gazing at the dazzling vision she made in the pastel pink organza dress; it had a hint of Medieval in its styling.

The wide seed pearl belt, dipped attractively at the back thus emphasising her trim waist. — Tonight, she was Helen Campbell, discarded were the combs, her hair was secured in the fashion of Rome, the front gently swept away from her smooth forehead and in the fashion of a pony-tail, appeared in a long loose tangle of ringlets trickling down her back. The wide sweep of her dress neckline, needed no more adornment than a simple gold chain bearing a single pink pearl drop, hung about her creamy neck.

"… Ye'll always be my first love," he said in a lowered voice. She reached up and warmly kissed him, gently on his lips while his arms slid around her and he held her close for one poignant moment, softly kissing her temple, and when she pulled away, her eyes glistening with tears were full of regretful fond affection; she stroked his face, saying …

"Yeel be fine with Fiona, she'll have fine sons for yer."

The moment was broken when Hannah bustled in, "Ye're a treat for these old eyes," Hannah told her, affectionately smiling, "And will be, to a great many more before this evenings done."

"You'll both have me conceited," Helen replied, blushing as she slipped into a matching pink satin evening coat.

"Will you be warm enough, lass?" Hannah asked, concerned.

"I'll be fine Hannah, the evening is warm, and I expect to see you at the party, later."

"Aye, I'll be there, Rory's father will come for me." She appeared thoughtful, "Och, there's just more one thing, ye've, forgotten your white heather aigrette, it looks so bonnie pinned to the side of your hair, it's the finishing touch."

Helen smiled, loving the idea all over again. — Swiftly returning upstairs to her bedroom, she selected a spray from the many she had received earlier in the day. She pinned the aigrette into position at the side core of the pony-tail, and then returned once again, to join them.

They first dropped Hannah outside her home, and within half-an-hour, had arrived at the castle gates. — Helen knew that Arrochar had a fair sized population, but to see the crowds making their way through the gardens, drew a gasp of amazement from her, "The Lairds' friends must be very popular," she remarked.

"They've come to see the traditional ceremony," Rory replied. "Yeel enjoy it too. The flowers and the heather, play a large part."

And it was so, for when they had arrived and parked the car, Helen could see that the castle proved to be in a abundance with flowers, both outside and in, "Your father *has* been very busy," she commented, while gazing wide eyed in wonderment at the colourful spectacle. — Baskets of flowers even lined the stone stairs, which led to the torch lit gallery.

Rory chuckled, "My father grew the flowers, but Mrs Roach, Hannah and some of the women from the village, arranged them about the castle last night and early this morning."

Rory suddenly looked uncomfortably concerned, as they stood in the doorway of the hall waiting to enter, "Helen ... I've something to confess."

She stared at him expectantly, "Well ...," she urged.

"The orchestra's here, we hoped that you would play."

Something plummeted in Helen, it wasn't exactly her spirit, but Duncan hadn't been all that keen on hearing her play earlier in the day. — She suddenly felt confused, hesitantly uncertain, "I ... don't think that it would be good idea,"

"Please, Helen, they've been rehearsing all day."

"I ... don't know," she doubtfully replied, frowning.

"Have I to say ... that you owe it to the Laird? His friends made a special request as a wedding present, and it is a way of making amends," he said slyly.

Helen's green eyes flew up to read his expression, but she compressed her lips and smiled, as she met the roguish twinkle in Rorys' grey ones.

"That was very below the belt," she said. "It seems that I have no choice. What have they selected?"

"There's only one real choice on such a romantic evening, "A Highland Medley, including the Dark Island, but they've strayed from the Scottish, the lady is from England, although she's gone for the French, she likes the Plaisir D' amore, which has been especially selected."

"Such irony," she murmured softly, a melody of love; one of my favourite pieces; how long have I got?"

"About an hour," Rory concluded, as they reached the doors of the hall.

Helen suddenly panicked, when she caught sight of Duncan's, tall, dark, imposing, foreboding figure. — This evening he had favoured tradition by wearing the MacFarlane hunting tartan, blue green and cranberry in colour, with a frilled shirt, over which he wore a claret velvet doublet, awe inspiring seemed to be the appropriate description. Jean stood at his elbow with Iain hovering in the background.

Despite the rising confusion, a puzzling thought suddenly struck Helen, the Grahams should also have been at the helm, as Eleanor would normally act as Duncan's hostess at such a large affair. But Eleanor, she suddenly realised, had made no mention of travelling to Arrochar for a party. She clutched at Rory's arm, "I'm going to the cloakroom," she hastily informed him, and before he could detain her, she pushed her way back through the crowd and sped up the flower decked stairs. She took so long hanging up her coat, and neatening her hair which didn't require neatening, that Jean came in search of her.

"You can't stay up here forever, Helen," she said kindly, "Your host is waiting, and so are your orchestra and your audience. Don't let them down, please."

Helen smiled, nervously, assuring, "I had no intention. I had an upsurge of nerves, that's all," she admitted truthfully, and walked from the room into the wide corridor, her step carrying her to the top of the stairs, with Jean following closely behind. — It was a trembling, but regal Helen who descended slowly down the wide, winding, staircase, Alex Craig would have loathed her, for her 'cool-aired' exterior had she seen her. — As she came in sight of the foot of the stairs, she paused in an attempt to control a further quake of nerves at seeing Duncan waiting, obviously for her. She shivered slightly, under his icy blue, unwavering gaze, as he watched her progressing descent again.

"Good evening, my Lord," she greeted, dropping a curtsy while managing to keep the tremble from her voice.

He acknowledged her greeting with a slight incline of the head, "I couldn't risk a further snub from you, so I decided to ensure that I led you to your piano, by waylaying you personally. — Do you hate me so much, Helen?" he concluded.

She lifted her eyes, bright with a rush of emotion, with the intention of speaking the words that she so wanted to say, but his eyes, as she met them, held only derision. — Her words withered on her lips, instead she replied, "Hate, is a very strong word, my Lord, perhaps, a slight feeling of resentment, would be more appropriate description of my feelings under the present circumstances."

He made no further comment, as she hesitantly took the arm he proffered, and oblivious of them, a few people were still milling about the entrance hall. They walked in strained silence between the great-carved oaken doors into the Feasting Hall. — There were people dancing, some merely standing talking, others were sitting at the various tables, strategically placed around the hall, the atmosphere was charged and very dry; someone passed her a drink. — The dryness suddenly caught at Helen's throat as they reached the Laird's party's table, causing her to cough and then sneeze."

"A glass of water, Jean, quickly," Duncan commanded, and placed a protective arm about Helen's shoulders, until the short fit had subsided. She sipped gratefully at the glass of water which he held for her, "Do you feel unwell, Helen?" he said, with a show of concern, while still holding her close to his side, and while silently cursing himself for exposing her to the epidemic of influenza which had swept the village, the previous year.

She tucked his handkerchief into her bag, "It's over, please don't concern yourself, it was just the Champagne bubbles," she assured, and reluctantly forced herself to move away from him, as the close confines of his arms were playing havoc with her reeling senses. — Duncan would be kind to any wounded puppy, she thought, as she seated herself between Jean and Iain. Duncan sat opposite her, studying her closely for a few moments, causing her colour to heighten and giving her a radiance, which she had long since lacked. She tried earnestly not to meet his gaze; something which seemed to be an impossible task, for the absence of his pipe began to trouble her again. She then felt relief when Jean leaned towards her.

"Rory is about to announce your recital," she said.

His announcement came clearly over the microphone; it was simple and to the point. — When he had finished, she stood to a resounding round of applause, followed by an accompaniment of cheers and whistles, when the Laird stood also. — Helen couldn't resist a shy pleased smile, but it wasn't for her self-esteem that she smiled; it was for Duncan, and the knowledge that he was a well-respected man.

There was too much noise to say anything, when he took her hand and held it, as they walked to the rostrum, but suddenly, a confidence welled up within her; her nerves seemed to abate. — She wanted to share the music with Duncan; it may have the desired effect, she thought, and relax him.

When they reached the rostrum, she inclined her head in silent greeting to her orchestra, and was immediately met by a professional tapping of instruments by them. — When their private applause had subsided, Rory stepped down to invite her to play.

She smiled at him, and then turned to Duncan, who still had possession of her hand, her eyes sparkling with the unexpected joy and excitement that she now felt, "Will you stay with me?" she asked, with a bravado that suddenly surged.

He held her eyes with his own for a moment, now soft with love, reading the plea within the depths of Helen's before replying, "I was under the impression that I made you nervous."

"Perhaps, nearly a century ago, you did," she said, without quite understanding the meaning herself.

He inclined his head in quiet acceptance, and when they took their places on the rostrum, — Helen at the piano and Duncan sat slightly behind her left shoulder, but still within her range of vision.

Silence reigned as she flexed her fingers; she smiled and then smoothly began to play. The haunting strains of the music seemed to cause a soft rosy hue to surround her; — she played for the man at her side, ever conscious of his scrutiny, while Fiona Drummond sang, and the guests joined in, softly humming and swaying to the much known words ...

Plaisir d'amour ne dure qu'un moment
Chagrin d'amour dure toute la vie.
The joy of love is but a moment long,
The pain of love endures a whole life long.
My love love's me, and all the wonders I see,
A rainbow shines through my window, my love love's me.
His eyes kissed mine; I saw the love in them shine,
He brought me heaven right then, when his eyes kissed mine.
But now he's gone, like a dream that fades into the dawn,
But the words stay locked in my heartstrings; my love love's me.

And finally, Helen played the first chorus alone, her orchestra never once overtook her, she swayed as she rode the crests of the crescendos with love and ease until the tinkling notes led to the last gentle chords dying with the strings of the orchestra. — Silence reigned again and for a few moments, she sat, head bowed, with hands clasped in her lap, feeling totally peaceful. — Then the applause broke; she stood and acknowledged them only once, immediately handing their acclaim to the orchestra and to Fiona, the singer. — She wanted only to see Duncan, to discover if the music had had the desired effect, but when she turned to face him, panic beset her again, on seeing his chair empty, and one glance around the hall told her that he was nowhere to be seen.

Chapter 25

None but the Braveheart

With heavy heart, she stepped down from the rostrum, realising that she had made a mistake in asking him to stay to bolster her confidence. He wouldn't have known that she had played for him, he had once before thought that she had played for Rory, and the chosen music this evening had been a melody of love. — She dispiritedly pushed her way through the crowd that had returned to the dance floor, and when she had reached it, found their table vacant. — The Roaches, she supposed to be dancing, and then she wondered, where to, Duncan had disappeared; her eyes frantically scanned the room.

"Will you dance with me, Helen?"

She whirled round, startled at the sound of his voice, feeling her confusion return, "Oh … Oh yes, I'd, like to," she annoyingly stammered.

She trembled when he took her into his arms, and steered her into a waltz. For a moment, she wondered if her legs would support her, but if they didn't then Duncan did, for he held her firmly against him, "I apologise for having had to leave you," he said. "I had a telephone call to say that our engaged couple have been delayed."

"Oh, that's alright, I managed," she replied, now feeling a fool, for Duncan would no longer concern himself for whom she played, — he was a man of firm decisions, and decided to take her word, and believe that she didn't want his life, "I hope that they weren't delayed by anything serious, they've missed their wedding present from you; I shall have to play again for them, later."

He nodded, "Serious enough for tonight. Apparently, there's something that they can't quite agree upon."

"Oh, I see," she said, feeling sudden sadness for the young lovers, disagreeing on the day of their engagement. — She glanced up at him from beneath a long fringe of lashes, but as she did, she realised that he was smiling at her, and he was the old approachable Duncan again, the Duncan that she loved. — She fought off the inviting urge to lay her cheek on his shoulder, for in reality, that was all that she wanted to do, but it did seem to be an appropriate moment to ask a favour of him. — She swallowed trying to find the courage, "Duncan …," she said, and hesitated, biting on her lower lip. She could feel his eyes searching her face, waiting for her to continue.

"It must be very hard to say," he remarked.

She nodded, "I … I need a job."

He stopped smiling and immediately veiled his eyes; her heart sank with despair at his curt reply, "Ryder offered to re-employ you — did he not?"

"Y…yes, he did," she replied, with some surprise, "But how did you know?"

"I paid him a visit when I travelled to London, and managed to shame him into it. It was the least I could do, after Charles had informed me that you were ill because you had lost your job. And, I knew that I alone was responsible for that."

"Charles told you, but Charles promised … Oh. …," she grumbled, "Is there no-one I can trust, no-one I can confide in."

"For you to feel the need to confide in anyone is a whole new role. And as I presume that you're applying to me for a job, then, that is also a new role, and a very confusing one, as you so adamantly informed me that my kind of life wasn't your kind of life. Besides, there is another drawback."

"And … what would that be?" she snappily retorted.

"Yeel have nowhere to live."

"I have Bracken Cottage."

Duncan shook his head, "You've forgotten — the cottage is no longer yours, you signed over the rights to the estates, this afternoon — I've let it. — No, you're better of in London Helen, doing what you want to do."

"You hold me … to *one* measly day," she stated, complaining.

"You had a moral obligation," he said sharply.

Helen felt choked; she bowed her head in a supreme effort to hide the threatening tears. "Please … excuse me," and pulling away from him, began to push her way through the crowd of dancers. — Leaving the hall, she ran up the stairs, turning in the opposite direction of the gallery, for no longer did she wish to gaze upon the faces of the long-dead, her feet sped along the wing containing the bedchambers, and randomly opening a bedchamber door, she entered, slamming the door shut behind her. — For a moment, she stood leaning back against the cool panelling, trembling, and fighting back the misery and the disappointment, "Fool, romantic little fool, Helen Campbell," she whispered to the darkened room, "Lulling your fine self, into thinking that he would agree to such an idea." — Suddenly — she sucked in her breath when the overhead lighting came ablaze — startling her. Her heart hammered noisily in her breast, even though she knew that it had been switched on from the outside of the room. Feeling his weight, she pressed back against the door as the knob turned noisily, and Duncan called through, his voice commanding …

"I mean to come in, Helen; unlock the door, or I'll use an axe," he threatened.

She wearily, resignedly, moved further into the room, she felt tired of running away, tired of being ill because of stubborn pride which forced her inside of herself. She wanted to be near Duncan, to see him each day, to hear him, even if she couldn't touch him other than to dance with him, she tried to convince herself, she could beg him to let her stay, something could be arranged.

"It isn't locked," she softly replied, without turning. — Immediately, she heard him entering the room, and close the door behind him and then lock it, she half-turned at the sound, and then held onto the bedpost for support.

"A small precaution," he said. "I don't want you slipping away again, just yet."

"Duncan, I don't want the village to die and it surely will if you forsake the idea of the Tourist Centre. Let me help, please, there must be something that I can do," she begged, feeling him come to stand directly behind her.

"You can help by accepting Ryder's offer. I can't allow you to stay just to salve your conscience, yee'll be ill again."

Helen turned to face him, her eyes glistening with tears; she said earnestly, "No, no, you're wrong, Charles is wrong. It wasn't you who made me ill, nothing that you *ever* did could make me ill. It was …," she hesitated before admitting, "It was … the thought of having to leave you, having to leave Arrochar. — Working for Ryder isn't the answer, but if I could stay here, to be a small part of your team, that would help, and you could lease Bracken Cottage to me. Please … Duncan isn't two months in a Swiss Clinic punishment enough for failing Mairie Campbell?" she pleaded tearfully.

For a moment, he searched her pale anxious face for the truth, until suddenly he reached out to gently draw her trembling form into his arms, and press her head against his shoulder, his anger abated, his sigh heralded the relief that flooded through his tense body, his throat was pained with tight constriction, "Helen darling," he said gruffly against her hair, "I've missed you so terribly, and lived in my own private hell. I felt so sure that I was responsible for making you ill."

There it was; the word that said it all, 'darling' he had called her, he still cared; — now she knew that he still cared, and that there was nothing more left to fear. She lifted her head, her eyes now soft with unashamed, love, "Oh Duncan, there's so much that I want to tell you, but I don't know where to begin … I feel so foolish."

He shook his head, speaking earnestly, "I've heard everything that there is to know about the events surrounding the twelve weeks that you spent here, except the one thing that I really want to hear, and only you can say it, Helen, I need to be certain, it's the rest of my life." he pleaded.

"You overwhelm me, my Lord."

He feverishly underlined the events, "After you had left, I stormed up here to the castle to find Alex, her evil tongue lashed out with all she had said to you about Mairie Campbell. — She screamed at me, something about history repeating itself, but when I questioned her, she refused to answer, and sneered instead about her arrangements with Ryder. — This morning, my mother phoned me after you had left, she said that you had confirmed Alex's story, but that you had told it with such precision, that she felt that you hadn't quite told everything. — My only guess now is that it's the same piece of the puzzle that Alex refused to convey. — She threatened you with the same fate as Mairie Campbell, didn't she? Helen, if you love me, tell me now, don't let Alex win, for if you do, Alicia Craig will have seen her day; — Helen, please, put me out of my misery, you rejected Rory … say it, say the words, just three," he pleaded, his voice still gruff, his own eyes a reflection of hers while smoothing away a tear with his thumb. — He kissed her moist face, and lifted the hand that lay gently on his pounding chest, and carried it to his lips with shaking hands, to kiss her finger-tips, "… or you're free to leave now, and I will forever hold my peace," he said, still gruffly, "Helen, tell me, *please* ... my own darling, my deere one," he gently urged, only wanting to end their torment.

She smiled through her tears; then freeing her captured hand, lifted it to gently smooth away the tired lines about his eyes, he kissed her palm. His face was beloved to her, and she could no longer hide the fact, nor did she have to.

"What I withheld, was for your ears alone, Alex only guessed at my feelings for you, she wasn't certain; I would never let her know anymore than Mairie would have allowed Alicia to know of her true feeling for Angus. But I don't want to tell you everything tonight, as my conversations with Alex are now unimportant, and will be something to laugh about in years to come, for you can't make me leave you, now."

He suddenly kissed her lightly on the lips, saying earnestly, again urging, "Helen, you're tormenting me, you still haven't said it."

She paused before saying, "Always so lordly, domineering, demanding and presumptuous; you tried to get me pregnant to keep me here; but I wouldn't let you." She nodded, "You're my laddie, Duncan; I could never love anyone else, as much as you. And I would be so honoured to bear the son's of the mighty ... Lord Lennox."

He stared at her in almost disbelief as the words sunk in, and as the relief and the joy suddenly flooded through him, he bent and scooped her up, one arm about her waist and one under her knees, enthusiastically, giving a yell that sounded like a Gaelic war cry while swinging her around the room, "Duncan, have you gone mad?" she shrieked, laughing with him, when he came to a standstill again.

"Mad with love, wench," he said, kissing her passionately before breathlessly, setting her back on her feet and holding her close in his arms, "Helen, tell me, how long have you known?"

"Since, Jean's party."

He looked surprised, "Even then, my Helen, you looked pretty murderous that evening."

"Immediately ... even then, you would have got your wish, had Alex not been there, — instead, I could only peevishly think, 'he's *my* laddie'," she softly replied, "... but I pretended that nothing had changed. — Then, when you kissed me for the first time in the gallery, I knew that the column was no longer of any consequence, but I had to be stubborn, covering the conference was the only way in which I could stay near you."

"But I offered you a job, and you cannae deny it now, it was a job which you enjoyed."

"I wanted to accept, but to see you with Alex everyday were a far greater torture than I could endure. It was proof enough on the day that I went to the Islands."

"Alex had something to do with that?" he said, questioningly, with a note of surprise.

Helen stole a look at him from beneath her lashes, "I called at The Loch House early, as we had arranged, but when I arrived, Alex's Cadillac was parked in the drive, and as Alex doesn't rise early, I ... reached the only possible conclusion."

Duncan chuckled, "You thought I had a breakfast visitor," he suggested, noting Helen's pink cheeks.

She laughed softly, admitting, "I did."

"I loved you, Helen, Alex had no place in my bed," he assured her. "It was you that I wanted to cuddle every morning, I still do," he revealed. "But to put your mind at rest, my visitor was Arnie. He called en-route to Greenock to advise that his cargo of film equipment had arrived in Britain, and would be arriving in Arrochar in due course."

"You were very angry with me, Duncan."

"I felt more worried than angry," he said, softly trailing caressing fingers along her jaw line. "I wanted to hug you, when you walked back through the door in one piece, but your damned singular attitude, caused me to lose my temper."

He heavily sighed as he gazed at the vision of loveliness that he held in his arms, Helen now looked radiant, and he felt confident that it was for him that her eyes sparkled so happily. — As she slid her arms about his neck, and raised soft inviting lips to meet his own, he made a silent vow that she would never suffer needlessly again. Mairie Campbell had been ill when she had been forced to leave Arrochar, all those years ago, pining for Angus and her home. She had returned, knowing that she would have to deny herself the love of her life, but she thrived once back in the village, being near Angus had seen to that, and now Duncan thanked Heaven that his judgement in bringing Helen back home, hadn't been wrong.

She sighed as his kiss deepened, and became more urgent, while stealthy fingers slid down her dress zip, "Helen, my darling, Helen," he breathed while pressing and moulding her into his hardening thighs, "You're so beautiful, you drive a man insane, you've tortured me," and feeling her passion rise to meet his own, he lifted her again and carried her to lie on the great four poster bed. Gathering her close, he continued to kiss her hungrily while loosening the pins from her hair.

Helen trembled in his arms when she felt his caressing hands travel over the soft nakedness of her breasts, his thumb paused to rhythmically tease her risen nipple, his hand furthering down, past her waist, smoothed over her belly and hips and between her quickening thighs, "It's been too long, and I hope, that this time, there are no steel fortresses in the way," he whispered, his voice hoarse with passion.

"I haven't taken anything for months," she promised.

"Then, can we *now*… please … get on with it?"

Helen chuckled, as she ran gentle fingers through the thickness of his hair, softly replying: "Is this a different Duncan; you've never asked before?"

"I know the needs of your body, my Lady," he gruffly replied, while swiftly, keenly, divesting himself from his doublet and urgently unbuckling his kilt. Her timorous hands reached out for him, her legs opened in an inviting way, and rose, to twine around him as he went into her; the release for both was swift, the seed was sown.

"I have so longed for you, my Lord," she whispered.

"Welcome home," he laconically remarked, while giving a soft laugh.

"I admire Mairie and Angus, but I couldn't live as closely as they lived, never to know one another …,"

Suddenly, he lightly covered her mouth to stop her speaking, to say, "Helen, don't be so nieve – when Mairie Campbell came back to the village, she was pregnant, the baby died, no-one spoke of such tragedies, of course things went on — I asked my mother not to tell you because I wanted to tell you myself. — Mairie became a- wet-nurse for my father, who was much younger than your own. — Angus watched this ritual everyday, — he was in the throes of negotiating his marriage to Alicia, — she couldn't do it, — and without saying a word, they privately considered the child theirs, it was easy meat for the gossips – Alistair just turned a blind eye, he was comfortable and possibly had another lassie stowed away somewhere, no other child materialised, the blood in our veins is independent.

"But not the milk, I knew there had to be something."

He gazed at her naked beauty, and kissed her again, gently this time on her lips and then lifted his head, saying, while sitting up and pulling her with him, "The blood has more riches — now come, we've been away too long.".

Helen covered her nakedness by replacing the bodice of her dress, which Duncan zipped up for her, and then proceeded to place delicious little kisses across her bare shoulders, he swiftly donned his kilt, while she vainly tried to return her hair into some semblance of order, giving a soft laugh at her failure, "leave it loose," he suggested, and then, "let me pin your bridal heather back into place."

A fleeting puzzled frown creased Helen's brow, but having replaced the heather, Duncan dropped a kiss on her nose, took possession of her hand, and was leading her towards the door before she could question him.

It took them longer than necessary to reach the top of the stairs, as every few paces they indulged themselves in many lost kisses, until finally, with mutual reluctance, they descended, "I wish I had re-pinned my hair," she said quietly, complaining, "It would have spared my blushes."

Duncan chuckled, revelling in Helen's pink cheeks and the gloriously disarrayed profusion, "I promise you, that no-one will notice a thing amongst this entire crowd," Helen smiled a trifle dubiously, but she had no alternative but to believe him.

The entrance hall was clear of people when they reached it, but the party still went on noisily behind the great oak doors. Duncan selected a red rose from an arrangement at the foot of the stairs and handed it to her. She inhaled its intoxicating perfume, and then smiling, held the bloom to her cheek, "You're such a romantic, Duncan," she gently accused.

He chuckled again, while taking her hand and tucking it through his crooked arm, "Only for you, Helen. — Now, if we slip into the hall to join the party, no-one will be any the wiser, that we had left," he said, steering her towards the hall doors.

They each pushed a door wide enough to walk through together, but they had only taken a few steps into the hall, when Helen came to a sudden halt, and stared about her, aghast, shocked, dismayed. — Immediately, Duncan slid an arm about her waist, curving her closely to his side as if knowing she needed support.

In their absence, the hall had been transformed. The great centre table had been replaced into its rightful position and now bore the settings for a feast. Thirty eight places were laid along the polished surface, a silver goblet beside each plate with stone wine jars standing along the centre amidst bowls of spring flowers. The other tables had been moved together along the window wall, and they were also laid in preparation for eating. — Helen's pink cheeks flamed anew, when the crowd in the hall fell silent and centred their attention on them. She turned, wide, horrified, questioning eyes to Duncan, who chuckled somewhere above her head and first giving her a squeeze for confidence, he slightly loosened his support and taking a hold of her wrist, he swiftly raised the hand holding the rose. — On their left, Rory suddenly moved, and leaping onto the corner of the great table, he raised his goblet, giving a yell — "Loch Sloy! — She's carrying the MacFarlane rose — Helen has accepted the Laird — Three cheers for the Laird and the Lady Helen Campbell."

Suddenly, pandemonium seemed to break loose as they cheered and raised their Champagne glasses in a toast. Helen clutched at Duncan's arm, her heart pounding, "What does it all mean?" she asked.

"I thought we'd do a little revelling," he replied, with a roguish smile while holding her trembling form closer, and when he glanced down, his smile swept her face adoringly, "It means that they acknowledge our engagement, and approve of my choice for a Wife."

"Your Wife!" she exclaimed, pointing out, "But ... Duncan ... you didn't propose."

"And chance a refusal," he replied, again roguishly grinning. "There's no turning back now, Helen. You've accepted the Laird's rose, it's an old tradition," he said, while taking a hold of her hand and sliding a sparkling white diamond ring on her finger, "And this is a another one, it once belonged to Bridget Macleod, I knew that it would fit."

"My Lord Lennox ...," Helen gasped, shaking her head, feeling overwhelmed and torn somewhere in between laughter and tears. — When Rory jumped down from the table, Fiona Drummond joined him, and they walked towards them bearing two silver goblets, which they had retrieved from the table, they handed them one each. — Duncan released Helen to shake their hands, after which, Rory bent to kiss her cheek, admitting ...

"I'm guilty of waylaying you this afternoon, Helen. The bunches of flowers which you received from the women today, is an old tradition which has been carried out for several centuries, to denote that they approve of, and accept the Laird's bride into their circle," he glanced at Duncan before continuing, "I think that the Laird would have preferred to have taken you himself, but he was engaged on other business."

When Rory and Fiona moved out of earshot, Helen turned starry eyes to Duncan and whispered, "What other business?"

"I had an appointment with the Reverend, whereby, I had to deliver a certain piece of paper in a hurry, or, we cannae be married on the morrow."

"Tomorrow?" she echoed, with a question in her voice, while realising that she and Rory hadn't made their proposed visit to the Kirk. "Duncan, what did I sign this afternoon?"

"A very legal and binding marriage contract," he replied, looking a little concerned. "There was so little time, Helen; I didn't want to chance loosing you again."

She shook her head in confusion, "But, I don't have any lands, and I don't have a dowry."

Duncan laughed, "Helen, Mairie Campbell was very shrewd, she left you the only piece of land in Arrochar that I don't own, Bracken Cottage. And your dowry ... is in the jewellery box."

"Helen just gaped at him, "Costume jewellery; — but how could you have been so certain that I would have agreed?"

"I wasn't. It was a pure chance that I had to take, but as our lunch progressed, I became more confident."

"I thought our lunch to be a disaster," she chastised. "You were so bad tempered, I put it down to the fact that you'd given up smoking, and you laid me to blame."

Duncan chuckled, "Would I have won an Oscar, Helen?"

"You did it all on purpose," she exclaimed, questioningly, "Why?"

"Well, I had already tried and failed being honest with you," he replied. "So rather than risk a further rebuff, I decided to be adverse, thinking that if you felt anything for me at all, you would respond as you always did, you're a sassy lass, Helen, I had plenty of hope."

Helen smiled gently, encouragingly; she was beginning to understand, he knew her so well, "Duncan, you're incorrigible, please continue, I want to know everything, I insist."

"Rory had already discovered that you didn't appreciate the idea of my abandoning the tourist trade, and then I saw your pleasure in the scenery as you strolled down the driveway of The Loch House, you were pleased to be back. They were hardly the reactions of someone who didn't care what happened to the village. I made a shrewd guess that you wouldn't read the papers, as it would have prolonged the agony of having to sign over your rights to the cottage, and your one chance of staying."

"You confirmed my worst fears," she replied. "I felt that while I had possession of the cottage, you might have still cared for me."

"Darling, you were right to feel like that, — Bracken Cottage would have remained in your possession for all time, for while you had the cottage, there was always a chance that you would come back to me, and I had no intention of removing that chance."

"And the piano?" she said softly.

Duncan smiled, as he pressed her closer to his side, "In perfect working order," he replied, giving another chuckle.

Chapter 26

Mairie Campbell's Last Laugh

"To you, my Lady Helen, my own true love," he said, raising his goblet, "Today's victory."

"To my Liege Lord, my love," she replied.

The twined their arms together, sipped their wine in a toast, and then chatted for a few more minutes until Hannah joined them to add her congratulations, "I felt surprised when you phoned me earlier this evening, Mr. Duncan. I've brought your pipe and tobacco as you instructed, and I must say that it's a relief to put the poor lass's mind at rest," she sighed, and then smiled at them affectionately, "It's grand to have you together again, even grander that yeel be together under one roof, where I can make sure that you're both eating properly," she wiped away a stray tear before kissing Helen's cheek.

"Thanks Hannah. And it's grand to be home."

Duncan shook her hand, and kissed her proffered cheek, "Keep my pipe until later, Hannah, I seem to have my hands full, just now," Helen laughed softly, realising that she hadn't been as subtle as she had originally thought.

As Hannah left them, Jean and Iain took her place, "I confess, that I don't understand why you insisted on having your wedding feast this evening," Jean remarked, addressing Duncan.

"We'll miss most of tomorrow's party, as I'm planning on taking Helen away for a few days, before the holiday season really gets under way."

"A sensible idea," she agreed, before turning to Helen, leaving Iain speaking to Duncan. "Forgive me for deceiving you this morning, Helen, but even if you won't, it was worth it just to see you both so happy at last."

"There's nothing to forgive," Helen cheerfully replied. "In fact, I think I'm indebted to everyone, for the part which they have played today."

"Your clothes, they're not at Talbert as I told you, Duncan took them to

The Loch House, as soon as he found you gone. – So … as you won't have time yourself, and also as it's bad luck to see your bridegroom before the ceremony, I shall see to it, that they're packed and ready for your journey tomorrow."

A fleeting concern crossed Helen's features at the latter, "Jean," she said, a little apprehensively, "Promise me, that it will only be straightforward packing."

Jean smiled in assurance, "There's no tradition of which I know that involves the packing of clothes, other than confetti."

Alone again with Duncan, she became curious, "Where are we going tomorrow?"

He replied with grin, his eyes full of loving mischief, he winked at her, "We have a little unfinished business on the Islands, although, I doubt they'll be a great amount of sightseeing done, there's nothing to stop us now, Helen, it's all out in the open."

Catching his meaning, Helen felt her colour heighten, "That being the case, my Lord," she replied coyly for his benefit, "… I'm relieved that we won't be staying here tomorrow, for in a village so steeped in tradition as Arrochar, I would live in dread of finding the ancient custom of 'bedding' still being carried out."

Duncan gave a soft laugh, kissing her lightly on the lips, saying, "I thought we had better leave, just to avoid the issue."

"We hate to intrude," came, a sudden familiar voice.

Startled, Helen faced the newcomers with a soft gasp, "Why … Eleanor! Henry! Oh, could anything else more wonderful happen?"

Embracing the radiant girl of whom she felt so fond, Eleanor sent up a prayer of grateful thanks, "Are you really so surprised to see us, Helen?" she said, smiling affectionately at the pair. "Duncan phoned me this afternoon, to tell us that the party would be going on as arranged. I knew when I saw you yesterday, that it couldn't be any other way but this. You couldn't hide the disappointment from your face, when you realised that Duncan hadn't come to meet you at the airport."

"Do you think that Mairie Campbell, would have approved, mother?" Duncan asked, curving Helen back close to his side, while smiling down at her.

"I think that Mairie Campbell would have been delighted. — In fact, I have a sneaking suspicion that she planned it. — In bringing together the two persons most dear to her, she would have found an excellent way to right a wrong."

"Oh no," Helen replied, shaking her head and frowning, "That couldn't be possible; she refused to allow me to visit her after my father had died. — She made the reason my career, feeling that a young girl would find nothing of interest in an out of the way village."

"That doesn't sound like the Mairie Campbell, that I knew," said Eleanor in surprise, "Your music, she loved, even though she knew from those early tapes which you sent her, lacked something of the polish which you have found today. But your newspaper career, she heartily disagreed with."

Helen frowned, thoughtfully puzzled. But Mairie Campbells' reasons weren't to be discovered just yet, for two more of their guests, joined the small group standing by the great doors. — She glanced up at Duncan, who shrugged, as if he were innocent of knowing from where they had sprung, but she knew that he did, and not wishing to spoil his fun, she silently wondered whom else he had hidden away, as she greeted, James Craig and his wife, Connie.

Alex had never appreciated her father's friendship with the sprightly, button eyed Connie, but then Alex's jealously had reined supreme, in all things.

"I have to tell you, Helen," Connie said, smiling nervously, "… that we didn't just meet you by accident in St. James Park. Your stepfather phoned us to let us know where you were."

Helen smiled in reassurance, at the time remembering, that it had been the first occasion since leaving Switzerland that she had been allowed to wander alone.

"When Duncan told us of Alex's lies and interference in your life," James continued, "We felt it necessary that you should learn the truth in the way in which you did. We saw it as a chance to make amends, but Charles made it abundantly clear that we were to wait until he felt that you were well enough, to cope with yet another trauma, also, enough to decide what it was that you wanted to do with your life."

Helen began to feel tearful again, as she reached up to kiss the large man's cheek, "I couldn't wish for better friends, I hope that you will be frequent visitors to Arrochar."

James smiled broadly in acceptance, "Be happy, lass," he said, in finality.

Back in his encircling arm, Duncan bent to whisper in her ear, "If you turn towards the door, you will see others whom you know, arriving."

Helen did as he suggested, letting out a soft gasp of pleasure, "Charles and mother! Darling, you've thought of everything."

"We cannae have a wedding without our friends and relations present, my Lady Helen."

Her eyes spoke volumes, she was longing to ask him how he had accomplished the family gathering at such short notice, but now, she, like him, were duty bound to remain patiently with their guests.

"Oh Charles," she murmured affectionately, as he hugged her tightly, "I might have known, that you had something to do with this."

He gazed down fondly at her, "Had I known that it would have made you so happy, I would have done something sooner. — Helen … I couldn't stand to see you so ill and unhappy. — When Duncan came to see me and told me all he knew, I felt angry with myself, with the whole world. At first, I wouldn't betray any part of your confidence, but then he told me that he loved you and wanted to marry you, but he wasn't certain that his feelings were returned. I told him that you hadn't indicated anything of a personal nature about him, and that as far as I knew, your illness pointed to the loss of your job. — He pressed me to the limits, but in fear of upsetting you further, I refused to divulge your whereabouts." He sighed, remembering, "He wouldn't want you to know this Helen, but when I sent him away, he was angry. I've seen men in love before, and I felt certain that his anger was a camouflage for his hurt, so I decided that if you ever uttered one single word, which indicated any lasting feeling for him, I would tell him and he could act accordingly. I did this with confidence, knowing that you would be cared for, for all time."

Helen swallowed the constriction in her throat, as she moved back into Charles arms, whispering, "Oh Charles, I don't know what I said, but whatever it was, I'm so glad that I said it."

"It was a very fleeing remark, Helen, but, ask Duncan, when you're alone. I know that he'd want to tell you himself,"

She nodded, and then turned her attentions to her mother, whom up until now had been speaking to Duncan.

"Oh dear," Glynis exclaimed, with a hint of a catch in her own voice, while scanning Helen's face, "… have my handkerchief, Helen, and do try to stop weeping, your eyes will be quite puffy, if you don't. — But I must confess that I too would be overwhelmed by all of this at such short notice, and you know that I always have a good cry at weddings, anyway. — Oh! I nearly forgot," she continued, "We've brought your wedding dress from London; a heavenly creation from Harrods. I'm certain that it will fit you to perfection, you always were so marvellously, stock size."

"I'm quite sure that it will be *white*, mother."

"Could there *be* another colour."

Helen grinned after her, as her mother moved away to speak to Eleanor Graham and she felt Duncan's arm steal about her waist, "You're too far away," he complained quietly for her ears alone.

Covering the hand firmly holding her to his side, she smiled up at him, "The hotel isn't closed for business, is it, Duncan?"

He chuckled, "No, but we had to tell you something, in case the idea of using the hotel's piano entered your head. I had to bind the Craigs and your parents, who arrived yesterday afternoon, to the confines of the hotel, in case again, you took into your head to wander about the village. But after tonight, any visiting relatives can stay in Bracken Cottage," he bent his head to kiss her gently, with warm lips, "Do you still love me, Helen?" he asked anxiously.

"I still love you, my Lord," she confirmed, reaching up and stroking his face.

Suddenly, he cast a glance over her head and sighed, "Sometimes, duty becomes such a burden, but here comes the last of our late arrivals."

Helen followed his gaze, clutching at his supporting hand as she excitedly questioned, gasping, "Oh darling, where did you find them?"

"Rita will tell you," he said.

"Rita! Gary!" she exclaimed warmly, as they approached, smiling, "I thought you were abroad, on honeymoon."

"And miss all of this, Helen," Rita replied, casting an encompassing hand about her, "Kidda, I've waited almost three years to throw handfuls of rice over you, and not even my own honeymoon would stand in the way of that, besides, we are abroad, and we are on honeymoon. — I have to admit though, that we fell foul of Alex Craig. She has a sharp tongue, a way of putting words into your mouth that aren't there." She smiled at Duncan, who gave her an encouraging nod for her to continue, "The Laird visited the Daily News offices to see Ryder, I might add, that the Laird won the ensuing argument, which I think everyone overheard. Ryders' tactics involving the Craig woman left a nasty taste in our mouths; we no longer wanted to be a part of his empire."

"You mean … you haven't jobs?" Helen enquired, with a concerned tone and a frown.

Rita smiled again, she replied, "We have jobs, Helen; the Laird made a special concession, and allowed us to open a photographic shop in the village, on condition, that we did the advertising photography for your Tourist Agency."

Confused, Helen stammered, "But, you said … oh, I don't care what you said," she decided, "Welcome, to Arrochar."

Rita stepped forward to kiss Helen's cheek before they moved away, "It would be an idea, to contemplate starting our own newspaper, Kidda, 'The Arrochar Herald' would seem appropriate," she winked.

Oh no, Helen replied, shaking her head while giving a mischievous grin, with so much dark history, it must be called, 'MacFarlane's Lantern' there's plenty to write about, in a sleepy Highland village, like Arrochar."

Chapter 27

So much to say

Duty done, Duncan whispered, "I haven't kissed you properly for a whole hour. I suggest that we go to make our report to Mairie Campbell before the roast beef is served," and with arms entwined about each other, they left the hall to make slow progress up to the gallery, "You're very quiet, my darling, is something wrong?" he said, quietly concerned after they rounded the bend on the stairs.

Standing still, Helen turned to face him with tears of happiness still glistening on her lashes; she swallowed, trying to find the words to express her emotion, "No, how could anything be wrong, I'm just overwhelmed?" she replied, shaking her head and then laying her cheek against his firm velvet clad shoulder, "Oh, I love you so much," she sighed.

He folded his arms about her, saying gruffly, "And that's all that I want, Helen; to know that you're mine."

"Will you tell me what it was, I said, that led you to do all of this?"

"You whispered to a mountain, - do you remember? You said, 'Perhaps, I am Mairie Campbell and he Angus' it was the only clue that you gave. Your mother mentioned it to Charles, and he in turn passed it on to me. — Hearing those words three months after you had left Arrochar; I knew that you were still thinking of me. — Charles wouldn't run the risk of letting me see you without first exposing Ryder for what he is, and then hearing the truth about Mairie Campbell. — With some help, I did the only thing left open to me. — My darling, I wanted to meet you at the airport, but I had to keep my promise to Charles. I would have done anything if there had been the slightest possible chance of getting you back; I had already made the fatal mistake of changing Mairies' instructions."

"I never stopped thinking of you for one moment. I think I must have sighed in final resignation, when I spoke those words," he kissed her gently before they continued to the gallery, "Will you tell me one more thing?"

"Anything, Helen," he whispered. "If it will only settle your mind and cast away the last nagging doubts."

"When I first met you in Bracken Lane, you mistook me for a tourist. It puzzled me, not for the first time this afternoon, being so like Mairie Campbell, and yet you failed to recognise me. I later had the impression that you had rushed off to meet Alex."

"With you only a hair's breadth away, I would hardly do that," he replied. "Helen, I seemed fated *never* to meet you, James will have told you how hard I tried when you first arrived in Edinburgh, and how I failed."

She mischievously chuckled, "His explanation was so visual."

Duncan grinned, although he felt indignant, "It was no laughing matter." She chivvied him to continue.

"When we finally returned home, it was too late in the evening to go decently social calling, and so I felt compelled to wait until the morning. I duly arrived at Bracken Cottage only to be informed by Hannah that you were on your way to the Kirk. I was in such a tearing hurry, that I didn't stop to consider that you might not have arrived at your destination. Seeing you so muddied and practically unidentifiable, I did take you for a tourist, until you pulled your hat off and your hair tumbled about your shoulders, thus revealing a beautiful, but very irate, Helen Campbell," they paused a moment to lightly embrace, "Darling, can you imagine my horror, after waiting so long to meet you, that when I finally did, I managed to mow you down, and not for the first time; your hair style, when I bumped into you in Edinburgh, wasn't how I remembered you. I didn't dare stay in the lane, but I still had the evening to face, and decided that you may not feel quite so adverse, if I sent you a note to break the ice."

"It was a very nice note," she happily replied. "But, by the evening, I had forgotten the incident until I saw you again, and then I was too busy being a reporter, for it to worry me."

Duncan suddenly chuckled again, "And I felt mistakenly lulled into relief when you didn't mention it."

"You acknowledged it, I admit that now."

He had to leave her for a moment, while he switched on the spotlighting beneath Mairie's picture. When he returned, he stood behind her to fold his arms about her, pressing her back against his chest as he addressed the canvas, "You see, Mairie Campbell, I have her, I have your granddaughter, and she's promised to marry me. — Soon, you will see the MacFarlane and the Campbell's blood mingle and flow in our sons' veins, and he'll *laugh* at long last, at the folly of our ancestors."

"I think she smiled, Duncan," Helen suddenly said. "I think she's the one having the last laugh."

Duncan chuckled, "A trick of the light, my Helen."

She nodded acknowledging his comment; she sighed, "My mother was overly insistent that I bought that dress, I hadn't ever seen the cloak before; I guessed that it must have had special memories, and had been stored away in a trunk along with her wine stained dress. Angus bought her the dress, intending it to be her wedding dress, but it was never worn in that manner; he painted a portrait of his true bride. Mairie wasn't invited to Alicia and Angus's wedding feast, there is no invitation, but she went anyway, and wore the dress, the aigrette and the combs, and in spite, Alicia threw the wine over her. My party was almost a modern replica of the wedding feast; I was the guest of honour, and placed in a position where Mairie should rightly have been, but she didn't reckon on Alex Craig's presence."

A very good deduction," Duncan replied.

Helen nodded, "I know that I'm right. The hair combs weren't in the dressing table drawer when I left the cottage in the morning, but very mysteriously, they were there when I returned in the afternoon; — they were the bait. — The last time I was here, I sat at the dressing table trying them out, Mairie came behind me, she demonstrated how they should be used, she studied me through the mirror; I think it must have been at that precise moment, she realised my resemblance to her, and an idea began formulating in her mind, she knew everyones' habits, the nice ones, like parties and the not so nice ones, like embarrassing relatives, also, my mothers' penchant for white dresses. — She hid the photos because I was wearing white dresses in every one, and by the time Crawford had handed them back to me, the party had long since gone, you had the real Helen Campbell, I *am* your legacy."

He turned her to face him, looking anxiously serious now, "Alex had been pressuring me for sometime for permission to use the castle for filming. I wouldn't agree, until one day, I received a certain letter from Crawford, which said, 'Helen Campbell has agreed to the terms of Mairie Campbell's *will,* and will be arriving on a date to be confirmed in September' those words, I thought I'd never see. They made me so happy Helen that I became blind in my judgement and reckless in my decisions, for as I have already said, I had waited so long to meet you, however, my elation was to be short-lived."

Helen stared at him with a dawning comprehension, and incredulous astonishment, "My eighteenth birthday corresponded with my Prom Ball, and my departure to France. Mairie sent me the Victorian combs and the silver aigrette to use, on the solemn promise that I would return them immediately into her care. — Along with the combs was a picture of an oil painting of a Victorian Lady, wearing the combs and the aigrette, obviously, the previous owner, the aigrette bears the MacFarlane coats-of-arms, the lady in the picture, I now have no doubt, was Bridget MacCleod, and also packed into the parcel was a cellophane box containing a single red rose, the card was signed with the compliments of, D R Parlan. I now put it to you, my Lord, that you loaned the combs to me, in the same way that Angus had loaned them to Mairie."

"Aye, I kept you dreaming along with myself, it pleasured me to think that you had worn the combs, although Mairie denied having been sent a picture of you wearing them, it was a real bonus when you sent a lock of hair wound into the combs." He continued awkwardly, also appearing a little sheepish, "Helen, I have a confession to make … when I stopped off at the cottage, my plan was to give you them to wear, just as you did. Hannah was ready to leave, and so I decided to put them into your drawer, but you had left Ryder's letter lying on your bed, I must confess, I read it."

She grinned, followed by a soft laugh, "Oh, now I understand, that's what you wanted to tell me, that you'd read my mail; — you knew, *all* the time, you knew,"

He nodded, "How the devil can you tell anyone, that you've read their mail? I tried, but there was never a right moment, and so many interruptions, I prayed that you would tell me of the difficulties of your own accord, but when you didn't, I decided that it might be best to let matters lay; at least you were *trying* to stay in the village for a further three months, it did hearten me, but I still got anxious, I knew what Alex was probably up to. I tried to spare you, but you wouldn't have it, and so I tried to keep her away from you. — On the day that you went into the village with Jean to collect the vaccine for Iain, I saw you both go into the Post Office, but so did Alex, I managed to steer her away, I took her into the Arms Hotel and stayed with her, until I felt that you had returned to Talbert, I then thought that I would waylay you with Jean, but you had other ideas. — I also commissioned Rory to keep an eye on you, Rory is the one person that Alex will steer clear of, he wouldn't tolerate her at any cost, despite your assumptions," he suddenly chuckled, "But I didn't expect him to be so enthusiastic about his job."

"You were so jealous, that you wouldn't invite him to the party."

"Aye, I wasn't taking any chances until I'd met you myself, that's why I sent Hannah as a chaperone."

"Alex deliberately scheduled the conference on my deadline."

"With a little assistance from Ryder," he injected.

"Alex was so jealous when she saw the jewellery. — Where's Bridget's painting?"

Duncan chuckled, "It's further along, and tomorrow, together, we'll move it alongside Mairie's. — It was underneath Alicia MacFarlane's, Mairie and Alicia kept switching them around. — I gave Alicia's portrait to Alex, as a going way present." Helen pressed her cheek against his hard chest, — immediately, he tightened his hold, they clung together, both feeling the regretted bitter pain of the harsh words that they had inflicted upon each other, on their ill-fated first visit to the gallery. "I hated the portrait, Helen, I wished that it had never been found, and removed it from display. I never considered for one moment that the years would have changed you, or that you would have grown so like her. But, as its presence took you away from me, so its absence sent you back."

Helen pulled away slightly to stare up at him, frowning quizzically, "Changed me? grown so like her?" she softly echoed. "I don't understand; you speak as though we had met before, and *why* so anxious to meet a stranger, someone whom you'd never seen?"

"But, I *had* seen you, Helen. I saw you for the first time, seven years ago."

"But, how?" she questioned, still frowning.

"Don't you remember, my sweet, it's fairly simple," he said, while tracing the outline of her lips with his index finger. "Rory, with your gran, drove me to the station on the day that you arrived for your last visit. I was purchasing my ticket for Aberdeen when your train arrived, there were only a few other passengers to alight, but somehow, you were the last, and as you stepped from the train, the Talbert breeze caught and swept back your hair from your face. You made such a pretty picture, that I immediately fell in love."

"Go on," Helen gently urged, smiling now.

Returning her smile, he gently dropped a kiss on her nose, "I stood with Mairie while Rory sorted out the luggage with you, hoping for an introduction, but it wasn't to be, my train came in and I had to make a mad dash to the opposite side of the platform."

Now I remember," she said, in wonderment, also remembering her vision at the station earlier in the day. — It was as though Mairie Campbell had tried to give her a clue, "I waved over to gran, and you smiled at me. It was the briefest of moments, for when I went to join her; I looked around wondering where you had gone, Gran said, 'The lad has caught the train'."

Duncan chuckled, "I had the greatest of difficulties in concentrating on my studies ever after that, for I had visions of Helen Campbell enjoying her holiday, doubtless with Rory Cameron, as he was very available and nearer to your own age. I don't think that I would have passed my scholarships for that reason alone, and when summoned home a few weeks later because of my father's accident, you had left Arrochar. — Two months later, your own father died, and only weeks after that, Mairie received a letter from your mother informing her that you were taken to Switzerland, as there was some concern over your health. Mairie mentioned pneumonia. I desperately wanted to meet you, and to care for you, I saw it as the ideal opportunity, so I suggested that you came here as …,"

"Arrochar is another Switzerland," Helen finished, smiling.

Duncan nodded, "She refused, commanding, *'The lass must remain in her mother's care. It's not for such as we to interfere.'* I remember those words as if they were spoken yesterday; they bore deeply into my soul, as I could see no way in which to meet you."

"Did you ever confide your feelings to Mairie?"

"No, I kept them to myself, but I looked forward to your letters arriving just as much as she did. A good few, she read out to me, which is how I knew so much about you. — Helen darling, I've wanted to tell you so many times, but either my courage failed me, or you wouldn't stand still long enough to listen, and then there were moments, when it didn't seem to matter."

"Everything is so clear, now," Helen ascertained. "Your mother's words were so true earlier this evening, when she suggested that Mairie had planned for us to meet."

"But Helen, she kept you away."

"Duncan, don't you see? It wasn't the right time. You were suddenly, unexpectedly, thrown into your duties as the Laird, and with all the in-house fighting to deal with, she tried to avoid a repeat of history, she didn't want to involve me, also, Mairie saw the dangers of a high spirited young girl swaying your better judgement by tempting you away from your duties, merely because she had become bored."

"But supposing you had met someone else."

Helen shook her head, "I may have, but Mairie thought of that also. Whenever I mentioned any romantic attachments, she warned me of the perils of marrying a Sassenach, and urged me on with my career. — A career, which we now know she hated, and she hated it because she realised, as so many others realised, how it was affecting me, hence the wording in her last note, 'Look into your heart, Helen, and yeel be sure to find a welcome in the heart of Arrochar, your heart Duncan, she was aware of your feelings, she saw your disappointment."

"I didn't think that you had even noticed me, Helen."

"Oh, but I had," she replied, while sliding her arms about his neck. "And now it comes to mind, in that *one* shared, fleeting moment, all those years ago, I too lost my heart, and what is more … Mairie Campbell … knew it."

EPILOGUE

Twelve months later, Helen sat at the piano playing a very different tune. She smiled at her husband when he came to join her, leaning on the piano lid, and as always, she basked in his blue raking gaze. — Blue eyes set in by sooty fingers, she had thought, when Iain had first placed Duncan's son into her arms, for young Robbies' eye lashes and hair, proved to be as dark as Duncan's, although the latter's hair at the moment, having recently returned from a tour of the estates, appeared a trifle unruly.

"Young Rory is making a grand job of Craigiemhor, Helen. I must confess that I felt dubious when he first approached me for the lease, but he seems to have settled down since he married the Drummond lass."

"He'll be settled even more, next year, darling," Helen replied, while tinkling at the notes of her lullaby. "They're to have a bairn, and so is Rita, and I do believe that Jean muttered something about a brother for little Rachael."

"A baby boom," Duncan thoughtfully remarked, raising his eyebrows. "I'm pleased that everyone has the future of the village in mind."

Helen smiled at his remark, but then her smile became replaced by a fleeting concern, "The village will always survive, won't it, Duncan? We have made sure of that."

He moved to her side and pulled her up into his arms to kiss her lightly on the lips, saying, "Have no fear, my Lady Helen, Arrochar will flourish, and we'll have more sons and grandsons to ensure that it does. Yeel be playing lullabies until you're an elderly, grey haired old lady, and I have a beard which sweeps the floor."

"You're so wonderful, Duncan, you always manage to say the right things," she replied. "But while we're on the subject of music, I've never heard you play the piano."

He appeared uncomfortable, "Hardly surprising, my darling, I can't play a single note."

"But, you said …"

"I *know*, what I said," he replied, appearing slightly abashed. "I hoped that you'd forgotten."

She gently shook her head in denial, "Tell me."

"I brought the piano for you, in the hopes that it would encourage you to relinquish your career, but that was at a time when I didn't expect Helen Campbell to be such a stubborn wench. — Helen, if any man has ever worked hard to win a woman's heart, I most certainly did."

She laughed softly, ending with a sigh, "Well, I think that it was just a sprat to catch a mackerel, but there's something that you still don't know," she said. "Come into the office, I've been sorting through some old paperwork which I found in the cottage." Moments later, she reached for an old folder and lifted it down from the shelf, "I have a letter for you, it appears to be from Mairie Campbell, it has twice been posted, but twice you haven't received it, — it was described by Mr Crawford as my letter of introduction and everyone surmised that it wasn't required, but I have opened the envelope and what it contains is a letter from me, to you, written after I left Arrochar at the prime age of sixteen, I asked Mairie Campbell to deliver it, but in her wisdom, she didn't. — I suppose that she thought that a young girl shouldn't be making romantic overtures to a young man, who might have been flattered, but embarrassed, or he may have laughed, or he may have even been stirred by fantasies, and in one way, Duncan, I'm glad that you didn't receive it, I would have been *most* embarrassed.

"It's mine to read," he said, scanning the envelope, it was addressed to: - The Young Laddie.

Hello,

I don't know your name, but mine is Helen Campbell, Mairie Campbell's granddaughter, and just to be clearer, you waved to me today as you left Talbert station. I wish I could have met you, as I thought you a handsome, bonnie laddie, even more handsome than Rory Cameron, you must know Rory, he is such fun, but I don't love him as much as I could love you. I hope that you won't mind if I dream about you, I don't know if boys have dreams about girls, but I will try to turn your dreams into adventures, if you will dream of me.

I could say, best regards; yours truly or even yours sincerely.

But, I would rather say, 'in dreams we'll meet, in *my* dreams of Caledonia'.

You will be my dearest heart forever, my bonnie Highland laddie. Love — Helen Campbell xxx

Duncan smiled as he refolded the letter, and replaced it into the envelope, "She did give it to me," he revealed. "It arrived at precisely the right time; I could hardly run off and marry someone else after reading that, it gave me the strength to fend off my peers. — From that moment, I knew that I was an anxious man in waiting, and so I memorised it, and asked her to keep it, along with your others; she agreed and said it would be best if Helen were to deliver it herself — and you just have."

"And, I don't take back one word," she murmured, sliding into his embrace, "It all went wrong, Duncan. If Alex hadn't been there, when we first met, despite everything, I would have said, 'you're the laddie' you would have got your wish," she underlined, "but I was angry with you on two counts, when I realised that it was you; I felt betrayed, disappointed and embarrassed."

"I was just as confused, myself," he confessed. "I just want us to enjoy ourselves. Helen, from the very first moment that I saw you, I realised how much I had missed, being steeped in duties and traditions to uphold, you simply, bubbled with life; something of which I felt Rory had had more that his fair share. Now, I want *my* share, and I know that I'll receive it, while I can make you laugh and see you happy."

Helen raised her head from his shoulder to assure him, "Oh, without a doubt, I am happy, Duncan, now that I have you and Robbie," she ascertained with a soft sigh. "Do you think it possible that Mairie Campbell knows how happy we are?"

"I'll guarantee it," Duncan replied, while revelling in his wife's beautiful, radiant face, adoring her, as did the amorous ghost, of the Castle … Drumbrae.

The End

JC/MFL/CH/1981-82

Now read: - Book two

MACFARLANE'S LANTERN

Drama!   Scandal!   Intrigue!   Mystery!   Romance!

Ralph Barrington was a very young man when he inherited the run-down Georgian mansion of Redwoods in Winchester. In accordance with Margaret Fitzgerald's *will*, Ralph was unable to sell his inheritance; therefore he and his teenage daughter, Roselyn, known as Ros, were forced to make the best of things and to live in just a few of the rooms. Ralph's wife, Charlotte, was a depressant: she had cruelly denied Ros at birth, and then, Ros re-meets Andrew Frazer MacFarlane, who has had an equally tragic and difficult beginning to his life; but not only has Andrew got himself entangled with a woman, who is determined never to let him go, but he also harbours a fearful, dark secret.

Set amongst some of Scotland's most dramatic scenery, this is a powerful tale as seen through the eyes of an eighteenth century, former daughter of the house, Marguerite Fitzgerald Campbell, an adventuress during the Jacobite uprisings, who suffered a cruel rape; she had a child. There is a mystery surrounding the child's parentage which becomes a vital link in saving Redwoods and the North and South Timber Mills from being demolished. And just *who* is the mysterious, Rafe Frazer?